The Conjurer's Boy
by award-winning author Michael Raleigh

"Like Raleigh himself, this book is deeply rooted in Chicago, but offers a vision of a much vaster world. Raleigh's tale of outsiders looking for a way in examines the resilience of the soul by way of a tour through the catastrophes of the twentieth century."

—Sam Reaves, author of *Mean Town Blues*

For Michael Raleigh's *The Maxwell Street Blues:*

"With his flair for vivid prose and his vesting of dignity in the humblest of characters, Raleigh *renders* a superlative work . . ."

— *Chicago Sun-Times*

For Michael Raleigh's *The Blue Moon Circus:*

"With no safety net, Raleigh takes a spectacular highwire route . . . making it all look easy . . ."

—Kirkus Reviews, starred review

The Conjurer's Boy

Michael Raleigh

New York

Harvard Square Editions

2012

Published in the United States by Harvard Square Editions

ISBN 978-0-9833216-6-8

Harvard Square Editions web address:
www.harvardsquareeditions.org

Printed in the United States of America

For my wife Katherine

prologue: Ghosts

Cities have their deserts, places where life has been leached out, and in such a place on a certain chill night in March of 1972 I saw ghosts, an entire room of ghosts. I saw the dead. Or hallucinations, whatever, call them what you will. I did not want these things. But there you are.

It is still winter in Chicago in March, sometimes for weeks to come. Even in late April, winter sometimes sneaks back in for a couple of days like a hard-to-kill villain, freezes pipes, kills the new plants, confuses the migratory birds, makes noise like an old fighter on a comeback. And on this night, a light snow began to fall around dusk and soon thickened until the sidewalk had a delicate coating of white fur. A harsh wind came off the lake and sent the natives scurrying. I was caught wandering – it is not quite accurate to say "far from home," for I had no home. I did have a room above a tavern at Quincy and Green but had not slept there for some time, for I owed the tavern keeper money for the past two weeks' rent. The previous night I had fallen asleep in an alley. When the heavy chill of night woke me, I staggered into a hallway where I found a dry corner and slept. At dawn I roused myself so that I wouldn't be in the hallway when the residents came out to start their ordinary days. I am quite certain that the hallway saved me: I believe I was within minutes of freezing to death in that alley.

The cold was the least of my worries. I was not well. I coughed incessantly and my chest was tight, constricted so that I could not draw a clear breath. The first few days of it, I told myself it was smoker's cough but when my scant supply of smokes ran out I still coughed, and my lungs hurt. I was hungry constantly and weak – more than once I wanted simply to collapse someplace out of the wind and go to sleep, perhaps forever. For the first time since a day in a clearing in Vietnam I saw the possibility of my own death. I was not troubled so much by the thought of this as I was by the idea that no one would know, for no one knew I had returned to Chicago. I could have been my own ghost.

Earlier that night, I'd been waiting to cross the street when a bus rumbled by and I felt someone watching me. I tried to make out faces but the bus was picking up speed so that the people in the windows were a blur. Then, just as it pulled away, I caught a glimpse of a face, a girl's face remembered from childhood. More than anything else, I saw the eyes, large dark eyes, nearly expressionless. Nearly but not quite, for even in that quick moment I thought I detected something like pity. If asked I would have said it was the face of a young woman named Rachel, who had been in and out of my life for nearly ten years, the last person to love me, before I left her. But as I squinted to focus I saw I'd been mistaken, it was the face of an older woman, a perfect stranger. The pity was there, though, I'd seen that clearly enough.

For several hours I wandered empty streets, and the wind had worn me down to the point where I was ready to face the tavern keeper. I walked east on the old Skid Row, West Madison Street. I should not have been there, of course.

"Knock on any door on Chicago's West Madison Street," a long-dead Chicago writer named Willard Motley had written, "and you'll find a Nick Romano." His Nick Romano lived a short troubled life, and Motley himself was long dead, along with the people of all kinds who had followed them down into this urban hole, for this was no longer a neighborhood. Just a sort of desert, a place where human life has more or less moved on. In the Spring of 1972 the street was a long line of empty storefronts, boarded-up saloons, here and there a burned-out three-flat. Homeless men and squatters lived in some of these places.

From almost anywhere on the street you could see the rocklike hulk that was the old Chicago Stadium, looking like a great mausoleum on a dead street. I saw few people as I walked: a huddled form shivering in a doorway, three men clustered over an oil drum fire, burning scrap wood torn from a back fence. Two cops in a squad car slowed down slightly so the driver could squint my way and see if I matched any faces he was seeking.

My walk took me past an old tavern. From what little streetlight seeped into it through its dust-caked windows I saw that it had died, this old place, simply stopped existing, all at once: the stools were still piled on the old

11

rectangular bar, chairs set carefully on tables, as though the saloon would open as soon as the porter swept up.

As I passed it, I caught movement inside. At the edge of my vision I saw activity within, light, unmistakable light, a crowd of people elbow to elbow at the bar, laughing and talking and listening to the music of a corner juke box, I could hear the music, old music, swing – Artie Shaw or Stan Kenton. I walked on a few paces and then came to a stop and turned. I could see it all, all of them inside, carrying on and living in that dead place. I felt giddy, flushed. For a moment I needed more than anything else to spend a moment in that place. I walked back toward it and saw that the light was gone. Up close, I peered inside, my hand cupped against the cold glass. There was nothing. Dark as a cave, a dead saloon from the days before the street became Skid Row, when all the taverns and cafes and diners might be filled on any night with people heading to the Stadium to see the Blackhawks, or Sugar Ray Robinson and Basilio fighting for the crown. Or simply packed with people for whom a hot, crowded tavern was company and entertainment.

Then as I began to turn away I stopped. There was movement inside, and as I focused on it, I saw shapes, the shapes of people, two dozen or more. I saw people laughing, drinking, arguing. I saw a woman singing along with the jukebox, another woman looking away from a man who pleaded with her – for what? Another chance, a fair hearing, to sleep with him?

If someone had asked me at that moment what I was looking at, I would have said I was watching a group of people trying very hard, in the face of whatever awaited them outside the saloon, in their lives, to have a good time, to secure just one night for themselves. A wave of longing rushed over me, a sudden fierce need to be a part of this even though I was a stranger. Another second and I would have gone in, embraced the smoke and the noise and the press of bodies. Then they left, they faded. There was no one. I remember that my heart beat very fast for a moment, and I wanted to call out into the night, to release my anger and disappointment. I had seen nothing.

I hurried away from that spot. A few feet from the corner – Morgan or Sangamon, one of those streets, I don't even remember – I stopped and tried to clear my head of the image of people celebrating in a tavern long dead. Something made me turn around, but this time my well-honed street instincts told me I'd probably see a more earthbound vision.

I had attracted notice. A pair of men, one white and the other black, were coming after me, gaining ground and making no attempt to conceal their intentions. I didn't even need to look around to see that there was no one likely to help me, or even witness what happened. I remember that the white man had one arm, and for some reason this troubled me, as though a one-armed man bent on harm must know something I didn't.

I turned to face them, gave them a long look, but it did nothing to slow them and I turned and headed for the corner. Behind me I heard the scraping sounds of their quickening footsteps, and as I crossed the street, I came to a sudden stop. Another man stood on the far side, as if waiting for me. I saw his face, the last face on earth I should have expected to see on a Skid Row street corner:

Farrell. Arthur Farrell. He seemed unchanged, his penchant intact for looking at once serenely at ease with his surroundings and yet out of place: he was hatless, his thick silver hair blew wildly in the wind, and he stood with his hands thrust deep into the pockets of a topcoat that very likely had been the height of fashion in 1955. Something in his pose told me he had been standing there for some time. I had no doubt he'd seen all of it, my vision of the life of the old tavern, my pursuit by the two men. I crossed the street.

At the far side I turned to face my pursuers again. They made it to the middle of the street before they stopped cold. It might have been the notion that mugging two people would be more complicated, but I saw the looks on their faces. They ignored me and stared at Farrell. Then the white man shot a quick glance at his companion and spun on his heel, the two of them moving back down Madison Street faster than they'd come up.

When I turned to Farrell, he was watching me. I wondered if the irony had struck him, that he had just reenacted, more or less, the moment in 1962 when he'd first come into my life.

"Farrell."

He pointed a finger up to my face. "You are dying."

"So much for small talk."

"Small talk has its uses. This is not one of them. You're dying, lad."

I stared at him and then realized I was shaking my head, shaking it over and over again. I was in one of those moments when one feels the need to blurt out a half dozen things at once, wounding things, killing things, and none will come. I bit back the impulse to tell him that he disgusted me, that he had no right to foist on me his notions about my health or anything else. Most of all, I suppressed, almost physically suppressed the urge to spit my accusations at him.

He stood watching me, patently studying the effects of the past five years on my face, on my health. He was shaking his head like an aging nurse. Years before, on a chill night not much different from this one, I had watched him emerge from a narrow alley behind Halsted, leaving a dead man behind him. I had no doubt that Farrell had caused the man's death. I had seen him do other things, things that were in my unsophisticated view unnatural. More than once, I'd wondered if his were unholy gifts. But I knew if I spoke to him of such matters he would affect ignorance.

Too much to say, without a means to have it come out right. And so when he made his arrogant pronouncement of my impending death, I said none of these things. I mustered my street bravado and said, "I'll admit I've felt better. Got a short leg now, complicates buying pants, but hey, that's life." When he said nothing, I added, "They weren't nice to me over there. I got shot, as it turns out."

Farrell hesitated, then said, "A near thing, it seems."

"Where'd you hear that?" I asked, though I already knew the answer. He had not actually heard, no one had told him.

"Your injuries are just an excuse. They removed the bullets, after all. Your modern field hospitals can do so much more than we could in our time. And it was several years ago, your wounding. You are just a sick man now."

15

I felt the anger rising. "Well, it's been great, Farrell." I stalked away and felt the blood pounding at my temples.

"I'll stand you to a nice hot cup of coffee, Thomas," he said. "It's been such a long time."

I waved him off without turning around and continued pounding pavement. When I was a block away I stopped, feeling foolish. I was chilled and tired, nauseated from hunger, and hours of walking on concrete had dealt my knee harsh punishment. In truth I wanted Farrell's promised cup of coffee. I wanted anything warm that would line my stomach for a few minutes, I wanted a place to sit and get in out of the March wind, but I was uneasy about spending time with Farrell. When I turned around to look for him, he was gone.

As I made my way toward Halsted the swirling snow stung my eyes. Ahead of me, near the corner of Sangamon and Madison, I saw the yellow light of a diner. I was down to two bucks and small change. I had been saving that last couple of bucks for three days, saving for some moment even more desperate than the present, but I wasn't certain I could make it back to my room unless I could get off my feet and out of the cold for a few minutes.

I pushed open the door and a waitress with salt-and-pepper hair measured me for trouble. There were four or five people in the diner and not one turned to look at me. I took the farthest booth in the place and sat staring at the cigarette scars in the wood table top. The waitress came and took my order for a cup of coffee and a glass of water, and I never looked at her.

After she brought my order I waited until she walked away. Then I reached into the booth behind me and

16

grabbed a ketchup bottle. I poured ketchup into the water until it was the color of new blood, shook it a little to mix it, then drank half of it in a swallow. It was revolting, as I'd suspected it would be, and I gagged and took a breath until the moment passed. It didn't taste like tomato juice or tomato soup or anything a person would willingly consume, but I'd watched a sunburnt street guy do this in an old Pixley and Ehler's cafeteria one morning in the '60's. I thought it was the most disgusting thing I'd ever seen anyone do in a public restaurant. But even then, in my teens, I understood that he was hungry, and I'd heard that normal humans have no concept what a truly hungry man will do for food. So in 1964 or 1965 I'd watched an old man in a cafeteria and been disgusted. And now, in 1972 I was taking his place in the world. I took another gulp and fought against my rising gorge. Then I shoveled sugar into my coffee and drank half of that even though it burned my mouth like a coal.

A man moved in a booth by the window. It was Farrell, and though I could not have said how he would know I'd come to that diner, I was not surprised.

One:

The Conjurer's Shop

My father left us in October of 1962. I remember odd things from that day, a day on which I was to run frightened into a second-hand shop near the ballpark and change my life forever. It was the time of the Cuban Missile Crisis, when all of America rose each morning to learn whether we'd finally have the inevitable war with the Russians, the one children had been prepared for from Kindergarten. Here now was the critical day of the standoff, and all around me people spoke of the outbreak of war. But for me these were secondary concerns, of little import. I was fifteen and my father was gone.

A lost boy if ever there was one. We were new to the neighborhood, just one more change forced by my father, the latest "fresh start" of many – five neighborhoods in six years. He'd moved us here and now had left us. Never a boy to make friends easily, I had just started at a new high school, a massive place where I knew no one. I remember coming home from school that day to the oddly quiet flat, to my mother perched stiffly on a chair in the kitchen waiting for me. I can still see the two of us sitting in silence across the improbably bright kitchen table, on blood-colored Naugahyde chairs, neither of us making a sound. I was old enough not to cry, and he had long since taken it out of her, the ability to cry over him, to express rage at him, to do anything but stare down at the table. He'd left without warning though they'd had a fight, in fact several of them in the space of a week. I remembered listening to the last one and thinking there was something odd about it: usually they fought when he was drunk, and he rampaged through the house bellowing his rage at his life, knocking things over and promising violence to different people for slights real or imagined.

Once, only once, he'd hit her. I remember the sound of the smack and my horror that one of them had been hit. By the time I got out to the kitchen – they never fought anywhere else, they talked, planned, drank, joked, argued there, debated life – she'd hit him back and then grabbed the meat fork. That was how I found them: glaring at one another, him running his hand through his hair in shame and confusion, my mother standing with a red handprint on one side of her face and holding out the two-pronged fork.

But this last fight was bloodless and oddly subdued, and long afterward I came to understand that he'd picked this one, a pretext for leaving. I never learned why he left, though I eventually came to understand that there are men who live their whole lives simply picking up and running. It is possible, from things my mother let drop here and there, that we weren't even the first life he'd run from.

But run he did, my father, and true to his form, left it to

my mother to tell me.

"Tom, your father's gone," was the way she'd begun. "He left. He left us," she added, the gratuitous syllable making the news impossible to misconstrue.

"What do you mean?"

"He's gone. His stuff is all gone, his clothes, his – his old kit from the bathroom, he packed it all up."

"What happened? I mean, why?"

"Who knows why?"

I wanted to scream at her, to mock the hoarseness in her voice, her Tennessee accent. But I just looked at her and she could not meet my eyes.

How could he leave? How could he not care about us anymore? I wanted to know.

She tried to explain the things that can happen between couples, told me it had nothing to do with me, but I didn't believe this. I had never been the prize of his life and I knew it. Eventually I went out and left her to sit there smoking her Salems and reliving the old fights, looking for her mistakes. I made my way down to the lake, to sit at the rocks off Addison. It was a cold autumn day with a low, heavy sky, and the gray lake water slapped at the rocks, flinging itself high and far, and even when the icy spray started to reach where I sat, I refused to move. I sat there and I raged at them both, my mother who couldn't keep our life intact, my distant father, who'd run from us in his old brown Plymouth, a car unreliable as he was, and felt pity for myself. Sometime later it began to rain but I sat soaking on the rocks till I lost all track of time and then, as the wind and cold finally worked through my clothes, I headed home, lead-footed with reluctance. For a moment I toyed with the idea that I too would leave, I would run off to some distant part of the country, it would serve them right, all of them. It did not really occur to me that there was no "them" in my life. We had few relatives left: my grandmother had died earlier that year, and we had no other family in Chicago. There was an aunt, my mother's younger sister, somewhere in Peoria, where my mother's family had lived for a couple of years after coming from Tennessee. I thought of my mother again and realized I had to go back eventually. On some level I began to understand that if anything she felt worse than I did.

The shortcut was a mistake. I cut through a tough schoolyard near Halsted. My acquaintances in the new neighborhood had already taught me to avoid the place and now, propelled by my anger, I cut through it. I was nearly across the schoolyard when I realized I'd been noticed. I looked behind me and saw them, two boys about my age and an older one, 16 or 17. They were following me and gaining ground. The older one was grinning. I did not wonder at all why they were coming after me, bored boys on a wet day, boys with nothing better to do than torment a stranger. A police car passed on Addison and I knew I could run to flag it down, but I was already cognizant that boys had rules to live by, illogical though most of them turned out to be, and I rejected this idea as undignified and shameful.

Up ahead I saw the shadow of the elevated tracks, and just beyond, the empty gray hulk of Wrigley Field. I turned and looked again and they were talking about me, I was sure of it, and the older one made a beckoning motion. I began thinking of a way to escape, to hide, to

21

disappear for just a few minutes so that I could get back to my street. I looked again and the boys were gone. My relief was momentary. From the corner of my eye I saw them again, on the far side of the street this time and only a few yards away. My chest began to pound. I thought of running but I was a slow-footed boy, no runner, and a child knows sometimes that nothing will provoke pursuit as surely as breaking into a run. As frightened as I was, I remember the rage swelling up inside me at the unfairness of it all, that on a day when a boy's world collapsed he would take a beating from three kids who didn't even know him.

I walked faster, an unnatural pace that would fool no one, and in my panic I was about to break into full stride when I saw the coin. It lay in the very center of the sidewalk, and it seemed to shine even under the leaden mass of clouds. It was an Indian head penny, and, startled, I took the risk, I could not pass this up even if it slowed me down for a couple of seconds.

I picked at it, then realized the coin was embedded in the cement. I was in front of some sort of junk shop, and I understood. I wanted to scream, at my life, at these three kids coming for me, at my hated father, at this shyster shopkeeper who tricked people with gleaming coins that they could not have, just to advertise his wretched business.

I glared in through the rain-stained window. In the dark interior I could just make out a man standing behind a counter. The larger of two signs in the window said simply, "BOOKS." A smaller hand-lettered sign said "COINS, STAMPS, ANTIQUES, MAGIC AND PARLOR

22

GAMES, MISCELLANY." Below the sign, the message, "A. Farrell, Proprietor," had been painted in a faded gold lettering.

I saw the three boys reflected in the shop window, now crossing the street. They had caught up with me. My fear choked me, perhaps squeezed off the flow of blood to my brain. I pushed the door open and went in and changed my life forever.

As I shut the door I shot a quick glance behind me and saw the kids hesitating at the curb. Then I looked around at my temporary refuge.

It was a cramped place, a jumble of a room, with books stacked on shelves along two walls and piled high in the front windows. On the other two sides were tables and long glass counters, each one covered by flat trays, trays upon trays of small objects: I could make out brass fittings and ceramic statues, Christmas ornaments and old lead soldiers and tin toys. Gradually I became aware of the smell, a composite of mildew and aging paper and dust and disintegrating books, and plaster gone to powder, a junk shop smell.

Two men were watching me in silence, old men, I would have said. The smaller of the two stood beside the counter and looked at me. He was dressed in a shapeless wool overcoat cut for a larger man and a sweat-stained black fedora. The coat too was stained, missing buttons; he looked like an aging gangster fallen on hard times. He was squat and unshaven, with sallow skin and dark circles under squinting brown eyes, and I remember that he seemed to be moving from one foot to the other like a fidgety child. His arms, I saw, were long for his size, as

23

though nothing quite fit him. He leaned there against the counter looking me up and down, assessing me and not shy about it. Despite his size and the ruined look of his clothes, there was a boldness to him. I disliked him on the spot.

This man met my eyes and let me see the arrogance there. He shook his head and gave me a knowing grin of crooked teeth, yellow teeth. He jabbed his badly shaven chin toward me and said, "Another one."

The man behind the counter studied me as though I were a curiosity. This one was taller, and thin, with thick hair gone nearly silver. He wore a faded sweater and a white shirt, and a narrow silver tie. He was clean-shaven with a long narrow face. I noted his eyes, watchful intelligent eyes, and he reminded me of the old engravings of Sherlock Holmes. And there was something tired-looking about him, as if he'd survived an illness. He said nothing, just continued to study me. Almost against my will I found myself meeting this man's gray-eyed gaze, a scrutiny even more unnerving than his companion's, and on a better day it would have driven me back out onto the street. But I knew what was waiting just outside the door.

The silver-haired man looked past me and indicated the three boys with a nod.

"Do you know those lads?"

"No."

He made an almost imperceptible nod. The door behind me opened and I turned to see them entering the shop.

"There he is," the oldest of the boys said

"Get out, please," the man said in a calm and level

voice.

The older boy blinked in surprise. He said, "Say what?"

Then the shorter man spoke.

"You heard what he said. Get outta here."

The boy blinked. "I don't have to get outta here."

"The man told you to get out, so go."

"Who's gonna make me? You? You old bum – "

The man in the hat made an odd little growling sound from the back of his throat and pushed himself off the counter, a hard new look in his eye. The boy took a half step back. He frowned, opened his mouth to say something smart and his bravado fled. He looked in confusion from one man to the other.

"I told you to get out," the taller man repeated, and the boy began to back toward the door. The younger boys fell back on either side of him. "And don't come back," the man said. "There is nothing for you here."

He still had not raised his voice but continued to stare at the three boys. I saw their eyes: he'd frightened them. They hesitated at the door and looked from one of the old men to the other. Then the taller man came out purposefully from behind his counter and took a couple of paces toward them, and the boys backed out and hit the street running.

The short man in the hat gave a snort and muttered "little pricks."

The man looked at me for a moment. "If you want to stay here for a while, lad, it's all right."

I don't even know if I answered him. I was grateful but embarrassed as well.

"Just don't steal nothing," the short one in the hat said, and laughed, a laugh drained of mirth. The taller man shook his head and looked annoyed.

I looked around and, now that my panic had abated, I realized I'd never been in a place where so much had been crammed into a few feet, so that I was afraid a sudden movement would bring down half the shop on my head. Indeed, I shot a quick look up and saw that the ceiling was covered with the old punched tin sheets, and these had rusted and rotted so that it seemed the sky would fall through. The back walls beyond the three long counters were filled with more books and figures, leather cases and wooden boxes and cardboard cartons. One long shelf held what seemed to be folders or scrapbooks, and a hand-lettered sign over them said "Stamps". On one bookcase, several of the shelves were bowed, nearly to the point of giving way.

The counter closest to me held long flat trays, the largest nearly overflowing with coins, a great mound of them. I leaned over and stared at them. All the boys I knew had some sort of rudimentary coin collection – to a child coins bring the possibility of finding treasure in your own pocket. But I could tell at a glance that I had never seen anything like what he had in that tray, large coins and small, and some in strange shapes.

"You can pick them up and look at them. They're grand, the coins of other places. The ones in that tray are all a quarter. The ones in the small tray next to it, those are fifty cents. The ones in the case below are a dollar and up. Some of them are actually quite rare."

I let my fingertips graze an odd coin with a square hole

cut in its center.

"Coins from all over the world," the man said, as though reciting.

This, I saw at a glance, was quite literally true: I saw coins from France and Egypt, Turkey and Japan, Russian coins with the hammer-and-sickle. I glanced at the smaller tray and saw in its very center an enormous copper coin that proved to be an Irish penny dated 1927. On one side was a harp, and on the other the profile of King George of England.

"Farrell's got coins from every place he's ever been to," the one in the hat said. "Selling your pocket change, eh, Farrell?" he asked with an amused look.

I looked a question at the shopkeeper. He shrugged. "Ah, pay him no mind. But it's partly true, lad. I collected many of those, and I suppose a few came from my own pockets." I noted for the first time his accent though it seemed to me a mix of things: he managed to sound both English and Irish at the same time.

Inside the case below I saw a group of ancient-looking coins. A label in a dark, tidy script said "Greek drachmas c.250 B.C.," and I looked up at the shopkeeper.

For the first time he smiled. "Drachmas, those are. Drachmas. No, I'm not that old."

His smile changed his face, made him look younger, and I found myself risking a small smile of my own.

"You sure about that, Farrell?" the one in the hat asked. "What's that on that coin? Looks like your pocket lint." Then he chuckled and kept his eye on the other man.

"Yes, I'm sure. Of that, and little else." He saw me staring at them and after a moment said, "I am Arthur

Farrell. And that fellow there, is Meyer. My – associate."

They were both watching me now. I recalled an uncomfortable time in a book shop on Clark Street, when an intense-looking older man had spent considerable time studying me before inviting me out for a Coke. These men studied me and for a moment I thought of bolting as the three boys had. I looked from one to the other and decided they weren't looking at me in that way.

Indeed, the one called Farrell seemed to be peering at me as though looking for something. A look of worry crossed his face. Then he seemed to catch himself.

"Well, now, you know our names. What's your name?"

"It's – everybody calls me Tom."

"You have a first name you don't care for."

I was surprised at this, but nodded. "My first name's Charles but –" Charley was my father's name. By family custom I'd long been called Thomas, and now by choice I wanted never to be called Charles or Charley, and would never use it again. One Charley Faye in the world was enough.

"You prefer to be known by your middle name. And Thomas is a grand name. Do you know who he was?"

This was a stupid question, I thought. "Doubting Thomas. St. Thomas."

He made a little shrug. "Misunderstood fellow in my view: the one among them who was most like the rest of us. *'Prove to me these things you say, prove them so I can believe them.'* All he was doing. Do you know about him, though? A long, wandering life if the old traditions are to be believed. It is thought he died in India."

"Is that in the Bible?"

He caught the note of doubt in my voice: I'd never heard nor read this business of St. Thomas in India.

"It is not. But it is found in other writings just as old, and I don't know why some of them would not be true. Brought Christianity to India, Thomas did, or so these accounts go. All that long way from all the people he knew. A fellow forever out of place," he said, and gave me a preoccupied look. Then he shrugged again. "Perfectly good name for a lad, though."

"I hate 'Charles'."

Farrell gazed at me for a moment, then said, "You hate things about your life. It seems to me."

I felt my face burning.

The one called Meyer chuckled. He tipped his head toward his companion. "He's good at this," he told me.

"It's not mind-reading. I have – a skill for reading people, you might say. And your life is all over your face, lad."

I thought of how I had left the house, my mother sitting alone and quietly distraught at the red kitchen table. Suddenly I wished I had said something to her and I thought my eyes were starting to fill. I turned away from the man called Farrell.

"I meant nothing by it, young fellow."

"You spook 'em when you do that," Meyer said, and sounded amused.

"I didn't mean to." He looked around, clearly hoping to salvage the moment. "Feel free to look around. There are many interesting things in my shop." He made a small waving motion with one hand.

I nodded but thought it was probably time to leave.

Farrell seemed to sense this. His eyes flitted around the shop as though looking for something I might enjoy.

"Are you interested in comic books? Do boys still read the comic books? I have old comics." He indicated the far corner of the room where shelves were dense with piles of comic books.

He now had my full attention. "I collect comics. I have a lot of them."

"It's good to collect things," he said. "And of course I have many books, hundreds of books," Farrell added, looking around at the crammed bookcases.

"Loves his books," Meyer said, shaking his head.

"Meyer prefers the comics."

"That's right. No illusions in them."

"Don't be foolish, they're nothing *but* illusions," Farrell said.

"And those books of yours, what are they?" Meyer snorted and dismissed the bookshelves with a wave. "What do all of them books do for you? I got no time for books. Not anymore," he added in a quieter tone.

Farrell gave him a patient shake of the head and Meyer looked at me.

"I seen the elephant, kid. Farrell, there, he's your Man of Ideas. Me, I'm something else entirely." I now noticed Meyer's accent as well, just the hint of one, and nothing like Farrell's. He winked at Farrell and the other man shrugged in resignation. I saw that they were replaying an old debate. It made me uncomfortable, and so I went to the comics and crouched down to examine them. There were actually hundreds, and they filled that corner of the shop with the beloved odor of damp, aging paper. Some of them I knew were very old, perhaps even rare: early *Superman* comics, *Archie, Blackhawk.* I glanced at Farrell and he motioned with his hand for me to sit. I planted myself on the floor.

"Take your time," he said, and began speaking to Meyer in a quieter voice.

Soon I lost myself in Farrell's musty-smelling old comics, lost myself and all track of time. After some time the door opened and an old man came in, a bent, hatless man in a coat even filthier than Meyer's. He was bald and wind-burned even on the top of his head, and there was a dark gash under the man's chin, a cut still dripping blood. His shirtfront was stained with it. Behind him, this man pulled a two-wheeled shopping cart with a load of junk. He paused just inside the door, blocking it completely.

"Hello, fellas," the newcomer said in a high reedy voice. "Whaddya say, Arthur? Hiya, Meyer."

Farrell gave him an indulgent smile as this visitor filled the shop with his stench. He passed by me and I held my breath against the smells of a body long unwashed, of filthy clothing, alleys and basements, rotten food, garbage.

"Had a fall, Timothy?" Farrell asked him, eyeing the cut.

"Ah, you know, it's always something."

I saw Meyer step back as though pushed by the man's odor. He coughed slightly and made an exaggerated wave as if to clear the air.

Farrell came out from behind the counter and tipped the old man's head back to examine the cut. He stepped back to get a better look at Timothy's face, then took both the old man's hands and glanced down at them. There was

31

fresh blood on the man's hands.

"Scraped your knuckles into the bargain."

"Ah, you know me, Farrell, I'm always falling."

"We'll get you cleaned up." He went into a back room and returned with a wet cloth. "Let's have a look, then," he said, as he began washing the old man's hands.

"Listen, Farrell, I got something I wanted you to have a look at. Found this behind one of them nice houses on Alta Vista. Brass, I think it is."

He held something out for Farrell's perusal.

Farrell took the object and turned it over, nodded, made interested noises, then gave it back to Timothy.

"Yes, it's brass. That is a drawer pull from a fine desk from the old days. 'Tis a grand piece." A few feet away I saw Meyer snort and shake his head but the man called Timothy didn't notice.

"Yeah, I thought it was brass," Timothy said. "Can I get two bits for it?"

Farrell looked around the room as though considering this price. I saw his gaze rest for the merest of seconds on Meyer's eyes and then he looked back at Timothy.

"Sure. Two bits. That's a fair price."

"You can get maybe half a buck for it, Farrell."

"Right you are." He reached into the open drawer of his ancient cash register and came out with a quarter. "Here you go."

"Oh, you're a pal, Farrell."

The old man held up his quarter and grinned. He was turning to leave when Farrell said, "Let me have another look at that cut."

He reached out and touched the old man's cut chin. He

32

nodded, said, "It's healing already. You're nearly good as new. Mint condition, Timothy."

"Show me that trick, Farrell, the one with the coin."

"Ah, that's all nonsense, Timothy."

"It's fun."

"All right, then."

Farrell took the big Irish penny from the tray and held it in the palm of his hand. He passed one hand over the other and the coin was gone. Then he leaned forward and appeared to pluck the coin out of Timothy's ear, to the old man's happy laughter. Farrell smiled, shot a glance my way and gave me a quick wink. He held up both hands and the coin was gone again.

"Look in your vest, Timothy."

Timothy blinked, felt inside his sweater pocket and came up, not with the original coin, but a quarter.

"That wasn't there before," he said. Then he frowned. "Where's the other one?"

"In your other pocket, I believe."

And so it was. Timothy handed him both coins but Farrell told him to keep the quarter for his "cooperation".

Timothy thanked him, then looked around the room for a witness. "Did you see that?" he said to no one. "That's magic!"

Across the room Meyer made a farting sound with his lips. When Timothy looked my way, I nodded. It had, after all been impressive. I hadn't seen Farrell's hands anywhere near Timothy's pockets.

"All right, then. I'll see you later, Farrell. You, too, Meyer," and then left.

I held my breath again as he passed and looked up at

33

him. The old man smiled at me.

"Hello, boy. Nice quiet young boy."

I think I said, "Hello," but I'm not certain, for I was distracted. I was noticing his chin, where just a moment ago there had been a dark bloody gash, the sort of deep cut that required stitches, and now there was a modest pink ridge of scar tissue like the old cuts around a boxer's eye. I glanced at his hands and saw no blood there, either. For a moment I thought I'd been mistaken, that the blood had simply been an old scab, but I glanced at the floor just inside the doorway and saw blood there. I watched Timothy leave, then turned back to other men. Meyer was holding his nose and laughing.

"Jesus Christ! He smells like a backed-up toilet."

Farrell seemed to be watching the old man leave, but I saw him chance a quick glance my way and understood that he was watching for a reaction.

I felt a sudden twinge of fear, compounded by confusion, a feeling of being off-balance. I was afraid of him. I stood up quickly, felt light-headed and wondered if I would fall. Now the shop seemed stifling. I stood there blinking and realized I was staring at the shopkeeper. Farrell met my gaze and then looked away as though embarrassed.

I became aware of a change in the light, understood that I had been in the shop far longer than I'd realized. I remembered the unhappy home that awaited me and tried to block it out.

"Probably time to be going home," Farrell said. "Your mother might worry."

"Okay."

"Come back again, though."

"Okay," I said, without feeling.

Farrell gave me an earnest look, the look of one giving counsel. "You should. We can – I can tell you about some of those old coins. Some very interesting coins in those cases."

I nodded to show my earnest intention, looked from one to the other and then left.

Outside, the afternoon had fled. I began walking toward my house. I walked quickly, puzzling over what I had seen: the trick with the coins, of course, but more than that. I thought of the cut that disappeared. I had seen it, it was gone, and seemingly at one touch from the older man called Farrell. That was something else, beyond clever tricks with coins. And I remembered the other thing, the frightened look of the three boys, the look in the men's eyes that seemed to hold menace. As I made my way home, what I had seen began to take on darker meaning. By the time I reached our block, I was running.

Sleep was slow in coming that night. I thought of my father and it seemed my life had lost its underpinnings. I even wondered what this shared disaster would mean for my mother. And I thought of what I'd seen in the junk shop – what I believed I'd seen, for I was no longer even certain. At first I tried convincing myself I'd imagined most of it. But the reality of it pressed on me: a cut healed in moments, a pair of shabby old men putting a fright into three cocky street kids merely by looking at them – because the kids had seen what I'd seen. I realized I had been to a place where the rules of life as I knew them were suspended or contravened. I sat up in the dark and

35

pondered the possibilities.

The next morning I rose to an empty house. For a moment I thought I had woken to my old reality, of a home with a father in it. In seconds reality intruded. I ate the cereal my mother had left out for me and went out to school, where, in my shame at the new, barren state of my life I spoke to no one all day. After school, I walked aimlessly for a while, then headed for the shop under the el tracks, I am not certain why. When I was no more than a hundred feet from it, I stopped. I found myself staring at it. I backed away. Through the dirty window I thought I saw the one called Farrell. He seemed to be watching me. I turned around and went back the way I'd come, and imagined I could feel his eyes on my back.

TWO:

The Old Dispensation

That week when I first stumbled across Farrell's shop, people all over America spent their nights huddled around their radios and televisions and waited for the almost certain war with the Russians, and my confused impressions of the strange shop on Addison faded in importance. Whether because I was unusually sensitive or because I had an unhealthy amount of time to fret over the more menacing possibilities of life, this became a doubly troubling time for me. My father's departure left me feeling many things – defenseless, for one. There was no father in my home to protect us. The notion of my runaway old man as the shield-and-buckler of his family now seems foolish, but I was just a boy whose father had abandoned him.

So I listened to my mother on the phone, eavesdropped on her conversations with my aunt in our kitchen, listened to the breathless reports on my transistor radio and convinced myself the world was coming to its bloody end over missiles in Cuba. Russian ships were on their way, our ships and planes would cut them off, and there would be a war. During the night I woke at street noises, once or twice thought I heard my father's footsteps and tried to convince myself that he had returned. At last I fell asleep hoping that I would awaken the next morning and the two of them would greet me at the red table in the kitchen. Instead I woke to the gray morning, my mother sitting at the table and forcing a smile as she stirred her instant coffee endlessly. It would be just the two of us and I couldn't imagine how we would be able to live. My mother apparently determined that the healthiest thing for me would be a happy parent and so behaved in those first few days like the mother in a television comedy. She hummed while doing her housework, greeted me with a cheery smile, asked me how my day was, in short, drove me crazy. I took to walking, endlessly walking.

From time to time in those ensuing weeks I would think of the junk shop at odd times and push it back from my consciousness. I considered the many claims of his front window – Antiques, Coins and Hobbies, Parlor games, Magic tricks – and though I'd seen little enough in the way of magic, I managed to convince myself that this man called Farrell was some sort of magician, a notion that I did not care to hold up to the light. In any case, I avoided the shop; I had no further need for unsettling things. Then, in the greater world, the Russian menace came and went: Kennedy backed the Soviets down and occupied for a brief time the place of national hero, a position he would hold for exactly one year before he was to be shot on a sunny Dallas street.

We were no longer threatened by missiles in Cuba. Inside the small back apartment on Roscoe Street, the insistent realities of life demanded notice. The departure of one person, even the source of the family's main worry, brings an odd desolation, as though a certain space is reserved in our lives for even the troublesome. The truth of her life ate away my mother's brave performance and my home became a dead place, presided over by a woman from whom life seemed to be draining even as the physical weight left her. And leave her it did, for she grew thinner by the week. The four rooms that had so recently seemed cramped were now cavernous, so that our voices seemed to rebound off bare walls on those few occasions when we spoke. Even in leaving, my father managed to dominate the house, like an unresolved conversation. I know that it must have been the shortening days of the fall season, the low angle of the sun, but it seemed to me that our house grew darker as well. I found myself noting the things that were now missing: the smoke in the kitchen from his long hours sitting at the table with a quart of Meister Brau and his cigarettes, the smell of his hair tonic or shaving cream in the bathroom. At night, the sound of his endless pacing, always he paced after we'd gone to bed, as he dreamt up implausible new schemes for making money or worried about the money he'd dropped. He was a relentless bettor, at the track or on ballgames, relentless and luckless. Money washed through his hands, always the fault of someone who'd deceived him or refused to come to his aid, or simply his luck. The finality of his leaving now dawned on my mother, who dropped all pretense and descended quickly into depression.

Of course I had no idea what was going on in my mother's head or her heart, only that she wasn't well, wasn't herself. At times I held her responsible for his leaving and grew angry with her again. At other times it seemed to me that he had left simply because he didn't love us, and for that I was at least as responsible as she was. I made an unconscious decision to withdraw in my own way. My walking became obsessive, I roamed the streets for hours, sometimes whole days, into neighborhoods I'd never seen before. I walked in the rain, heedless of the condition of my clothes, and more than once shuffled into the house, oblivious to the time, only to find my mother sitting, tense and worried, asking me where I had been. And I could only say "walking."

Winter came like a dull ache, and the holidays, for the first time something to be gotten through, something to survive. I was eventually to see worse holidays in my life, including one spent on the streets, but that one stands out among them all, the first Christmas after the old man hit the road, a cold morning in our badly heated flat amid our garish and now out-of-place attempts at decorating – the things of Christmas will mock a family in distress. But survive it we did, almost in spite of my mother's attempts to force a Christmas on us.

Sometime after the New Year I made my way back to the strange shop on Addison. From time to time I'd thought of it, but now associated it with unpleasant things: the time of my father's leaving, the tough kids chasing me, and of course what I thought I might have seen. But one afternoon under a low sky pregnant with snow I found myself on Addison, with the black steel skeleton of the el hanging over the street. I assured myself that I wasn't deliberately going by the shop, it was just that our flat was in that general direction, but when I reached the shop I stopped. For the first time I saw what passed for Farrell's window display, a jumble of antiques, books, lamps, junk. On my first visit I had had no time to stop and peer into it. Now I did, and I was transfixed, he had things that would have held any boy: he had a Civil War era canteen, a display of pocket knives, and an old sword in an ornate scabbard.

I made a sudden decision to go in. As I pushed open his door, it occurred to me to look for the penny, the embedded penny that had stopped me on that first visit. It was gone. I was annoyed by that, that some luckier kid had come along with the leisure to dig it out with a pocket knife. Annoyed and perplexed, for the penny, embedded though it had been, had left no outline of itself in the cement.

But I went inside, into the musty air, barely heated – I learned later that neither of them was fond of a warm room. As soon as I stepped in I could smell the damp paper smell of the comics that had held my attention on that earlier visit. It might have been the light, but the place seemed smaller, more crowded than I recalled, and the two of them were both there, one at each end of the counter. Farrell was peering at what seemed to be a photo album. Meyer was looking out at the street. When I closed the door behind me he jabbed his nose in my direction and said, "This one again," as though I were bad news in the mail.

Farrell looked up, said "Hello, lad," and went back to his cards. I made a slow circuit of the various collections and counters, spent a few moments on his old coins and

41

then made my way over to the comics. I did not stay long: it was a test, to see if he bothered me, or if the troubling atmosphere of my first visit would be a permanent feature. Nothing happened: a couple of customers came in, one bought a lamp, the other browsed and left. I could have been sitting in any small, cramped junk shop in Chicago. I bought a tattered early *Superman*.

"That's five cents, my boy. And how was your Christmas? A grand Christmas, I hope."

"It was okay," I said, not meeting his eye. I handed him my nickel.

"Well, a happy New Year to us all, young fellow. A better one than the last," he said and I was certain he meant this for me, as if he knew I was lying.

"Thanks," I said.

"Come again, lad," he called out as I left went out.

And "come again" I did, within that same week. Four times in the next two frigid weeks I went to the shop. A sort of rhythm settled onto my visits. I came in, answered Farrell's greeting, perhaps nodded at Meyer and then went over to the vast pile of old comics or pored over one of the trays of coins. The two men would resume their conversation. At first I made no attempt to learn what they discussed. When their talk intruded upon my consciousness, it seemed an odd stew of minor and major topics: baseball, not the actual teams but the concept of it, a leak in Farrell's roof, the likelihood of eventual war with the Russians, the death of an acquaintance. This last seemed particularly troubling to them both. I remember that Farrell spoke slowly as though distracted, and Meyer seemed for once at a loss for words. I recognize now that this death, whoever it was, reminded them of their great loneliness even as it intensified it. The recent showdown with the Russians, on the other hand, had made them both furious.

"*Amadans* and fools, damn them all, the bunch of them," Farrell said with surprising heat. Meyer paced back and forth and muttered under his breath, much of it profane, as though the possibility of a war were a personal affront.

But they addressed none of this to me. Later that afternoon an unkempt bald man entered. He smelled of pipe smoke and old paper, and though Farrell addressed him as "Leo," I was eventually to meet this man, a Professor at DePaul, and to learn that he loved argument, on any subject. In no time at all the professor managed to get into a verbal streetfight with Meyer on the subject of Israel. It was the most demonstrative of debates, the professor waving his arm frantically so that I thought he'd rip his coat, and Meyer moving back and forth in short paces as though looking for an angle from which to sucker-punch his opponent. The professor was at a natural disadvantage in this dialogue, for he had a soft voice that didn't convincingly project assurance or even irritation. It was hard to imagine him hailing a cab let alone debating an angry opponent. Meyer had a voice to match his face, all ground glass, hard and sharp and grating. He also fought without manners or scruple, interrupting the professor constantly. After one such spate of interruptions I saw him steal a sly glance at Farrell, and his eyes were smiling.

At his most provoked, the professor threw his arms

open wide and barked, "What does this matter to you, Meyer, for God's sake? You're not even a Jew."

"The fuck I'm not," Meyer said in a low voice.

"The lad is here, Meyer," Farrell said. Meyer just shrugged.

"Don't be ridiculous," the professor said. He looked to Farrell for support but Farrell just watched them.

"So you're a Jew, now? That's news to me, Meyer. Maybe to everyone."

For a long uncomfortable moment Meyer just glared at him. Then he said, "That's right, I'm a Jew. Just another fuckin' Jew."

I stared at him, as startled by this admission as by his insertion of profanity into what had been a friendly argument. A few feet away Farrell shook his head like a disappointed parent.

For a long moment Meyer glared at the other man as if daring contradiction. Then he looked away, the argument was over. The professor looked a question at Farrell. Farrell shrugged. Soon he and the professor were in quiet conversation over Napoleon and the Duke of Wellington, clearly a less prickly subject. For his part Meyer moved from his constant perch at the counter and went to the front window to stare out at the street. He glowered at the passersby and I saw his lips move. I thought he was crazy, the first person I'd ever known who was actually insane.

And, for that matter, my first Jew. I'd never known any, knew nothing of them except what I had heard from my father, that they were sly and preternaturally gifted in the making of money, that a man like him never stood a chance in a business deal with a Jew. But Meyer's assertion of Jewishness seemed to puzzle the professor, and it was clear that something here had gone over my head. I was, of course, to understand later. I was to understand all about Meyer.

On my next visit I stopped just inside the door when I saw that Meyer was there but not Farrell. I had not yet been alone in a room with Meyer and was reluctant to enter but just as loath to go back home. Telling myself Farrell was probably not far, I entered quietly. They had actually turned up the heat against the growing cold, and the shop was warm. Still, Meyer wore his overcoat and filthy hat. He nodded to me and then looked past me, staring with his strange eyes out at the street, his cheek puffed out with a load of hard candy. The wrappers sat in a careless pile on the top of the counter. As I made my way to the comics I looked around for Farrell, and Meyer growled, "Farrell stepped out. There was a problem, something he had to do."

I nodded and knelt down beside the comics. Behind me, Meyer said, "Don't buy nothing till he gets here. I can't work that goddam register."

I rooted around for a comic I'd been looking at on my previous visit and tried to read but I was intensely conscious of Meyer's presence. He shuffled around, paced back and forth like a dog in a kennel, and made an array of odd and disturbing noises: he cleared his throat, clicked the candy against his teeth, sucked at it, swallowed, snorted, and muttered.

The first time he spoke I looked up quickly and said, "What?"

"Wasn't talkin' to you," he said, with perfect

nonchalance. A few moments later he muttered again and I looked out the window to see what had caught his attention, but there was nothing.

Finally Farrell returned, his face pale. He moved slowly and I would have said he was ill.

Meyer studied Farrell's face for a moment, a strangely eager look in his eyes. "So?"

"No good."

"She gonna die?"

Farrell nodded. "Yes, poor soul."

Meyer nodded, then remembered me. "That kid's here again."

Farrell turned slowly and it seemed to take him a moment to focus his attention. "Good. Hello, lad."

I said "Hi," and as he walked to the back room I heard him say, "A little company can be a tonic." I had no idea what he was talking about, but I was taken aback at his weakened appearance.

As I sat in my nook with a pile of old, damp smelling comics in my lap, I strained to follow their conversation to see who it was that Farrell thought would die, but they gave me nothing. There were times in that shop when neither one said anything for a long time. I have since experienced this phenomenon among older people: the ability of two acquaintances, even two friends, to sit for hours without speaking, and in no apparent unease in such silence.

As I crossed Addison to head home that day I saw a man standing in the doorway of a small grocery store across the street from Farrell's shop. He was a thin man in a faded denim jacket. His hair was gray and dense but he was going bald on top, and he had an ashen look to him. And though I passed directly before him he kept his gaze on the shop, as though I didn't exist, and squinted at the shop as if to see through its filthy windows.

On several of my subsequent visits the man in the doorway was there, either before I went to the shop or when I left. One day as I passed the small grocery on my way to the shop, the doorway was empty. As I went by, from the corner of my eye I caught a movement in the gangway beside the store. I turned and found myself facing this man. He hung back in the dark gangway and watched me. Up close he was even more desolate looking, with the pallor of influenza. His eyes were close-set and dark, and gave him a fevered aspect. He took a nervous puff from a cigarette, glanced at the shop across the street in clear distaste, then seemed to study me for a moment.

"You oughtta stay away from there. From them."

"What?"

"You're not like them, you're not one of them. You should stay away from that place. It's a bad place." He nodded in the direction of the shop and I noticed that his left earlobe was gone. "There's evil in that place."

I did not know what to say to this, and my silence seemed to provoke him. He leaned forward, urgent and angry and I took a step back from him. He moved closer.

"You don't know what they are."

He took a hasty puff on his cigarette and blew out smoke, and it seemed that his pale self blended into it, as though he were himself made out of smoke.

"You don't know. You got no idea." Then he gave me a disgusted shake of the head and went away quickly, muttering to himself and leaving a smoky trail in the air. I had not felt threatened but he'd unsettled me. For a long moment I stood there trying to decide what to do. I remembered the odd things I'd seen there and on some level thought I understood what the man meant. After a while I rationalized that no one in the shop had ever done anything to bother me, and crossed the street. They were both there when I went in, and looked up at me simultaneously. It seemed that there was something different in the way they looked at me, and I could not meet their eyes, either of them. After just a few minutes looking at the comics, I left, muttering "Bye" as I pushed out through the door. I did not want to see how they watched me.

Three: Laws of Nature

My next visit interrupted an intense conversation between them, a sharp exchange with Meyer waving his hands and Farrell shaking his head, and when they saw me they lowered their voices like conspirators caught in a corner. Then Farrell nodded to me, said, "Thomas," and Meyer just watched me. Each was in his way annoyed at my presence. I left after a few minutes.

Other things preoccupied me, other concerns, the problems of being a teenage boy in a desolated house, a boy with no connections in his life. A teenager who has no actual social life will imagine one, and so I began to create a fantasy life for myself. My walks made this easier, for they allowed me to put miles of real space between myself and my life. Winter helped. Snow and early darkness sent the populace scurrying inside, and I became less self-conscious of the solitary nature of my walking, for the streets were nearly empty. I sought out the tree-lined streets far from mine, streets where each family owned the home they lived in.

With the wisdom of hindsight it is clear now that I was looking for perfect families. I peered in the windows and imagined people with orderly, untroubled lives, well-dressed girls with perfect faces, families that sat down to dinner together and had conversations. I lost myself in my imaginings, envisioned myself with a girl from one of these perfect homes. And so I marched and fabricated, lost all track of time or location and at times found myself on streets so strange to me that I wasn't sure I could find my way back home. By the end of that year I had probably been on nearly every block of the north side, and was developing an encyclopedic knowledge of the city.

For some reason I began to play basketball obsessively, not with the kids in the neighborhood gym at St. Andrews but at the more distant Hamlin Park, a rougher place near the projects between Clybourn and the river, a place full of tough kids and gym rats who came to know me casually and didn't bother me. This was precisely what I wanted: acquaintances, not friends.

Shortly after that I began to see the signs of true panic in my mother. Several times I came home to find that pieces of furniture were gone. The first was a small TV that we'd kept on a counter in the kitchen, then several things of my father's, his easy chair – which neither of us had sat in since he left – and his bar, his ridiculous mahogany bar filled with a dozen kinds of fancy glassware. The bar, when he'd bought it, had been the cause of one more fight: she couldn't understand why a family with so little would need something like a bar. He thought it was exactly the touch of elegance his life was lacking. So I wasn't surprised when she decided to sell it. But the sale of our other things frightened me. I understood very little about money or our finances. From conversations with my schoolmates I understood that ours was one of the few households without a car. But selling our things seemed a dramatic step, a final stage in the dissolution of a family. Each time I came home and saw an empty space where a chair or table had stood, a hard knot of fear and depression grew in my stomach. I had once, in one of my wanderings, made it up into Uptown on a day when an old woman was being evicted. She stood there, a thin black woman in a man's sweater, and stared at the street as the Sheriff's police carried her belongings out of her home and deposited them at the curb. I watched for some time, and saw that a small crowd had gathered for this terrible scene, standing far enough from her to pretend they weren't watching. There seemed to be no one to take the woman in, and I wondered for days what became of her, and how a person could arrive at so final a pass in her life.

And here in my own life those questions were being answered: it was clear to me that we had begun whatever descent brings a family to the point of eviction. My initial reaction, of course, was anger. I asked only about the television. She told me in a quiet voice that she had to sell it, that when we got through this she'd buy another one. I did not see how we were going to get "through this."

So I bit my tongue and watched as she reduced the contents of our flat, and added this transgression to the others for which I held her responsible. Somehow the new barrenness of the apartment crystallized my rage at her. I deliberately did things to provoke her, stayed out past curfew and dodged the cops, engaged in an endless series of verbal combats with her over the most trivial things. Several times I came upon her silently weeping in the kitchen, and her sorrow somehow made me angrier with her.

51

One evening I was coming home from my wanderings and I was startled to see my mother sitting alone on a bench at a bus stop. She sat looking down, unaware of my presence or, it was clear, of anything else, heedless even of the cold. I had the odd notion me that she was looking at the dark scenes of her life and I thought I had never seen anyone look so despondent. A bus came, slowed down and, when she did not even look up, sped along without her. She could have been a homeless woman whiling away her time. Without actually thinking of what I was doing I slipped into a doorway to watch her. As I did so, I felt a slight light-headedness and a new image seemed to superimpose itself over her, like a descending shadow. For a moment someone else was sitting on the bench, a girl, a young girl. And as I looked at this new person, I understood many things about her: I saw a barren life, poverty, I saw a man striking her. In this sudden image the girl looked up and was my mother. Still a girl but my mother. I did not recognize the man who struck her, but the image was terrifying. I looked away in confusion and when I looked back the defeated woman on the bench had returned. I slid out of the doorway and retraced my steps. As I fled, I was struck by the conviction, chilling and unshakeable, that I had just glimpsed my mother's life. I moved faster, putting distance between myself and what I thought I'd seen, then told myself it had not happened. To prove this I replayed the scene mentally, trying to reconstruct it in all its elements. But the scene reappeared, perversely intact in every detail. I saw this younger version of my mother in some past stage of her unhappy life, noted that the blouse she wore was wrinkled, noted the dark stubble on the man's chin, saw his eyes now and recognized a far more dangerous look in them than mere anger, I saw his deep frustration at his life. And as though it were happening at that moment, I saw the scene continue, impossibly, saw the man strike her and knock her to the floor and then storm out in shame at what he'd done. I saw her sitting on the floor, and I saw something else. Just as a witness will call up unrealized detail when questioned by a streetwise cop, I saw more. The girl in my mind's eye faded and once more I was looking at a forlorn woman on a bench. And now I saw another person across the street, also watching my mother. In the fading light I saw this second person only in silhouette but I knew it was Farrell, and it was perfectly clear to me that he had taken in all of it, my mother on the bench, me watching her from a distance and saying nothing. And I suddenly had the ridiculous notion that he knew somehow what I'd seen. In a panic I forced myself to walk faster. After a few paces I shot a quick look over my shoulder. Farrell was nowhere to be seen, but I took the rest of my trip home at a steady run and sprinted the last block.

I began looking around for work in the various businesses along Southport, and eventually found a part-time job. A couple of afternoons a week I swept up and carried out boxes and other trash for a dog-eared store grandly named the Southport Department Store. It was a single wide room with a low tin-covered ceiling. The owner, a short man in thick glasses, sold a little of everything one might find in the bigger stores, Goldblatt's or Wieboldt's or Sears. His business was irregular: at times the store was busy, at others the only sound would be my own footsteps on creaking wood floors worn nearly white by decades of customers. Some weeks he didn't need me at all.

In the meantime I kept to my recent patterns. I was beginning to notice more, understand more: I saw men in gym shoes and thin coats begging on the frigid corners and wondered if they would live out the year. Street incidents I witnessed as well, and two of them stood out, for they each involved one of the old men of the shop, first Farrell and then Meyer. These two occurrences opened my eyes to darker possibilities in these men.

One night I was walking in my neighborhood near the Music Box Theater when I witnessed an accident. A car ran a stop sign and barreled into a delivery van. The van spun round from the force of the collision and struck a man I had seen many times in the neighborhood and once in Farrell's shop, a man my mother referred to casually as a "ragpicker". In my mind's eye I can still see the van spinning across the intersection, its rear end catching the small dark man just as he stepped off the curb and throwing him like a stuffed animal against a parked car. I heard the *thunk* of his head hitting the fender of the car, and a second sound, stark and final, as his skull hit the pavement.

People began running toward him, and I joined them. When I got within a couple of feet I recoiled from what I saw. His eyes had turned up into his head so that only the whites showed, and his thin body was contorted in an unnatural position. He shook, seizured as though his bones were no longer quite connected, and then he was still. The breath caught in my chest and I took several steps back. For a long moment no one went near the man on the pavement.

Then a man in a tie bent down and felt for a pulse, first at the throat and then the wrist. He gave a small shake of his head and quickly stepped back. I saw several of the bystanders move away to avoid the taint of this man's final bad luck. For some reason I noticed that the ragpicker wore no gloves despite the cold.

"Somebody call an ambulance," a man said.

A woman ran for the grocery store down the block and the rest of us looked down on the stricken man.

Then I saw Farrell. He was standing at the periphery of the growing crowd. For a moment he stared down at the man and made no movement. Then he began pushing his way through, saying in his grave, dignified voice, "Let me through, please. I know this man."

The crowd parted and Farrell knelt down. I could not hear him but I saw him mouth the words, "The poor man." He seemed nervous, his hands were shaking, and he took the man's hand in his. He felt for the pulse, shook his head as the other man had done but continued to hold onto the ragpicker's hand. Like the ragpicker he wore no gloves. I saw him touch the man's throat as if feeling for a pulse there, and then he picked up the man in his arms.

"I don't think you're supposed to move 'em," a woman said, but Farrell sat there on the cold asphalt and held the man to him. He shut his eyes and clasped the man to him, and an onlooker might have thought that here was the dead man's brother holding him close to fend off death. Gradually Farrell's eyes opened. His gaze moved over the faces of the bystanders and fell on mine and I saw no recognition there. And as he held the frail body in his arms Farrell began to rock back and forth. The ragpicker's fingers curled once and then straightened.

"He moved!" the same woman's voice said. There was a general murmur from the crowd and the ragpicker's head jerked slightly. And then I saw Farrell's eyes. They had regained their focus and rested on me as though noticing my presence for the first time, and what I saw there chilled me. For the faintest moment in time he was changed, his eyes were changed. I remember thinking that they looked like my father's eyes had looked when he came home drunk and raving as he threw wild punches at the hostile forces in his life, and recognizing none of us in his rage. That is what I would have said at that moment, that Farrell didn't know me, and that I should not be there. More than the cold light of his eyes, a wave of hostility, of malice, seemed to emanate from Farrell, toward me, and I moved back into the crowd. A man stepped in front of me to get a better look and I turned and ran. I had no doubt I had seen something I was not meant to see.

That night I slept little. When I did sleep, my dreams were troubled by images of old men pursuing me down streets where no one would help me, forcing me into corners. The men had no faces at first but eventually became Farrell and Meyer, and of the two I feared this vision of Farrell far more.

February settled on the city like the plague. On a dark afternoon I hiked over unshoveled sidewalks, made it all the way to the icebound lake and stood there listening to groans of the water trying to break through. I imagined the fish frozen in place, waiting for life to begin again. In that first winter after my father left, it seemed life would not resume, not for us or for anything else. I don't know how long I stood there but eventually the cold seeped through my clothes and I began to shiver. My feet were already nearly frozen, and I was tired from the long trek there. It was nearly dark when I began heading for home. When I looked up to get my bearings, I could see the dark skeleton of the el in the distance. I cut south on Halsted toward Roscoe, where we lived, and then I saw Meyer. Without thinking, I stepped into a doorway.

He was coming out of a small tavern attempting to stuff a bottle in brown paper into his coat pocket. After a moment he gave up. The snow on the sidewalk had been ground to slush and then iced over, and he stopped just past the tavern door and looked down at the ice. Then he began gingerly making his way toward me, without looking up. He wore his ill-fitting wool coat, heavy black work shoes, no boots or galoshes, and one of his white socks had slipped all the way down into his shoe so that his ungodly pale ankle showed. He was muttering to himself and shaking his head, and he couldn't have looked crazier. Two dark shapes crossed the street toward him. I recognized them, a couple of the older kids from the neighborhood. One of them was more or less notorious among the younger kids. People called him Pez and it was rumored that he had spent time in the reformatory at Montefiore or St. Charles. His constant companion was a heavy-set redhead named Rooney, and they seemed to spend their days standing on corners smoking and trying to get a rise out of people passing by. On this chill Chicago afternoon Pez and Rooney had spotted a victim. They hustled toward Meyer and walked a couple of paces behind him, laughing silently as Meyer slipped and lurched on the ice. They were all coming in my direction though no one had noticed me. I saw Pez come up behind Meyer and wink at his companion.

"Meyer," I called out, and as he looked up, Pez pushed him from behind. Meyer's feet slid out from beneath him and he landed heavily on his back with the thwack of bone on pavement. The bottle shattered and bled its dark contents over the snow. For a moment Meyer made no sound. His eyes began to roll up into his head, and his mouth came open. His bony legs stuck out from his trousers.

The one called Rooney went as pale as old Meyer's skinny ankles. I saw him mouth "*holy shit.*" Pez took a sudden step back and thrust his hands in his coat pockets as though to distance himself from blame. We stood there, the three of us, staring at the motionless old man on the sidewalk. I was certain he was dead. Then Meyer made a harsh gasping sound. He sat up, swore to himself and began to get to his feet. On his first attempt he fell back onto his behind, which elicited more cursing. I saw the two thugs exhale in unison and share a relieved glance, and then Pez stepped forward.

"Hey, old guy, you fall down and go boom?"

He laughed and grinned at Rooney, and then bent over Meyer. He took a grip under the old man's armpit and gave a tug, yelling out, "Up you go, guy." With very little effort, he had Meyer on his feet. Meyer made a feeble try at brushing himself off, got almost none of the snow from his coat. He glanced down at the pool of wine spreading at his feet, a red stain I now noticed on his pants and on his solitary white sock. He looked at me without apparent recognition and then turned slowly on Pez.

"Busted up your bottle, there, Pop," Pez said in a cheery voice, but there was a new wariness in his eyes. I couldn't see Meyer's face. He stood motionless for what seemed a long moment, snow falling from his back. Then he seemed to gather himself.

"Here, want me to brush you off?" Pez asked, and he never saw the first punch. Meyer's right fist caught him high on the cheekbone with a loud smack. Pez lurched back, slipped slightly on the ice, then righted himself. He put a hand to his cheek, where a red swelling was already forming.

"Hey, you old fuck," he said, but his eyes showed confusion. He took an uncertain step toward Meyer and shoved him. The old man lost his balance and tumbled against a car.

Pez pointed a long finger at him. "I oughtta kick your old ass, you old – "

Then Meyer bounded off the car toward him. Rooney came between them, yelling, "Hey, what are you, goofy, you old asshole?" and he was about to say something else when Meyer smacked him in the mouth. Rooney bent over and held his hands to his bleeding lips.

"This old fuck needs his ass kicked," Pez said.

For a moment the three of them seemed frozen in a gray tableau: Rooney licking at the blood on his lips, Pez to one side, glaring, and Meyer bent low, his gnarled hands balled into fists. He breathed through his mouth and a wild look had come into his eyes, a look of perfect hostility. They came at him and he crouched low, weaving from side to side, and he put me in mind of a great four-limbed spider caught in a corner. Then they both went at him, hit him at least half a dozen times, I could hear the steady thump as they landed their blows. I thought they would kill him, I thought I was watching a man being killed.

"Leave him alone!" I heard myself call out, but no one heard me. Meyer covered his head, ducked a punch, then sprang, punching and snarling at them. He threw wild blows with his improbably long arms and I saw him hit Pez high on the forehead, then squarely on the nose. He hit Rooney as well, and the big redhead backed away. Meyer turned on Pez and the two men traded punches, Meyer making guttural sounds deep in his throat.

None of it seemed possible. After his quick attack Meyer moved back up against the car again. He had lost his hat, and I could see the bald spot at the top of his skull. It made him seem fragile.

A woman with a small child came by in the growing darkness, shot a horrified look at Meyer but hurried on toward the safety of her world. I looked around and saw that there was no one else around. The Town Hall police station was two blocks away but might as well have been in the next county.

The two kids moved in on Meyer again and Pez came at him from behind.

"Behind you," I called out, and Meyer spun round to face Pez. They traded punches and both landed. When he stepped back, Pez was bleeding from his nose, and I remember thinking that he looked surprised. But he came forward and now Rooney came at Meyer from the other side. The old man got his back up against the car and snarled at them, and each seemed to be waiting for the other to make the first move. Finally Pez threw a punch, and then Rooney, and Meyer took a long swipe at each of them but hit nothing. A cut had opened across the bridge of his nose and dark blood ran down past his mouth. He looked from one to the other, his face contorted, horrible, and he was growling. Spittle was dribbling from the corner of his mouth and his breath whistled back in his throat.

Pez threw a punch that missed, and Meyer caught him with a counterpunch that made a loud smack. Rooney made a sudden move, slipped a little on the icy pavement and Meyer caught him on the side of the face, and Rooney went down in the snow with a wet sound. Then Meyer lunged at Pez, grabbed him by the neck and sank his teeth into Pez's ear.

Pez howled and swore. They fell to the sidewalk and rolled in the gray snow, and what I saw of the infighting was terrifying. I saw Meyer claw the other man's face, gouge his eye, thump the side of his head with his fist, I saw him put both hands to Pez's throat. Then Rooney pulled him off by the back of his filthy coat. Pulled him off, yes, but stepped back.

Meyer and Pez got to their feet, both of them, and Pez moved away, clearly terrified.

His face was a mass of blood and the gouges from Meyer's long nails, and dark blood had already started to clot at the top of his ear. His hand went to the ear and he stared at the bloody fingers.

"Jesus Christ!"

Meyer was panting, and grinning, and there was blood on his teeth, they could have been fangs. Rooney and Pez exchanged a quick glance. Both were bleeding, gasping and clearly confused by what was happening. For a moment I feared that they would try once more, and it seemed to me that Meyer must be hurt himself although he was grinning.

I yelled out, "There's a cop."

Pez gave me a dazed look as though noticing me for the first time. And then they both spun round and ran into a nearby alley. Meyer glared after them. As they disappeared from view, he looked around and saw that there was no police car. He glanced at me and then turned his attention to his snow-covered clothing. I saw him look at the dark stain on the snow and I could smell it now, the wine, a sour smell I was to forever associate with the sight of an old man fighting two punks with his back to a car, fighting alone.

Then he pointed a finger in my face. "You helped me, kid. Twice." He seemed surprised. Then he added, "You don't come around Farrell's no more."

I didn't have anything to say to that. For a moment I stared at him: blood ran down the side of his head from a scalp cut, and he bled as well from the gash across his nose. "I think you're hurt," I said pointlessly.

He seemed to find this amusing. "From what? From this, these two clowns? Fuck, no." He touched the cut on his nose, bent over and put snow on it. He looked at me again, the blood turning the snow pink on the bridge of his nose. "This here, what you saw?" He jerked his thumb behind him as though the fight could still be seen in the fading light. "This ain't nothing, boy."

Just to be saying something I said, "Sorry about your wine."

He shrugged. "Wasn't for me anyhow." Then he gave me a measuring look. "You're smarter than you look." He smiled and showed me his bloody teeth again. Then he nodded. "See you around, kid."

I watched him trudge back toward Addison in his lunging walk, the heavy shoes slipping with nearly every step. I stood there watching him until he was lost in the distance and the dark. Suddenly I was very cold. I could not seem to stop shuddering. I noticed the blood now, blood all over the gray snow – whether his or the two boys' I could not tell. I thought of what I had seen, the malicious violence of the two young men, then their clear and well-founded terror. I thought of Meyer's startling transformation. I wasn't sure how the fight might have ended, but it was clear that despite his age and size in solitary fight Meyer would have taken either one of them, might even have killed one of them. This realization was as disturbing as the violence itself had been. With a final glance in Meyer's direction, I headed home. That night I was unable to get warm. My mother pushed me into the bathroom and ran a tub of hot water for me, chiding me all the while for staying out on the streets in the coldest week of the year.

That night I slept badly. Near dawn, before sleep finally came in earnest, I thought of what I'd seen in the company of these old men, the things that happened either

63

in their presence or due to their agency, and decided I wanted no more of it. Meyer was a madman and Farrell something more complicated and therefore more troubling. I feared the taint they could bring to my already damaged life.

"You don't know what they are," the man in the doorway had said. I wanted no more of either of them.

Four:

A Shoebox Full of Life

1 formed a sort of truce with my mother. As the weeks
went by I was able to put out of mind the night I'd seen
her sitting at the bus stop, but I'm certain that experience
had something to do with my change in attitude toward
her. For her part she seemed to calm down a bit. She sold a
leather-topped card table, kept for parties and thus never
once used, there were no parties in her life, and then she
stopped selling things. I brought in a little money, and she
got a small raise and an additional half-shift at the diner,
so that money was, for the time being, no longer a cause
for panic. I also believe that she'd sold off a few pieces of
her jewelry from an old box she kept under her bed, and
this had convinced her that she had a primitive version of
a nest egg. Some of the jewelry was hers, some had
belonged to her mother. Once I came home from playing
basketball and she was sitting at the kitchen table listening
to big band music on her red radio and looking with
something like reverence at each piece. When she noticed
me, she invited me to sit down. After just a moment's

hesitation I decided I could do her this small kindness. After a moment I realized these things were a connection with her past, and so with mine, something I knew nothing about.

One of the items was a tiny watch, no larger than a locket.

"It was my mother's," she said quietly. "And she got it from her grandmother, who came over from Scotland."

"I never saw one like that," I said. It seemed a stupid thing to say but apparently it was just what she wanted to hear.

"I never did either. I'm afraid to even wear it."

Then I heard myself asking her questions about this long-ago relative. Many years later I was to learn of the horrors of these ocean-crossing voyages, the coal-smelling ships that crammed hundreds into fetid quarters below decks and arrived in America laden with the dead of whatever country they'd set out from, whether the despised contents of the ship's hold were African slaves or Irish fleeing famine, or Swedes and Germans hoping the cards would be kinder to them in the new place.

My mother told me what little she knew of her great-grandmother, and then her other ancestors, and for the first time I understood that there had been a long, complex family and a thousand kinds of trouble and suffering before the line produced me. After a while I asked what seemed an impolite question: what could she tell me of my father's people?

She gave me a long look and then shook her head. I thought I had upset her but she was merely embarrassed: she knew nothing about him, nothing about his family, for he had never been willing to discuss such things.

"He mighta been born the day before I met him, for all I know about him. Man with no past, and I went and married him. Said he thought of himself as a traveling man, a man who needed to see the world. But that's what some folks call a drifter. Came into my life, stayed a bit, then he left, might as well disappeared in a puff of smoke, and I can't tell you a thing about him you don't already know. I'm sorry, Hon."

"No, it's okay."

She went into her room and came back a moment later with a shoebox. She gave me a shy smile, then set it down between us and took off the lid. It was filled with photographs, a small mountain of photographs large and small, in no particular order.

"One of these days I'm gonna buy a big old album for these, sort them out, you know." She shrugged. "They're all in there, all the people of my life."

I stared at the pictures and understood that for a woman who had outlived most of her family and friends, this shoebox contained not only her history but her sole connection with it. Her youth, her childhood memories, the things she'd seen and done, were all in that box. It is nearly impossible for children to understand the people their parents were, to imagine them in youth, propelled by ambition, anger, fear – *lust*, for God's sake – but as she spread the photos out before me, I watched her and saw her as a person for the first time in my life. I'd seen some of these photos before but the people in them had no connection to my life, and the little girl in the photos, though unmistakably my mother, had never quite seemed real to me. Now I made an attempt to understand the people in these pictures, to understand my mother's life.

Photographs are the great irony among our keepsakes: the people in them are forever smiling, carefree, fearless, their faces giving little hint of the troubles in their lives. The people in my mother's discolored photographs grinned and mugged and gave no indication of their need, frustration, disappointment. I watched her study the faces, saw how she paused at a photo taken of her at age fourteen, smiling at the photographer and shading her eyes against the sun, saw the sadness in her eyes as she compared the bright face of childhood promise with what she knew of life. Then she was looking at me.

"The future's so different from what we expect, Tom. Not always worse, but – different, always different. You should remember that. Your life's gonna be different than you expect."

I said nothing. She would not have expected me to understand. In my silence she produced a photo of my father. It was one of only three or four pictures, and the others were of the two of them, during the early days of their marriage. The black-and-white photograph she held before me showed a handsome boy of nineteen or twenty, posing with one foot on a hydrant. Clybourn Avenue, I would have said – just a long stone's throw from where I played ball. He was sure of himself, of his looks and his future. The other pictures showed me he was certain of her as well.

"There he is, in Chicago. Always told me he was from Texas. But one time he admitted he lived here for a while."

"You don't think he was from Texas?"

"Coulda been. But nothing else he ever told me was the truth." She gave me a rueful smile. "I'm not even sure his real name was Charlie Faye."

She gave me a long look and I could see her suppressing the next thought, though I knew what it was: *He's never coming back: that, I'm sure of.*

As I undressed that night I recalled her phrasing, that my old man might as well have disappeared in a puff of smoke, and I realized that more than once I'd had such a thought, that it almost seemed at times as if he had never really been there at all.

At about this time my mother also stopped badgering me with her questions. I could tell she was still troubled by my long hours away from the house, though she didn't mind if I was leaving with a basketball under one arm. I'm sure she asked herself how much trouble a kid could get into playing basketball.

One night as she sat at the kitchen table I came in and, without actually having made the decision, announced that I was going to be looking for a better job. I remember that I felt on the verge of adding, "to stop the bleeding." At the time I thought it an odd phrase to pop into my head, and was glad I hadn't spoken it aloud. She gave me a rueful look, then a sad smile.

"You can work for spending money, Tom. But I can take care of us now, I can. I got a few more hours at the restaurant."

As I was leaving the room she said, "I made good tips this week. I been making good tips lately for some reason." She pulled out the small coin purse in which she held the family fortune and came out with fifty cents.

"Go get yourself some ice cream. Or a Coke or something."

I went out to spend her money and understood that we'd come through the hardest part.

My mother and I surprised each other, I think, by not puncturing the delicate fabric of our cease-fire. I made a conscious effort to be more patient with her, and she learned how to give me space. Two other things occurred at around that time, both my mother's doing, which helped me in my ongoing quest to have a normal life.

For my sixteenth birthday in April my mother threw up her hands in surrender at what to give a teenage boy and put twenty dollars in a card. My delight was obvious and took her by surprise, and I was happy to have given her something to smile about. I knew exactly what I'd do with it. By the end of the day I'd bought a used Schwinn 3-speed, what we called a middleweight bike then. It was an odd choice: by that age, most boys had started thinking of ways to get hold of a car, and though I fantasized about myself in a red Chevy Impala convertible, the events of the previous year had made me a realist in ways my acquaintances could not dream of. There was no red Impala in my future. So I bought a bike, took it home and stripped it. I removed the useless tank, the carrier, the front and back fenders, and I was in business.

With the bike I was mobile. Oblivious to the April cold, I traveled farther and farther across the city, covered the lakefront, rode the deserted and wonderful beach and imagined it full of girls, explored strange neighborhoods. I learned of huge parks on the west and south side, parks with lagoons where strange kids chased me, I learned of a tiny, hidden beach just beyond the Planetarium, I found full-sized ships moored by the long piers jutting out into the lake. On one of my rides down along the lake I had the sobering experience of watching the police divers pull a man from Belmont Harbor. As they took the man from the water I caught a glimpse of his face, unearthly white from the icy water, and could not turn away. For a moment I saw this face in life, I saw this man in a room with no lights on, I saw him alone and despondent. Later that night I dreamt of this man, I dreamt of his life.

I made my lonesome circuits of the city, never venturing near the shop on Addison. At night I read, voraciously, books of history and especially books that told me of the exotic corners of the world. Occasionally I drew. I roamed, I watched baseball, I drew sailing ships, and in this way I spent a perfectly solitary summer. I stared at the girls till my heart ached and told myself I would have one, and soon, though a part of me knew that was a lie.

When I finally did meet a girl, the first of several, it was a girl to suit my odd life, a girl in a fortune teller's window.

They come and go, these people – usually women – sprouting up like dandelions when people's fortunes dip and the credulous go seeking protection from the future. Within a mile of my house there were at least a half dozen fortune tellers, palm readers and a tarot specialist and a woman who studied charts of the skies. Eventually fortune tellers would develop sophistication, relying on the careful placement of small but ridiculous signs to announce their presence and their varied gifts – a blue neon eye staring out at Halsted Street, perhaps, or a glowing sign of the Zodiac or the trusty old moon-and-stars motif.

In the 60's most of them still worked out of basement flats or they rented storefronts and sat in their windows. Street legend had it that all fortune tellers were gypsies, and so I assumed that my neighborhood must be nearly overrun with gypsies to have so many fortune tellers. The closest was a hard-faced woman in a basement apartment on Addison, who left her blinds open and always seemed to be talking to the same worried looking man. The second, whom I was eventually to meet at Farrell's shop, called herself "Madame Volga" and held court in a tiny space on Clark Street near the ball park between a couple of moribund taverns, that is, when she was not actually in one of the taverns. The third told her fortunes in a storefront on Sheffield that had been a dry cleaners, and I could have sworn that in its former incarnation, she had also been the woman behind the counter taking in people's shirts. Whenever I passed by her shop, she was in the window, sitting just below a hand-made sign, thick paint put on through a stencil, proclaiming her to be "Madam Georgina". Below the name was the admonition, "Know your future". "Future" was spelled *"Futur"*. But her spelling seemed not to trouble her. Indeed she appeared to be the most jovial of fortune tellers, for she grinned at me and held up a deck of cards or made some sign indicating that she could be of service.

Then, one morning I passed her shop and sitting in the window was a dour-looking young girl of around my age, a dark young woman with thick black hair. She was sewing, and as I walked by she looked up and met my gaze without blinking or showing interest. She had odd eyes for a young girl, a grown woman's eyes in an impassive face, the face of someone difficult to surprise. I thought she was beautiful. I nodded and realized that I was staring, indeed that I was powerless to do anything else. Suddenly the older woman materialized in the window beside the girl. She indicated with broad gestures and her strange grin that the girl was somehow for me, that I should come in, that wonders of the flesh awaited me. She pointed at the girl and then at me and leered, and I know that my face burned red. The girl gave her a disgusted look. She spoke and I read her lips: she said, "Stop it."

I took one more look at the girl and walked on to hide my confusion. A boy of that age can convince himself of nearly anything where young women are concerned. Thus I managed to convince myself that what I'd taken for a gypsy fortune teller's parlor was really a low-rent house of prostitution, and that at the age of 16 I had just been propositioned. I was both exhilarated by this sign of my long-anticipated manhood, and disappointed as well that the pretty young woman in the window was a prostitute. But prostitute or no, I thought of her that night, in fact every night for weeks and in every possible stage of undress or sexual congress until I thought I would never sleep again. In days to come I wondered if I was haunted.

One afternoon I rode to within a few yards of Farrell's shop. For several minutes I waited there, straddling the bike, and watched the door. I saw people enter and leave with their purchases, it might have been any small shop in the great wide city, and I had the odd feeling that I was being left out of something. I watched for a few minutes more and then left.

After giving me cash for the bike, my mother engineered a second minor change in my life: she pulled a string or two and found me a job, and managed to make it seem I'd obtained it myself by pointing me in the general direction of a job she'd "heard" about. It was an actual job with regular hours in one of the innumerable diners that once thrived on nearly every arterial street in the city. This one was on Clark Street, and there was another one just like it on the next block, another on the block after that, and one across the street. The owner was a Tennessee woman named Millie who had once worked with my mother and was happy to send a few dollars our way. She put me to work as a bus boy and general errand boy. I was paid cash straight from the register, and almost against my will the diner worked itself into my imagination. It was garishly lit and seemed to be a sort of collecting place for dislocated southerners. I loved it. It was raucous and busy, the air dense with the smell of frying food, so that when I went home my clothes smelled of onions and hash browns. There were no quiet moments, it seemed steeped in something I thought of as *Life*. Customers called out insults to one another and harassed the waitresses in barnyard voices. The conversation was unschooled, unadorned, often salacious, and they all loved it. I soon became the butt of some of the humor, and so understood they'd come to accept me. Years later I was to see an Arthur Miller play called *A Memory of Two Mondays*, about a college kid working in a Depression-era factory, and it brought back the year or so I spent in Lou's Diner. There was no Lou, by the way. Millie thought a man's name sounded better, but informed me once that if she ran a tavern, it would be "Millie's".

"Men understand a woman runnin' a ginmill won't take no crap," she explained.

And so I worked and made money and rode or wandered around the city. I fought for normalcy without knowing it, telling myself I was doing all right. More than anything else, I fought to suppress the fearful, skittish boy I had been a mere year before, a boy whose days began and ended in one sort of dread or another. I convinced myself I was afraid of nothing anymore. The school year ended and one of Millie's busboys quit to go back to Tennessee, and she put me to work more or less full time. I worked, I went to movies by myself, I hung out at Hamlin Park and once or twice passed a bottle of wine around. I wore out the tires on my bike and dreamed about the girls.

One Saturday toward the end of my aimless summer I was sweeping the kitchen floor when Millie sent me on a delivery. The address meant nothing to me: a business on Addison, a Denver omelet sandwich and a burger with raw onion. It was a blazing day and I was delighted to be sent out of the diner. Halfway to my destination I had a premonition of where I was headed, and was not at all surprised when the address turned out to be Farrell's shop. The last thing a young man wants to do after escaping the people and places of a phase in his life is to revisit them, and in my case I feared being drawn back in. I stopped a few yards from the shop and was close to tossing the bag in a trash can. Then I went on. It was my job, after all. Besides, you can do many low things in life, but you can't take away someone's lunch.

I pushed open the door and Farrell raised his eyebrows. Meyer made a little snorting sound and said, "This one again."

They were in the same places I'd seen them before, as though time had stopped when I last left the shop and resumed now that food had arrived. For a moment I was nearly able to forget the unsettling occasions when I'd last seen each of them.

"I believe he's brought us our lunch," Farrell said.

I looked from one to the other and made a show of reading the carbon of their bill.

"Denver on wheat toast, burger with onions."

"Yes, that is our order. A pleasure to see you again, young Thomas."

I nodded and tried to look around casually. The dreary afternoon when I'd first taken refuge there seemed far in the past.

Meyer took the bag from me and began rooting through it as though there were money in the bottom. Farrell paid the bill and handed me a dollar tip. Back then it was a large tip for such a small order, and I was embarrassed.

"Take it, lad. Most places don't deliver small orders. This is special service for us. Saving us a trip out in this ungodly weather."

I looked back out the window, where the late summer sun had bled gold onto the street, then realized I was being had. Farrell gave me a faint smile at his small joke, and I felt myself smiling at him.

Across the room, Meyer saw no joke. "Hate this goddam weather."

"Well, you wear a hat and coat whether it's January or August."

"So?" Meyer said, and gave him a belligerent look.

"Just keep the change, Thomas," Farrell said, studiously ignoring the other man.

I thanked Farrell for his generous tip and looked around, and I could feel his eyes on me. My discomfort hung in the air between us. I remembered the last time I'd seen him, the last time I'd seen Meyer as well, and the man who watched their shop. For just a sliver in time I wanted to blurt out that I'd seen things that cried out for explanation or denial but something made me hold my tongue. Perhaps it was Farrell himself, for he did not behave like someone with anything at all to hide. In fact, he behaved very much like a man who had been waiting for his lunch.

He glanced at me, then at Meyer and went behind his counter, spread out the waxed paper and picked up his sandwich. He took a bite and nodded. When he saw me watching him, he made a small toward Meyer, who was savaging the hamburger.

"I like a nice hamburger now and then meself, but a Denver omelette sandwich, now that is a lovely American invention."

I must have smiled, for he winked and returned his attention to his lunch. After a couple of bites he pointed to his coffee pot, where something black and viscous had settled.

"Help yourself to a cup of coffee, lad."

"No, thanks. I should get back."

In the end I became not so much relaxed as distracted, distracted by my surroundings, by the jumble of improbable items on his shelves, by the weight and presence of all these old things, and I stayed for a few minutes. Across from us, Meyer looked around the room with an enormous bulge of hamburger in his cheek. It seemed he had already forgotten my presence.

"How have you been?" Farrell asked.

"Fine. Thanks." After a moment I remembered my manners and asked about him.

"Oh, the same."

A few feet away, Meyer nodded at this and mouthed the words, "the same," then gave a silent laugh, as though this were a fine joke.

"School is going well? It is boring at times, I know, but you are a good student."

I shrugged. I was better than average but Farrell wouldn't have known this. I started to leave.

"I don't suppose you have much interest in the comics anymore."

"Not much, no," I said, even though I still had a collection of my own that I looked at regularly. I'd begun to think of myself as a collector. To the old comics I had added an interest in old boxing magazines, fascinated particularly by the photographs of legendary fighters, old bare-knuckle boxers and fans in straw boaters. So my statement that I no longer had time for old comics was disingenuous, and I wasn't even certain why I lied to him.

"I've got to get back to work."

"Of course. And how is your mother?"

"She's fine."

He nodded and suddenly seemed preoccupied, as though a new thought had occurred to him.

"Well, it was grand to see you, lad. Stop in again sometime."

Across the room, Meyer raised the gnawed end of his sandwich in salute and looked away, dismissing me.

I yanked open the door and heard Farrell say, "Stop by and visit anytime, you know. I have more than the old comics. Boxing magazines and so on."

I refused to turn around, just nodded and went out. My face was burning. I pulled the door closed behind me. In the glass of the door I saw the reflection of someone attempting to enter the shop, and I pushed the door open again and stood aside.

The newcomer was the girl, the dark-haired girl I'd seen in the fortune teller's window.

I almost said, "Oh."

I stood there with my hand still on the door and chanced a look at her up close. She was indeed my age, and pretty in her solemn way, dark hair and eyes and olive skin. She wore a white top and shorts. And try as I might, helpless under the onslaught of my hormones, I stole a glance at her brown legs. When I met her eyes I saw an odd look, part amusement, part surprise, perhaps at seeing someone her age coming out of the old shop. I wasn't certain she recognized me, wasn't sure I wanted her to remember the circumstances.

"Hi," I said.

She said "Hello" but didn't hold eye contact. She

thanked me for holding the door and this seemed to release new strength, so that I gave the door a sudden push. It banged against a brass statuette inside and I heard Meyer bark "Don't wreck the joint for Chrissakes." I waited for a heartbeat to see if she'd turn around and of course she didn't. Without looking at him I could tell Farrell was still watching me. The girl said something to him and gave him a breezy wave, a gesture of easy familiarity. She made her way to the back of his shop and the great groaning mass of his bookshelves. I stepped out into the street and inhaled the scorched air of Chicago in August, with its grit and smells of sun-softened asphalt and cigarette smoke. For all I knew the air could have been ripe with the smell of sex.

For the rest of my shift that day I thought about her. A young man without other female company was of course going to think about those brown legs, and I did, but I also thought of her eyes. They were striking eyes, but it wasn't that. I'd seen something interesting in her eyes, in her face, something I could not put a name to. I'd seen many, many girls that caught my eye – my God, at that time in my life they all caught my eye – and on my walks into the better neighborhoods I'd seen girls from good families, girls in fur-collared coats and high boots or knee socks, girls I couldn't have, girls who would have been at least mildly amused at the notion of going out with a boy who rode a bicycle and couldn't tell you the whereabouts of his father. It seemed to me that all of them were beautiful, that there were whole neighborhoods in the city where all the girls were beautiful. This girl wasn't beautiful in that way, but she was far more interesting. Once she'd reintroduced herself into my fevered consciousness, she was to remain there for a long time.

Five: Many Faces

A couple of weeks after that trip to the shop on Addison, I contrived to pass the fortune teller's on Sheffield. As I passed the window, I made a show of looking at my watch while scanning the shop from the edge of my vision. The girl was inside and I caught the movement as she noticed me. I pretended to be unaware of her. I pretended to be unaware of her the next three or four times I went by the shop, I did all the stupid things a boy could do to prove lack of interest in a girl who has already begun tormenting his nights.

Then one morning I was late for work at the diner, running, in fact, and as I passed the fortune teller's window I forgot my strategy. I slowed down and looked inside. The girl was sewing – perhaps the old fortune teller had gone back into the cleaning business? – and met my eyes with an odd look that was part challenge and part amusement, as though she'd seen through my pretense, as she'd seen through a hundred others like me. I could no longer feign disinterest, not now, and as I moved past her window I met her eyes and gave her some sort of nod. Then I put my head down and ran the rest of the block, feeling as ridiculous as if I'd lost my pants. Later I decided I'd made a fool of myself, and for a time I found another route to the diner, hoping even as I avoided the gypsy's place that I'd see the girl on the street or in a store. Or in Farrell's.

As a result, after months of avoiding the place and the two men in it, I began once more to drop by the shop. I was a distracted visitor those first couple of times, sitting on the floor like a small child and paging through Farrell's *Ring Magazines* and comics while keeping an eye on the door for the dark-haired girl. As I did so I fell into my old pattern of eavesdropping on the conversations in the shop, whether they were Farrell's intellectual debates with his friends or his short, terse discussions and occasional arguments with Meyer.

I found that, as I varied the times of my visits, the character of the shop seemed to change: in the evenings it was a place full of talk, about books, philosophy, politics, films. And argument, often ferocious – although none quite as angry as Meyer's argument with the professor. More often than not, Farrell himself took part in these debates – "vigorous disputation," I was to hear him call it. In fact, I eventually heard Farrell argue convincingly with Professor Leo for the existence of God, and with a young minister that there was no evidence at all for a God. These "disputations" made my head spin, and I was not at all comfortable that a man could one day argue for God and the next day flatly assert that there was none.

In the afternoons, Farrell "received guests" – people coming to him for one sort of favor or another, people like old Timothy, the fetid old street scrounger whose

83

suddenly healed chin had given me my early fears of Farrell and his shop. Time and again Timothy returned to the shop, blowing into the place in a sudden blast of chill air, lurching and bruised like a dropped apple, grinning perhaps at his great good luck in having survived another night in the alleys, and willing to talk to anyone breathing. Once I was his victim, on a day when Farrell was busy with a customer, and so Timothy talked to me of his worldviews and his life on the streets for nearly an hour. I uttered no more than three or four words in response, but apparently this was sufficient to keep convince the old man he had a receptive audience.

Timothy, yes, and others like him, a homeless man named Ray, and a tiny shriveled woman called Alice, who struggled through Farrell's doorway towing rather than carrying a shopping bag that smelled of old fruit. She often brought Farrell suspicious food items that he stared at and promised to enjoy later at night. Farrell fussed over Alice, treated her as a prized guest and made her tea. To Ray Farrell spoke quietly, inquired about the man's innumerable physical ailments and wounds of the street. When Ray left, I listened to Farrell and Meyer speak of him and understood that Ray was dying of half a dozen different diseases and complaints.

Others there were as well, men and women, some coming to sell him things which Farrell bought whether they were worthless or had value. Some came to talk, just to talk, and once or twice I saw him work his small sleight-of-hand tricks to their appreciative laughter.

Strangest of all his "guests" as he sometimes called them, Madame Volga herself came in, not the "gypsy" woman with the dark-haired girl but the fortune teller from Clark Street. Her name, I learned, was Zoe, and I wondered why, with a name like *Zoe* she'd needed a professional name. Madame Volga bustled into the shop, a bony woman with an odd bent-over walk, wearing a blue sequined turban over silver hair.

She called out, "What's new, Farrell?" in a barmaid's voice, asked for coffee, then took her turban off and placed it on a corner of the counter. The silver hair came with it, revealing Madame Volga's own thin gray hair, bobby-pinned flat to her skull.

"Meyer," she said. "What's new with you, hon?"

The idea of anyone calling Meyer "hon" so startled me that I had to look away to keep from laughing. For his part, Meyer snorted, waved, said, "How ya doin,' Babe."

Then "Madame Volga" lapsed into a brassy four-way conversation with Farrell, Meyer, and Leo the Professor, during which they made small talk about common acquaintances and she revealed that the fortune-telling business was, in her words, "A moribund enterprise."

I became aware of other features of the shop as well. The back rooms, I learned, were Farrell's living quarters though Meyer sometimes slept there, or on the floor of the shop itself – when he wasn't flopping in a doorway somewhere. And the shop had the power to make Meyer crazy: Farrell had more than a dozen clocks, all set, and when they chimed the hour Meyer would growl or curse.

I observed – no, it is more accurate to say I spied on Farrell. I listened to his stories, noted his oddly anachronistic speech: an ashtray was a "smoking stand" whether it had a stand or not, a vacuum cleaner was a "carpet sweeper", a record player, any record player, was a Victrola, whether it had a hand-crank or not. And the bus was always "the streetcar". I heard him speak of his scholarly interests but learned he was a devoted fan of baseball. When a customer asked why, Farrell explained, "'Tis the one game without time, beyond time. There is no clock to it, d'you see? In theory a baseball game could go on forever." He turned to me then and winked. I didn't know why.

But I was keen to learn about him, and so I spied on him in his interactions with his customers and guests, I watched for any further sign of the small miracles I thought I'd seen, and the other things as well. He fed them, these old people of the street, fed them and gave them tea or coffee or cold drinks, even gave one or two of them items of clothing – a sweater or a scarf (a "muffler" he called it), or a pair of shoes. He bought their questionable items and listened to their stories and sent them out with the admonition to return soon. Several times, with the more physically damaged of these old street people, I watched surreptitiously and saw him put his hands on them. I fancied that they left the shop changed, renewed in ways I couldn't have put to words. More than once at these times I saw him look my way with suspicion.

But whether they came to escape the emergent winter or to have someone listen or to sell him something, there were dozens of them, and he knew their names and their stories and their latest injury at the hands of the world. Some returned time and again, so that their names were impressed upon my consciousness whether I wanted to know them or not: Alice and Ray, hard-faced Mary, who carried her burdens in a laundry cart and announced her intent "to do some business, Mr. Farrell," a small sickly man named Walter, fragile and colorless, who seemed content to sit for a time on a small chair and say little.

Most of the people to come into the shop were white, but from time to time Farrell was visited by a light-skinned black man named Pickett, who called Farrell "Arthur" and seemed possessed of nearly bottomless knowledge of the wide world, having served on a heavy cruiser in the Pacific for nearly twenty years. Farrell was cordial to all but always seemed genuinely glad to see Pickett, and the two men sat sometimes for hours speaking of the wide world and what they'd seen of it, and what they would visit if such opportunity ever came back. There was a tone to their talks that suggested neither one would ever travel again.

Once Pickett chanced, as he was leaving, to see me reading an old *National Geographic* article on Russia.

"There's a place I'd like to see, young man. Never made it there."

I looked up at him.

"They weren't sending heavy cruisers to that place. I would have liked to see it, though. You should see some of the world, even if it's just the States."

"I want to," I told him, and of course it was true. I wanted to see some of these places I'd read about, and for the first time had begun to imagine a life somewhere beyond the barrenness of my own. In my fantasies I had money in my pocket, a car, good clothes, the interest of women, and my life was playing itself out in French

Polynesia, or Greece, or Brazil. An article in the *Tribune* Travel section convinced me I might find a life both exotic and erotic in Tahiti, of all places, where there was apparently a need for English teachers. For a time I saw this as my destiny, and I pictured myself in a white tropical suit with a dark slender girl on my arm.

What I never realized was that I had become a part of this small, disordered storefront, accepted by the customers, many who seemed to know my name and some who were willing to talk to me.

And finally there was Warren, to me most interesting of them all, small and menacing and sure of himself, troubled by drink, a former boxer and the first Indian I had ever met, a tough little Menominee from Wisconsin. He chatted with Farrell about old-time fighters and spoke in a near-monotone of his many adventures inside and outside the ring.

There was no end to the surprises in that place. One day a man came in with an address written on a piece of paper. He looked around, confused, spoke to Farrell in Spanish. Farrell nodded toward Meyer. The man took his paper across the room to Meyer, who looked at the address and then, in what seemed perfect Spanish, told the man how to get there. When Farrell saw the look I gave Meyer he nodded.

"He knows many languages. One of Meyer's gifts. A man of parts, your man Meyer."

Of his own life, Farrell offered no account, not intentionally, but I learned to listen when people brought up old events, or brought in objects to sell him. More than once the things they brought him told me small things about him, his life.

On one such occasion a small furtive man came in with a tattered shopping bag. Farrell stood with one hand on his hip and watched the man produce one item after another. From across the room I watched Farrell's eyes. It seemed to me that he paid little attention to the sales pitch, instead studying the man's face, his shaking hands, his entire aura of nervousness and fear. From the bag he took out the flotsam of his life: a lamp – people were always bringing Farrell lamps, the shop groaned with the weight of a hundred useless lamps and he always bought them, always – a lamp, and a long ornate serving spoon, and a pewter mug and a camera long since sunk into obsolescence, souvenir cups, decorated thimbles, a woman's watch.

Finally, at the very end of his speech, the small man produced a helmet. I knew from my reading that this was a World War I soldier's helmet. The man held it out and for the first time Farrell moved. He stepped forward and took the helmet. For a moment he seemed to study it, the seller speaking enthusiastically all the while. An uncle, it seemed, had brought it back from "the First War". The man said he knew it was a British helmet, thought it funny that his uncle had come back with such a dubious souvenir.

"I mean, other guys come back from that war with German stuff, swords and that. Officers' pistols. My uncle comes back with a helmet from our own side."

Farrell nodded. "Yes. Poor Tommy wore this. Tommy Atkins," he said, and I knew he was speaking to himself.

"Tommy Atkins? That's who it belonged to?" The man

frowned.

"No. That's what people called them, a nickname for them: Tommies. The British Army in the Great War. Tommy Atkins, the typical British soldier. Like your G.I. Joe."

"Oh."

Farrell hefted the helmet as though weighing its metal content and looked past the man, out toward the street. His face transformed, if only for seconds but I saw it, unmistakable, a look of tremendous sadness. I lowered the magazine in my hands and for a moment wondered if I should do something. Then the small needful man broke the silence and the spell.

"So? Can you use it? Any of it?"

Farrell looked at him as though just recalling his presence.

"Now, I'm not looking for a lot of money. I thought, the lamp, maybe a couple bucks and the camera, now that camera still works, that's a good camera – "

Farrell rested the helmet on his counter and gazed at the camera. Then he nodded.

"It's grand. And the lamp, yes, my friend, the lamp as well."

"So whaddya think? I'll take five bucks for the whole bag." When Farrell didn't respond immediately, the man said, "I think the helmet's worth two- three bucks by itself."

"I'll not buy your helmet, my friend," Farrell said. He spoke with authority: this clearly was a matter beyond haggling. "I cannot use it. There is a fellow on Belmont, near Riverview, who specializes in such things. In war *memorabilia.*" He mouthed the word "*memorabilia,*" a second time and then added, "That's the lad you want."

The man took back the helmet. "Okay."

"But these other interesting items, I'll give you three dollars for the lot of it."

The man brightened. "Three? Okay. That's a deal." He held out his hand and they shook.

When the man had left, Meyer spoke from the far side of the room. "You bought another bag of crap, Farrell. To add to your crap collection. Three bucks, for Chrissakes."

I'm not certain Farrell even heard him, but when I spoke a moment later he heard me.

"Was the helmet real?"

"Yes, it was genuine. Worn by a man long dead. A man who was killed in the War."

"How do you know?"

"I was there." After a moment, he added, "British soldiers wouldn't just hand their helmets to their Yank allies as souvenirs. Someone took that off the field. From a dead man."

"Is that why you didn't want it?"

"One reason. Of many."

I looked around his shop, aching to ask the obvious question: what of all these insignia, buttons, medals, weapons, yes, the weapons?

He watched my gaze, saw where I looked, moved to intercept: "Why do I keep all these other things, then? A good question, but most of them saw no combat, these buttons and lapel pins and shoulder patches. And those old rifles likely sat in an armory and grew a patina of dust till someone saw a way to make a nickel off them."

"What about the swords?"

We both looked at the beautiful crossed swords displayed on his back wall, each hung gleaming and spotless just above its scabbard.

"Ah, the swords, yes," he said, and I could see his mood lighten, if only for the moment.

"Those are the ceremonial swords of the Knights of Columbus, lad, our nation's last line of defense. When the Goths and Tartars of old return to sack our cities, those lads will face them in the street and sort them out."

Then he laughed quietly. I had seen them in parades, the Knights of Columbus, white-haired Catholic men strutting in capes and bicorn hats with ostrich plumes and brandishing their fierce swords, and I laughed with him, as much at the fact that I'd gotten Farrell's joke as at the old Knights themselves.

He was still smiling, doubtless at his suggested image of those old men in capes fighting the barbarian hordes. I felt emboldened to prolong the rare candor of the moment.

"You told the man about a place where he could sell his helmet. Have you been in it?"

"I have not. I have no interest in such a place. *Military memorabilia.* Indeed. I will tell you, lad, a man who has stood on the field when the bloodshed is finished, who has looked around at the dead, the piles of dead thrown up like windrows, has no need for *memorabilia.*"

His tone suggested that the conversation was ended. But he gave me few such openings, at least in those days, and so I was loath to let it go.

"Were you in – did you see fighting?"

"Aye. I saw fighting. All the fighting."

Something odd was happening to his speech, it seemed. His brogue grew more pronounced, as though he were acting a role.

I pushed on. "Which battle were you in?"

He had been gazing out at Addison Street and for a moment I thought he hadn't heard me. Then he gave me a long look. I met his eye, I knew these battles from my endless reading, I wanted him to know that, for once, I knew something.

"There was only the one, lad. Just the one battle. It went on for four years, but it was the same battle."

I thought of what he'd told the man about the English soldiers. "You were in the English Army," I said.

"Aye, I was. His Majesty's Royal Dublin Fusiliers. Paddy dying for his English King, poor Paddy whose loyalty was questioned even as he died in battle. The Dubs served at Mons and Ypres – they gassed us at Ypres. And of course, the Somme."

I saw Farrell mouth *the Somme* to himself as though he'd momentarily forgotten me.

"Did you ever get wounded?"

He gazed out at the street and I believe he was deciding whether to answer.

"Sooner or later, boyo, all of us were wounded. Killed or wounded."

"And that's why you didn't want the helmet."

"'Tis. I would not see those fields again. And if I had that poor dead fellow's helmet here, I have no doubt I would see them again."

I did not understand what he meant, and before I could ask another impertinent question he went into the back of the shop and began fussing with a new pot of coffee. When I turned around Meyer was watching me. He was grinning, like a man who has gotten hold of a fine secret that he will not let go of. For the remainder of that afternoon Farrell was silent, gray-faced and silent, as though he had been taken ill.

When I left the shop that afternoon I experienced an odd feeling of shame, as though I'd seen something I had no business looking at.

Six:

The Wandering Jew

Perhaps it was nothing more than an extension of my impulse to eavesdrop in the junk shop, but I began to follow Meyer. The first time was complete chance.

I had already learned Meyer's proclivity for disappearing, sometimes for a week at a time. More than once Farrell had spoken of Meyer's walks, made reference to Meyer "falling off the earth," as he put it, at least once every couple of years. I learned that this was the great overriding pattern of Meyer's life, this incessant roaming, whether of the streets of the city or the roads of the wider world. One day when Meyer had been gone for several days I was in the shop and someone asked Farrell where Meyer might be. Farrell shook his head and said, "I know only that he is on the loose, and no good can come of it."

I looked up at that and saw that he was smiling, but there had been a trace element of the truth in that statement.

But on a warm Sunday in late September, just after school had started again, I chanced to see Meyer. He was on the far side of the street, and even at my distance I could see he was talking to himself. I watched him for a moment and then began to follow him, keeping to my side of the street.

He walked bent over, head forward, his heavy coat flapping behind him. As he strode belligerently ahead, he took the center of the sidewalk, several times forcing people to walk on lawns to avoid him. Eventually he crossed the street, cutting in front of traffic. A motorist gave him the horn and Meyer absently gave him the finger. A block or so ahead was St. Andrew's Church, a handsome red brick building that took up most of a block. Meyer was looking at it as he walked.

When he reached the church, he began pacing back and forth as the well-dressed parishioners went inside. I took a spot behind a tree and watched him muttering to himself, chain-smoking and tossing the butts on the sidewalk. Finally, about ten minutes into the Mass, when the last stragglers had gone up the staircase, he went into the church. I gave him a minute and then followed him inside.

In the back of the long rectangular church I found a place to stand, ignored an usher's attempts to guide me to a seat, and scanned the crowd. I found him in seconds: I merely looked for a place where the congregation looked very uncomfortable, and there he was, in the middle of it. He hadn't even removed his hat. He'd inserted himself into the end of an already crowded pew about midway from the altar and taken the area over with his bellicose presence and, no doubt, his smell. In the pew directly behind him, I saw a slight, white-haired woman fish out a small handkerchief and put it to her nose.

Meyer ignored them all, just sat with his arms folded

across his chest and his head tilted to one side and studied the priest on the altar. As far as I could tell there was nothing unusual about the mass, and the priest was unremarkable in every way, a middle-aged man with a thin face and a droning manner of speech. Around Meyer the faithful went through the required actions of their service, stood when they were going to sing, knelt at the right times, sat, chanted their Latin responses – these drew a sardonic shake of the head from Meyer – and tried without success to ignore the filthy man in their midst who did none of these things. Then the unsuspecting priest began his sermon.

In the silence that met the first moments of his oration, I could hear the thousand sounds of a restless congregation, the coughing, moving about, rustling and shifting as people attempted to stay awake and pay attention despite the man's monotonous voice. Several minutes into the sermon, however, I began to focus on what he was saying, for it was clear that this priest had not prepared a dull speech for his congregation but something like a confession. He leaned forward on the pulpit and addressed them with an earnest look, and spoke of the challenges of faith, the challenges *to* faith. The first time I glanced at Meyer he was sleeping, his mouth open, and drawing hostile looks from those around him. When I looked a moment later, he was awake and studying the earnest priest with new interest.

"We accept much on faith," the priest was saying. "We never really stop to tally up the things we are asked to accept on the basis of faith: the history of our Church, the lives of all these saints pictured around us in painting, in our statuary, in the stained glass of the windows. We accept the miracles of these martyrs and the existence of the angels and the archangels whom we mention in our Creed, and so many other things that we are asked as part of our faith to believe."

Meyer rose slowly in his pew, as though he had been waiting for this moment. He was grinning at the priest, and around him people were watching him with wary looks.

The priest looked his way for a second, made an obvious decision to ignore this challenge from the pews, and went on for several moments. He was in mid-sentence when Meyer gave battle.

"What about 'em, those angels?" Meyer barked out. "You seen 'em?"

The priest said something innocuous like "Excuse me?"

"I said, you seen these angels? What do they look like?" Meyer's voice grated through the silent church even though he was not shouting.

"Like that?" He pointed up above the altar, where statues of twin angels looked over the church from on high. "It's all garbage, you know it's all garbage. Where's these angels, priest? Where they been hiding all these – what? – thousands of years? What, they on vacation? Maybe lunch hour or something?"

Around the church the congregation began to wake up. Someone said, "Is he drunk?" I heard a woman a few pews behind Meyer mutter something about disrespect, and a man called out, "You shut up." Near me, another man said, "Somebody ought to shut him up."

The priest, to his credit, remained patient. "You're

troubled by the reference to angels, my friend. Only angels? Not the rest of it?"

"*Troubled?* Yeah, I'm troubled. I'm troubled by all of it, but your angels, they're the biggest joke." Meyer looked up at the stone angels and shook his head. "Those are them? White guys with wings! Is that what you believe in, these white guys with wings? They look like ducks with blond hair, like something out of Flash Gordon."

A kid a few pews behind him laughed at this and drew a nasty look from his mother.

Meyer glanced at the statues and shook his head. "Your angels, they look like those, those flying monkeys from the *Wizard of Oz.*"

"Oh, that's too much!" a woman said, but here and there I heard chuckles from the parishioners, for nothing is so well-loved as an open display of madness.

"My friend, what is it that I can do for you?" the priest said. He leaned forward against his high pulpit. A little color had come into his cheeks and I saw that Meyer had actually woken up the fight in this priest. Which was, of course, had been his intention.

"For me? You can't do nothing for me, priest. But I can tell you there's no angels here, not the way you mean. There's no guys with curly hair and wings waiting to protect us. There's none of that."

The priest shrugged. "Maybe not. And maybe you're wrong. Why does the question trouble you? In all the things I've worried at over the years I've never lost an hour of sleep over the angels."

"But you talk about 'em. You tell people to believe in 'em. If you seen what I seen of the world, priest, you

99

wouldn't be filling the heads of these people with stories about angels, tellin' 'em there's angels protecting them. You'd know there's just us."

"Us and God, perhaps," the priest said quietly. "Do you believe in God? Or is that part of it?"

"Him, I don't know about, but I'm pretty sure about angels, these white guys with wings."

"If you are troubled by artists' representations – " the priest began.

"No, I don't care what kinda silly things some artist paints. I care about the truth."

"If you know the truth, my friend, you're far ahead of me."

Meyer looked at the priest for a moment. He seemed to be trying not to smile and I didn't follow any of it, though now I understand he'd just realized the quality of his opponent. He gazed around him at the hostile, shocked people and shrugged.

"I don't make no claims about the truth. But I know there's no angels, not that kind. If you seen what I seen, you'd know. I've seen thousands of people killed, waiting for some kinda help, looking for heavenly armies. Heavenly armies. And I can tell you there was no angels in none of those places." He gritted his teeth and said, "There was none of that."

Several ushers began to make their way toward Meyer but the priest surprised me by calling out to them.

"Ushers, go back to your places. Leave the man alone. This is the house of God, it's not some Clark Street saloon where we throw people out into the street."

After a moment the priest asked, "Are you speaking of

the war, sir? The camps?"

Meyer looked at him, gripping the top of the pew tightly, but said nothing.

The priest nodded, looked down for a moment, then met Meyer's eyes. "You are Jewish, sir."

Meyer muttered something that sounded like "smarter than you look." Then he said, "Yeah, that's right. I'm a Jew." He made a long slow turn, taking in as many of the parishioners as he could, nodding and meeting their eyes. "I'm a Jew," he said. After a moment he added, "I wasn't born one. I am now, though. I'm one of 'em."

I recalled Meyer's earlier argument in the shop, the professor's puzzled question: *"What does this matter to you, Meyer, for God's sake? You're not even a Jew."*

I waited for Meyer to say something more, but he just looked at the priest. The priest seemed to be giving him the last word, then nodded again. Something had been finished between them though I didn't understand what. Meyer slid out of his pew and stared at the ushers. One, younger than the rest, seemed poised to grab him in spite of the priest's injunction. He adopted a lineman's stance and a hard stare. Meyer paused, gave him a long look and dropped a shoulder, and the kid usher had the street sense to back off. The old man trudged down the aisle, staring straight ahead. When he was nearly at the great oak doors he turned and looked right at me. I suppressed the impulse to duck.

Meyer's face was flushed and his eyes were wide, and I understood that it didn't matter to him that I was there, but that he'd just had a fight over the truth.

Over the next two years I was to encounter Meyer on

the street several times, I was to see him involved in trouble both visited upon him and of his own making. There seemed neither pattern nor sense to his wanderings, and if asked to ascribe a purpose, I would have said he roamed the great breadth of the city looking to pick a fight. At first I assumed the massive chip on his shoulder was intended for his fellow man, any fellow man, but that would have been to miss the point. Meyer sought another sort of fight entirely.

For several days afterward I was bursting with the need to speak of this to Farrell but did not know how to explain that I'd followed Meyer, and into a church, no less. Then one afternoon he asked me to run an errand for him, to pick up a sandwich, and this seemed an opening of sorts.

"I saw Meyer go into a church and I went in – "

"You went in, did you?"

"I don't know why."

"Of course you do. To see why Meyer of all people was going into a church of all places. And what did you see from that improbable combination?"

"Meyer started yelling at the priest about – "

"God, I would guess. Or the efficacy of prayer." He gave me an interested look. "Or angels."

"It was angels, yes. So – why? What's his thing with angels?"

"*His thing*, indeed. He finds the common belief in angels to be foolish. He finds most types of belief foolish. His life has – " Farrell looked around the room and I saw that for the first time he was being evasive with me, that he was actually uncomfortable. When he went on, his response was disappointing, a cliché.

"He has had a difficult life."

"Is that why he has a chip on his shoulder?"

"Of course. He is angry."

"With who?"

"*Whom*. With whom. Humanity, all of it. He's seen us at our worst." Farrell gave me a candid look. "And God, of course. That is why he is interested in churches, in the people who are drawn to them. He is angry with God. If God were to appear to Meyer in corporeal form, I have no doubt Meyer would take a swing at him. More than once I myself have seen Meyer at work in a church or temple. I've seen him escorted out by ushers, I've seen him *deck* an usher or two. It is not advisable to put hands on Meyer." He seemed to ponder this for a moment. "Yes, lad, he's angry with God. You might say he's looking for the Big Fellow. Meyer is looking to settle things with the Big Fellow."

This seemed another opening, a hole so large I didn't know which of my hundred questions to fill it with, and I heard myself asking, "Do you believe in God?"

"Well, I'd as soon hear your views on that as tell you my own. That's a subject for another talk and another time, Thomas."

He nodded and then handed me the money for the errand, and dismissed me.

And once, not so long after that, I spied on Farrell. It was late in the day, a chill Friday, and I was walking down Addison when I noticed a man watching the shop. Deliberately I walked by the man and took a good look: I'd seen him once or twice, a wreck of a man, filthy, sunburnt, his eyes watery. His clothes hung on him like a tent, and his skin bore numerous eruptions and scratches. As I watched he moved from one foot to the other as if unable to keep warm. From the nearest corner I waited, and when a customer left Farrell's shop, he shuffled slowly across the street on legs that clearly pained him.

I followed. I stood at the very edge of Farrell's unwashed window and watched. The man lurched in and leaned against the counter, and Farrell spoke to him. The man shook his head and then his entire body was rocking, he wept. Farrell came around the counter and the man's knees buckled, so that Farrell had to grab him to hold him up. I watched Farrell take the man into his back room. For a while I peered in, cupping my hand against the glass, but I could see nothing. After a while they came into view again and the man was carrying a paper cup, coffee or tea, and what looked like a half sandwich. I moved back and slipped around the corner of the building and watched him walk by. It seemed to me that he moved more freely, as though his legs no longer gave him pain. But even in profile, I saw the desolation in his face.

I watched him until he turned the corner. When I turned away, Meyer was standing at the edge of the sidewalk, smoking a cigarette, his eyes on mine.

"You think you're gonna learn something by spyin' on him, but you won't. You won't understand what you see. You won't understand shit."

Then he went inside and I went home. For a time I was too embarrassed to visit the shop again.

Seven:

Shades and miracles

It was the fall of 1963, and for me a dark, cold time, not only for the chill that fell on the people of the United States with the murder of their president, but because of a sense of uncertainty that seemed to permeate my life. For it was around this time that I became aware of my mother's mortality, the first time I was given cause to fear for her life.

With school and work, my free time was more limited, and my visits to Farrell's shop grew less frequent. But the universe runs on irony, and just as I had begun to go there less often, my mother discovered it. She had been riding the bus home from work one afternoon just as I came out, and she was puzzled to see me there: I had never mentioned it.

Her need to know what I was doing was compounded by the fact that she was ill, dying in fact, and probably aware of it on some level, thus driven to prove to herself that I was all right, that I would be all right if something happened to her.

She still worked long hours to bring in money, slept

little, began to look haggard. Most significant, she had developed a rash on her arm, in the crook just above the elbow, and she scratched it till it bled. At odd moments I caught her staring at it, and I could see in her face that it troubled her. Eventually I saw that it was spreading, darkening, and as she scratched at it, of course it bled. She put off a visit to the doctor but eventually broke down. Our doctor had a small walk-up office on Southport. He was a tough old Montenegrin named Kapitanic, with a massive shock of silver hair, and after my first few encounters with him, I imagined Montenegro as a place in the Carpathians where vampires yet lived, and men like Dr. Kapitanic hunted them down and drove stakes into their hearts. When my mother came back from her visit she was ashen, but I saw that she had set her mind on not saying anything about what had transpired.

"So what did he say?"

She gave me a pretend look of surprise. "About me? Oh, I'm fine. He wants me to sleep more, that's all."

"What about – that, you know, that thing on your arm?"

"Oh," she began, and then she pursed her lips and shook her head, and the lie wouldn't come out because she had not rehearsed one, and she began to cry.

"Mom?" I moved toward her and instinctively reached for her arm. She held up a hand and shook her head.

"He doesn't know what it is, the old fake. Some doctor."

"What did he say?"

In a voice leached of hope she said, "He thinks it might be cancer." She sighed and looked away. "Some kind of cancer."

That night I lay in bed and listened to the sounds of her prowling – a glass of milk, a cigarette, ten minutes with the TV on, half hour in silence – and told myself I would soon be alone in the world. Children who have experienced loss find it perfectly reasonable that loss might come again, and it seemed possible, even likely, that I would now lose my mother. I tried to imagine what might happen to me if she died. *When* she died. When I'd indulged my darkest self-absorbed imaginings, I turned my thoughts to her, and I felt worse, conscious of the barrenness of her life and the possibility that it might soon be over. I remembered the night I'd seen her on the bench, remembered the images that had come to me, and I wept for the luckless woman I lived with.

The next day after school I went to the public library near Belmont and Broadway and sat at a corner table reading about cancer. When I broached the subject to my mother that night, not speaking of it as "cancer" but merely "that thing on your arm," she headed me off with the statement that Dr. Kapitanic had recommended a specialist. She emphasized the word *specialist*, as though this were simply the logical next step, not a serious, even drastic measure.

After that she said no more about her arm, but it was clear what she thought it all meant. Her concern about her own mortality had the immediate effect of making her infinitely more vigilant where I was concerned. At odd moments I would look up from the television or the newspaper and find her staring at me. And I could read her look: *what will happen to him?*

She began to pay more attention to my comings and goings, and at times behaved as though I'd suddenly done something to deserve scrutiny and mistrust. She asked more questions about what I did with my time, and we both began to see the holes in my version of my life. One day I came home with a stack of old magazines and when she asked where I'd gotten them, I mentioned Farrell's shop for the first time, and it was clear she'd been waiting for this moment.

"I don't like that place."

"What?"

"I've seen that place. I don't like you hanging around at some old junk shop with old men, you ought to be out with your friends."

"Sometimes I am. But I – " I stopped short of saying I liked it. That, of course, was no longer the reality of things. "It's interesting," I finished.

"It's not right. I don't even know who these men are. Sometimes old men like that – you don't even know what they're like."

"They're just a couple of old men, Ma."

She looked away and I saw her face change. I knew what she would do. She scratched the rash on her arm and I knew what she would do.

To stave off the inevitable I did not go to the shop for more than a week. Instead I walked all the long way to Hamlin Park and played basketball. Three nights running, I stayed until the gym closed. When I got home the third night, my mother was sitting at the kitchen table.

"I went there, Tom." When I said nothing, she added, "To that old place of yours. That junk shop."

"I know where you mean."

"I don't know what else to call it. It seems – not very respectful to call it a junk shop, I'm sure some of it is –" She sought to dress her judgment in politeness. "– I'm sure he has good things in there. I mean, it's what he's got, it's all he's got to sell. And he has books."

I stood there with a basketball under my arm and refused to make it easier for her to say anything. When she finally spoke I was taken by surprise.

"He's very nice, that Mr. Farrell."

She watched me and I nodded, forced by her patience to respond. After a moment I asked, "Did you meet the other one? Meyer?"

"No. Just Mr. Farrell. And another man came in and I think borrowed money."

"He gives money to a lot of people."

She nodded. After a while she added, "I guess it's okay for you to be there. But it's still not the same thing as having friends your own age."

"Ma, I got friends my own age. And I got times when I don't want to see them."

The first part was only marginally true – I had acquaintances, mostly the ones I played ball with. A couple of times we'd all chipped in and bought a bottle of Richard's Wild Irish Rose. But they weren't friends. I had grown comfortable in this image of myself, a romantic way to dress up the fact that I had no real friends: I was a loner. I'd already established that reputation among my acquaintances. I had even managed to convince myself that a solitary life was something to be embraced, a thousand movies and television shows paid homage to the man who is attached to no one.

"I talked to him for a while. He's a nice man. He called you a nice, polite young man."

My mother laughed then, an odd, slightly embarrassed laugh. "He said he'd buy me a drink sometime. Do you know, he drinks at Mindy's, where we used to go with Grandma?"

For a moment I could not speak. I was already taken aback by the fact that my mother and Farrell had met, but I was unwilling to accept the notion that they might get to know one another, meet socially, have a drink together.

She misunderstood my silence. "You know, Mindy's over on Belmont?"

I nodded.

"Anyway, he's a nice man, and it's kind of an interesting place, I guess."

She was finished. The conversation turned to dinner, and her readiness to drop the subject allowed me to tell myself that her visit there made no difference. I pushed it out of my mind.

About a week later I came home in the late afternoon to an empty house. This would have been the time to find her in the kitchen, working her minor magic, her gift for arriving home from work and putting together something resembling a dinner in a half hour. She wasn't there. I looked at the stove and saw no sign that she'd even been home – there looked to be no dinner, nor any chance of one. For some reason I found the silence troubling. Just before six I was startled by the sound of the phone ringing. A singular feature of that house was our silent phone, no one ever called us, the thing might have been dead. And now I rushed over to put an end to the jarring sound of the phone. When I picked it up I was even more taken aback to hear my mother on the other end.

"Tom?"

"Ma? What's wrong?"

She laughed. "Something's gotta be wrong 'cause your mother calls you! Nothing's wrong, hon. I'm sorry, I don't like you to come home to an empty house. But I'm at Mindy's!" She seemed delighted.

"Oh."

I wondered what this could mean: she liked a highball now and then but she was no drinker. Hanging out in taverns in her desperation, perhaps? Then she let me hear the rest.

"I've been having a nice talk with Mr. Farrell. And now it's nearly dinner time. So why don't you come over and we'll go someplace for a sandwich." When I said nothing, she added, "You can say hello to Mr. Farrell if you get here soon enough – I think he's going to go soon."

"Okay. I'll – give me a few minutes."

"Time stops in Mindy's" I had once overheard a man say in a diner. It was a tottering relic of an earlier time lodged in an old frame building on Belmont whose foundations had shifted over the years so that it appeared to be leaning away from the west wind. The painted sign in the window said its true name was "The Oakwood Inn," but to my knowledge no one ever called it that, and as a boy I always had the odd feeling no one but me had ever noticed the sign. It was a dark tavern within but oddly cheerful, its walls and back bar covered by cartoonish paintings of round faced drinkers with handlebar moustaches and

111

pastoral scenes of some unnamed but romanticized European country with men in lederhosen and a great many sheep. And signs above the back bar, all encouraging some level of debauchery and bonhomie: "There's always fair weather when good friends get together," "If you drink, you'll die. If you don't drink, you'll die. So drink."

The room was dominated by a gigantic juke box that flashed gold and yellow light into the eternal dusk of the room, and the whole was presided over by a tiny, high-voiced man named Pete. I never understood why in a bar called "Mindy's", the only bartender was a man named Pete, but so many other mysteries were to present themselves in my life that I had little time to ponder this one.

My mother was sitting at the bar with Farrell when I came in. She was laughing. I must have given her a look – I hadn't heard her laugh at anyone or anything in what seemed years – for she broke off, stubbed out her cigarette and looked as though she'd been caught out in some plot. Farrell turned slowly, half-smiling, and I would have said he knew it was me without turning. He had a cigarette going: I rarely saw him actually smoke his cigarettes. Rather he would light an unfiltered Chesterfield or Camel and hold it in cupped hands, sometimes studying the blue smoke as though watching it ascend to heaven.

"Hello, Thomas," he said.

"Tom, Arth – Mr. Farrell was telling me a funny story about when he was a boy."

I nodded and sat down beside her. I noted the pause over his name – I had already struggled with that myself.

In the end, I would call him Farrell, with some misgivings. Strangely, I never had this problem with Meyer. I called him "Meyer" always. I suspected almost from the beginning – correctly, as it turned out – that Meyer was an alias. One of many, I am certain.

They bought me a Coke and Pete put a cherry in it, just to annoy me, and my mother went on speaking with Farrell. I couldn't quite make out what they were talking about though some of it did indeed consist of Farrell recounting childhood tales. My mother shared a couple of her own, small warm memories that I had never heard. It struck me that these two quite solitary people were recounting festive occasions from childhood, times marked by the press of people in crowded rooms, united for the day – a stark contrast with their current lives.

A few feet behind me, Dean Martin sang of "Amore" and I remembered hearing his voice over a record player in my grandmother's house on Goethe, a damp crowded place where we managed to shoehorn two dozen of us on Christmas. A sudden rush of memory came to me: my grandmother, a short, stout woman with a face like a well-fed chipmunk, greeting us at the door, her round cheeks already flushed from the overheated air in her kitchen, greeting us, a wet kiss for her favorite daughter and then a bone-crushing embrace for me. Her clothes smelled of her cooking and her house.

It struck me that my mother and I were nearly the only ones left from those times. Many were dead, and the ones that still lived had scattered across the map. Not a family blessed by fortune, nor even its simpler cousin, stability, but such patterns were not apparent to me. I looked up and saw Farrell watching me over my mother's shoulder, and for just the merest fraction of a second I had the odd notion that this memory was somehow connected with him.

And then they were finished. Farrell took a last sip of his highball, put out what was left of the unsmoked cigarette and gave a short stiff wave to Pete. And, though Pete was seventy if he was a day, Farrell called him "Lad." Then he went out the door, letting in a rush of cold Belmont Avenue grit.

"He's such a nice man, Tom. Just such a nice man."

She looked in her purse, seemed to consider what she found there, and then surprised me for the second time that evening by suggesting we move to the little dining room in the back and have dinner.

"Here?"

"Sure. Why not? We never go out," she said, and the tone in her voice said it made a difference to her. "Unless you have something else to do. Were you gonna go out?"

I told her it was fine. I'd seen the look in her eye and wouldn't have said no even if I'd had plans. She needed to be out. Except for a quick drink with the other waitresses once or twice, she hadn't been out anywhere since long before her husband had left her. And so we sat in the steamy back room of Mindy's Oakwood Inn, the only two dinner customers until the cook's sisters stopped by, and we had chicken dumpling soup, followed by some sort of fish for her and fried chicken for me. And I thought I had not seen her so relaxed or talkative in years. By the end of dinner she had me talking, too. She wanted to know my opinions of some of the new singers, got me talking about the Bears, wore me down until I was actually enjoying myself. Toward the end of dinner she put her purse on the table to look for her money and I saw her arm. The rash, her rash which I'd seen her scratching last night till it bled, was gone. Not better. Gone.

I said nothing until the following day.

"Your arm's better, Ma."

She gave me the look of a person caught in the act of theft. She looked at it, shook her head, looked back at me.

"I know. It's just – gone. I don't even know when it got better, but it's gone. I don't know how it happened. Mr. Farrell even commented on it, because he noticed the rash the first time I went to his shop. He's very observant."

"It's really gone, Ma."

"It is," she said, clearly embarrassed to have made such a fuss over a passing inconvenience.

I studied the place where it had been, lest I miss some evidence that this was merely a trick of the light. But the rash was gone, there wasn't even a healing patch to show where she'd torn the skin with her incessant scratching. I felt a sudden rush of relief: she was not to die of this strange rash, or drive herself mad fretting about its implications. And then a new thought cut this one off, the recollection of Farrell touching an old man's bloody chin with his tobacco-stained fingers and cutting off the bleeding. I tried to push the scene from my mind. I wanted to reject the notion that Farrell could have had anything to do with my mother's recovery, it seemed critical that I find a more ordinary cause. I wanted her to be cured by God, by nature, by good fortune. Not by an old man in a junk shop who could not be accounted for in the world I'd been

115

brought up to understand. For the first time I realized that, while I was content to spend time in Farrell's shop, to watch and observe and eavesdrop, I did not want the shop or anyone in it to intrude into my own life. I had no idea, of course, that the time for such fine distinctions had already passed.

And if the rash had indeed been cancerous, had Farrell not, by the merest passing of his fingers over her arm, cured not just a nasty rash but cancer? An image came to me unbidden, of Farrell's face the night he'd done whatever it was that he'd done to the ragpicker, of his eyes. As kind as he had been to me, and now to my mother, I recalled those eyes, and the Farrell that I had seen that night was a man to be feared. I shuddered and my mother noticed.

"Are you cold?"

"Little bit."

She looked at the old radiators along the walls. "It is a little chilly here."

The more I worried at these things, the more convinced I became that Farrell had done some unholy thing. I wondered again at the nature of his power. But my mother was cured, and as I studied her, it seemed she'd been cured of more than this physical affliction. She gazed around the room oblivious to my conflict and for the first time in years looked perfectly relaxed, as near to happiness as I'd seen her, as near to health as she'd been in years. For that, at least, I was relieved.

I should have been grateful as well but I was furious, I felt violated, as though my life were no longer entirely mine. It was one thing to witness the strange comings and

116

goings in Farrell's shop, but to a boy who had striven for and failed to obtain anything remotely resembling a normal life, this was just one more humiliation.

That night I lay in bed and determined to go to the shop the next day to confront him, to tell him I knew what he'd done, to tell him he'd turned my life into a freakish thing, to announce that I wanted nothing to do with him. Of course a teenage boy would have no idea how to go about saying such things to an adult, and in the end I decided that it was indeed good that this poor woman had one less thing to worry about. By the next morning, the notion that Farrell had cured my mother seemed too ridiculous to speak of. With the passage of a few days I was able to convince myself that I had not really seen anything to suggest that Farrell – or Meyer, for that matter – possessed any kind of power, that circumstances had contrived to make me think I'd witnessed these things, or, worse yet, that all of this was the working of my disturbed imagination. I even wondered, briefly, if these ideas that plagued me from time to time about Farrell, these odd beliefs meant that I was losing my mind.

Eight: The Errands

1 spent perhaps a month working these matters out and in the end, through my own circuitous logic, came to several conclusions. The first was that, if Farrell had indeed done something to my mother, it was merely some form of folk healing, and the greatest favor anyone had ever done her, or me. If, as was far more likely, he had done nothing, it was some sort of freakish medical development and there was no harm done in any case. Finally, I had begun to think about that afternoon when he'd told me about the British helmet and the dead soldier who'd worn it. I remembered his face, drawn and sickly-looking and, just for that moment, vulnerable. I felt a new emotion for Farrell: pity.

From this cocktail of reasons and excuses I determined that I owed him something. On my next visit to his shop I offered to run errands for him. What I actually said was that I would be glad to help out in the shop on my days off from Lou's Diner. He held his lip between his fingers and looked around the shop with his head tilted to one side.

"Well, here's the thing of it, lad," he said, pronouncing it *"da ting of it."* "There's times when I need an able-bodied fellow to go places for me, and, ah, you know, make deliveries and pick up a book here and there."

"Fine."

For the remainder of that year, an otherwise socially barren junior year in high school, I ran errands for him. At first Farrell sent me only to deliver things people had already purchased, odds and ends from the shop. These deliveries took me to odd places: the first was to a wizened book collector in a coach house off a vacant lot. I knew him from the shop, a washed-out man named Ralph who put me in mind of fragile things. At my knock his door opened wide enough for Ralph to put a nervous eye to the space. I moved forward, saw him blink and realized I was so close to his own eyeball that he could see only another eye. I backed off and he said, "Oh!" then pulled the door open. He literally cackled when he saw his package from Farrell.

"This will be my book, the Donnelly." He pulled it from its paper bag and rubbed it with a loving hand. It was a 19th century sort of book, with title and art on the cloth of the cover itself – as was done before the paper dust jackets came into vogue. Farrell had told me he had several customers who collected such books for their covers alone.

He held it up for my approval. I looked at the title: *Atlantis the Lost Continent.* I didn't know what to say to that, but he saved me the trouble.

"Most collectors seek serious books. I collect the odd and the remarkable." Here Ralph stepped back and indicated a small apartment that seemed to have been given over completely to the collecting of books. There was little furniture.

"I have almost every book written in the past hundred years on lost continents, mythological kingdoms, other worlds. And now I have Ignatius Donnelly, the fellow that started the modern interest in Atlantis. Farrell is trying to find me a copy of *Islandia*. Do you know that book?"

"No." I felt stupid. Just to be saying something, I asked him if he believed in Atlantis.

"Goodness, no. But then, my knowledge of the world begins in Milwaukee and ends here, behind Halsted Street!" He grinned and gave me money to take back to Farrell, and a quarter tip.

A few feet from his home, I stopped, my attention caught by a sort of coffee house. It was a dark place, filled with foreign-looking men: dark-haired, almost all of them with dense mustaches. They were drinking their coffee out of small glasses, and something in their attitude, something in the comfortable way they laughed and chatted, drew me, so that I almost went in. The man behind the counter noticed me and waved, beckoning me. I waved and shook my head.

Thereafter Farrell sent me for books as well: purchases he'd made earlier from shops in other parts of the city. It was never clear to me whether the negotiations for these books had taken place over the telephone or Farrell had actually been into these shops and simply taken a while to decide that he would meet the dealer's price.

Some of the books were clearly purchased to resell. Others, just as clearly, were for Farrell himself: he delighted in works on the Arthurian legends and in the Irish saga of the hero Cuchulain, a tale he referred to as "*the Tawn*" – the *Táin Bó Cúailnge.*

"Read that, boyo," he said, "and your Greeks and Trojans will seem humble fellows indeed. Our lad

Cuchulain fought off an army."

Most of the time, though, he either took his purchases with a quiet "Thank you, Thomas," or quietly added, "There's a book for you to look at sometime."

And so I did even though there seemed no connecting thread among the books, the many books he encouraged me to read: C.S. Lewis on *Miracles,* an early and battered set of *Butler's Lives of the Saints*, tattered 19th Century tomes on folk medicine and folk healers, books of New Testament Scholarship.

I paged idly through the Lewis book, the point of which seemed to be Lewis's belief that miracles do indeed occur from the intervention of the Deity in our lives. I told Farrell I had no interest whatsoever in old "saints", but a couple of weeks later, chanced to see the book atop a counter and read a few pages while Farrell cleaned his darkly encrusted coffee pot. Predictably he had put a strip of paper to mark the entry on St. Thomas the Apostle. I read it in a few minutes and learned only what Farrell had once referred to, that an ancient tradition held that Thomas had taken Christianity to India. I had always, from the Gospel story, thought of Thomas as something of an outsider, always out of step with those around him, and this seemed a terribly long journey to make alone, this pilgrimage to lands he doubtless had never even heard of.

Other wanderers there were in these books, some of them books of adventure, whether novels – *The Prisoner of Zenda, The Man Who Would be King, Lost Horizon* – or non-fiction accounts of exploration to the wind's twelve quarters. These he encouraged me to borrow, all except the Anthony Hope book, for it was a first edition. And at that uncertain stage in my life, they seemed the perfect reading for me. I read of the conquistadors' exploration of the Americas, of the search for the source of the Nile, mad voyages to both Poles, the journey of Lewis and Clark.

The bookmark became a feature. The books he left out, whether specifically for me or merely occupying a corner of his counter, were now marked. In a thick volume on World War II, he had marked a page of photos. In one, a group of grim-faced Poles stared at a camera, all of them armed. The caption identified them as members of the Polish Home Army. The other photographs showed the aftermath of the Warsaw Rising: a line of captured fighters, men dead in an alley, watched over by soldiers.

Another bookmark held its place in a scholarly discussion of God, recording the debate between two scientists as to whether there was a God who took an active role in the doings of the world and the lives of men. The discussion was far over my head, like a fight in the clouds.

A favorite of Farrell's was H.G. Wells, both as a writer of fiction and as a historian, and he prized Wells's *History of the World*. This book he left out on a counter one afternoon, a dog-eared copy with heavy notations in the margins, and I opened it to a bookmark. There I found an odd quotation presenting the views of the English explorer Sir Harry Johnston, that the clash of our Cro Magnon forebears with the Neanderthals may be recorded in our ancient legends of ogres and other "gorilla-like monsters". It was certainly an interesting notion but I could not see why Farrell thought it worthy of passing on to me, I could not see its application.

He also left out poetry despite my frequent assertion that I didn't "get" poetry. But still the thin, plain volumes were left out, often with a particular poem marked: a somber passage in E. A. Robinson's *Merlin*, Emily Dickinson, so briefly, on loneliness, heart-broken verse by Thomas Hardy, a volume of T.S. Eliot marked with what I eventually learned was Farrell's favorite poem, "The Journey of the Magi," a moody poem of a man late in life who is filled with religious doubts. When I read it, I realized I'd heard him recite it, at least the last part of it, on a morning when I came into the shop and surprised him emerging from his back room.

But poetry was a source of joy for him as well, whether reading or reciting it aloud, and more than once during this time I came upon him reciting it for visitors, indeed several times he recited for me alone, coming to a stiff pose, hands in his pockets, as he declaimed his favorite verse, Robert Frost, at times – he was fond of "The Death of the Hired Man" – and, predictably, Yeats, whose verse he recited in the voice of an aging druid. These poets, too, he left out for me but I was not ready for either of them.

Several times his bookmark took me to anti-war poems, and these meant little to me at the time. One, though, stood out from them all. The poem was called "Dulce et Decorum Est," by Wilfred Owen, a poem describing a soldier's awful death.

The central image of the poem caught me, I understood a man was dying, horribly, but the rest, terse language and poetic syntax, confused me, the images troubling: "foundering like a man in fire or lime…" With another poem I might have just dropped it but this was different, it seemed somehow critical for me to understand what was happening in this poem, who this man was, and so I went through it again, taking the lines one at a time, then pairing them. I went back to the beginning and read it once more and understood. Perfectly. A man had died – was dying, here in these lines, with me as his witness. I sought explanation and found a note at the bottom of the next page that Owen's unit in the First World War had been gassed, and this was his bitter remembrance of that day, that Owen himself would be dead in a bloody pointless assault mere months after writing these lines. I stared once more at the image of the dying man and my consciousness flooded with this scene, as though I had witnessed it myself. I saw an English boy of not much more than my age, I saw him in "the ecstasy of fumbling" with his gas mask, I saw the gas take him, I saw him staggering toward *me*. His eyes rolled and he gasped and choked. And this boy long dead appealed to me to help him, to do something to end his suffering, and I was utterly certain I was witnessing not a dramatization of the poem but the death of the boy who'd provoked it.

I slammed the book shut and closed my eyes. I could hear my own labored breathing, I was soaked with perspiration. For a moment I forced myself to breathe calmly, as though to reassure myself that his awful death had not somehow spread to me, to my own lungs. Farrell had caused this, I was certain of it: I looked around for him, then recalled that he had left the shop and had not yet come back. Across the room, Meyer stared out at the street, oblivious to my presence.

Shaken, I put the book aside, vowing never to read

Wilfred Owen again. In the coming years, I would come back to him many, many times.

Other poets there were, not nearly as disturbing as Owen, and though the poems themselves seemed to share little except a lugubrious subject or tone, I was years later to see the pattern and understand. And when I understood the connection, it meant I understood these varied poems, I understood all of them.

And on my own I discovered books about the streets, Willard Motley and Nelson Algren, and when Farrell saw my interest he sent some of these my way: *Studs Lonigan* – "*A lad of Chicago should know this book*" – by his namesake James T. Farrell – "*Any relation? Well, all Farrells are cousins*" — and Farrell's short stories, and my favorites of them all, James T. Farrell's five books about a smart street kid named Danny O'Neill, destined always to be an outsider.

But other tasks he had for me besides my education, other errands to run. Two of them stand out from that time. On a warm afternoon Farrell asked me if I had time to look in on "a friend." The friend was a Catholic priest, "A lovely fellow giving a retreat over there at St. Bonaventure's, Father Mackin is his name, and he –" Here Farrell was at an uncharacteristic loss for words. "He may need someone to help him."

"Help him do what?"

"Small errands. You know. They've given him quarters in the school hall. And, well, I don't know what he will need you to do, but I'm certain there is something. It will be helpful to him. He is – he has a great many things on his mind, poor man. He lives hand to mouth, and not well."

"Sure thing," I said, though none of this made sense. Was this some sort of homeless priest? In any case, I rode my bike to St. Bonaventure's and went to the school hall. There was no answer when I knocked, and the lights inside were off. I knocked again and was about to leave when the door opened, filled with a creature out of a small child's nightmares.

He was a most forbidding man, priest or no. He was at least six feet five, probably taller since he seemed to spend his life stooped over, as if a lifetime of ducking doorways had changed his posture forever. His hair was black and tangled, and he continually ran his hand through it in a futile gesture at order.

He was gaunt and hollow-eyed, sunken-cheeked and pale, dark with whisker stubble. As we looked at each other a name came to me: John the Baptist. This was, I had no doubt, what John the Baptist had looked like. And if the Baptist had worn a long black cassock like this priest's, I had no doubt it would have had food stains and burn holes in it. He looked disoriented, and I guessed that I'd woken him from a nap.

"Yes? Can I help you, son?"

"Farrell – Mr. Farrell from the, the shop on Addison Street, he sent me to see if you needed anything, he thought you might need something," I rambled, knocked completely off my balance by his clear lack of comprehension.

"What would I need?"

"He didn't – he didn't know."

For the first time his stare softened and a hint of humor came into the dark eyes. "He didn't know what I might need, just that I needed something." He nodded and under his breath I heard him mutter, "a guardian, he probably thinks I need." To me he said, "Come in, son."

I followed him into the school hall and he took me up onto the stage, where I saw both the gadgets and equipment of his retreat and the spare trappings of his existence: a cot, a small black suitcase, a bowl, a glass, his toilet kit. On a folding chair, a tiny hotplate plugged into the far wall.

"I'm fine here," he said, apparently reading my look. "It's comfortable."

I doubted it. "Farrell said you might need me to, like, go on errands."

"Errands." He regarded me with his large sunken eyes and now I was reminded of Jack Palance in one of his barbarian roles. John the Baptist and Jack Palance: any kid would have been afraid of either one, and here they both were in one body. The dark priest regarded me and I could hear his slow breathing.

Now he was nodding. "Yes. There is something. I need food." He walked a few paces to a cardboard box behind the cot. He bent over and fumbled around in it, came up with a half loaf of Silvercup bread and a box of Lipton tea.

"I have bread but – " He peered down into the box. "I know I had some tea left."

"It's in your other hand," I pointed out.

"So it is. At any rate, I have tea and bread but I could use more soup."

I nodded as though this made perfect sense.

"Potato soup. That's my favorite. Do you like potato soup?"

"Sure," I said though I found it hard to tell potato soup from wallpaper paste.

"Can you go to the store and get me soup?"

"Sure."

"I could go myself but I have to prepare for the retreat tomorrow. Get some potato soup. As many cans as possible: eight or ten cans."

He fumbled in his cassock pockets and came up with a single dollar bill. He gazed at the bill for a moment and shook his head.

"I don't think that will be enough, do you?"

I looked at his wrinkled bill: the face of Washington looked withered, as though he were having a hard year. I shook my head.

"No, I don't think so either." He felt in his pants pockets and we both heard the jingle of coins. His face brightened and he brought out a handful of change, primarily pennies.

"This is more like it," he said. He poured his change into my hand: twenty-three cents. "I hope that does it," he said. "That's all of it."

"Sure, Father," I said, embarrassed to have all of any adult's money. A dollar and twenty-three cents. And how to tell a priest he didn't have enough for his soup?

Then he went over to his small table and wrote something down on a piece of paper. He handed it to me. It was illegible.

"I wrote you a note so you won't have trouble remembering."

I nodded and stared at the scribble. He sensed my discomfort and took the note from me.

"It says 'eight or ten cans of potato soup.'"

"Okay."

Then he smiled at me. I looked at him and his face was transformed. It seemed I had never been in the presence of such a person. I didn't know what to call it, and at the time simply thought of it as his kindness, that you could actually see true kindness in a person's face and I was seeing it in his. For the first time I relaxed in his company. Even as I did so, I noticed something else in his eyes, something beyond his kindness but I did not spend any time puzzling over it. I beamed at him and left to run his errand, leaving him there in the doorway, still holding onto the hieroglyphics he'd written for me.

I bought him ten cans of Campbell's potato soup, and of course his buck-twenty-three didn't cover it, so I used some of my own money, spent it gladly for the reward of his beatific smile. When I returned to the rectory I rang the bell, and when he answered I would have sworn he'd already forgotten me and my errand.

"Ten cans of potato soup," I said.

"Oh, my dinner." As he took the bag from me, he muttered, "And tomorrow's breakfast and lunch and dinner," then smiled at me again.

"Did you have enough money?"

"Sure."

He looked doubtfully at the bag and back at me. Before he could express his misgivings I said, "Soup was on sale."

"All soup?"

His gaunt face lit up once more, amazement mingling with hope. I saw the potential for disaster here with this guileless adult who would clearly believe anything and decided it was unkind to elevate his hopes. "No, only Campbell's." And then I added, "and just potato."

He shook his head slightly and I wondered if I had overdone it. Then he looked at me, tilted his head to one side and said, "You're a good boy." He looked around him at the little stage where he lived and it seemed I could read his thoughts: he saw his existence the way another might see it: a barren life, lived alone and the great part of it on the road, as it were.

He turned to me. "You wonder why a grown man would live like this."

"No." Farrell slept in the back room of a shop. Meyer on floors; sometimes in doorways.

"I am so used to it that it doesn't bother me at all. Not sleeping on a cot, or living for a week behind the stage of an old school hall, or eating potato soup off a hot-plate." He smiled again, a sheepish smile this time and I felt myself smiling at him. No, I knew I was grinning as though the two of us were sharing a rare joke.

He chuckled now at himself, his ridiculously austere life, ran his hand through the tangled hair and shook his head. "You wake up one morning and see that you have become a certain person with a particular, in my case, a *peculiar* life, and you cannot see quite how you got there. But it is what you are. And you must accept it or start anew. But I like it. I give retreats."

"Farrell – Mr. Farrell told me."

"Do you know what a retreat is?"

"Religious talks. And stuff."

"Indeed. Religious talks and stuff. Are you – are you Catholic?"

"My mom – " I began, and then broke off.

"You don't get to church much."

"No."

"But you are a good boy, as I said. Will you come again to fetch soup for me? I'm here until next Saturday."

I was suddenly filled with the zeal to fetch soup for him from all the points of the compass, soup from Seattle and Katmandu if need be, I had no idea why. He gave me the smile again. Then a more serious look crossed his face as though something had just occurred to him.

"You will have an interesting life." I don't know what my face told him but he felt compelled to add, "You will. I know about these things."

I didn't know what to say to that. I nodded and said good-bye, then got back onto my bike.

When I returned to the shop, Farrell was directing a man to a shelf of novels along the far wall. He raised his dense eyebrows in question.

"He sent me for soup."

"He lives on soup. Did you have enough money?"

"Yes."

Farrell gave me a doubtful look but just asked, "What did you make of him, Father Mackin?"

"He looks like John the Baptist."

Farrell laughed. "Why, that's exactly what I would have said. At least, that's how I've always imagined the Baptist. I've known him for years. He's a lovely fellow." When I said nothing to this, he said, "Children are sometimes afraid of him. But what did you think of him?"

"He's – I like him."

"I wanted you to meet him, you know. To see what you

131

thought."

I said nothing.

"It is well to be in the presence of goodness. That's my opinion on it."

He went back to his work then. He was going through a box that someone had sold him, trying to separate the dross from what he might actually sell, and he paid me no further notice.

The other task he gave me proved more complicated in its effects. On a day when the sky hung dark with the promise of rain, he sent me to the home of a woman. He gave me a package to take to her home, a small frame building on Racine. The woman answered her door, a remarkably tall woman leaning on a cane, and ushered me in to a room in which most of the furniture was covered with sheets. She saw me looking around and said, "I keep most of the furniture covered. It gets dusty and I can't keep up with the cleaning." Then, under her breath, she added, "And anyways – " She broke off and gazed around her apartment. As though just noticing me, she said, "My name is Helena."

Without waiting for a reply she beckoned me out to her kitchen where she poured me a cup of tea without asking whether I wanted any, then set about opening her package. The brown wrapping paper – Farrell frequently packaged his sales in brown paper and string, an old-country eccentricity. He saved bags, for what, I never learned, he had hundreds stuffed into various places. The paper held three items: a packet of postcards, a chocolate bar, and a book.

She took out the postcards, turned each one over, then

held up one for my inspection.

"This is where I grew up. And this is what it looked like then."

It was a sepia photo of a small town in Wisconsin at the turn of the century.

She set them down, looked at the chocolate, then at the book, which made her laugh. Her laughter surprised me, the voice of a young girl. The book was *Bleak House*, and she held it up for my reaction.

I didn't know what to say, so I just asked, "Do you like Charles Dickens?"

"Of course," she said, distractedly. She opened the book from the back, looked inside, nodded.

"Nine hundred and sixteen pages!" She laughed again, delightedly. Then she noticed my blank look.

"You're too young to understand. Nobody's got a sense of humor about it, that's the thing." She gazed at me for a moment and then I understood. She was dying.

"You see?"

I thought I did, then, part of it. Farrell had sent me to the home of someone who was dying. I didn't know why he wanted me to have that experience, or to experience this woman called Helena. But I was certain she was dying. I had no sense of sadness in her though more than once I saw her looking around her at her things with a sort of distracted concern. When I left, she tipped me a half dollar and gave me part of the chocolate bar. I said good-bye and she winked.

As she closed the door I heard her mutter "Nine hundred pages!" and burst out laughing again. I was too young by far to see the joke.

When, two weeks later, I asked Farrell about Helena, he shook his head. "She's gone, poor lady. A lovely person, she was."

Nine: The Art of Business

At around this time I learned that there was more to Farrell's shop than I had seen. On the weekends it was transformed, as though infused by a new energy that seemed to change even the light in the place. And I came to learn how he actually stayed open.

I learned that this sort of business thrived by negotiation, and I never missed a chance to watch one in progress. I was interested in those moments when one human being made money off another, in the secret of it, if there was one. I came to understand that there are many for whom the negotiation itself is the prize.

I was no judge of the worth of things, but I knew that more than once I had seen Farrell throw his money away when confronted by the destitute. I never once saw him turn Timothy away, no matter what sort of trash the old man dragged into the shop. But for the ones who knew the value of things, the collectors and the more darkly streetwise of his sellers, rag pickers and the humblest sort of con artists, he saved his energy, his knowledge, his many weapons. In these encounters he was more street fighter than junk seller. He knew a little of everything, it seemed, but was most formidable on two subjects: books, and his beloved coins. Arguments over his coins I saw him dismiss out of hand, meeting each objection with a half dozen examples to support his own position. He knew the history of his coins, knew what to look for, understood fakes.

Once, when a teenager attempted to sell him a Standing Liberty quarter of serious value, Farrell just smiled at him. He hefted the coin in his palm and then flipped it in the air so that it landed sharply on the glass of his counter, but with an odd flat sound. The kid frowned. Farrell smiled and slipped into the genial Irish shopkeeper.

"Counterfeit, lad. 'Tis the monetary equivalent of lead shot, a sinker for yer fishing line."

"But it looks real," the boy countered, clearly lying. It didn't look real to me. It was a dark gray, like the sides of an old ship.

"Ah, well, that's the counterfeiter's art. 'Tisn't money at all. Melt it down for toy soldiers." He flipped it back at the kid, who caught it in the air and left without a word.

Another time a man tried to sell him a rare penny. Farrell listened to the man's spiel, never really looking at the penny but at the seller. After a while he deigned to look at the coin, through his heavy magnifying glass and shook his head.

"The mint mark has been removed, d'you see. This was a Denver mint coin and somebody's gone and rubbed off the 'D'."

The man expressed first doubt, then outrage that someone had tampered with the coin, though it was clear who Farrell believed had done this.

Two walls were devoted to his books, hard-cover and paperback, but behind the counter he kept others, perhaps fifty or sixty books, on small shelves along his back wall, and I learned from my nearly constant eavesdropping that these were all more or less rare. An early history of Chicago by A. T. Andreas ("A most idiosyncratic work, it is."), a first edition of a story collection by H.G. Wells, a garishly-decorated version of *The Wonderful Wizard of Oz* ("Your man L. Frank Baum lived here when he wrote this, Thomas, over there by the little donut factory on Webster Street."). And though I was now something of a reader, these books were of no interest to me. But such is the way of life that things we pay no conscious attention to insinuate themselves into our lives. More than twenty years after that time, I can tell at a glance the age and approximate value of an edition of *Tom Sawyer*.

But it was Farrell's performance with the dealers that proved most entertaining. One, a tall youngish man with no affect whatsoever, came in from time to time and attempted to part Farrell from his rarest books. One afternoon I noticed him staring at the books. He shot a quick look at Farrell and then said, in a musing tone, "*Lee's Lieutenants.*"

Farrell said nothing, and I understood that this was merely the introduction to a formal dance of negotiation and mental combat. "Nice looking set. What are you asking for it?"

Farrell glanced over his shoulder at the books, a small gesture of his used primarily in such contests, a look that seemed to say, "Do I have such a thing in my shop?"

He squinted, frowned, ran his hand over his hair, said, "Twenty dollars."

The expressionless man trotted out a reaction. He

smiled, shut his eyes, shook his head. Disbelief.

"Sir, I can buy that set for ten bucks. Twelve at most."

"Ah, but your set won't have the signature of Himself."

"That's an autographed set?"

"'Tis."

"Douglass Southall Freeman signed it?"

"The very fellow."

The dealer opened his mouth, in protest or dispute, and Farrell headed him off.

"The ones on the top shelf there are all autographed by their authors. Sometimes it seems a sort of small felony even to sell them." Here he looked directly at me, and the next remark was for me, I knew. "Touched by their creators, they are."

The dealer stared across the space and read off names, names that meant nothing to me. He bought nothing that day, but returned a week later and bought the three volumes of *Lee's Lieutenants* for twenty dollars without complaint.

Other sorts of visitors entered the shop as well, small-time crooks among them. One afternoon as I lingered after delivering sandwiches to Farrell and Meyer, I heard Meyer mutter something through his mouthful of food. Farrell acted as if he'd heard nothing – but I later learned he tried never to acknowledge Meyer when he spoke with his mouth full.

So Meyer chewed a moment more, then said, "This guy again, Farrell, your favorite."

A man entered and paused as though uncertain where he was. He moved cautiously to the counter and produced several small bags from inside his coat, then encouraged

Farrell to look inside. As Farrell rummaged through the bags, the man looked around the shop. He shot a quick and practiced smile in my direction but looked away when he met Meyer's eyes. Meyer gave him a sardonic look.

When Farrell had finished he shook his head. "Nothing there I can use, my friend. Nothing at all."

He spoke quietly but managed to sound both precise and impersonal, and there was no trace of the genial Irish shopkeeper. Merely a man of business pronouncing sentence on a proposed deal.

"No, huh? None of it?"

"I'm afraid not. Good luck, sir."

The man tucked the bags away and left the shop, and the look on his face suggested that he was already forgetting the conversation, for he was planning his next stop.

One other time the nervous man came in, with the same result, and I felt emboldened to ask why Farrell never bought anything from him.

"Because the fellow steals, lad. His 'merchandise' is all stolen, and I've no use for such things."

"Can you tell just by looking at it?"

"No, but I can tell a great deal by looking at the man himself. The truth is in the man's face."

"'*The poor man*,'" Meyer mimicked. "Goddam thief is what he is, Farrell."

Farrell looked out on to the street. "He is that. And a poor one, no good at all at his business. I've seen him on the street at night, standing on a corner as if he had no idea where to go, a man literally without a place in the wide world."

"There's plenty of us," Meyer said.

"But you at least have accepted your peculiar condition."

Meyer snorted. "I ain't accepted nothing. Nothing." He glared at Farrell as if daring contradiction, but it was clear that Farrell had no interest in a fight.

Later that afternoon, as I sat in a far corner reading, the girl came in, the girl from the fortune teller's window.

"Ah, my young friend Rachel," Farrell said.

She answered in a low lovely voice, something I could not make out, perhaps because my ears were ringing with her name. She made her way back almost to where I sat, and I saw her glance my way before moving closer to Farrell's bookshelves. From the corner of my eye I saw Farrell watching me, and buried my face in the book though I didn't read a single sentence thereafter. A short while later, she bought a couple of paperback books and left. I fought the urge to follow her.

One night after that old Chicago rite of spring, the late March snow, I was heading home for dinner, having made my last delivery for Millie. An afternoon thaw had melted some of the snow. When the sun went down, it all froze over and the slush became a new sheet of ice. I picked my spots with care. Behind me, a man slipped and went down with a loud thump. I stopped to help him up and, as I watched him brush the wet from his clothes, I saw, just a few feet from us, another man looking my way. Something about the stiff, watchful way he stood told me I'd caught him following me. There was something vaguely familiar about him, but I couldn't see his face. I resumed walking home, conscious – or at least it seemed so – that he was still behind me. Finally I turned onto another street, waited a few seconds and came back around the corner just in time to see him slip between two houses.

I went quickly through the nearest gangway and emerged in the alley about the same time he did. The man was looking behind him toward the street, obviously expecting pursuit, and did not see me for several seconds. He was about my size, thin, and despite the cold wore a denim jacket and a watch cap, an underdressed bundle of tension. It struck me that by pursuing him I'd put myself in harm's way, but he had been following me, he would follow me again if I didn't confront him. And I wanted to see his face.

"What do you want with me?"

He froze, then turned suddenly and I recognized him: the sickly man who had once warned me against Farrell and Meyer, against the shop – *"You don't know what they are."*

He set off at a run and I went after him. But he ran like something wounded, he ran limping and hunched over, and when he shot a panicked look over one shoulder I had no heart for such pursuit. I stopped and yelled after him to leave me alone, to stop following me. He lurched off into the darkness of the alley and I heard him drop something – a piece of metal, a length of pipe. He ran off and I let him go. I said nothing to Farrell or Meyer about this experience.

141

Ten:

Interpretation of the Signs

The cold weather made one or two more half-hearted comebacks but May is inevitable, even in Chicago, and winter left us at last. For several weeks I did not see my gray-haired pursuer, and then he reappeared. With the coming of baseball season and good weather, the neighborhood filled up, and one consequence was that it was easier for a man to hide. On a Saturday afternoon when the Milwaukee Braves were in town, I stopped by Farrell's shop to see if he needed anything. He was engrossed in a debate with a customer, and so I left. The el had just deposited its load and I walked right into a thick crowd of people on their way to see Hank Aaron, Warren Spahn, and company. I waited to let them pass, then crossed the street. I was midway to the far side when I saw him in the dark space under the tracks: the gray-haired man who had been following me a few weeks earlier. He was dressed just as he had been that earlier time, a denim jacket and a dark wool cap, and as I moved in his direction he seemed to separate himself from the shadows, a gray apparition among the living. He gave me a humorless smile and nodded.

This time he did not run, just continued nodding slowly and when I was just a few feet away he began talking. To a passerby it would have looked as though he was speaking to the air, and the baseball people began to give him a wide berth. I moved closer, reluctant but drawn to him, and to my horror I realized he was speaking about me. He pointed me out.

"There's one," he was saying, "there's one who knows about this evil, he's one of them. They're over there in that little junk shop, and they're evil, all of 'em, I know because I've seen. I've seen!"

I stood there transfixed by his mad talk, then realized few if any of the people passing us were paying me any attention at all. They watched him, some uneasy in his presence, some openly amused.

The man went on, shouting now in a harsh voice that made his words unintelligible, and I finally yelled at him to shut up. He laughed in my face, said, "You're afraid for them to find out, aren't you?" and then he took off through the crowd. I saw how he hobbled away, knew I could catch him before he got twenty feet but I let him go, I let him run into the dark steel cavern of the el. Once he had gone into that place, I was afraid to follow.

Still I made no mention of this man to Farrell, and I soon understood what this reluctance suggested. For several days after that I watched for this gray man, once from a doorway, another from a gangway, and then, on a cloudy afternoon the following week, I positioned myself in the shadows under the tracks on the opposite side of the street from where I'd last seen him. I waited and finally he appeared, almost as if he'd been conjured to the spot.

He stood on the sidewalk across the street and stared at the shop, shivering, smoking and talking to himself. For some time I watched him, both transfixed by the strangeness of the man and frozen by indecision. Then I forced myself to move. I crossed near the corner, walked up behind him in silence, and I was only a couple of paces from him when he realized I was there.

He gave a start, said, "Sonofabitch!" and took a step backward.

Up close he was a wreck, with the sort of street-worn face that could have been forty and just as easily could have been sixty. I was shocked at what the street had done to him in hardly a year and a half: he was unshaven, pale, his face covered with blotches and what seemed some sort of bites. I noted once more the rough red place where his earlobe had been. His clothes were filthy and he smelled, of alleys and unwashed clothes. He shot a look into the alley, as though preparing to flee. Then he seemed to face down his urge to run, and he looked at me.

"Figures you'd catch me from behind."

"Nobody's catching anybody. Why do you – Why are you watching them?"

"I told you. I told you about 'em, but I think you knew already. You're one of them."

He spoke in a hoarse voice, perhaps damaged from sickness or from exposure. Now that I could listen to him carefully, there was the faintest hint of an accent.

"I don't know what you're talking about. I only know

you tried to jump me, and you stand out here acting crazy. I ought to call the cops."

"Why don't you?" He sneered but his eyes were uncertain.

I made a show of backing out from the tracks to look for a cop.

"I know you're with them," he repeated.

"I don't even know what that means. So why don't we find a cop – "

"What, you don't know who he is? That one you're with?"

"In that shop? His name is Farrell. He owns it. He sells books and coins and – "

The man gave a quick impatient shake of his head. "Not him. I mean, he's one of them, I'm sure of it, but I'm talkin' about the other one. The short one in the dirty coat. Him, I know about. That's the one."

"Meyer," I said.

"That's not his name. Just what he calls himself now. When I knew him it was something else. He can call himself whatever he wants, but I know who he is."

"So who is he?"

He shook his head and smirked. He coughed, then perversely fished a cigarette out of the jacket pocket and lit it. He puffed at the cigarette for a moment. He stared at the shop now, finished talking, it seemed. I gave him a shrug of confusion to bait him into disclosure. I sensed that this man could not stay silent for long about these things that angered him.

He spat a piece of tobacco out. "You really haven't figured it out?" He shook his head and muttered, "Fuckin' stupid kid" to himself. To me he said, "He's not who he says, he's not who you think. Everyplace that one goes, they die."

"Who does? Who dies?"

"Everybody. Anybody." For the first time he appeared frightened.

"He's just an old man," I countered, seeing the lie of this before it was even out of my mouth.

"He's not just an old man, he's not – he's the fucking – he brings *death*. He's like the Angel of Death, he fucking causes it all. Yeah, go on and look at me like I'm crazy, but I know." He tapped his head. "I know. 'Cause I seen him, and every place he went, the other people all died and he come out of it. He was on work crews where everybody else died, went on details where nobody else come back, other things, too: he was in the same barracks as men from our village, they all died one way or another except him. Most of 'em got sick and died, wasted away, but not him. And finally they shot him. He oughtta be dead like all the other ones."

"Where did this happen?"

"In the War, the camps." He looked at me and repeated, slowly, "In the camps. They shot him in the camp I was in. Took him out and shot him. And then he was dead, like all the other ones. And here he is now."

I could not make sense of this, and my ignorance provoked his anger. He rolled up a sleeve and showed me blue numbers tattooed onto his arm.

"The camps, you stupid fucking kid. In the War," he added.

I took a step back, I wanted to walk away but he'd

managed to provoke me. "It can't be the same guy."

He closed the space between us till he was just a foot from me.

"It is. I saw him there, I saw *the body*. They shot him. I saw. They shot him and a dozen more men, they shot four men that I knew. One of them was my uncle, my ma's brother." In his agitation his accent grew stronger, he sprayed spittle in my face, I could smell his breath. I stepped back but he just put his face closer to mine, urgent and relentless.

"They shot him, I was on the *burial detail*, I shoveled dirt on him, he was dead. They stripped the dead and piled the naked bodies in a ditch, and I saw him: he was dead. His body was gray like all the others and he had bullet wounds in two places. And he's still here all these years later. He oughtta be dead like all the others, that sonofabitch but he's not, so what does that make him?" He watched me, saw that his words had taken effect. After a moment he added, "And I'll tell you something else, he looked just like that, too, like he does now. I was just a young guy, and look at me. So what do you think that means?"

"How would I know?"

"You know. This was right at the beginning, when the Germans came into Poland, twenty-five years ago. Twenty-five years ago and he looked the same," he said through gritted teeth. "Think of it, kid: twenty-five years ago, he was sixty years old, maybe sixty-five. Look at him now."

"It's gotta be another guy. Has to be."

"Oh, no, kid, I seen him close up, close as you are now.

He's got a thing here, a purple blotchy thing," he pointed to his cheekbone. "Like a big busted vein. The guy I saw in the camps, he did, too. Same guy, kid."

For a moment I could say nothing: Meyer did indeed have a broken vein in his face, a dark starburst of old blood in one cheek.

"I don't know about that. But they're not – there's no evil power in them, they're just – "

I couldn't finish, my defense of them weighed down by what I'd already seen, what I knew whether I admitted it to myself or not.

"No evil power, huh? Remember this, you." He pointed a tobacco-stained finger in my face. "Evil can come dressed up as good. You can't tell the difference. Not at first."

I opened my mouth to protest again but could not speak, and my silence was the final infuriation.

"Fuckin' kid," he snarled. He made a sudden move toward me and I put my hands up to ward off a blow, but he just walked around me, shaking his head, and then he was gone. My first impulse was to go back to the shop but knew I couldn't speak of this yet, not to Meyer. That night I dreamt of the dead. In the dream I saw bodies piled high, naked human beings, bony and taut-skinned, the flesh pocked and scarred with the evidence of their torment, and amidst this tangle of humanity I saw Meyer. Or a version of Meyer, younger and smaller and in death more vulnerable than the hostile creature I knew. He was dead, his pallid skin stretched across the points of his skull, one eye heavily encrusted with blood and pus. And in my dream the young Meyer opened his good eye and looked at me, and I felt a pressure in my chest as though he were squeezing my heart. I awoke, gasping and covered with sweat. It was several long minutes before I could reassure myself that I was in my room, that Meyer wasn't there. I felt exhausted but for the rest of that night I refused to close my eyes, fearful of sleep and its messages.

For several days I avoided the men of that shop, walked the streets in widening circles. On one of those nights I had the dream again although in this version Meyer was indeed dead like the others. Gradually as I stared at the mound of the dead I became aware that someone was watching me. I turned and saw the man from the alley. He looked from the bodies to me and back again, and the dream ended.

Later that week I went back to the shop. Farrell read something in my face as I entered and I refused to meet his eyes. Meyer was not there and so I buried my attention in the magazines. Farrell was polishing the lenses on a prized possession, a telescope – more than once I'd heard Meyer mock his interest in "the goddam stars." From time to time he tossed comments my way, about the weather, about the deplorable state of the Cub pitching staff. I took the bait and offered my half-hearted thoughts, and in the middle of this discussion, when I thought Farrell was about to speak of the upcoming series with the Cardinals, he caught me unawares, as he'd planned.

"What is it that is troubling you, lad?"

"Nothing," I said, feeling transparent.

"That is not true. Anyone can see that. And whatever it is, I think it concerns us. Or me. Is it something about me?" He fixed me with a look of interest and concern.

Evil can come dressed up as good.

Once or twice before I had come close to asking what I wanted – what I needed to know, to ask him about his abilities, his hands.

I've seen you do things with your hands, I've seen you touch people's hurts, I've seen you with a dying man who didn't die. I know about you.

We both became aware of the silence: his last question hung in the air.

Yes, of course it's you, I thought. I met Farrell's eyes and looked away. After a moment I shook my head.

"No. It's not – it's about Meyer."

"Meyer – bothers you." I heard the slight hesitation when he would have said *frightens.* "You have seen him in the street more than once, I believe. He has told me, you know." A half-smile and I thought I detected relief that this was to be about Meyer.

"It's not about that. I saw a man in the alley. He – I've seen him before, last year a couple of times, and then he went away. But he's back and he watches your shop. And I talked to him."

"Did you, indeed? You spoke to him. You are an interesting boy. What sort of man is he?"

"He's not big. He wears kind of raggedy clothes. He looks kind of crazy but he's just – I mean, I don't think he's dangerous. But he's a little crazy."

"Why? What did he tell you, this raggedy man?"

"He said Meyer was – he said wherever Meyer was, people died, that he was kind of a Messenger of Death. Or something like that. The Angel of Death."

"That is what they called Mengele: the Angel of Death.

Do you know of that man, Dr. Mengele, the Nazi doctor?"

I knew the name, it had come up in school, along with others: Eichmann, Goering, the war criminals. Just names to me, though, interchangeable Nazis. Interchangeable evil.

He watched me for a long while, seemed to read my eyes and then asked, "Did he tell you why he thought this?"

I watched his eyes. Something in them changed, they grew harder, and I bit back what I'd been about to say, the strange things the man had told me, that he had seen Meyer's bloodless corpse, had buried him, in fact, that he had not aged in twenty-five years.

"No," I said. "I didn't talk to him that long. He sort of ran away. He's probably just crazy," I finished.

Farrell shrugged. "I don't know about people dying wherever he goes, that sounds like a lot of foolishness to me. But Meyer was in the camps. He seldom speaks of it. You understand about the camps, do you? The concentration camps?"

"The Nazis ran them."

"Yes, although there were others as well who had camps. A popular idea of the 20th century, a camp in which to *concentrate* large numbers of suspected enemies of the state, refugees, undesirables. A delightfully dark use of English, by the way: 'undesirables'. People who are – *not desired.*"

"Meyer was in a concentration camp?"

"Oh, he was in the camps, my boy. Aye. More than one. The prisoner of more than one country."

"Why?"

"Does it surprise you that some government would put a man such as Meyer in a camp?"

"No."

"What else do you know about this fellow who watches my shop?"

"He's angry. I don't know why."

"If he was in the camps as a lad he doubtless has a right to his anger."

"He has a number on his arm."

"As Meyer does. He just doesn't show it.

I thought this over and for the first time saw the possibility that the man in the alley had been telling the truth.

"What happened to Meyer in the camps?"

"That is a question for Meyer."

He watched me. I saw that he was interested in my reaction to all of this, in how I would deal with it, so that I took my time answering. And he had angered me slightly by his refusal to give me a straight answer. It occurred to me that I might catch Farrell off his guard for once.

"He said Meyer is the Angel of Death. So? Is he?"

He snorted. "And why in the world would there be an Angel of Death?" He sighed. "Angels again. Angels of Death and Avenging Angels and cherubim and seraphim and ophanim and thrones and dominations and powers and all the rest of 'em." He looked at me as he spoke but I sensed that his rant was meant for himself, as though I were no longer in the room.

And when he was done with his little litany of angels, he seemed to collect himself. He smiled and it seemed he might even humor a stupid question, and I nearly blurted out, *Is he evil?* But I held my tongue. Farrell looked out onto Addison and when he looked back at me he seemed amused.

"Yes, you should ask Meyer about himself, about the camps. And by all means tell him about your man in the alley. He will be interested."

I thought of Meyer's bristling ferocity. "I don't know if that's such a good idea. I mean, maybe he'll do something to that man."

"I doubt it. But he will be interested in what you have to say."

After a while I added the final detail. "He said Meyer is older than he looks. A real lot older."

Farrell looked at me with new interest.

"I wouldn't know anything about that," he said, and I understood he was lying.

Two days later I entered the shop and Meyer was there, and as always they were arguing. The last time I'd heard them in verbal combat, they'd been arguing about corruption in government. The subject this time was hot dogs, and whether one could eat them uncooked. Meyer was holding a pack of hot dogs out to Farrell, who gave him a look of disgust.

"Of course you don't eat them raw, for the love of God!"

"They're cooked already," Meyer said. "You can eat 'em out of the pack. Watch," he said and slit open the pack with a pocket knife – one of several he carried, I knew. He pulled out a hot dog and gnawed off the end with the side of his mouth, where his best teeth were.

"See?" he said through his mouthful of food.

"I see a barbarian, I see a Hun, a Visigoth."

"Ah, you're just – what's the word?" Here Meyer looked accusingly at me, as though I'd purloined his vocabulary.

A word came to me unbidden, a word I'd encountered in a novel read for school, about a fussy man like Farrell whose shirts had to be just so.

"Fastidious," I said, and looked apologetically at Farrell.

"That's it! Fastidious! Good one, kid. Farrell here is an old fuss-budget, he's fastidious."

Farrell was smiling as well. "You've been reading again, lad. Beware, for once started on books, a man never stops." Then he turned on Meyer.

"Sometime in the murky past, ten thousand years ago (*"ten t'ousand years,"* he said), my forebears made the decision to come down out of the trees. Yours elected to stay there." Farrell looked at me. "Look at him. You, Thomas, do you eat your frankfurters uncooked like a Hun?"

I refused to be drawn into it, but I looked at Meyer, chewing contentedly on uncooked hot dog, and I know I shuddered. I remembered the gray man in the doorway and it seemed important to bring this subject up.

"Did you tell him about the man?" I asked Farrell.

Farrell seemed to hesitate a moment. "The fellow's right there, lad. You can tell him yourself," he said, and it seemed the humor of a moment before had left him.

"Tell me what?" Meyer mumbled as he chewed. "What man?"

"There's a man that watches the shop. He's here a lot. He stands in the doorway of that grocery store. He talked to me. He says – he knows you."

"He does, huh? And?" Meyer said, suddenly hostile.

"He thinks you're – " I fought the urge to look to Farrell for help with this. My nerve had fled, these things seemed too ridiculous to voice.

"He thinks I'm what?"

"Bad luck, like you're some kind of bringer of – misfortune."

He squinted, irritable. He chewed for a moment, slowly, then took the time to swallow, his eyes never leaving mine. "What else did he say?"

"He said wherever you went, people died."

Meyer shrugged. "They do that anyhow. Shit, they could say that about you."

"He said – he said you were in the camps, that's where he knows you from. He was in the camps, too. And he said he saw you – he thought you were killed back then. Shot, with a bunch of others."

From the corner of my eye I could see Farrell looking down in the way of a man witnessing another's embarrassment.

Meyer stiffened and I had the sense that he was fighting the urge to look over at Farrell. He stared at me and I couldn't tell whether the look he gave me was a challenge or contempt.

"What's he look like? How old?"

"Not as old as you. He's small and he's got – " I thought about it and details seemed to present themselves. "Blue eyes. And there's something wrong with one of his

155

ears, there's - "

"No earlobe. Right? He's got no earlobe."

I nodded.

For the first and only time, Meyer looked confused. He swallowed again and looked past me.

I looked at Farrell. There was something clinical in his gaze, and I saw that this time it was Meyer he studied.

Finally Meyer spoke. "He was just a kid. And he was small. Looked sick, even when he wasn't. Most of them – most of us got sick sometime, but that kid looked sick always. I thought for sure he'd die, he'd be one of the ones to go."

"You remember him?"

"Yeah. The earlobe. Nazi bullet did that. Half an inch closer and it would've gone into his skull. Maybe he'da been better off. All these years."

"He showed me his number."

Meyer wasn't paying attention. Then he seemed to realize what I'd said. Not what I'd said, exactly, but what I meant: that I knew now about the significance of the numbers.

"Like this one?"

He pushed up the coat sleeve and the discolored shirt within, and showed faint blue numbers on a patch of oddly discolored skin. He studied his arm and shrugged.

"I tried to rub it off, put acid on it, burned it. Then I decided it was useful in its way. So he showed you his number, this guy?"

"Yes."

"What else did he tell you?"

"He said you're older than you look."

"Don't waste my time with bullshit."

I looked to Farrell, who merely nodded, prodding me.

"Is he telling the truth? About you, and the camps, and, and what happened to you?"

He gave me a long look. "Never mind about that. I wanta know about this guy. Where does he go, do you know?"

"No."

Meyer nodded as though I'd given him information. "I can find him."

"What are you going to do?"

He shot me an irritable look. "I wanta talk to him." He looked at Farrell. "I'll see you, Farrell."

Farrell said nothing, merely raised one hand in a casual wave as Meyer left the shop, stuffing the package of hot dogs into the deep pocket of his coat. For a long moment neither of us said anything. Eventually the silence grew oppressive to me and so I forced conversation.

"Meyer's a little crazy, too, isn't he?"

"No more than most," Farrell said without feeling. Then he looked at me. "Well, I've oversimplified. Yes, most people would say he was crazy. It is after all a term used to cover so many sorts of people and behavior. A convenience."

He was watching me as he spoke, measuring me.

"And what do you think of these things the fellow told you about our Meyer?"

I hesitated before answering: I was certain that Farrell in some way knew the other things I'd held back, that he was asking me how I felt about those things as well. I suppressed the sudden urge to shrink back from Farrell, as

157

though he might strike me.

"You mean about being the Angel of Death? I suppose it's goofy. And I don't think there is an Angel of Death," I added, trying to navigate a safe course.

"Why would there be such a *crayture?*" he said, and I understood that he was speaking to himself. At length he seemed to remember he was not alone. He gazed at me with his sad, pale eyes and said, "Don't trouble yourself with all of this, Thomas. You are becoming a young man. It is a time of great change for any lad." Then he added, "For you especially, a time of great change," and I was vaguely troubled by his words.

When I said nothing, he said, "Meyer is a difficult fellow to comprehend, even harder, I think, for a young lad such as yourself to be comfortable with. As you have seen, he is given to violence though if you had lived through such horrors as Meyer, you might be prone to violence yourself. And he is unpredictable to a far greater degree than you know. But he is no bringer of death or Angel of Death or any of that nonsense."

A new thought occurred to me, something neutral to ask: "What's his real name?"

A shrewd flicker crossed his face and I understood he might lie to me about this. In the end he shrugged.

"Who knows? It is whatever name he chooses to take, same as you. If you want to call yourself Finn MacCool or St. Joseph, it's your business, and all the same to me. He has been Meyer as long as I've known him."

"How long – "

He anticipated the question and answered before it was even out of me.

"Years. Many years."

Then he seemed to recall something, as though what he'd just said was more complicated than he'd made it sound, but he said nothing.

For just a moment it seemed I might at last have a chance to make not-so-subtle inquiries into the other mysteries of that shop, but there was something final in his tone and in his eyes. We would speak no more of Meyer that day.

Later that week I came into the shop just as Meyer was leaving. He seemed preoccupied, and did no more than grunt when he saw me. Inside, Farrell was dickering with a man over the price of a coffee table art book.

Neither of them said anything further about the man who watched the shop, and for a time I did not see him, not until I'd nearly forgotten him.

The warm weather came to stay, and change, change enough in my life to prove, when I looked back on it from the vantage point of another year or two, that among Farrell's gifts, whether he would ever admit it, was the ability to sense things about one's future.

Eleven: Another Orphan

A child can grow accustomed to the oddest of life's patterns, convince himself that all is well and his life is normal. Thus it was that, so long as my mother's mysterious illness kept in abeyance and I wasn't thrown out of school, I was able to persuade myself that I had a life like anyone else's. The summer passed in a blur, uneventful and lonely in ways I had grown used to. I did not consciously avoid Farrell's shop but a man who came frequently into the diner offered me a job working at the public library downtown, a job that gave me more hours than Millie could and paid better. So I had less time to visit Farrell and Meyer. On the few occasions that I did, Farrell seemed slightly wary, guarded. Meyer said little, stared when I came in, frequently did not respond to my greetings, seemed to forget my presence immediately. For a time it could have been any junk shop in the city. I saw nothing unusual, heard no cryptic conversations.

The young have little in the way of short-term memory, and I more or less forgot the dark haired girl. There were girls aplenty downtown, and toward the end of that summer I even had a handful of dates, which came to nothing in the long run but helped me with my continuing illusion that I was normal. My first sexual experiences came this summer, and will forever be tied inextricably with memories of Grant Park, hot nights, fumbling under a summer dress and failing to get a bra strap undone, then plucking from my slim wallet a condom I'd carried for months in sanguine belief that I'd someday use it. In the end I needed her help with that, too. Shortly after a similar night's experience, behind a hedge near North Avenue beach, we parted company by mutual agreement.

On a crisp fall Saturday when I was getting ready to go to work, our doorbell rang. It was in the first place one of the most jarring doorbells I ever heard, so that it was always startling to hear it. My mother was in the back, shuffling cans in the pantry, and so I went to the door.

A man stood on the doorstep. He was tall and thin, with a deeply furrowed face and large brown eyes, and it was clear that he was taken aback to see me. Though he was twice my size I would have said he was nervous, and that I'd caused his discomfort.

"Morning," he said. I nodded, perhaps even said hello, but we had no male callers and this didn't look like a handyman or plumber.

"Is, uh, your m – " He cleared his throat and started anew: "I come to see Elizabeth."

He pronounced it *Lizbeth,* but even so, it was odd for me to hear someone call her by her name, odder still to hear it coming from a man, and I think I let us both stand there staring at each other for a moment.

"I'm a friend of hers," he added in a Tennessee-flavored voice. He could have been Millie's brother.

From the back of the house I heard my mother call out,

"Who is that?"

I blurted out, "A friend of yours, Ma. There's a – " I wanted to say, "There's some hillbilly here that says he knows you" but I caught myself in time. "There's a guy here."

The man nodded and looked even more nervous, and something made me drop my defensiveness. I liked him. He reminded me of the good-humored men in Millie's little diner, he seemed a man who would always feel awkward in the world outside his small existence. And it was clear that he'd intended to make some sort of impression wherever he was headed, for he gave off the heavy aromas of what passed for working class male grooming: Old Spice aftershave and a hair tonic that might have been Wildroot – he'd used enough so you could smell his hair. And this shy Southerner had put on an unpressed sport coat and buttoned his shirt all the way up to his chin, in what I came later in life to understand as the style of simple men who want to feel dressed up.

"Roy? Elroy Owens? Why, hello, Roy," my mother called out, and when I turned to look at her I saw that she was as nervous about the occasion as the shuffling man on her doorstep. I began to sense the purpose of his visit, and allowed myself to wonder what sort of name *Elroy Owens* was.

He was smiling now, a tentative smile, and his hand went to the top button of his shirt collar, God forbid it come undone at this dramatic moment.

"'Lo, Betty," he said, and dipped his head slightly, as though he were assuming privilege to use her name. And the name itself was strange to my ears. My mother's name was Elizabeth, and to my old man she'd been "Liz" or, when he was pleading for something, like forgiveness, "Hon". I understood she was still called "Betty" by people who'd known her in the old days, but it seemed odd to hear her called by this name now.

"Hello," my mother said, unaware that she'd already said that. Then, "Come in. And this is Tom, my boy."

"Hullo, Tom," he said, still shy of me and held out a hand, a long hand with broken nails and what seemed to be grease stains on the knuckles. We shook and I thought my hand looked like a young girl's in his.

When she'd finally coaxed the poor man into our flat, pulled him into it, literally, my mother looked at me.

"I've known this man – twenty-five years, at least."

"Longer than that," he said, clearly uneasy correcting her.

They looked at each other and I realized she was still holding onto his hand. I know I must have stood there looking from one to the other and I was startled at what I thought I saw in their eyes. They moved to the kitchen at the back of the flat and she banged around for a moment in the way that she had, making four times as much noise as anyone ever needed just to make coffee and "fry up a few eggs and some sausage," as she was fond of saying. I went on my way and my mother said good-bye to me in a voice laden with distraction. Later I was to realize that early in a relationship cooking for a man is a declaration of intent.

They began seeing one another almost immediately, and the change in my mother was startling. Beyond the superficial – she sang around the house more than ever, smiled more, became as chatty at home as I knew she had once been among her friends – beyond these obvious and expected ways, she changed on a fundamental level, in the way she carried herself, her tone of voice when she expressed an opinion, and something far more subtle, a look in her eye that told of a new confidence about herself. But there was something else, I would have sworn her coloring had changed, her movements became more assured, more graceful, as though she'd gotten a burst of whatever life force had been ebbing since the old man had left her. Quite simply, she was prettier.

A month later Roy moved in. I felt blindsided – one morning I woke up and there he was, coming out of the bedroom, buttoning up his shirt. My mother took me aside to explain, or rather, to defend herself.

"He's a good man, a real nice man," she told me. I more or less knew this but another man had moved into my life and, like any teenage boy, I was committed at least to a certain mute resistance to the change, if not outright hostility. So I listened to the poor woman justifying herself and stared off into the distance as if I were hearing none of it. But she was smarter than I gave her credit for, always, and she read my mind.

"Your father's not coming back. Not ever. I think I always knew he'd do what he done, and I'm sorry. I apologize 'cause I should have done something. Maybe told you how he was, maybe left him first. I don't know. But I do know he's not coming back to us, and I divorced him. I divorced him –" I heard the defiance in her voice – "and I'm not married to him anymore."

One more surprise from her, this last news, but I

refused to respond. She let me have my silence for a moment and then said, "Roy's good to me." She left the rest unspoken: *And I deserve something in my life.* Unspoken, but I heard it all the same.

"All right," I said. It wasn't much but it was apparently sufficient to the moment. She had heard what she needed. She patted my hand, called me a good boy, and went out of the room.

For a few days after that I tried to do what any adolescent boy would have done at the cold-water shock of a new male presence: I was sullen and unresponsive, stayed out as long as possible or kept to my room, and demonstrated the remarkable ability of most boys to answer almost any question, regardless of its depth and complexity, in a single syllable. But he wore me down, Roy did, with his quiet good humor, his kindness, and his total lack of guile. And my mother was right: he was good to her. He worked, he brought home his check, he bought her small gifts, even flowers. The first time he did that, I realized I'd never seen flowers in our flat: my father would never have thought of it, and my mother would not have been comfortable spending money on anything so ephemeral. I was surprised she had a vase.

It took some time to sort out my feelings for all of it, for Roy himself, for his intrusive presence in our flat, for the change in the dynamic of that house. But I was fated to see human beings accustom themselves to life changes another might have found truly bizarre, and this situation was fairly painless. Ironically, Roy's presence caused me to become preoccupied with my father. Initially after his escape from us – that's how I thought of it, his escape from people who weren't worth his time and attention – I thought of the old man in terms of what he'd done to us, of the hole he'd left in his wake. And I thought in terms of running him down someday, of catching up with him. Now for reasons I couldn't have said, the notion of confronting him no longer interested me. After that, from time to time, images of my father came to me at odd moments. Several times I dreamt of him, and once in that time just after waking, I imagined him in a strange place, on a street corner, one hand thrust in his pocket and the other gesturing with a cigarette, speaking non-stop, the anger clear in his voice. There was no one else in the scene. He was speaking to himself.

Roy did not bring back my old life but remade our home. He was a source of constancy, of self-effacing steadiness. For the first time since the old man left, there was someone who could fix things, who could handle a hammer and a saw, who could put a new pane of glass in a broken window and change an outlet. None of these things were his responsibility, but when my mother insisted that she call the landlord and demand action, Roy just said, "Naw, Betty, I can do it."

For a time I tried not to engage him in actual conversation, lest by this sort of attention I give tacit support to the new configuration of the household. But Roy was cheerfully stoic in the face of my mulishness, and without even understanding how it came to be, I found myself growing comfortable with this newest phase of my life.

Even the most intractable of us will adapt when given limited options, and I was no different. These new patterns of my life were the only ones I had, and we all, my mother, Roy, and I, slipped into something like a life. So it was that by the coming of the cold weather I'd begun to accept Roy as a part of our household. And though I might have been loath to admit it, his presence, not just his good-hearted nature but the mere presence of a third human being in the house, gave us the closest thing we'd had in years to a Christmas.

Thereafter, Roy's presence as an element of my life was unquestioned.

The spring brought changes. The first was that Roy and my mother pooled their money and bought a maroon Dodge, ugly but serviceable, and I quickly learned that Roy knew cars, more importantly, knew car engines. He worked on the Dodge more or less constantly in his free time and it was clear that this was as close as he'd come in his life to a hobby. I was of course interested in the car, and I paid as much attention to his work on the engine as I did when he took me out practice driving down by Montrose harbor. And when Roy showed me the many small tasks that could improve an engine's performance, his smile made it clear that there were few things as holy as the internal combustion engine.

And so we had a car, like normal families, and I was soon able to drive it – and if I had scoured the great city on my walks beyond number, I now went farther into the streets and neighborhoods I'd never even heard of, near giddy with excitement, for there is nothing so liberating to a kid who's never been anyplace than a car, even a maroon Dodge.

And I provided the second great change in our lives

that spring of 1965, announcing to my mother and Roy that I had applied for college. I'd begun looking at college catalogues in the public library, there were loans and grants, and it seemed I might be able to afford to go to college, something that had never occurred to me before. The quirky Chicago branch of the University of Illinois, having driven out thousands of Greeks and Italians on the near West Side, was to open a new campus.

"College!" my mother said, then looked at Roy and repeated the word several times.

To celebrate, Roy took us to dinner, and toward the end of the week, took us to a ballgame, a Sunday doubleheader with the Cardinals – this was as much for Roy as for us, I knew: the Cardinals were the closest major league team to a southerner in those days.

I have only three distinct impressions of that day: the much-lamented former Cub Lou Brock ran wild on the base paths, Cubs lost both games, and I thought I had never seen my mother happier. And inasmuch as my mother's happiness was Roy's primary goal in life, he beamed at me for most of the day.

For many years thereafter, I was to look back on that spring, and a few brief weeks of summer that followed it, as a sort of high-water mark in my life.

Twelve: Rachel

For other reasons that summer proved memorable. Among other things, I had my first romance, and true to form in a life where normalcy seemed to have little place, it was an odd romance that began in minor humiliation.

Like countless kids before me, I fell in love with the seemingly endless lake. On certain days I could almost convince myself that at its farthest edge was another continent, where a young guy whose life hadn't quite worked out might start another one. On Sundays and Wednesdays – my day off from the library – I took to walking along the beach with a towel and a paperback book. When I grew tired of walking I dropped the towel and book and plunged into the water, whether I was on one of the long crowded beaches or on the less-frequented areas called "the rocks." I had the vague notion that a pretty blond girl from the library spent afternoons down here somewhere, tanning her golden self, and I was more or less attempting a "chance" meeting. If she was there, I never saw her, but I wandered the lakefront nonetheless.

It was on one of these lakefront meanderings that I saw in the distance a dark-haired young woman reading on a beach towel. She was too far for me to make out in detail but I believe there are moments when we recognize people by their aura, and I recognized hers. It was Rachel, the girl I'd met at Farrell's shop.

There were, in fact, several girls much closer, but my heart clamored as though I had entered harm's way, and I moved as close to her as I dared. Without so much as a glance in her direction, I set down my towel and book, put my wallet in my shoe, and walked to the edge of the hard concrete surface. I stood on the yellow painted warning that said "No Swimming/No Diving" and dove, just missing the edge of one of the great jagged rocks that lined the shore there. The chill squeezed my bones till they ached, but I went under, swam and surfaced and swam again.

When I came out, I collapsed on my towel and affected interest in nothing save my book of Ray Bradbury stories. From the edge of my vision I saw her give me a look. A moment later she got up and dove into the water herself. I didn't budge, I moved no muscle, not even my eyes, staring a hole in the page. When she emerged from the water her path took her close to me, and she even scattered drops of water on me as she shook herself off. And now I had to look. She wore a two-piece suit and as I stared at her brown skin I could see the goose-flesh from the icy water. A short while later she dressed, and when I thought it was safe I watched her. All young men believe the most sensual sight is a woman undressing, but there was something riveting about watching her put her clothes on. When she was finished she looked right at me, caught me staring, had the good grace not to smirk. A moment later

170

she left, passing close by, and I mustered nerve enough to face her and say, "Hi."

She nodded and said "Hi" and I decided she'd given me proof that she remembered me. I watched her walk away, hips swinging slightly, and crushed my impulse to follow her – at least for that day, I suppressed it, for the following week I saw her in the neighborhood and followed her for several blocks before she went into a grocery store.

On my days at the lake I looked for her along the rocks between Belmont and Diversey, but for a time she wasn't there. Then, perhaps three weeks after that first encounter, she was there again. We said hello, I forced myself to remind her we'd "met" more or less.

"At Mr. Farrell's bookshop," she said. I was amused to hear her refer to it that way. I'd heard it called half a dozen other things, junk shop, resale shop, second-hand shop, even coin shop, all depending, it seemed, on what people wanted from it. I introduced myself and pretended I didn't already know that her name was Rachel. After an awkward moment, I held out my hand. She smiled and took it, then she looked at my towel and at my book.

"So you like to read, and you're interested in the Aztecs."

"Aztecs?"

She gave me a small smile and nodded at my beach towel. "The Sun and the Moon on your towel. They look like Aztec symbols."

I understood who the Aztecs were but wasn't sure why a young girl would make that connection. I nodded. She was reading a book by Robert Graves, one of the *Claudius* books. Farrell had given me the strange and exotic *Count Belisarius*, and I leapt at the chance to ask if she was interested in ancient Rome.

" 'Faraway places with strange-sounding names,' " she said. Seeing my confusion, she added, "It's from an old song. My mother sang it to me when I was a girl."

And without a hint that it was so, I understood that her mother was dead, long dead. She looked out at the lake and this seemed to signal the limit of conversation. So, having made far greater progress than I'd ever expected, I said, "Well, I guess I'll be moving on." And so I did, feeling a certain combination of elation and embarrassment that I believe is the unique province of adolescents in the throes of a crush.

For a week I fantasized about her, about taking her out, about kissing her, about having my hands all over her body, my very pale hands on her brown skin. It cost me hours of sleep, night upon night, so that I nodded off on the el home from work.

The following Wednesday she was there down by the rocks again. There has probably never been a moment in my life that I rehearsed so intensely. My mental screenplay included contingencies for half a dozen different scenarios, including the one I most feared, that I would come upon her lying on her beach towel with a handsome lifeguard-type and would then have to walk on as though I hadn't noticed.

But she was there and I hit my marks and went through my lines, and within five or six minutes I had asked her out. She said no. Just "no" and a short shake of her head, and then she looked at me as if to assess the damage. I looked out at the lake and composed myself, waited for the red to leave my face. I was about to excuse myself when she said, "Sit down."

I did as I was told and she led me through small talk, and when I was feeling nearly comfortable she said, "Thanks for asking me out. It doesn't happen all that often. But you shouldn't go out with complete strangers. I shouldn't, and you shouldn't."

I nodded and tried to interpret all that she'd just told me, trying to sort the gold from the pyrite.

"Okay. I guess."

And she laughed. Her face changed totally when she laughed, became a younger face, lost much of the distance and maturity I'd come to think of as her overriding characteristics. And I realized I'd never really seen her in an unguarded moment.

"I don't want to make you uncomfortable, which is clearly what I did. I'm sorry."

I stared out at the lake, without the faintest idea what to say: I'd envisioned her turning me down, even laughing in my face, but not turning me down and then asking me to sit.

"So why do you go to the bookshop?"

I began to list the things I found to immerse myself in: the old comics, the boxing magazines, the coins, yes, the books. And as I talked I felt the tension leave me, saw myself in an unreal situation, one I'm not certain I thought I would ever experience, given the odd patterns of my life: I was sitting at the lake and a pretty girl in a bathing suit was listening to me talk. And so I talked on about the unique things I'd noted in Farrell's shop but stopped short

173

of revealing my fascination with the two men or giving any hint of the stranger things I had experienced there.

"So that's my side. What about you?" I asked her.

"It's where I get most of my books."

"There are a lot of bookstores. And libraries."

She hesitated and I watched her face. My first reaction was pleasure that I'd now managed to make her uncomfortable, for it was clear she was considering her reply carefully. For a moment it seemed she might not even answer. Then she gave me a frank look.

"I love it there, I really can't explain why. I like old shops, and I go into a lot of them, every one I find, actually. But that little place is different. And I feel different whenever I'm there, I mean, it's just a smelly old shop, with a couple of old men in it, and some of the people that come in there are like – " She turned to face me. "Hoboes come in to see him, and bag ladies. And there are one or two that I think are really crazy."

"Oh, I think there's more than one or two crazy ones there."

"That's what I mean. It's not really the nicest place, although Mr. Farrell is a sweet man."

"How about Meyer? Is he sweet, too?"

She grimaced, blushed a little, aware that she'd sounded sentimental, this serious young woman. "I don't know what the word is for Meyer. He has seen a great deal of sadness, I think."

This took me by surprise. I had never quite made it past Meyer's harsh persona to see anything pitiable.

"Anyway, when I walk into that little shop I feel like it's a place where I'm supposed to be. There's almost always someone there talking to one or the other of them, or the two of them are arguing about something – *God* sometimes, if you can believe it."

Indeed, I could, for the subject of God had come up in my own conversations there.

"They argue about God," she said, shaking her head, and laughed.

"I know. I've heard them do that. Farrell, especially."

"And every little thing in the store is where it was the last time I was there, I can almost convince myself that time stopped since my last visit. I feel like I belong there."

This last statement threw me off balance for a moment. Once or twice I'd had this feeling that she had just put into words, but mine was a more complicated experience with the two men, and I understood that I had no simple expression for it.

The girl misunderstood my silence.

"That sounded silly, right?"

"No, not really. It made me think, that's all. I've never, you know, really understood why I go there, but I've been doing it for a couple years."

She was watching me, frowning slightly, assessing me. I would have said that she was measuring me for trouble. I was a year older than she was – a surprise to me, given her self-possessed air. We talked on for a few minutes, neither of us, I noted, speaking directly about our families. And for this I was thankful, for I would have been mortified to describe what passed for a family in my life.

Yeah, my real father left us, without money or a backward look, and now a drifter from Tennessee lives with us and sometimes I pretend he's my father.

175

At some point we struck our first conversational gap and, unaccustomed to such awkwardness, I excused myself. She told me she didn't get down to the lake often but that this was her spot, and I understood that it was an invitation of the vaguest sort.

She had never asked me where I lived and did not offer that information about herself, and I saw this as a simple defense against a boy who might be as strange as anyone she was likely to meet. But we managed to run into one another again at the lake, and once more after that, and finally I asked her out again and she accepted. With the greatest reluctance she told me where she lived: above yet another storefront, with the woman she referred to simply as her aunt. When I started to ask if it was the strange fortune-telling woman I'd seen in the window that day, she just held up her hand and said, "My life is weird. I don't think you want to know about it."

When I picked her up that first time, the older woman was there, lurking in the background. At one point I saw her craning her head around a doorway to get a look at me, and I almost laughed. When Rachel came out, putting keys in her purse, she saw the old woman. Something in her face fell but she recovered in an instant and smiled. She nodded toward the old woman.

"That's my aunt."

I waved and the old woman ducked back behind her doorway.

We went out the rest of that summer, not so long at all: perhaps ten or twelve occasions in her company, and despite the turmoil that was to develop in my life later that summer, Rachel dominates that time in my memory, for I

176

thought of little else. The first time we kissed, seriously, she bit the corner of my lip bloody so that I had to make up an improbable accident for the half dozen or so people who wanted to know if I'd been in a fight.

Toward the end of August I was accepted at the newly opened Circle Campus of the University of Illinois. I had no particular illusions of myself as any sort of student, nor did I have an idea of a profession. I was going to college entirely for my mother, who reacted to my acceptance as though I'd been knighted. It was not just that no one in her family had gone to college: no one had ever even considered it a possibility. Roy treated me like Babe Ruth.

And in the other odd relationship of my young life, Rachel was delighted for me, a girl born for books, for an education, but resigned to the odd burdens of her life.

I see now that for me, at least, time had come to a stop. I lived for the day, for that summer, and managed at least until late August to think of little else but the present. It was unlikely that Rachel, more grounded in the adult world as she was, would see things the same way. At some point during that ephemeral time she dropped her guard, her odd reserve, and I learned about her life, if only in the vaguest terms. Her mother was indeed long dead, and it was clear that Rachel had never gotten over that moment at the age of eight, when she had lost her. She had lived in other places, other states, so that more than once, when speaking of her own future she said, "Wherever I'm living then." Her father was still alive but not living in Chicago – "as far as anybody knows," she added. She would say nothing more about him. The "aunt" that she lived with was actually her mother's aunt, a messy, dotty woman, not unkind toward Rachel but distracted and disorganized and frequently living on the edge of bankruptcy – hence the slightly hysterical willingness to try whatever would bring in a dollar, even if it meant pretending to tell fortunes.

"She actually thinks she can do that, though, tell fortunes," Rachel told me. "She's really a little bit crazy. And she's growing senile. But I can take care of her."

I remember watching her as she stared out at the last boats coming in off the lake at dusk, and thought I understood what might have been termed her gravity, the deep seriousness that never seemed to leave her for long, not even when she was laughing. I came to think that she was a person who was never, even for a moment, "carefree". As though she could read my thoughts, Rachel leaned her dark head against my shoulder, and for the first time, the first moment since I'd seen her that day in the window, I was uncomfortable in her company. Even as I stroked her hair, I shrank inwardly from the closeness, the implied responsibility.

Perhaps my sudden coldness was easily explained: as it turned out, my own troubles were resurrected the second half of that summer, for my mother grew sick. At first she was tired a great deal, bled of energy after simple tasks. She told me it was nothing, extra hours at work, sleeping badly on hot nights, a touch of the flu. With each lie a dull foreboding grew in me. At first there were no outward signs save the dark circles that grew beneath her eyes – she did not lose weight, not at first, and her color gave nothing away, pale as she was. For a time I bought the stories she fed me, because of course I wanted to. Roy was another matter.

He saw immediately what was happening and I read the changes in his eyes. He had once said in passing that he'd watched both his parents die, and in his unschooled way he recognized the presence of death. At first he seemed frightened of it, as though it had followed him all the way from Tennessee. Then he got hold of himself.

To me he spoke of it only once. We were in the living room watching a ball game and my mother, who had been napping in her room, came out to get a drink of water. From the kitchen we heard her coughing, a cough that could have been anything but had Roy's complete attention. When she padded back into her room, he turned to me and said, "Your Ma's real sick, son."

"How sick?"

He stared at the ball game to buy himself time for his answer.

"I'm takin' her in to that doctor. Then we'll see. But she's real sick."

His tone, the simple evasion of his answer – *real sick* – confirmed my belief. She was dying.

There followed a series of visits to doctors: to Dr. Kapitanic, twice to a specialist, my mother's drawn face after her tests, then hospitalization. My mother told me not to worry.

"It's just to get me checked out," she said.

"I'll come see you," I said.

"No, you got plenty to keep you busy." She smiled. I had told her about Rachel and she was giddy with joy – and relief – that her boy had finally found a girlfriend.

"I'll be out in a few days anyhow."

179

I nodded and said "Sure" and looked away to hide my sudden terror. Whether she came out of the hospital or not, she had very little time.

The day she went in to the hospital, I decided to speak to Rachel about this new trouble. To that point, I had said nothing.

We went to the zoo, saying very little, and gradually I became aware that she was forcing herself to be charming, attentive. That she was preoccupied. I wondered if she had begun to sense my distance, and felt a sudden urge to somehow make things right.

We were leaning against the railing around the lagoon, watching couples in rowboats, and she put her hand on my shoulder and told me she was leaving.

"What?"

"I'm moving. *We're* moving. My father's back."

She paused after *back*, and I realized she meant he was back in her life.

"He's been back about three weeks. He quit drinking, at least I think he did, and I'm moving in with him. He has a place in Rockford. I don't have any choice: my aunt's sick and she's going to live with one of her daughters in Missouri. I can't be on my own, not yet. And besides, I – I have to take care of him. He'd laugh if he heard me say that, but it's true."

"You're too young to be taking care of other people."

She raised her eyebrows at that. "I've been doing it for years. It'll – it'll be all right."

I had no idea what to say. My reaction was shock for myself, combined with no small sense of relief. But I was also terrified for Rachel. This seemed no life at all.

"Rockford's not that far – "

"It's far enough."

"You'll be – " I stopped short of expressing whatever I'd nearly blurted out.

She smiled, looking for the moment, years older than she was. "Miserable? Nuts? Yes, to both of those things. But I've been that before and it didn't kill me."

I felt the familiar pressure in my throat and turned away lest I begin to cry. She took me by the chin and looked in my eyes and kissed me, hard, for a couple of seconds and then broke it off.

"This is how life is," she said, and gave me a genuine smile, a smile for my sake, and I understood that at that moment she was most sorry for causing me any sadness. "My solitary boy," she said.

"We could keep up – "

But she was shaking her head. "People don't do that." I didn't know how she could be certain of this and, just for a brief moment, wondered if she had had to do this before.

I opened my mouth to say something and then, for the only time that day, showed intelligence. I stroked her hair and pulled her to me. And as I held her I saw a young dark-haired girl in a room, perched at the edge of a narrow bed, a child, and I wondered if this was how she had looked the night her mother had died. I put my hand on her hair and muttered something about things getting better, hearing the utter hollowness of these words.

Thirteen:

A Pair of Deaths

My mother returned from the hospital, beyond cure. She had continued to waste away in the hospital, and it was clear to anyone with eyes that she had little time left. She slept much of the time, which I recognized was a small mercy. When she was awake she asked me about my life, about my new life as a college student, about Rachel. I couldn't tell her Rachel was gone from my life, I knew what she wanted to hear. As for my classes, I was sleepwalking through them.

Roy hovered in the small flat and drove her to quiet exasperation. The stricken way he looked at her gave voice to my own fears and I wanted to assault him. Though I had not seen Farrell in some months, one final time I contrived to have her visit his shop, have Farrell work his strange effects, but I saw in his eyes the moment she arrived that there would be no "magic," no reprieve. There was no rash to wipe away. He did his best to entertain her with his stories and his manner, introduced her to half a dozen people as his "good friend Elizabeth, young

Thomas's mother," and made her laugh. It was the last time I would hear her laugh.

The week she died she tried to make a show of working around the house, cooking and cleaning as though there were nothing wrong. Three nights running she made dinner even though she had to lean against the stove as she cooked. The day before she died, I came home from work as she was lying on the couch, and she tried to get up before I saw her. She made it into a sitting position and then collapsed against the back of the couch.

"I'm feeling better, Tom," she told me, even as all color drained from her.

Later that day, as Roy clumped around in the kitchen putting together a supper of ham and eggs for us, my mother asked me to bring out the pictures. And so on that final night of her life we sat in the dim lighting of the living room – "the front room," she'd always called it – and looked at old photographs, of her family and herself as a girl, and the photo of my elusive father on Clybourn Avenue.

My mother shook her head at the photo. "A handsome man, your father. But handsome is as handsome does."

She put the photo away and brought out the pictures of her youth, and these she set down lovingly, as though they were brittle parchment liable to crumble at her touch. She interpreted each one for me, named the people, all of them long dead, and for the first time in many weeks she seemed calm, relaxed, free of pain. Only once did she rouse herself: a photo of me as a baby. She gazed at it, then looked up suddenly, her face showing her alarm.

"I'm all right, Ma," I said to her clear but unspoken

question. And then I pointed to a picture I'd seen a dozen times and said, "Now who's that again?"

She was dead by morning. As Roy made the necessary calls I sat at the foot of her bed, numb.

There was a small funeral, really just a one-night wake with a brief service at an Irish funeral parlor on Southport. A handful of her co-workers came, as did Millie and two of the waitresses from the diner, who all made a fuss over how tall I'd grown. Her sister Mary came up from Peoria – Roy had gotten hold of her. I had very little to say to these people. I spent most of the evening off to one side, staring at my mother in the coffin, conscious more than anything else of the need to say things to her, what things I didn't know. Toward the end of the evening I was startled to see Farrell making his way from the rear of the room. He spoke briefly to my Aunt Mary, nodded to Roy though he could not have known him, then made his way over to me.

"A sad time, lad. A lovely woman, your mother."

Emboldened, perhaps, by my loss, I said, "Once, when she first met you, I thought you had cured her of whatever it was."

This took him aback. He looked around the room and I saw that he was composing an answer.

"Cured her? No, I'm no healer. If I've learned anything in my life, it is that."

He studied me to see if I'd bought any of this. I glared at him, not so much in anger that he could do nothing for my mother but at his refusal to acknowledge what we both knew I'd been talking about. In the end I simply looked past him, at my mother, and he took his leave of me. He stopped a moment at the casket, I saw him touch her hand,

and then he was gone.

We buried her the next morning in Rosehill Cemetery, a hundred yards or so from a tall statue of a Civil War soldier.

I went home, numbed by it all; now I would live with Roy. I changed clothes and marched down to the lake, walked all the long way to North Avenue Beach, with its great white boat-shaped beach house looking like a grounded ship. I hadn't intended to go there but was perhaps impelled by memory: one of my earliest recollections was of a trip to that beach. I remembered my mother taking me into the lake water so cold that I gasped. She laughed.

But it was nearly October, and the beach was deserted. I sat for hours, outlasting the daylight, then made my way back home. When I returned, Roy was chainsmoking in the dark.

"You all right, Tom?"

"More or less. You?"

"I'm not much good. But I didn't just lose my ma." I was heading for my room when he called out my name once more.

"Whatever happens, I'll do right by you."

His voice had changed in those recent weeks, so that he continually sounded like a man who had just left off crying. My sense was that he was drinking more though I never saw him intoxicated, and his drinking was a private thing: it did not make him talkative, or aggressive, or abusive. Just his private narcotic.

"Thanks."

I will give Roy some credit: for several months after my

mother's passing, he labored at the illusion that he and I could go on living together in the small flat on Roscoe Street. He sat at the red formica table in the kitchen and scrawled lists of tasks, thick pencil on scratch paper – the back of a receipt or an envelope. He wrote like a man for whom school is a vague distant memory. Sometimes the lists were food items to buy, and he would call out to me.

"What else we need, son? Hey, Tommy? What we need from the grocery store?"

For my part I worked at tolerating him. One night I came in late from hours prowling the streets to find him quietly weeping, a pile of cigarette butts in the ashtray. Without an accompanying image I nonetheless understood that he was no stranger to such a moment. I backed out of the room before he saw me. That night as I lay in bed I reflected on what I'd seen, on the things at work in his face, sorrow and loneliness and a kind of fatigue. I knew that he wept for my mother, but also for himself, for the loss of a last chance.

The next morning he cheerfully made me scrambled eggs and bacon before I went off to a day of classes and then work. In the evening when I got home he was gone, and although I could not have pointed to a single piece of evidence that there was anything out of the ordinary, I knew he was gone for good.

In the refrigerator there was ham and Swiss cheese – he'd made a final stop at what he always called "the German store" – a delicatessen presided over by a pair of dour sisters. There was a quart of milk – "sweet milk" as he called it. I made the quick circuit of the flat to confirm what I believed. His clothes were gone, his battered leather toiletry kit was no longer on the bathroom sink. He was gone. And with him, I had no doubt, had gone the car. I should have felt angry about that, for it belonged to all of us, but I didn't. Somehow I understood that to a man facing life's final ignominies a car would seem to hold vague promise of a new start. I wondered how far he had already gotten, if perhaps he'd driven straight without stopping, all the long flat length of Illinois and crossed the Ohio River to Paducah, into his beloved South.

On my dresser he had left me money and a bank receipt to show he'd cleaned out the small savings account. He had split four hundred dollars with me. I sat on the bed and pondered my prospects: the apartment was mine for three more weeks and I had, counting my own cash stuffed into the pages of a school text, another three hundred. It seemed, in the fall of 1965, a great deal of money.

For several days my frame of mind swung madly between elation and despair – elation at the freedom every kid dreams of and despair at the unimaginable solitude of my life under that empty roof. At school I began to hang out with two guys I knew from my classes. They had an apartment in a building on Morgan that smelled of mice. They drank more or less constantly, with the abandon of young men on their own for the first time. Not my introduction to liquor, but it was the time I began to drink regularly. On a fairly frequent basis I crashed there after a night of drinking, unaware that I had become that caricature of college life, the drunken guest sleeping it off in a corner.

With the help of the alcohol and my already solitary

habits, I created without intending to a life with little true human contact. I spoke to no one outside of class, I worked as many hours as I could, I hung out with my drinking companions. And though my classes were filled with girls, I met none of them. I developed the conviction that I stood out in a hangdog way, that even among a population where shabbiness was a fashion, I had a rundown look.

I began to take an occasional drink during the day, particularly before leaving for my classes. We joked about this sort of thing, my friends and I – I'd seen each of them gulp a bloody Mary on a Sunday morning after a raucous bout of drinking the night before – but I was the only one I knew who drank frequently in the morning. It put me in a fog, sometimes gave me an odd giddiness that was as close to optimism as I was to feel all day.

Eventually they shut off the power in the flat and though I might have managed to pay the electric company, I just let it go. I got hold of an old extension cord and ran it from the landlord's outlet in the back up to our flat. When he found out about it, he threatened to evict me. The rent was now due for the next month. I had that, too, but little more, and was determined to hang onto it. And so I lived for several weeks that way, in total darkness except for a couple of my mother's old decorative candles, and drank alone in the flat and when I was deep enough into the drink, brooded about my lost life. One night I thought I heard my mother in the kitchen, padding back and forth between the stove and the sink, mixing things and whacking the wooden mixing spoon against the sink to get something to come off, and singing along with her AM radio station, harmonizing with Nat King Cole.

I brooded on what I had seen already in life and added it all to the dark stew of my complaint. At some point I stopped going to classes, began to show up late for work, and I see now, from the vantage point of hindsight, that I was striving mightily to wreck my life.

On a cold Sunday night I was on an endless walk, I'd walked all day, much of it drunk. The liquor was beginning to wear off, though not its effects: the depressive thoughts followed quickly by odd moments of elation, then a sense of foreboding. Once or twice I saw people giving me wary looks and realized that I'd been talking to myself. Up ahead of me I saw a man cross Clark Street, too far to make out his face, but there was something familiar about him. He paused at the curb's edge, looked around, glanced my way and then back the way he had come. I recognized my gray acquaintance, the man who watched the shop. For a time he stood on the corner as though uncertain which way to go, and I saw him glance once more the way he had come. He turned his gaze toward me and I tensed, wondering if I were sober enough to defend myself. But the gray man didn't recognize me at that distance. He had other worries, it seemed: I saw him bend over, hands on his knees, and for a moment he seemed poised to lean against a parked car. Then he gave a shake of his head.

He walked on, dragging his feet, up Roscoe toward the elevated tracks, and as he disappeared from view, a second figure, dark and lurching and single-minded, crossed Clark Street in clear pursuit. Meyer.

I thought of running away but was drawn to this confrontation, I needed to see them together, these two remnants from the world of death camps and misery, and so I followed. I rounded the corner just in time to see Meyer enter the alley. I stayed across the street, hidden by the rusting girders of the train structure. In the glow of a single light I saw them face each other. The gray man stood leaning against the back of a building, as though unable to stand any longer. Meyer moved slowly toward him and I saw the man's hand come up, pointing at Meyer, his face enraged. They were too far for me to make out his words but I'd heard the gray man's accusations and knew he was repeating them now. Meyer stopped a few feet from the other man and stood for a time with his hands in his pockets. After a while he pulled out a cigarette and lit it. He took a puff, blew out smoke, and then startled me by handing the cigarette to his accuser. Reluctantly the man reached out his hand and took the cigarette. He puffed at it, then went down on one knee. Meyer stood a few feet away, hands back in his pockets, and waited. Finally the man sank onto the cold floor of the alley and leaned back against the wall. Meyer watched him for a time and then came closer. I saw the sick man point at Meyer again, saw him speak, his face contorted in physical or emotional suffering. Meyer said something, short and sharp, and the man shook his head. Finally Meyer moved to within a couple of feet of the other man, crouched down and spoke, his face thrust forward as though there were some urgency. He spoke for longer than I'd ever seen Meyer speak, and several times the other man interrupted him or just shook his head, over and over again.

At length it was finished. Meyer stood up, lit two cigarettes this time and leaned over to hand one to the other man. He stood there for a moment, puffing at his cigarette, said some final brief thing, and left. He moved quickly, never looking around him, and was gone by the time I came out from behind the girder. In the alley I could see the sick man, smoking, shaking his head slowly from side to side as though he would refuse all he had heard in that alley.

I took a few steps and then stopped. At the corner, across the street but just a few yards away, Meyer was talking to Farrell. He gestured behind him, and then he was gone, crossing Clark Street in the midst of the late night traffic. A cabbie honked his horn and Meyer bounced the lit cigarette off the cab's windshield, then marched off into the cold night.

Now Farrell entered the alley and stopped just a foot or so from the man on the ground. They spoke and I saw the stricken man shake his head, slowly now, weakly, his eyes closed. Farrell crouched down – with difficulty, reminding me of his own age and presumed infirmity – got down onto one knee and spoke to the man. The man said nothing at first. Then he opened his eyes and said something to Farrell, and his eyes seemed to flash. For his part Farrell merely lowered his head and stayed there for a time in that odd posture, half-kneeling, silent. Then he spoke to the other man and for the first time the man in the alley nodded, weakly. I saw Farrell reach out and put a hand on the man's shoulder and the man was speaking. Farrell inched closer, moving awkwardly, until he could reach out and touch the man's face. Then he placed his hand on top of the man's head. He said nothing, and the man in the alley moved his head slowly from side to side. I moved closer, took a spot behind a car and watched: I could see the man breathing, open-mouthed, and his chest seemed to heave with the effort. And then he was still.

Farrell stayed in that pose for a moment, his hand on the other man's head. Then he braced himself with one hand against the ground and got slowly to his feet. He looked up and down the alley, peered in my general direction for a moment. Then, without another glance at the man on the ground, he walked out of the alley, pausing once to brush off his knee where it had touched the pavement. It seemed to me that he moved very slowly, as if he were ill.

I waited until he was gone, then moved cautiously across the street. I entered the alley and approached the man on the ground. He did not move. I called out, something like "Hello," but he did not turn to face me. I stood before him and he appeared to be sleeping but this was no place to sleep, no night to lie on an alley floor.

"Are you all right?" I asked him. I fancied that he moved at the sound of my voice but this was clearly my imagination. I moved closer.

"You can't stay here – we should get you up off the ground. Can you walk?"

When he didn't answer or move, I knelt down beside him. He was motionless. I leaned forward, still fearful that he might suddenly reach out and grab me, pull me down and attack me. But nothing about him moved, his perfect stillness told me he was dead.

I reached out and touched his face and his skin was already growing cold. I touched the side of his neck: no warmth, no pulse, no life.

I heard myself say, "Oh, no." I wanted to call out to Farrell, to shout, "What have you done?"

I said "Oh, no," again and I sank back onto the pavement. For a while I stayed there, in that position, sitting a couple of feet from a dead man, and it seemed important, it seemed that I was his company, his only visitor at the time of his death. I studied his face, noted again the torn earlobe, and then my eyes seemed to blur: I saw him alive, he was a boy, on a road crowded with refugees, carrying a bundle of his things. And around him, occasionally touching him as though to reassure him, were a man and two women, his family, I was certain. And what I saw in the boy's eyes was heart-rending, for he looked wide-eyed ahead of him, clearly seeing their destruction, impervious to their attempts to calm him. My heart pounded with this lost boy's terror and I pulled back, heard my own breathing.

The scene left me and I looked at him again. I touched him once more and then left the alley where I understood that a murder had taken place. At the corner I saw a squad car and thought of flagging it down. I realized I had no story I could give a cop about the body in the alley, and I went home. As I made my way back to the empty place where I lived in darkness like a bat, I understood in a vague way that my old life was gone forever.

Fourteen: Talk of God

One night in early November I went out and began walking aimlessly though I'm certain I knew on some level where this walk would take me. At a bar on Sheffield where the bartender knew me I bought a half pint of Old Crow. I drank it all in one sitting in an alley, eight ounces of straight bourbon in less than twenty minutes. After the first lovely glow it rose in my gorge and I had to hold my breath to keep from vomiting it all out. I found a place to sit, somebody's back stairs, and sat there rocking, trying to control the sudden spin of my head, the quick loss of focus, the flashes of heat and nausea. I resumed my walk, now drunk.

Farrell's shop was dark and I cursed – aloud, apparently, for a passerby stopped, took in my glazed eyes and walked on. I was aware that I was weaving, and adopted, I am certain, that stiff walk with which a drunk compensates for his condition. I stood for a moment in front of the darkened shop and knocked, just once, a not very assertive knock so that I could say I'd tried, and before I could turn away to lurch on home, Farrell opened the door.

"Hello, Thomas." He looked me up and down, assessed my appearance, then said, "Come inside with you."

In the small main room of his tiny flat he was watching television, some sort of special on the comedy shows of the past. A narrator was explaining the genius of "The Honeymooners."

"My Ma watched that," I blurted out, just to be saying something. "That was one of her favorites."

Farrell looked at me for a moment, then back at the bluish screen of his tiny box of a TV set, where Jackie Gleason and Art Carney were arguing over something. He indicated them with a half wave.

"They're Irish, you know. The both of 'em. Sit down."

I lurched over to a chair, lowered myself onto it and nearly fell off. He squinted at me and, for the first time since I'd known him, I realized he was uncomfortable in my presence – whether with my grief or my obvious drunkenness, I couldn't have said.

"You need coffee."

"I don't need nothing. Especially from you. I'll be all right, Farrell. I'm not gonna – I'm not gonna die or anything."

"All right, then," he said as though my imminent demise had been his main fear.

The room was moving slightly and I tried to make my brain work. I couldn't even remember getting to his shop. For a moment I sat there taking deep breaths and Farrell turned off his television. Then he fetched me a cup of coffee anyway, which I ignored.

"I don't need anything, Farrell," I repeated. Then an

odd thought came to me and, even now, all these years later, I know that I grinned at him, grinned at the opening he'd given me.

"Actually, I do need something. I need – like information. No. I need knowledge."

"Knowledge, is it? Well, what sort of knowledge, my friend, Thomas?"

He gave me a faint smile but a look of resignation, even a faint glimmer of anger came into his eyes. When, in my drunken state, I didn't answer him right away, he repeated his question with the tone of a harried teacher.

"I want to know so many things I could fucking scream."

He winced at my unaccustomed profanity but faced me, did not look away.

"What are these things you want to know?"

His calmness took me aback. I'd rehearsed this moment a hundred times, expected any of a half dozen strategies: evasion, sympathy, feigned confusion, any of a number of distractions and his effortless conjurer's misdirection.

I tried to focus my thoughts. The room seemed stifling, I was conscious that my face was covered with sweat, that we could both hear my wet labored breathing. Farrell waited.

Every drunk wants to talk, liquor seems to release a primal need to be heard, understood, taken seriously. I strained to marshal what I needed to say, to put order to my thoughts, and to my horror it all came out in a torrent as if my feelings had been pumped out of my gut.

"I want to know why she died when you could have saved her – "

"I could not."

"Yeah, shit, yes, you could because you did the other time, and even if you couldn't, why did she have to die?"

He muttered something like "the poor lady."

"Never mind that."

I said many things, most of them forgotten within seconds of their being spoken. But even as the liquor wiped clean my short-term memory I said things I'll remember till my own death. I battered him with questions so relentlessly that he had little time for his answers. I asked him why my mother had had such a short, dead-end thing of a life. I asked about my own life, which seemed to me to have run nearly its entire course. I asked him about God, whether there was a God, what kind of a God he was, I asked him if he, Farrell, was God and finally, after suffering my rant for some time, he spoke.

"Do you believe in a God who would be content with a life such as mine?"

Half a dozen responses clogged my brain. I know I said something eventually, something marginally coherent. Whatever it was, it provoked the most subdued of responses, a small half shrug and a slow sad shake of his head, as though the level of my thought had disappointed him. His response ignited me again and I became not the Grand Inquisitor I had been playing at but a raging, weeping teenage boy who'd lost his mother, his world, his sense of an order in the world. At some point I rose from the chair and began pacing as I talked. I remember that all I wanted to do was weep but that I felt some sort of duty to give voice to my accusations, and the things I said to him are seared into my memory.

"And I want to know about you two old bastards, I want to know who you are, you sonofabitch, 'cause I know you're somebody more than just an old man that runs a piece-of-shit junk shop."

"I am an old man who is just as lost in this world as you are, Thomas, I'm just – "

"No!" I leaned forward and pointed a finger at him, and almost fell out of the chair once more. "No, I know about you, you and him. I know about you both. I saw you."

Something changed in his face and I would have said he had just heard a long-expected piece of news, a confirmation of coming misfortune.

"What is it that you saw?

"You. And him, Meyer. In that alley. The two of you, you know what you did, you know what you did to that poor fucker."

He blinked and I waited for him to express ignorance of whatever I was talking about.

"We did nothing to him, Thomas."

"Yeah, you did, I saw! I fucking saw, I saw him with Meyer, he went with Meyer, and then later he was sitting on the ground against that building. And you went into that alley, and a few minutes later he was dead. And you –
"

And here I stopped, unable to give voice to this most awful of accusations.

"I did nothing."

"Then it was Meyer, and you went along with it. I saw both of you there. And I waited, and then I went in."

"Did you," he said quietly.

"Yeah, I did. And he was dead."

"And how d'you know that?"

"I touched him."

"Good lad," he said, and seemed to mean it. This made no sense to me and, as I tried to make it scan, I grew more confused. The liquor, I thought. I tried to focus, tried to sober up in an instant, as every drunk who ever lived has tried to will himself to become clear-headed, sane, eloquent.

Farrell watched me in a guarded way and it struck me that he actually might fear a sudden burst of violence. I became conscious of his age, my quicker hands. It had never occurred to me that I might hurt him. Emboldened by the thought, I got up and made a sudden lurch toward him as though I'd come at him, and nothing changed but the cast in his eye. He was unafraid.

"You guys killed that man."

"He was already dead. When Meyer found him, he was dying. By the time I arrived he was already dead." He frowned: I was being stupid.

"No, that's not right."

But he seemed certain, unshakeable. Could I have imagined it?

"Why would we kill a man? This man or any other? Think, Thomas."

"To make sure. He knew about you."

"He knew about Meyer – little enough at that, so few people really know anything about Meyer. And whatever he knew, 'tis nothing to kill a fellow over, lad."

I glared at him for a moment. "Who are you? The both

of you?"

"*Da botha you*," he mouthed, mocking my Chicago accent. "You are welcome to sleep here tonight, Thomas. Or not, as you wish."

"I want an answer. Who are you?"

"I am a fellow not so different from you, *quare* as that may seem. The questions you've asked, you'll answer them yourself in time, if you are patient. The ones that have answers."

"What – some of 'em don't? Which ones don't?"

"Your mother. Such a good woman. Why is she dead? And well you may ask."

He frowned – I was wobbly, sweaty, unsteady. I seemed to be swaying with the room.

"Sit."

"No."

"Before you fall. And break things."

I sank back onto the chair and it wobbled, and for just a moment thought I'd take it down with me to the floor.

"So come on, Farrell. I want to know about you. You and him."

Farrell shook his head. "Read."

"What? Read?" I shook my head. "You bastard." I tried to get up, fell back, decided a few minutes' rest would do me good. Farrell sat across from me and waited, his hands on his knees like a pupil awaiting a recital. I remember that I gave him my best baleful stare. He nodded and looked around at his room.

When I woke up it was light outside. Farrell was not there. I took a couple of swigs of the cold coffee he'd offered me the night before, then left. It was perhaps six a.m. and the robins sang to announce their satisfaction with their lot.

A couple of weeks later, I dropped out of school, sold everything left in the flat – furniture, clothing, pots, pans, flatware, dishes – to a sweaty guy on Damen who ran a resale furniture shop. It was all probably worth, in the prices of that simpler time, a little over four hundred bucks. He gave me about thirty cents on the dollar. As he made his offer he kept his counter between us and watched me as though expecting assault, which he probably should have been. But I just wanted cash. I had most of Roy's money, four hundred of my own, and another hundred and a half from the bandit on Damen. There was now a couple of weeks' rent due on the flat but the landlord knew my mother was gone and was happy to cut his losses and rent the place anew. I got a duffel from an Army surplus store on Lincoln, packed clothes and a few other things and prepared to walk out of the flat on Roscoe and out of that phase of my life.

Eighteen and footloose and, despite my underlying sense of abandonment and of being cheated in life, I was near giddiness with my newfound freedom. The night before I left Chicago, I sat up half the night and thought about my life in that shabby small place, and my mother – it seemed I was cutting out the last physical tie, the last evidence of our life together. And I thought of what I'd seen and heard in the shop on Addison, and what had become my place in it. For the first time a pattern seemed to manifest itself, I saw myself and Farrell in a dozen different conversations, and now I thought I understood what he'd been doing these last months. I determined to visit him once more before I left. Not that this was my sole motive: a boy must announce such dramatic changes in his situation and I had no audience save this strange old man.

"Well," he said in response to my announcement, and then he said nothing more. He moved around his shop, straightening things, gazing out at the street, and finally, with his back to me, he said, "I suppose you've thought of the many ways a lad such as yourself might come to harm, out there."

Half a dozen smart-ass remarks suggested themselves, but what came out instead was something I'd not planned.

"How much worse can it be than the way I live now?"

"You've had a bad time of it, yes. But for a lad your age to be without a roof over his head –"

I had been expecting this, and reverted to my young tough guy role. "I've got money, and I can work. I'll find a place wherever I decide to stop."

"Ah, the streets are full of men and women, poor souls, who thought it would play out that way for them. You've seen them, Thomas."

"Yeah." *Dying in an alley*, I wanted to say but it seemed a hard matter to bring up again, and he'd managed, after all, to plant doubt in my recollection.

He shrugged, went into the back and came out with a pot of coffee. "Sit, boy," he said, and I grabbed a chair.

He sipped his coffee, made a pleased face even though it was quite as bad as usual, then looked at me almost fondly.

"Listen," he began. "You must be careful, Thomas. There is no point in recklessness."

202

"Is there a point in anything?"

"Ah, that's the question, isn't it. Is there a point in any part of life? That was at least a part of the 'knowledge' you spoke of during your last visit."

"I was drunk."

"Aye. You were. But what you wanted to know about was real enough. So many questions: who is Meyer, who am I? *'Are you a killer, Farrell?' 'What about God?'* Indeed, what about him, the Big Fellow? If he is big."

I said nothing, sober enough now to be embarrassed.

"Like I said, I was drunk," I said again. "I just – it seems I don't have the answers to anything. And you do."

"You've heard our debates here, mine with Professor Leo, or Meyer's with anyone foolhardy enough to talk to him about such subjects."

Here I thought I'd caught him. I pointed a finger in his face.

"I've heard you argue both sides, Farrell: I've heard you explain the existence of God with one guy and argue that there is none with somebody else."

"A man of intelligence can see both sides of complex issues, and this is a complicated thing, a thing that cannot be proved. But if you've heard learned people speak of these things, lad, you know no one, least of all meself, has the answers to these questions." He sat back a bit, gave me a sly look. "And about your other questions, you'll have to find the answers to them yourself. But the thing of it is, Thomas, this is a desperate course you've chosen. You need to be careful."

"I'm not going out on the road looking for trouble."

He gave me a doubtful look. For a moment he pulled at

his lip, his eyes flitting from one object to another as though trying to settle on a proper going away present. But I know he was fighting for time, trying to put to words what he thought most critical for me to remember, and I waited.

"You notice much, my young friend, and suppress it. You hear things, whether you are meant to or no — 'tis a quality I saw in you from your first visits here. I cannot tell what sense you make of all you've heard or seen but I know you are a fellow who misses little. I've seen you following it all, the odd talk and the debates, and I have no doubt you are as attentive out there. I'd say you note as much as anyone. Learn what you can learn, all of it."

"Like I said, I'll keep my eyes open, I'll be careful," I told him, and he shook his head as though clearing it.

"No, I didn't mean that. When the time comes you will either be alert to what will happen or you won't. That is not what I mean. I mean for you to listen to the people you meet, to watch them and take what they will tell you, for they will tell you more than they know. And I know you have a –" He paused, clearly embarrassed.

"A what?"

He shrugged and finished, "A gift. For this listening." A clumsy finish, I thought, but he wasn't done. "Yes, this is your gift. One of them, at least."

I was about to ask what he meant by this and stopped. I didn't want to know. And now I saw that, if I was ever to say what I truly felt, this was my chance. I had imagined myself delivering a small oration in that dark musty shop, but now all that came out was another accusation.

"I spent half of last night packing my stuff, the other

half thinking."

"About the things you spoke of before. About Meyer, about me – "

"This is different. This is about you and me. I know what you've been doing to me. All these past months, sending me places, giving me these errands to run, having me see these people, all these different people with their, you know, their troubles. I know what you've been trying to do to me."

"And what have you determined?"

"That it's all been for one thing, to get inside my head, to plant things there, about you. To hide what I might come to realize otherwise. All these places you've sent me, all these people, the ones that are by themselves and the ones that are dying, it's all to disguise who you are."

"I've no control over what you think of me, Thomas. It would surprise you greatly to know that I believe I've been more honest with you than you think. But I cannot prove it. Would you like a cup of coffee?"

I was already standing. "No, thanks. I don't need coffee. I don't need anything from you."

"Perhaps not. I wish you well, Thomas. Take great care of yourself, and be –" He dug for the right word. " – patient."

"About what?"

"All things. Yourself especially."

I had no idea what he meant, and just said, "See you around."

"I have every hope of that."

On my way out I bumped, literally, into Meyer, knocking him slightly off balance. I stopped, watched him fight his initial impulse to belligerence. Then he saw it was me.

"Oh. You. Watch where you're goin'."

I nodded and walked away, and it struck me that Meyer in his own way had just given me the same advice Farrell had.

That night I took a bus, my first of many, out of Chicago, heading west if only because that was what people did.

Many months later and thousands of miles into my "new life," on a night of sleet and driving rain I took shelter in an abandoned shack, a coop or pen of some sort. I had had to run to get to the shack, and at first the only sound I heard was my chilled gasping for breath. Gradually my lungs recovered and I came to breathe more normally, and I understood that I was not alone. I fished in my pocket for the small jackknife I carried, then got up onto one knee. As I waited for an attack I became aware of an oppressive sense of fear. This of course made him – whoever he was – more dangerous, and I prepared to meet his assault on me.

I wondered if I would die there in that dark rank shack at the hands of a man whose face I'd never see. I nearly pissed myself in terror. I resolved to make a fight of it, felt a fierce surge of my own anger, I'd kill the sonofabitch even as, no doubt, he killed me. And then I saw his face though he was still in pitch darkness. I saw a pale glow and it seemed he was little more than a boy. Improbably, as I stared across the room I saw this man in childhood, then, rapidly, other images of him, ending with a scene of this man walking down a city street at dawn with all his belongings in a small valise and a look on his face of lost hope. For some reason I thought of sad-faced Roy driving off in his ugly car, and then, for no reason I could think of, I thought of my father. I wondered if he'd had this look of defeat on his face the morning he'd run off from his life with us.

The man in the darkness moved – away from me, it seemed by the sound, and I felt a sudden sense of abandonment, of a despair so grave I sank back under the weight. I wanted to cry out, to announce my surrender, but I remained in that pose, knife in hand, ready to fight.

He made a single sound, as if gulping air, and I felt a bottomless fear not my own. He panted now, and I followed his movements in the dark by the slow scraping sound he made as he circled the edge of the shack.

"I just want out of the fucking rain. That's all I want. I'll stay here and I won't bother you. Or I'll fight."

I heard him crouching down, sliding down against the wall, sinking rather than settling onto the damp floor. For what seemed an hour we watched each other's dim form across the shack. Then I began to drop off to sleep, and as I did, even as I fought it, I heard him snore, startle himself awake and then doze off again.

At dawn I awoke with a fierce need to urinate. Outside, crows called out to one another. My adversary was gone. When I emerged from the shack, the crows laughed. I have always thought crows laughed at us, at me. Poe's weary scholar may have told us it was a raven, but I have no doubt he was visited by a crow.

As I began walking toward the highway, I recalled

Farrell's odd suggestion that I possessed a gift for listening. I thought of what had transpired in the night, my sudden intelligence of this stranger's life, if that was what I'd seen. I recalled the other time, the night I'd watched my mother on the bench and, more terrifying, the sudden flow of images I'd experienced standing over a dead man in an alley. For the first time I thought I understood what Farrell had meant, but this was no gift I wanted. I tried to tell myself these were coincidences, product of an unstable imagination, bad liquor, fatigue. I thought of Farrell again and cursed him aloud, and told myself that a man on foot in the mist of morning with neither money nor prospects had no gifts of any kind.

Fifteen: Detective

My experience in the abandoned coop took place just outside Omaha. By that time I was 20 and had been in more or less constant motion for more than two years. I zigzagged across the country in all the directions of the compass. In a couple of places out west I managed to be solvent, worked odd jobs and made enough money to keep a room and supply myself with liquor. In Billings, Montana I found work in a used bookstore. The smell and the pace reminded me of Farrell's shop. The similarities amused me at first and then began to trouble me. I left soon after that.

Along the way I managed to make considerable trouble for myself. My drinking and the chain-smoking I paired with it did nothing for my health, and my frequent intoxication made me a target. Several times I was mugged. Once it was just for money, a couple of times just because a drunk is easy to attack. And I was belligerent, unwilling to wait for someone to pick a fight, so that I picked my share. The last time, outside a bar in Tempe, Arizona, they broke my nose.

Twice I was homeless, twice – so that later, when I found myself on the street after Vietnam, I knew how to do it. To be homeless is to know desperation or simple, mind-numbing want, and after these experiences I concluded that Farrell's "gifts" amounted to the occasional hallucination and a general but not pronounced tendency toward survival, as though on an unconscious level I had not yet quite made the commitment to a life.

I understand now that I was attempting to put as many miles as possible between myself and my old life, but also that I had a moonstruck notion that I'd roll into a place someday and I'd see immediately that this was the perfect place for me to start a decent life. More than once I thought I'd found such a place: Santa Fe, San Antonio, one or two others, but in each place, in a matter of days, I felt myself growing more distant from the people around me, as alien as if I'd come from the far side of the sun. In my inept way I tried. I made acquaintances and called them friends. In each place I came to I found a bar, soon knew most of the regulars, picked up their bad habits and a share of their troubles, woke up in strange beds.

In this moribund fashion I managed to piss away nearly four years of my life. Most of that time is, understandably, a blur to me. Three experiences stand out. The first, ironically, occurred in Chicago. The second took me to a carnival. The third, most painful of all, was as close as I was ever to come to a normal love affair.

Somewhere in the back of my heart I think I knew I would someday return to Chicago. More than once I fantasized about showing up years later, with money and clothes and a swagger, meeting old acquaintances and shrugging off their surprised looks. When I did make my way back, the first time anyway, I did so the way a fugitive might. I hid in the midst of the city. I avoided old haunts, old faces. I took a sardonic amusement that no one in the entire city knew I was there. And that was just as well, for I had no plans as yet to stay there. My travels, such as they were, had merely brought me close enough to Chicago that I thought I might find work there for a few months. And so I did, the oddest of jobs. I became a private detective.

I was nearly out of money again, and I found myself in front of a liquor store near the corner of Wells and Division, at the frayed edge of the old area near Lincoln Park fittingly called Old Town. I was wondering if I had enough pocket change for a half-pint when I noticed a handwritten sign beside a doorway that said, "Help Wanted. No Experience Necessary." I went in, up the stairs past a boarded-up second floor to the third, where I found three signs: a more or less professionally-done sign announcing Pinnacle Investigative Services, a second, hand-lettered, for Pinnacle Employment Services, and a third, just saying, "Come right in."

I went through an interview with a man named Harry Hogarth, who introduced himself as "Company president" but barely kept a straight face as he said it. As he went through the "interview", he looked around us at his unpromising surroundings, winked, and ascertained the things he needed to know: that I was broke and in no position to haggle about wages, that I was able-bodied and could pound the pavement for him, and that I had very few fears about the street. When he asked me about that I saw him take in my streetworn face, the newly-broken nose, and he was nodding before I finished my answer.

I worked for Harry Hogarth for almost a year. He was a paunchy man with dark hair and an improbably round red face. He wore rumpled sport coats that had never been in fashion, faded shirts with ties that clashed. I was told that the secretary was his sister, and he had three "operatives": himself, a skeletal man with pale red hair named Nelson, and me. At first he used me simply to make phone calls and ring doorbells, but he began taking me with him when he made what he referred to as his "calls". I watched him work at his craft, the ferreting out of information from reluctant informers. Soon Harry found other uses for me.

By this time I had discovered one small talent, unexpected in one of such solitary habits: people did indeed open up to me, sometimes in the most disquieting way, revealing all manner of personal and painful things. Looking back over my life, I could see that I'd had this "thing" as far back as childhood. And Harry Hogarth recognized it – noted the way Nelson and Judy the secretary told me their stories. He began sending me out to question people who had given him nothing. And he promoted me from his glorified runner to a full-fledged operative. Even at that age, I understood that to be a private detective in all states one required a license, and that to acquire said license one must meet certain criteria.

I pointed out to Harry that I was not licensed to do this work.

"Neither am I," he said, shrugging.

"You're not?"

"No. You don't need it. I mean, I was licensed but they,

you know, they took it. But here I am, still doing the work, you know? So what's the difference?"

"Why did they take your license?"

"I tapped a guy's phone." He threw his hands up at the perversities of the law. Then he tapped his chest. "I got skills, kid, a lotta skills. They don't want anybody tapping phones except theirselves. It's a racket, like everything else."

I nodded at this version of his mantra, "Everything's a racket." And as I watched Harry his face changed, he looked off into the corners of his office and blinked, and just for a second, his mask dropped and he seemed fatigued, as though the life had been sucked out of him. An image came to me of Harry Hogarth sitting in a battered car on a flat stretch of country road. He was smoking and staring in manifest panic out at the empty countryside. This version of Harry shook his head, seemed to come to some decision. For no reason that I could have explained, I knew at that moment his name was not Harry Hogarth. The image faded.

Harry regained his emotional balance, shook his head and chuckled at it all. He grinned at me and I decided that, regardless of what kind of back story Harry Hogarth had, I liked him.

I became an *operative*. I no longer called people but conducted "interviews" with "subjects". I took notes in a small spiral notebook, walked the streets for Harry, looked for people who did not wish to be found. More than once during this time I came across someone I'd known in what I thought of as "the old time". When this happened, I nodded and looked away as though I didn't recognize

213

them. And they were never sure: I was older, I'd grown a bandito mustache, my hair hung over my collar – everybody had longer hair then – and so no one during this time ever buttonholed me.

One night when I'd been back nearly six months I found myself in an Indian bar on Sheffield, a stone's throw from the old ballpark and therefore from Farrell's shop. For all those months I'd avoided it, tried never to think about it. Twice I dreamt of it, and once the dream was nothing more than a rerun of that night in the alley. I finished my beer and went to see it. At Addison I turned the corner and got a blast of lake wind in the face that brought tears to my eyes. I wiped my eyes and looked across the street and saw that the shop was gone. The storefront was empty. I crossed the street.

A sign in the window promised a *taqueria* soon. I cupped my hand against the glass and peered inside. The place had been cleared out, every book and odd bit of junk, all the furniture and the sagging bookshelves, and someone had cleaned it as well, so that there was no hint of what had been there before. I felt an odd mix of disappointment, nostalgia and relief that it was gone. For the rest of that night I thought of the shop and the two men, and it struck me that now, finally, they might both be dead.

For a time I threw myself into my work for Harry Hogarth. I liked best the personal visits, the conversations, some with small-time con artists or the families of men or women fleeing from one life into another. I developed some of Harry's "skills". I could tell when someone was lying, could even tell at times whether the lie was prompted by confusion or fear or guilt. I worked with Harry's methods, learned to use his knowledge and my own instincts to anticipate what people might say or do. Without realizing it, I'd begun to take on some of Harry's streetwise persona – I even began to talk like him. I relished the work, I enjoyed the small challenges of finding people, sorting out what I was told. For just that short time with Harry Hogarth and his "agency", I fell into the sort of life routine any other person might have. This "rut" left less time for drinking, as did the occasional puzzle Harry threw my way, and more than once I spent hours over multiple cups of coffee trying to see a solution.

On an overcast day in May a well-dressed young man came in, paused just inside the door and adjusted the knot in his tie. There was something oddly familiar about him though I was certain we'd never met. He glanced at me and looked quickly away, and I understood that whatever he was going to tell Harry was a lie. Harry invited him into the little cubicle that served as his imaginary office. He winked at me and I left. When I came back, the well-dressed man nodded to me and left. He had a confident sort of smile I'd seen on men who counted themselves successful, a confident smile and a fine suit and a perfect haircut, and that nod, a polite greeting to someone of a lower station: he looked like a million dollars, except for a distant pain in his eyes, pale gray eyes, they were. At the door he slowed down for the merest fraction of a second, took in Harry Hogarth's office with a look that bespoke his misgivings, and then was gone. Harry was already working the phone, going through his "people", the various contacts he had with the utility companies, the newspapers, another agency. When he got off the phone, he called me over.

"I think this one is yours, kid."

He held out a photo, tapped it with one finger. "Her."

"For Christ's sake. This is like from World War II."

"C'mon, it's not that old, it's from the fifties. Well, yeah, to you, that's like the middle ages, right?"

I took another look: in the photo a plain young woman shaded her eyes against the sun. In the background were buildings I recognized. I could see Riverview, the old amusement park, in the background.

"Clybourn Avenue."

"Good, kid. Yeah, the projects on Clybourn."

"So why do we want to find her?"

"We're being paid for it. To perform this, uh, service."

"Why?"

He grinned, nodded. "You don't like him, he smells like a broad and dresses like Prince Albert. Here's the thing, kid. That's just his dust jacket. You know, on a new book, you got that fancy cover with a nice picture? Well, everybody's got a dust jacket. What we work at. For some of us – " He looked down at his soup-stained tie and smiled. " – it's not so impressive. For other people, like our client, it's pretty fancy. But the guy inside, he belongs to this world." Harry tapped the picture of the projects. "Same world as you and me. So, here's the thing: this guy is a lawyer and he's got a client. Client wants to find her." He held up a hand to forestall protest. "And we know where she is. Well, more or less. But people ain't gonna give her up. She's got other people looking for her, and the people around her now, her family, I guess they are, they

216

protect her. This guy, our client, he tried going out there himself, and you know how that turned out." He gazed at the young woman in the photo.

"So how am I supposed to get to her if people won't talk to me?"

"You'll figure something out, I know you will."

"This sounds like something for a professional, Harry."

"A professional is somebody that can do a thing somebody else can't do. That's what you are, kid."

I looked at the woman in the photograph and shook my head. "Why does this 'client' want her? What if he's gonna bring her trouble?"

Harry rubbed his chin and nodded. "That's a good question, kid. Tough call: sometimes you worry you're just causing people trouble, yeah. But in this case, I don't think so." He watched me and I understood he was holding something back and waiting for me to see it.

I remembered the well-dressed man's look of unease, the pain in his pale gray eyes.

"He doesn't have a client. *He's* the client."

Harry winked.

"And if that's the case, then, I don't think he's trouble for her. He's embarrassed to be using a detective and he's nervous about whatever it is. At least he doesn't mean her harm."

"There you go, kid," Harry said, and smiled.

Names are no surprise to a kid who's not sure what his father's real name was, but judging just from her names and aliases, this woman had lived more lives than a cat. Born Loretta Davey, she now went through life with a half dozen names strung out behind her like ribbons. Marriage

217

and other harrowing experiences had made her Loretta Thomas, Loretta Klein, Loretta Argulin, Loretta Kummel, Loretta Brown and most recently Loretta Mack.

I spent three days going through the Lathrop projects. I had one address, and that proved to be a vacated apartment facing the river. When I walked in, four women were going through the place to see what had been left behind. I remembered this from childhood, that when a resident left a place like this, the neighbors scurried in to see if anything useful had been discarded. The four women were black and they gave me an uneasy look – a strange white man standing in the doorway. I told them I was looking for a woman named Loretta. One shrugged and said "These people gone."

Harry's assessment had been accurate: they weren't giving her up easily, and so I found myself going door to door, starting conversations on the corner, behind the ballfield in the center of the complex, even along the river. The people in the projects gave me nothing. Once or twice I'm certain they even lied, several times sending me to non-existent addresses. Sometimes the people I spoke with were black, sometimes white, once a woman I was certain was Indian. They stonewalled me, all of them, whether out of protection for Loretta Mack, or just closing ranks against an outsider who asked questions, I couldn't say. So I walked, went up staircases, talked to everyone I could. And I dallied there. Something had struck me the moment Harry Hogarth had shown me the woman's photo, not the woman herself but the background: Clybourn Avenue along the projects. I recalled another photo, the one my mother had shown me that day just before her death, of

218

my father standing in the middle of the wide street, squinting into the sun, blond and cocky and grinning. No matter what stories he told her, no matter where else he might actually have lived, I knew he'd lived here.

And so even as I wore myself out asking about Loretta Mack and her gaggle of personas, I was thinking about my father, wondering about his life here. On the last morning there, I asked an old man if he'd ever heard of a family called Faye. He shook his head.

Finally I wore them down: perhaps they were unaccustomed to someone returning day after day to ask his questions. In any case, on my third afternoon there I became aware that I was being followed. I let him tail me for a while, then went down to the river, clambering over tree roots and bushes down to the water itself. I figured I'd lose him or learn whether he was serious.

He was serious. Young, grim-faced, serious, a light-skinned black kid. I read his eyes: he was doing something he wasn't necessarily overjoyed about but willing to go through with. As he came awkwardly down the riverbank, slipping once and almost tripping headlong down the slope as his foot caught on a tree root, I waited with my back to the river.

He slid unceremoniously down the rest of the way, dirty now and embarrassed. He faced me, brushed off his pants and his forearm where he'd broken his fall. Dirty or not, he was a handsome boy, African features but light skin and eyes. No doubt he had a small speech prepared, but I didn't give him a chance to use it.

"What do you want?"

"You been asking people about somebody."

"What's that to you?"

"I wanta know why. And who are you?"

I shrugged. "You first."

"My name Aaron."

"My name's Thomas." I waited.

"I want to know why you lookin' for Loretta."

"What's she to you?"

He folded his arms across his chest and spread his feet. "I don't have to tell you nothing." He pursed his lips, looking ridiculous.

"Then we're even." I turned and began to walk away.

"You ain't gonna find her."

Over my shoulder I said, "I think I just did. I just have to follow you. Or have somebody else do it."

I went on walking, heard him take a few steps and then stop, and I could almost feel the kid's confusion. I turned.

"I'll tell you what you want to know, and you'll tell me who you are. And don't tell me 'Aaron' again."

"Loretta my mother. That who I am." He tapped his own chest, feeling more confident now. And I noticed the eyes again, large gray eyes, beautiful eyes, actually. I stared at him for a moment longer than I intended, and then I thought I had it. I fought to suppress a grin.

"I have to talk to your mother. It doesn't have to be where she lives, I don't need to know that. I just need to talk to her."

"Why?"

"A man wants to find her."

"She don't want to see him. He done run off long time ago."

"Your father?"

"Step-father."

"I don't think so. This is a younger man. Thirties."

"What he want with her?"

"I think she'll understand. And if she doesn't want to see him, she doesn't have to. And she's got you to protect her. This guy's not dangerous to anybody."

"He could send somebody."

"I don't think so."

In the end Aaron agreed to bring Loretta to see me there, by the river. I agreed not to ask where she lived, and not to bring anyone else. Aaron told me to come back around seven.

I was there before them, and I waited, watching the river. Just when I decided they had backed out, they were there, just a few feet from me and watching me.

"Ma'am," I said, and nodded to Aaron. He stepped back.

She walked toward me and after a moment's hesitation, held out her hand. "Loretta Mack."

"Yes, ma'am. My name is Thomas Faye. I work for the Pinnacle Detective Agency. I've been hired to find you."

I saw her flinch at "detective agency" but she kept her eyes on mine. She was perhaps fifty, maybe fifty-five at the outside, and the years had worn her out but with a little makeup and a new dress she might attract notice. Up close, anyone would notice her eyes.

"Who wants to find me?"

"A gentleman." I thought again of the distressed gray eyes of the lawyer, the wary gray eyes of Aaron, took in the beautiful gray eyes of Loretta Mack. "If I'm right, he believes you are his mother."

Only once or twice in life have I actually seen someone so startled that you could see the physical effects of their shock. She went pale, then flushed, and she seemed to sag but did not stumble or lose her balance.

"What?"

"He's looking for his mother. And I think you are his mother."

"What's his name?"

"It won't ring any bells. He is a lawyer. His name is William Dietrich."

I saw her mouth the words *William Dietrich*, and then she pulled nervously at her hair.

"You could be lyin'," she said.

"What would be the point of that?" I asked, and she was nodding before I was even finished. I stepped closer to her. "I can tell you two things that might help you with this: he's got that boy's eyes, the same eyes. Your eyes. And the second thing is, he's nervous. Nervous we won't find you, maybe nervous that we will and it won't work out for him. I mean, after all – "

Her first smile.

"After all, I give him up. All those years ago. Just a poor little baby boy." She looked at the river, then met my eyes. "It's no excuse, but I wasn't but sixteen. Sixteen and not real bright. No kind of mother."

The boy moved up closer. "Mama? You all right?"

"Yeah. I'm all right." To me she said, "I guess I'm all right. I'm a mother again." And she sighed. "Oh, my Lord. Oh, my Lord," she said to herself.

I left them there to sort out the new dynamic of their life. She'd given me her phone number for William

222

Dietrich to call. As I walked away I looked back and she had her head on her young son's shoulder. I resisted the impulse to call out to Aaron, *Your family's just gotten more complicated*.

Grinning to myself I turned to leave and something made me look at Loretta Mack once more. In her place I saw a pretty young woman who had stopped to chat with a young blond man, a good-looking boy, full of himself, and their mutual attraction was clear. The young blond was, of course, my father. I felt the familiar wave of lightheadedness. For a moment I just stared Loretta's way. Then the image passed. I waved to them and Loretta waved back.

All the way back to the office I thought about what I'd seen, and wondered if it could be true, and if so, what had come of that moment long ago when a young Loretta Mack ran into a young Charlie Faye, if indeed such a moment had happened. I thought of going back, perhaps sometime in the future, to speak with her again. Then I realized how foolish it would all sound, how unlikely. But when the well-heeled William Dietrich came into the office a few days later, I gave him a long look as I wondered if our lives were in some improbable way connected. Tangled. Many years after that, I found his name in the Yellow Pages. From the size of his ad, I would say he prospered.

But I lay awake that night after speaking with Loretta Mack and tried to convince myself that I'd imagined what I'd seen. I told myself I'd developed an odd habit of mind, that I brought on these moments. I told myself I just had a unique way of seeing into people, a certain intuition. But I believe I understood the truth all along, even though I could not have put a name to it.

A couple of weeks after that, I came into the office to find Harry staring at an official-looking letter. He read the letter quickly, then I saw his eyes return to the top line and read it over. He wet his lips. He shrugged. And now he noticed me.

"Hey, kid." He held up the letter. "I guess this is it."

"What is it?"

"They're shutting me down."

"For what?" I asked, though the answer was obvious. For existing outside the law, ignoring it, cutting corners, shucking and jiving his way through life. This wasn't even the first time I'd seen him reading worrisome mail from a branch of the government.

" 'Operation of an unlicensed practice.' Like that's some kinda news. Anyhow, we're outta business, Tom. I'm through." After a moment a thought seemed to strike him. "At least for now."

"What are you going to do?"

He grinned. "Hit the pavement. Find a way to make money." His eyes flitted from one piece of his office furniture to another. "I got a guy that'll buy most of this from me."

"You gonna be all right, Harry?"

He nodded and then gave me an odd look. "You're outta work too, kid. You shouldn't be worrying about me. I been on the canvas before. Literally. For a while there, in the fifties, I was a fighter."

"Any good?"

"No, but I was smart." He wiggled his eyebrows.

"Fought under three names, used somebody else's license when they took mine.

He took out a checkbook from his desk and wrote out a check for two hundred bucks.

"Here's something to tide you over, kid."

"Thanks. Judy know?"

He looked over at his dour secretary's empty desk. "She quit two days ago. I pissed her off." At that moment he reminded me of Roy, a man treading water in the deep end of a dark pond. I wanted to say something to make him feel better. I started to assure him that at least he had family in town and he stopped me with a shake of his head.

"She's not my sister. We, ah, we go way back."

I had nothing to say to that. I nodded and we shook hands, effectively ending my career as a private detective. A month later, grown weary of my surreptitious existence on the fringe of my city, I left Chicago again.

Sixteen: Carny

1 hitched, rode buses, walked across the map of America, never once feeling enough a part of any single place to think of settling. I drank more, ate less, lost weight. Somewhere in Kansas I began a soul-killing succession of odd jobs and temp work, sometimes enough to pay for liquor and a room, sometimes just enough for the liquor. I missed Christmas that year, drunk in the back room of a Wichita saloon. The porter let me sleep on the pool table.

I made it as far as Denver this time. At the end of my first week in town I woke up, left the room key on a dresser for the landlord to find, and left. I dozed for a while on a bench at the edge of a park. When I woke up, the sun was climbing and I started walking. I walked for hours. Just east of Denver, on a vacant property not far from a school, I saw a Ferris wheel, looking as out of place as a whale on sand. Around it was a blur of size and color and movement, and as I drew closer, I heard voices, the irritable voices of men working in a hurry to do something. In this case, to take down a Ferris wheel. A carnival.

A long tractor-trailer up ahead bore the legend, "The

Bighorn Teton Carnival, Rodeo and Sideshow." It sounded like a name you'd come up with while staring at a map. I saw trucks, a couple of small animal trailers, piles of equipment. Nearby a red-faced man watched me, an odd look of amusement on his face.

"Looking for work?"

I started to shake my head but then shrugged. "Yeah."

He slapped his wide chest. "Frank Bauer."

"Tom Faye."

"That your gear?" he asked, politely refusing to stare at the canvas bag carrying my things.

"Yeah."

"Put it in that trailer, then fall in with that crew there on the big wheel."

And fall in, I did. I worked and they showed me what to do and told me what an idiot I was when I did it wrong, and that night I slept like the dead after the hardest day of work I'd ever seen. If there is a hell, if there is a nether world for the sinners of this one, it's an endless carny crew taking down and putting up a big Ferris wheel, in a hurry, forever in a hurry.

I learned that for a carnival or a small circus – and the Bighorn Teton show was a little of both – there is no such thing as leisure. You blow into town, set up, and everybody has at least two or three jobs. When it's time to go, you take it down in a hurry to get on the road for the next town. I was with Frank Bauer's carnival for a little over two months and I thought it would kill me. As I suspected, there was no rodeo, despite Frank Bauer's high-flown name for his show. Nor was there a sideshow.

"Had to shut 'er down," Frank explained. "Had a

Strong Man with a short fuse, went after a couple of local fellas. It got ugly."

What he had in his mangy Plains carnival was a small selection of rides, a few of the more predictable games, and a menagerie containing some of the most boring animals I was ever to see: an armadillo that slept most of the time, a pair of homicidal llamas, a miniature pig, a dwarf pony of some sort and a tortoise that might have been dead.

And of course, the staff. The other carnies were an assortment of misfits: a handful of kids from small towns with few work prospects where they came from, a couple of old drunks, a college kid who clearly thought he was living in the Old West, a pair of crusty women in their fifties, and a little man named Jimmy who ran the kids' rides.

About a month into my *apprenticeship* I was securing one of the countless cables that held the show together when I became aware that Frank was watching me.

"Something wrong, Frank?"

"Just trying to figure out where you fit in."

I wondered if this meant he was letting me go, and it showed on my face.

"No, no, nothing like that, Tom. Here's the thing. Look around you: you see people that's here because they don't know where to go, like young Billy Carr, whose last job before he signed up with us was a Dairy Queen in Minot. And then you got old Henry there, he's too old to do the work he did all his life, so he's with me, and you got young Joe Fairs, and I'm not so sure he's not on the run, not even sure Joe Fairs is his name. And we got our ladies that are just making a few dollars for the summer and I might see 'em again next season and I might not. And you got your college boy Alec," and here Frank laughed, "he thinks he's having an adventure!"

He gazed around him at these various people as he spoke, then winked at me.

"And then there's you. And I don't think you're any one of those things."

"Maybe not. What about you?"

"Me? Oh, I'm where I belong, oh, yes. There's a certain kind of fellow that is born to do just this, run a crazy little show from town to town, living in trailers and tents. In another time I mighta been one of those men in the painted wagons in the old days. Some men are born to do odd things, I learned that from an old circus man named Lewis Tully. I'm one of 'em."

"Maybe I am, too."

"Yeah, I think you might be, but what thing? What's your odd thing?"

"I'm beginning to wonder if I'll ever figure that out."

He was nodding before I even finished, and I understood that this was at least in part the point of our talk. Then he pointed in the direction of the miniature train.

"I'd like you to work with Jimmy. He can use the help and the other men don't have patience with him, even though he's as smart in his own way as any of them."

"Okay."

As I finished what I was doing, I watched Jimmy and wondered about this new assignment. Jimmy was like no one else in the show. He was very small, perhaps five feet tall, and what people in the old days called "*slow*". I thought he was retarded, perhaps even brain damaged. When he wasn't working the rides he tended to sway from side to side like a blind musician. Facially he could have been twenty but for a single oddity, an eyebrow gone completely gray. He was quiet, even-tempered, smiled more or less constantly, and was crazy about the children, whom he squirted from a pink squirt gun as the little train or moving caterpillar or dragon took them past Jimmy's station. They giggled and shrieked and he laughed with them and his face became a child's face. I was never to see such easy joy in another man.

I became Jimmy's assistant. The other men were amused, made all the predictable comments about being an assistant idiot. I shrugged it off. Jimmy showed me how to take the small rides down and put them up, how to make certain the safety features were working, what to watch out for when the kids were getting on and off. He was one of many people I was to encounter in life who was tremendously gifted in his hands: he could repair things easily, and not only the equipment he was responsible for. Several times I saw him repair toys the kids had brought with them, or the cheap prizes they won at the games. He worked in silence unless there was something he wanted to show me, and I was at a point where I was grateful for silence.

He was a devoutly religious and attended, once a year, a national conference for youthful Christians held somewhere in Oklahoma. On break, I'd smoke and he'd sit a couple of feet away reading the Bible. On those occasions when we actually spoke, his conversation was an odd amalgam of homespun evangelism and guarded suggestions for my life. I found this perfectly inoffensive: he was clearly trying to get me off the street. At first this amused me, for there was no question, once I got to know Jimmy, that he was indeed a step slow mentally, and the concept of life advice from a retarded man holds a certain innate humor.

But I listened to little Jimmy, first to learn what he had to show me about the job, and then because I came to understand that somehow Jimmy knew about me. Whether as a compensation for the other things his brain was incapable of, or simply from an innate shrewdness, Jimmy knew about me. From what he let drop, he knew about some of the others as well.

One morning as we were taking a break from the tear-down of the rides, I lit up a smoke and saw that he was watching me.

"Those things'll kill you."

I smiled: he was quietly insistent that the Lord didn't hold with smoking or drinking.

"If not these, Jimmy, something will."

"I know you've had a hard life."

"How do you know that?"

He frowned. "I just do."

"What else?"

He frowned in what would have been a caricature of concentration in anyone else.

"I know it'll get better someday. If you don't die first. It'll get better, but not the way you expect. Your life will be different."

A quick chill went through me and I laughed to conceal

it, but he seemed to know anyway.

"Different don't mean bad. Just different. Don't nobody get what they really expect." He smiled, shyly, and waved an arm around him. "I never expected this would be my life. But it's what I got, and it's good."

"Must be, Jimmy. I think you're the only happy man I know."

"Boss is happy. This here is all he wants."

"Do you know that, too?"

"Sure," he said, as though it was self-evident. "But you'll get something, you will. You'll see. Lord'll give you something."

"Maybe I'll just stay here with you." I meant it as a joke but he shook his head.

"No, you won't. This is not for you. Shouldn't be here in the first place."

He smiled, sensing this might be taken the wrong way, but I just nodded. Then he clapped his hands and said "All right. Back to work."

Toward the end of the season, when we were someplace in Iowa, he left the show to attend his Christian festival. Before he went to catch his bus for Oklahoma, he clapped me on the shoulder.

"You take care of yourself, Thomas."

"See you when you get back from Oklahoma," I said.

"I don't think so," he said quietly, and then he was gone.

A few days later, we were setting up in a town near the Mississippi. We had just put the last of the cars onto the Ferris wheel and the other guys had gone into town to get beer. I was standing alone at the edge of our grounds and I heard someone behind me.

"You miss Jimmy yet?" Frank Bauer asked.

"Yeah, I do. I think he's – he has – "

"Goodness," he said, grinning. "He's got goodness. The genuine article. It's healthy for a fella to be around goodness, don't you think?"

"Yeah."

"Specially when you're not sure of things," he said. He might have been talking about himself but I was fairly certain he meant me, at least in part. I didn't say anything.

"So you'll probably be going back into it?"

"Into what?" I asked, but I understood this part, too.

He nodded toward the east. "That. Life. Your life, whatever it was."

"I don't know. I hadn't really thought about leaving."

"No, but you didn't belong here in the first place, that's one. And every time you're by yourself, you light up a smoke and kinda look to the east. That's where you're from, I'd guess."

"Yeah."

"Might be time to be getting back there. But you're welcome to stay on. I just don't think you will."

"Tell me, Frank. Do you believe everything happens for a reason?"

"No. That's one of the stupidest things folks ever came up with. If I stub my toe getting out of bed, that wasn't the Almighty's plan or my fate or Karma or whatever high-flown name people want to give to it. It was just my clumsiness. It doesn't mean anything to anyone, nobody's affected."

He finished his smoke and ground it out thoroughly, a

man accustomed to careful measures to protect the few things he owned. On the road I'd seen men with no more than what they carried in a plastic bag, and they were more meticulous in tending to their belongings than a man who lives in a palace.

Frank Bauer started to walk away and then looked at me with amusement in his red face.

"But you coming here to work with us, in the great Frank Bauer carnival, I think *that* happened for a reason." Then he turned and with his back to me, waved.

Just before Labor day, Frank Bauer brought his show to Elgin, Illinois, a small dog-eared city on the Fox River. We spent a week in Elgin, set up in a Boys' Club ballfield. When we finished, Frank told us we'd be following the Fox River down through other Illinois towns, St. Charles, Batavia, Geneva, and he thought we'd swing across Illinois to the west and hit Missouri. I was physically exhausted from the work, mentally tapped out by so many other things. I knew I could hitch rides and be someplace quite different by the end of the day – Milwaukee or, if I caught a trucker going around the bend in Lake Michigan, Detroit. I decided to jump ship.

When I went to tell Frank, he laughed and said, "Told you."

"Maybe that's when I started thinking about it."

"I doubt it." He paid me and said, "You ever get stuck, you know my route. I expect I'll be doing this for some time to come, Lord willing."

I spent four days just knocking around Elgin, to see if the town had anything for me. I found a cheap room and roamed the streets, and just about the time when the cops

234

made me for the vagrant I was, I hooked up with a small auto repair shop and junk yard, working for a pair of brothers: when a customer came in looking for a door for a Dodge or an engine for a dying Plymouth, I helped haul it all out.

I worked and drank at a small place not far from a college called Dave's Tin Pan Lounge, an odd saloon that had once been a bowling alley and still had four working lanes. One afternoon when I left work, a kid ran by carrying a football and dropped it as he crossed the street. I bent over to retrieve the ball, and when I straightened up I sensed that someone was behind me. I tossed the kid his ball and before I turned around I knew exactly who it was.

"You," I said. "Jesus Christ."

"Do you remember me?" Rachel asked. I suppose it was an honest question but it seemed the craziest thing she could have said. She fought to smother a smile at this vulnerable moment.

"Rachel, what a question. Why are you here?"

She shrugged. "I live here." She tilted her head to one side. "Do you?"

I fought the urge to blurt out *I don't live anywhere.* "More or less. What are you doing here?"

"We came here a couple of years ago, my father and I. His brother lived here – my uncle."

"Uncles and aunts again, huh?"

"Not anymore. They're all gone now. It's just my dad and me. I take care of him. He's sick."

"What kind of sick?"

"All kinds. The kind that comes from hard living." She shrugged. But at "hard living" I saw her give me a quick

235

glance that took in my face and my clothes, and she missed nothing.

She met my eyes and the smile burst out, and I thought she was beautiful. Beautiful, yes, but other things as well. Her face was still youthful but she had aged. It showed in her eyes rather than in any physical manifestation.

"This never happens," she said.

"Well, it must sometime, 'cause here we are." And we both laughed. I have no recollection of what we said to each other, only that we talked in the street for almost an hour until she told me she had to get back to make supper for her father. For a moment I thought this meant I'd lost her again, two old friends meeting and chatting for a while and going their separate ways.

"How can I get hold of you?"

She gave me her address and told me to come by for dinner the next day. Then she reached out and took my hand in a way that no one had done in years. For a moment I just stood there and held onto her. All these years later I can still see us, on an Indian Summer day in that improbable place, smiling and refusing to let go lest we lose one another again.

I went to dinner at her home the next day. They lived in a weathered frame house with a sagging porch. She'd planted a small flower garden in front. Like the house, her father was a wreck of a man, tall and gaunt, his clothes hung on him as though borrowed from a bigger man. Surprisingly, in view of Rachel's dark coloring, he was blond, his hair in need of cutting. But he combed it, and he'd shaved in the patchy manner of a man grown unused to the razor. He asked me questions about myself until

Rachel made him stop, then shifted gears and regaled me with tales of his war adventures in the Pacific. Then after exchanging looks with his daughter, he saluted me with his beer can and left us. Rachel sat for a moment looking at the door through which he'd left. She shook her head.

"What?"

"It's just funny. He's checking you out."

"So? He's your father."

"I take care of *him*. I've been looking after him for years, so it's just odd for me, that's all. But he likes you, holes and all."

"Holes?"

"In your story. Anybody can tell you hold things back. You say things like 'So then I knocked around for a while.' God knows what that's shorthand for."

"Some of it I don't like to talk about. Some of it I can't even remember."

She said nothing for a moment as we both realized what I'd just implied about myself. But I was her dinner guest, so she bit back her questions.

I took her out the next night and lingered long afterward in her small living room, the two of us pressed close together as we talked. I said more than I wanted, revealed things long smothered in my heart in the hopes I'd never think of them again. I talked till I felt naked. At some point I forced it back at her, and she spoke dispassionately of her peripatetic life with her father, in Joliet, in Rockford, Illinois, in Milwaukee, and here two blocks from the tracks in Elgin, Illinois.

In the midst of her narrative she stopped herself, got up, pulled me by the hand to her room, not to bed me there as

237

I hoped but to show me the room. This I understood. I looked around in it and let her show me her things and what was important to her, for the room was where she kept her life, preserved as if under a glass sheet for some later time when she might be free to do as she pleased. One wall was covered almost to the ceiling with a massive bookshelf put up, surprisingly, by her father.

"In one of his better times – sober for nearly a month."

I gazed at the books, quite certain that some of them were from the old shop on Addison. As though reading my mind, she asked about it, about Farrell and Meyer.

"The shop's gone. Some kind of a Mexican restaurant was about to open there. I think they're probably gone, too," I added, and felt a sudden hollowness at the truth of this.

"That's so sad. I always felt they were very lonely, that they needed the people who came into the shop."

My darker images of that place rushed back to me now, and to forestall any more talk about Farrell and his shop, and Meyer, I changed the subject. I pointed to her small manual typewriter.

"So what do you do with that?"

She shrugged and I saw that for the first time I'd embarrassed her.

"I write. I write stories and short plays. And I send some of them out and they come back rejected. I save the rejection slips, though: they're kind of my proof to myself that I'm doing this."

"But you're a writer? I never knew."

"How would you? It's just something I started a couple years ago. Probably nothing will come of it but it makes me happy."

She had moved closer to me, put a hand on my upper arm as she spoke of her writing. I put my hand around her waist and pulled her to me, and then I kissed her. We stayed there, kissing standing up for a long time and eventually we adjourned to her bed, and I slid my hand under her blouse, worked my fingers under the cup of her bra, felt her nipple. I worked my hand around her back to unfasten it and she stopped me.

"Not here. Not tonight."

I straightened up and nodded, no questions. She'd just told me what I needed to know. When I left we stood on her porch and kissed again, and I had the sense that it would have pleased her if a nosy neighbor had lifted up a shade to watch, to see that she had a male caller.

Two nights later I brought her to my room, excitement overriding embarrassment at the seedy place where I lived. I'd washed the sheets, at least. For some reason I blurted this out to her and she laughed. I made love to her and thought my heart would burst. When we were finished we lay there, coiled in the wreckage of the bed, and listened to the wind. It seemed I had just finished a long perilous trek, that I was in a place in life where I could rest, where I could start over with this lovely, good-hearted girl who, it seemed, had waited for me over the years and the miles. This was where I could at last be happy. And no sooner had I dared this thought than a new one touched my heart like an icy finger, the old familiar notion that this would not last, it was inevitable as night.

A month or so later, I moved in with Rachel and her father. He never said anything to me about the change in arrangements, never questioned my presence. Once or twice I caught him looking at me from the next room, eyes owlish with his obvious question: what did this mean for his daughter, his treasured girl? He was never anything but pleasant to me, welcomed me into his home and his life, and only at odd moments did I see the doubt there, for I believe one drifter can recognize another.

And for a time my life in that house, my life with Rachel, was all I could have asked for and more than I ever thought I'd have. And I told her that. And although Elgin, Illinois seemed the least likely place on God's earth for me to establish a life, it began to feel like my home. Indeed, for the first time in four years I spent Christmas with other people. Rachel glowed with her carefully suppressed happiness, and I told myself that even if I accomplished nothing else, I'd brought something to her, that this was my achievement. For a time it seemed we were a matched pair in ways I would not have expected: I'd lived in the wagon ruts of the world, and was grateful for the mere fact of normalcy in my life. For her part Rachel had learned to assume nothing, to expect little, and had developed a talent for appreciation, a gift for life's smallest joys. It was intoxicating just to be around her.

Winter settled on the world and our life fell into patterns. I noticed no change, not at first. The old man seemed to take my presence as a permanent thing and Rachel asked nothing of me, there were no guarded conversations about changing our status, about making formal commitments.

But I began to see the signs of our – my unraveling. I found myself thinking at odd moments that I had become

240

an adjunct to someone else's life: she worked, she took classes in writing and drawing at the local junior college, she took care of the house. Once or twice I stood at the doorway to the room where we slept – "our room," she called it, but it was not – and looked at her typewriter, frequently adorned by a page in progress, either a scene from a story or a page of a play, and at the small drawings she'd done, and felt intimidated by her sense of purpose. The irony of her drawing was not lost on me: a boyhood talent that I'd long since given up.

And on the most basic of levels I felt stifled by that ramshackle house. I did not for a moment ever want to be homeless again but I began to remember the odd early moments on the road when it seemed to me that I had begun a life of perfect freedom. So I heard the train whistles in the night and wondered what distant part of the continent they were traveling to.

Though he never bothered me, I became more conscious of the old man's presence, of his drinking, his chronic health complaints, his nocturnal wanderings. One night I came out of the room to find him in the living room, on the sofa in drunken conversation with his lost wife, apologizing for leaving, for being a bum, remonstrating with her for dying young. I backed into the living room and had a sudden mental image of this man running. He was younger, heavier, terrified, running somewhere in the night in a place where there was water. I could not see his pursuers but it seemed I could hear them, several of them, and the look he gave them over his shoulder was a look of pure terror.

I stepped back into the bedroom and slipped under the

covers, shook my head to clear it of the terrible picture, felt Rachel's warmth beside me.

One night I watched her sew the seam in one of her father's shirts. She smiled as she worked. I was aware of the sound of the radiators coming to life, of the passing of cars outside on a slush-covered street, and I was revisited by an old image, one that had come to me so long ago in those early days of my relationship with Rachel. I saw her again sitting at the edge of a narrow bed in her mute grief, and now it was clear that it was her mother's bed, that her mother lay in it, and perfectly clear that her mother had just died.

I watched Rachel and then without really intending to, said, "So you were there, the night your Ma died? You were with her?"

She blinked, frowned, looked puzzled and wary at the same time.

"Yes. How did you know that?"

"I think you told me, or at least you said you were there. I assumed that meant you were with her. Like in the room with her."

She stared at me for a moment and then nodded. "I was. I knew she had died but for a long time I just sat there at the foot of her bed, convinced that if I stayed there, she'd come back to life, she'd sit up and I'd realize she'd just fallen asleep. I stayed there for hours, and when I finally understood she was gone, I didn't know who to go to, or who to call. I wanted to run out of the house and scream that my mother was dead, for someone to come help me. But it was the middle of the night. It seemed to me you couldn't just run out into the street like that in the middle of the night. I spent the night just sitting there, I felt like someone should stay in the room with her. I know it sounds stupid. But that's how I thought."

"How old were you?"

"I was eight."

"You poor kid."

She shrugged. "It was a long time ago, and not so different from things you've gone through."

She went back to her sewing and I said nothing more on the subject. But I watched her and pondered the scene I'd just witnessed, and asked myself if I'd actually seen into her life for the second time. I reached for my cigarettes and saw that my hands were shaking.

We lasted for a little under a year. Toward the end of that time I began drinking more. Rachel didn't pay it much heed at first – she lived with an alcoholic, after all, and my drinking couldn't touch his, not at the beginning. But I began to do more and more of it outside the house, to perch on a barstool until I closed the tavern, then to stagger home long after she'd gone to bed. In this way, since I got up after she'd left, we frequently had entire days when we saw each other for just a short while, around dinner. More and more often, unwittingly at first, I managed to avoid her for the better part of a day. Once she came to find me in the tavern where I drank. The next night I sought out a bar I'd never been in, far from our place, where she'd never think to look for me. One night soon after that, I went home with the waitress in a diner. I said nothing about this to Rachel but she knew what had happened, what it meant.

On one level I fought for separation between us, as

though the true object were my own independence. And all the while a part of me watched with clinical detachment as I engineered the perfectly gratuitous destruction of the life that had been offered me.

In the end I couldn't have pointed to a single thing that caused me to walk, but walk I did.

"I never thought you'd leave," she said, and I listened for betrayal and heard only disappointment. And as I packed she managed to remind me of the fundamental difference between us, in our ability to love.

"You won't have a *home* anymore."

"I know."

She came closer, her eyes brimming, and though she made no sound her tears began streaming down her cheeks. I bit back the impulse to kiss her cheeks. I just shook my head.

"Leave me alone. It has to be this way. This is how I am."

I heard my words and it seemed they were the most honest assessment of myself I'd ever made to her. And it seemed I was powerless to do otherwise, to stay there in that life I'd tried to make. A sudden surge of rage swept over me, and at just that moment Rachel put her hand on my arm. I turned and grabbed her wrist, yanked at her and tossed her halfway across the room. She fell and caught herself against the side of the bed, winced as the bed frame caught her in the ribs. I had no intent to cause her pain, only to show her that this was no pretense. I was leaving.

It worked. She stared wordlessly at me as she got to her feet, the blood draining from her face. I made a placating gesture but she silenced me with an upraised hand.

"Now you have to go. You've put hands on me."

"For that, I'm sorry."

She folded her arms across her body and made the faintest of shrugs. Then she left the room. I thought she might be waiting at the front door when I left but I had apparently burned that bridge behind me.

We carry our moments of joy and pain with us forever, some of us more successful than others at suppressing the times of pain, but I have never forgotten the sight of Rachel watching me throw things into my duffel, her eyes wide with her unasked question, "Why?"

And so I walked away from that life, and from that girl with her writing and her books and her puzzling gift for accepting whatever life brought her, me most of all. It seemed I had managed to bring her little more than pain, and that given her nature, her kindness to me, that this was the worst thing I'd managed to do yet in life.

Seventeen:
Soldier of the Republic

I resumed my old life almost immediately, made no attempt to settle anywhere. I traveled, on certain days determined to go as far as I could without stopping, as though the accomplishment of distance were my new goal.

Shortly thereafter I hit a stretch where I managed to stay drunk for several days on end, woke up mornings with my head spinning and my stomach turned inside out and began drinking almost before the sun showed its face. In Rapid City, South Dakota I was hauled in for a drunken fight outside a tavern. To this day I cannot remember why I was fighting. There I spent my first night in a jail cell. There was another man in the cell, a drunk who slept and snored the entire night, leaving me to stare around me at those gray walls – literally gray, they'd been painted gray, God knows why that struck people as a good color for a place where the angry and the depressed would be cooling their heels. That night in the gray cell I had an attack of sheer panic. I sensed an overwhelming sadness, a desperation, far beyond my own, as though the gray paint were an adhesive holding onto the heartache of the men who passed through. At one point I began to cry, I could not have said why.

The next day a battle-weary judge heard my case. I was led into the courtroom and met there by a rotund man in a too-tight sport coat. He was tying his tie. He introduced himself as my defense attorney, adding, "I just now found out."

I didn't know whether it meant he'd just learned he was an attorney or that he'd just been assigned my case. The judge was a red-faced man with a long scar down one side of his face that gave him a menacing aspect. I was to be tried by a scar-faced judge in a strange place and defended by a man still getting dressed for work. I had no doubt I would back in the terrible cell by lunchtime.

The judge watched my attorney, frowned, called him over and they whispered a very one-sided conversation in which the judge seemed to be taking the lawyer to task for a cavalier attitude.

"So you'll need to take some time here – " And then the judge stopped himself. He gave me a long, interested look, the look of a man seeing something he's seen before many times. He sighed. "Come here, son." The bailiff indicated I should stand before the judge.

The judge squinted down at the day's caseload. "Thomas Faye. Is that you?"

"Yes, sir."

"'Your honor,'" he corrected.

"Your honor."

"Disturbing the peace. And – " He squinted up at me, took in my bruised face. " – losing a fight, seemingly. So why were you fighting?"

"I don't remember, your honor."

"You were intoxicated."

"Yes, Your Honor."

"Is that a state to which you are accustomed?"

"Lately. It seems so."

"How old are you?"

"Twenty-one. No, twenty-two."

"Easy to lose track when you're having such a high old time."

This drew a titter of laughter from the courtroom. The judge didn't smile. He tilted his head to once side and studied me. As he did so I studied the scar and his perfectly impassive brown eyes, and in my mind's eye I saw him sitting on a rotting pier somewhere and fishing. And it seemed to me that he was not fishing for the joy of it or the entertainment, not entirely, but for the order of it, that he was a man who fought to put order in his life lest he lose his grip on his sanity. I was spared, thankfully, any sudden visions of his life, I did not see how he had come by his scar, but I understood that this daily routine in his small courtroom was his reason for living. And I knew as well that he was going to try to be fair to me. He blinked, suddenly, surprise in the brown eyes, and I would have sworn that at just that precise moment he knew I was thinking about his life.

"Where are you from, Thomas?"

"Chicago. Originally."

His first smile. "Originally. I'm not going to ask where you're from now. Do you know how far it is from Chicago, Illinois to Rapid City?"

"No, Your Honor."

"A little over 900 miles. So my question is, why are you here?"

"Your Honor, I have no idea."

He nodded as though I'd answered correctly in a classroom.

"You don't belong here. What did you think of your night in our jail?"

On another day I might have made a predictable comment about the alleged "cold cuts" on my sandwich. But I heard myself saying, "I hated it."

"You need to get your life in order. You need a way to put space between you and these things you've been doing to yourself or you won't see twenty-three. Have you been in the service?"

"No. Though I've thought about it."

The judged leaned forward and looked into my eyes in what seemed an odd manner. "I'm hesitant to do this – there's a good chance you'll see combat, and getting shot at hasn't straightened out anyone since Sergeant York. But you need to get your life in order. When court is adjourned, I will have someone take you to the Army recruiter, who happens to be just up the street."

And so he did – he had the bailiff drive me there, and I enlisted in the Army.

At that time we had troops in a dozen or more places, and I fantasized a tour of duty in Germany or some other European location. By late summer, I was in Vietnam. The moment I stepped onto Vietnamese soil, I felt a strange current run through me, and if asked to identify it, I would have said it was the foreknowledge of my death.

It remains a blur to me, Vietnam. Two months into my

tour of duty: an ordinary patrol in an endless series of patrols. A scattering of houses, not nearly enough to be called a village. Beyond them, the wall of jungle. I remember the smells most vividly – I was, from my first moment in-country, struck by the smells of Vietnam. Like most of the poor men's sons serving in that conflict, I had seen little of the world, certainly nothing like the jungle. I saw colors new to me, smelled the earthen odors of decay and growth, mismatched twins. When I wasn't obsessing about my impending death, I listened to the alien bird and animal sounds, smelled the foreignness of it all, and imagined myself here in another time, a joyous young explorer.

Just beyond the town we entered the jungle – or, rather, it ingested us, swallowed our patrol, all of us. I walked, listened to the birds from deeper into the trees, and I noticed, almost as an afterthought, when the birds fell silent.

Behind me someone said "fuck" in a low whisper, and then "They're here."

When we came upon a place where the jungle fell back a few feet on either side, a miniature clearing, the trees around us erupted in gunfire. I heard the sound of leaves ripping apart before I heard the actual shots, and the kid just ahead of me, another new recruit, was killed instantly. I turned and fired my weapon at the sounds. I am certain I was hit several seconds before I even realized it, looking down at the hole burned into my shirt. I wanted to scream but could make no sound. I turned and the man behind me was sinking to his knees, a red hole where his eye had been. I was shot a second time, this one in the knee, so that I could no longer stand.

I landed with my face in the ground, smelled the damp earth and jungle plants, and the burnt cloth of my shirt. My knee hurt terribly but I knew the real wound was the one in my stomach, that I was bleeding to death.

Then the shooting was finished. I remember thinking that I should be able to move but could not. I lay on the ground, the side of my face pushed into the soft earth. My leg throbbed relentlessly and I heard a low humming sound. It took several seconds before I understood the noise was coming from me. I grew thirsty, intensely thirsty, and soon it didn't matter how badly I hurt, I was aware only that I needed water.

I heard a low coughing sound and realized it was the kid next to me, Kloppstein was his name, a German kid from Milwaukee, just short of his nineteenth birthday, and what I was hearing was him sobbing with his face pushed into the ground. I lifted my head and saw that he'd been shot in several places, the back of his shirt soaked red. I shut my eyes and felt the weakness taking me, and for a moment I know I had decided not to fight my death. Kloppstein wept softly and as I listened to him it seemed to me that no one should die in such despair. I was unaware of any selfless impulse: it was clear I could do nothing for myself. I crawled on my elbows to him, bit my lip at the shooting pain in my leg, and put my hand on the kid's back. His body heaved with his sobs, and I patted him and told him it was going to be all right. At some point I just rested my hand on him, told him over and over that it was going to be all right. He quieted down after a while, and I could feel his body move with his breathing.

And then it stopped.

I became aware of movement as the Cong emerged from the trees on either side of us. They moved quickly, not in silence, exactly, but with a quiet economy of movement, and they spoke in low voices to one another. They were backlit, like shadow, perhaps a dozen of them. I remember remarking to myself how small they seemed, yet they'd filled the clearing with dead Americans, they'd killed me.

I became aware that someone was standing over me. My rifle was within reach but I knew I was too weak to do anything with it. Instead I kept my hand on Kloppstein, patting his shoulder one last time as though to keep him calm.

A Cong soldier moved into my field of vision. He looked at me and said something to another man that I could not see. Then he moved off to join the others, pausing to take Kloppstein's rifle.

The second man crouched down between us. He leaned close to Kloppstein, touched his face, then turned to study me, and I had time to memorize his face, a face I still recall in the most minute detail even to this day. He wore a kind of half-assed version of a helmet common to the Cong, a small pith helmet with camouflage netting, and the netting was festooned with little pieces of green ribbon. He had a stubble of facial hair above his lip, like a boy attempting to grow his first moustache, and a small mole on the side of his face near his ear. And he had one eye, with a slash mark across the other socket. The eyelid hung down, covering most of the injured eye, but the white part of the eye was darkened with old blood. And as

I stared at the Vietcong soldier's face he was transformed, for mere seconds, and I saw him as a child, he was standing with a row of children and several women, and some men came to their small hut and laid down a cot, and the women threw themselves at the dead man on the cot. The boy stood back, looking on in disbelief before he began wailing, his face turned not toward his dead father but to heaven, protesting to heaven.

The Viet Cong soldier kept his hand on the side of Kloppstein's face but he was gazing at me with no expression. I wanted water, wanted this to be done with, waited for this man to finish me, or to tell his comrades that one of us was still breathing. Instead he stayed in his crouch and studied my face. I noted his dark, flimsy clothing, his simple equipment. His rice bowl hung from the back of his belt on a loop, just a small green bowl that you might have seen on a breakfast table in Chicago or Detroit. And he had a makeshift canteen, a plastic bottle jammed into a canvas pouch on a webbed belt. A homemade soldier. After a long moment he leaned toward me and put his hand on me, on my back. He muttered something and I remember thinking he was saying a Buddhist prayer for a dead American. I grew faint, and when I looked at him again his face would not come into focus. He was reaching for his belt, and I understood he was going to give me water though I did not know why. He let me drink and then I lost consciousness.

I woke in a hospital, tethered to the world by IV tubes. I recall a certain older doctor with the face of a bookie who spat out his words as though they took too much of his valuable time. He displayed a morbid wit that embarrassed the younger doctors assigned to him. One morning I woke to his face peering into mine.

"Not dead, yet, eh? Then you're probably not going to die, not from this anyway." He gestured more or less in the direction of my stomach. "That was a good one. Should have killed you but the bleeding stopped. From the bleeding, or infection, that's usually a fatal wound. Sometimes you get lucky. You got lucky, kid." He pointed to my knee.

"Your dancing days are done, though. No more tango for you, Romeo. But what do you care? Kids these days don't actually move their feet when they dance, do they?"

"I don't dance much."

He shrugged. "Well, you're lucky. We got a roomful of luck here." He pointed to the black kid in the nearest bed, a Houston boy named Archie.

"That guy gets shot up in the jungle and has to get hospitalized to find out he's got a hit record back home. He's some kinda singer. That Soul music they like."

I looked over at the kid called Archie, who was sleeping off his various medications.

"Well, that's something to go home to."

The doctor looked at me for a long moment and then said, "Home, any home, is something to go home to, son. Whatever's waiting for you, be thankful it didn't end for you here."

I wanted to tell him that these things applied only if one actually had something like a home, but I had no energy for such disputation.

Within weeks I was discharged. I had lost some of the bone in the right knee joint, so that I now had a limp which

I tried to disguise by keeping up a brisk pace when I walked. It hurt only when I ran, and I got used to that. But I was free again, and tired and terrified to be going home again. Nonetheless, for lack of a better idea, I headed back with the greatest reluctance, to Chicago.

Chicago, City of youthful promise.

PART 11

eighteen: sick

I had been back home only a couple of weeks when I realized I was unwell. It wasn't the leg or the occasional odd spasm of pain but far more frightening things. At odd moments my surroundings, the very streets filled with people, seemed to fade into shadow, as though diminished by something beyond, and I fancied I could see other people, other buildings more real. Once or twice I lost my awareness of my situation, found myself standing on a street corner without knowing quite where I was or how I'd come to be there. More and more I saw the wary looks of passersby and wondered what about me troubled or frightened them. Drunk or sober, I was consumed with imagined angry confrontations with the people in my old life, my father, my mother, Farrell, even Rachel. And of course God, wherever he might be. Once I saw a man step wide of me on the sidewalk and realized I'd been talking to myself.

I spent hours in the great gothic public library on Michigan Avenue, where I'd worked in more hopeful times. There, in a building overrun by eccentrics, derelicts and would-be lovers seeking a partner for the night, a man living on the edge would go unremarked. I spent many hours poring through magazines to read of the many mental ailments and disturbances said to afflict soldiers coming home from Vietnam. I looked for myself in these pages but found no one like me.

I was chilled, always, no matter where I was, and tired, for I could no longer sleep through the night, and had developed a deep and wracking cough. For a time I ascribed my odd visual experiences and behavior to my diminished physical condition. But a part of me suspected that the explanation couldn't be that simple. Shortly after my return I had several street encounters that left me shaken.

One night I was coming home from a bar on North Avenue to my rented room on Willow Street and I passed a newsstand, a narrow wood shack painted green. The paper stand was run by a kid, just a small boy by himself. Three in the morning on a tough street corner, and here was a child out in the night selling papers. An odd kid at that, dressed like some kind of immigrant boy, suspenders and an old-fashioned striped t-shirt.

I bought a paper and gave him a buck. He fumbled in his little change apron, shivering in the cold. The wind was coming off the lake and it just tore through my Army jacket, and I could see this little boy out in the middle of the night was frozen.

"Awful late for a kid to be out selling papers."

"It ain't so bad, Mister. It's my own stand." He came up with my change finally and I told him to keep it.

"Thanks, Mister. You're a good egg."

A good egg?

I walked away smiling to myself over the kid's odd choice of phrasing. Something from an old movie, or something he got from a book, perhaps.

The next time I passed that corner, the little newsstand was gone, and I wondered about the kid. I asked a guy passing by what happened to the stand and he just looked at me.

A week or so later I was coming home and it was nearly dawn. The sky over the lake was beginning to show blue and the robins were announcing that they'd made it through another tough night, and I passed the corner where the kid's paper stand had been. An old man was there, clearly drunk, standing at the curb and trying to muster enough sobriety to cross the street. He put one foot down from the curb and then had to stagger back as a cab made a sudden turn in front of him.

"You need to get across? Come on." I grabbed his elbow and more or less pulled him across North Avenue, one drunk leading another.

"Thanks, buddy," he said, breathing muscatel and bad teeth on me. "I'd buy you a drink but I'm flat broke."

I gave him a buck. He protested but eventually I forced him to take it. I patted him on the back and left. As I walked away he called out, "Thanks, pal. You're a good egg."

I stopped and turned to look at him but he was on his way. For a moment I watched him staggering south on Larrabee toward a badly lit section of the street. I realized a cabbie was staring at me. I turned and made my way home in the frigid wind off the lake and I was asleep as soon as I hit the pillow, for I believe there are times, at least a few, when we can will ourselves to sleep.

I stayed away from that part of town – Old Town, again, where I'd worked for Harry Hogarth. As a child I'd had the odd idea that there was a town under the one I knew. Maybe there was. In any case, I stayed away.

Sometime after the two encounters on North Avenue, I was wandering up Halsted when I passed an old coffee house. I remembered passing it on one of Farrell's curious errands. It was an old one-story building, covered with cheap wood-paneling and tar paper, and the shop itself was indicated only by a small handmade sign on the door with the word *Coffee*.

Now, on this chill afternoon when the air was heavy with the lake odors of dead alewives and smelt, I stopped in front of the coffee house and remembered that time on Farrell's errand, to the dying woman named Helena, when the men inside had invited me to come in. I could smell the coffee, a dense, rich smell, and suddenly I felt I couldn't live ten more minutes without a cup of coffee. I went in.

The door was warped, and scraped the frame as I opened it. A roomful of men looked up to see who had come in. A half dozen or so sat along a counter, and three or four pairs sat at small tables. On two of these tables there appeared to be chess games in progress, at the others, conversation. All of them drank from small glasses, the steam rising from the dark coffee inside. Some of them had beards, most had thick moustaches, they were all smoking. The one behind the counter, a dark man with Zapata's moustache, smiled at me and beckoned.

"Come in, come in, boy."

I could not move. I stood in their doorway, and it

seemed that every face in the room was waiting for me to come in or go away. I was embarrassed, but I felt something stronger, a warmth that seemed to emanate from all of them at once, and the man behind the counter was waving to me.

"Come in," he said, and then added, "if you want. If you no want, okay."

And so I did. I entered their smoky enclave, found a place at the counter and ordered coffee, which the man with the moustache served me in a narrow glass. I put change on the counter and took a sip of my coffee. I nodded to the counter man but he was already moving back up the counter where he was in heated conversation with three other men. They spoke in a foreign language that I did not recognize but it seemed only politics could generate such exuberant debate.

I looked around and a couple of the men smiled at me or nodded. At one of the tables the chess match ended with the winner smacking his hands together and cackling, and the loser muttering to himself. Two of the men at the counter called something out to the loser, who clearly told them in his native tongue where they could both go. Almost all of the men in the place joined in the laughter, and I remember that I started to laugh myself, self-consciously but openly. At that moment it struck me that this was the first genuine human moment I had experienced since coming back, a roomful of men laughing and calling out in a language I didn't know. They had welcomed me into their room and now I shared their moment of laughter. My initial impulse had been to drink my coffee as quickly as possible and get out, but now I just sipped it and listened to them. They might have been speaking Greek, it might have been Armenian, or Turkish, or some tongue from the heart of Asia, but their laughter was genuine.

The counter man filled my glass again and I pushed money toward him. He shook his head and said, "No, no," and went back toward his friends. Along the back wall of the room was a table with a small record player and a stack of perhaps a half dozen albums, and now one of the men went over to the table and put on a record. In a moment the room was filled with a high-pitched woman's voice, the song propelled by a tinny stringed instrument, and soon the men were clapping. Predictably one of the men got up and began dancing and soon they were all laughing, singing, clapping, calling out encouragement though it was clear they thought he was no dancer. The counter man shot me a quick look that mingled his delight at the moment with a slight embarrassment that an outsider was viewing all of this. I smiled and began clapping. The counter man grinned and gave me a nod, and as he turned away I had another glimpse of him, as though someone had shown me a photo of him. It lasted for the merest of moments, but I saw the smiling counterman in grief, his face gray with his pain. I saw the man sitting stiffly on a chair in a darkened room. He was wearing a suit and facing a bed on which a woman lay dead. In death she wore her finest clothing, as though to match his suit. Then I saw this man trudging up a narrow road through a rocky place, and from his drawn face I could see that he was starving. It was jarring, and I felt slightly chilled even though the shop was quite warm.

Something tightened in my stomach and I watched the men now rather than the dancer, and although I received no sudden images of their lives I was certain these men had each suffered greatly. The singer paused, the dancer made a show of being exhausted, and then a new song came on, faster than the first and the dancer kept time, and I clapped along with all of them. Eventually I felt I might overstay my welcome and so I left. At the door I turned and waved but not to anyone in particular, to all of them really, and the counter man held up his hand.

"Good-bye," he called out. "You come back, is good place for you," he said, and I nodded. He could have meant any of a half dozen things but I knew exactly what he meant, and did not doubt for a moment that he'd seen into my heart as I'd seen into his. As I walked from the coffee house my chest was pounding.

I continued to roam the city like a stray dog, looked up people from my past but made no connections, drank in taverns familiar and strange, stayed in rented rooms and spent the rest of my pay from the Army. I walked the length of the lakefront, from Evanston to East Chicago, Indiana, wore out shoes but built up my legs, even convinced myself the limp was less obvious. My sunburn darkened so that I looked like a sailor, my hair grew long, I grew my moustache again, shaved it, started it over. My wanderings took me everywhere in the city except places where I might be recognized, and I paid little attention to direction. So it was that I didn't pass that block again for nearly a month.

The day was warm but overcast and the gray lighting softened the edges of the street. It was different in other ways as well, for the coffee shop was gone. The shell of it was still there but all trace of habitation was gone. For that matter, the roof and back wall were gone, and planks had been hammered across the door to keep out vandals and enterprising kids.

"Yeah, they're tearing all of this down," a voice said. I turned to find myself being studied by a cop, a sergeant in a crisp white shirt. He was a type, this one, a red-cheeked man with childlike blue eyes and as I met his gaze he smiled. He was trying to figure me out, with my army jacket and peeling sunburn.

"There was a coffee house here."

"Here?" He frowned and then nodded. "You know, you're right, there was. Some kinda Middle Eastern place, I think. Turks or Armenians, something like that." He grinned. "Don't tell the Turks and Armenians I mentioned 'em in the same sentence. Those Old Country feuds. That coffee house, that was an interesting place. That was a while back, though."

"I was just here. Maybe a month ago."

He gave me a long appraising look. He put one hand to the back of his neck, looked at the traffic on Halsted, then he nodded.

"Maybe. Coulda been that recent. I thought the place was long gone, but you go by a place every day, you stop seeing it, you know what I mean?"

"Yes."

I saw him take in the wreck of the building even as I gazed at it and saw the signs of a building long vacant.

His next question startled me though I should have seen it coming. "You all right, son?"

263

"More or less."

It sounded like a stupid answer to me but he nodded as though it was enough.

"I seen you before, walking around. You walk around a lot, I think."

"Yeah. Helps me think. I'm trying to get started. So I walk around a lot."

"You were over there, right?"

"I was."

"Bad?"

"I can't recommend it."

He seemed to find this witty. He gave a sort of silent laugh and then looked me in the eye again.

"You know, if you ever want somebody to talk to, I don't know what your religion is or anything. But there's a priest over at St. Vincent's, Father Costello, he served in Korea. Not, you know, not as a chaplain, he saw action. He knows about – this stuff."

This stuff.

I was mortified that he could see so much, that it was so obvious. I wondered if people had begun to point me out, if the local cops were taking note of my presence on the street. But he was embarrassed himself, this well-meaning cop, he'd plunged into sensitive turf and really had no idea what to say or do. I coughed then, a long drawn-out cough, and he winced.

"Thanks. Maybe I'll look him up."

"Well, I got to get back to the 'serve and protect' part. You take care, son."

I thanked him, and a moment later I waved when he turned to look at me, as I knew he would.

When he drove off I stared at the ruin of the little coffee shop. I smelled the odors of rain-soaked plaster and wood left to the mercies of the elements and no longer wondered whether my account or the cop's was correct. I remembered the way the police officer had watched me and hoped I was not losing my mind.

Nineteen: Full Circle

But I did not, of course, visit the well-meaning cop's priest or anyone else, merely continued what I began to understand as a descent to the bottom of life. And so it was that I came to be wandering on West Madison Street the night I had my "vision" into the abandoned tavern, the night Farrell's appearance forestalled an assault. And I looked up from my booth in the diner and there he was as though he'd been there all along.

He was pouring milk into a cup of tea, a habit I remembered from the earliest times, how he would pour milk into a cup of tea until no one but a chemist could tell it had ever actually been tea. He looked over at me and I glared at him. In response he merely raised his eyebrows. I sipped my coffee, took a swing of the revolting mess I'd made with the ketchup and water, gagged on it, looked studiously away. When I let my gaze wander he was still watching me. I gave up. I shrugged or something to indicate capitulation and he beckoned me over with his Old Country nod.

As I slipped into his booth I saw him shoot a quick glance at my table. He'd seen the business with the ketchup and distaste registered in his eyes, but he'd been hungry more than once in his long life, and his good manners overcame his revulsion.

"Have you decided to take me up on my offer?"

"I've already got a cup of coffee over there."

He beckoned the waitress to bring my coffee over to his table. I saw her make a face at the water glass full of ketchup. But she'd been around the block, this one, she'd seen it all, and she just held the glass up to me and lifted her brows in question. I shook my head and looked away. Farrell pretended he'd seen none of it.

The waitress set down my coffee and looked at Farrell. He told her to bring me a hamburger. I told him I wasn't hungry.

When she was gone, he shrugged. "You have to eat something. It is the first step."

"I'm fine."

He gazed at me for a moment, clearly running down the nearly limitless responses to this lie. In the end, he said simply, "You don't belong down here."

"I'm surprised you haven't asked me how I wound up here."

"Well, you wouldn't know, boy. But you don't belong here, that's clear. This is a place where people end their lives, poor souls."

"I'm not ending anything. I just need some time to get back on my feet."

"You're not well, Thomas. You have been through many things."

"I'll be all right. I just need to figure out – "

He was shaking his head before I finished my sentence.

"You're a sick man. Sick and injured and other things

as well. I know about these things, Thomas. As well as anyone."

There was nothing to say to this. I drank down half my coffee and the waitress materialized and filled the cup again. I dumped cream and sugar in it till it was nearly as white as Farrell's tea. When the hamburger came I tore at it and swallowed half chewed bites until it was gone, then crammed fries into my mouth as though fearful someone might take them. As I ate, Farrell politely turned away and studied the room but in his fastidiousness I know he was embarrassed to be sharing his table with a hyena.

"Would you care for another?"

"No. It was good, though."

"I like a nice hamburger now and then, it's grand. I've grown fond of American food."

I stuffed several fries at once into my mouth. Farrell was studying my unshaven face, my pallor, my matted hair, and I was provoked. Grateful as I was for the hot meal, this was not the man I would have chosen to be with, starving or not. I recoiled from what I believed him to be, from his implied connection with my life, from the sermonizing he clearly thought his right.

"Stop watching me like I'm going to do something weird."

"I wasn't."

"And I'm not dying."

"Perhaps," he said, but looked away. Something occurred to him and he turned back with a smile. "Our cousins the Sassenach," he began, delighted in having thought of some small joke at the expense of the English. The "cousins" part was a fond fantasy of his that I was

268

Irish like him. In truth I was perhaps one-eighth, but apparently it was enough.

"The Sassenach, despite their limited gift for language, have many fine expressions to describe the vicissitudes of life. An Englishman would say you've made 'a dog's breakfast' of things, Thomas."

He laughed then for the first time, his breathless quiet laugh, turning full red in the face and repeating "a dog's breakfast" to himself twice more, as though he'd never heard anything quite so hilarious.

"Have a good time, Farrell. And what do you care what I do?"

"What a foolish question, lad."

"Why?"

"Don't be obtuse. I have ever fancied meself a gentleman, and a gentleman looks after his friends, even if his friends find his concern intrusive. And even if his friends are intractable."

"Is that what I am?"

"I wasn't necessarily speaking of you. At least, not solely of you."

"Meyer, then?"

"Yes, well – Meyer, you see, is a bit more. Meyer is a responsibility."

"So how is Meyer?"

Farrell hesitated, then said, "Oh, he's gone, you know." He said it quietly but I'd caught troubled tone, whether from loneliness or concern for Meyer's volatile nature, I couldn't have said. He looked out at the street to avoid meeting my eyes.

"Gone away? Or, like, *gone*?" I stopped short of asking,

"Is he dead?"

"Who ever knows with Meyer?" He looked at me and forced a smile. "He's like the wind itself. My mother, rest her soul, used to say that about me when people wanted to know my whereabouts as a lad. 'Oh, he's like the wind itself.'"

I let myself imagine this, Farrell as a wayward boy in an Irish town in a distant time, and a worried mother looking out for him. Did she know her son was unlike any of the other boys?

I heard myself blurt out a question, though not the one I wanted to ask. "What did your mother want for you, Farrell? What did she want you to be?"

He grinned. "Think, Thomas! She was a good Irish woman in a poor village, what sort of dream do you suppose she had for her youngest son?"

I thought a moment and then said, "She wanted you to be a priest."

A rueful smile this time. A priest, of course. I was going to make a joke about this but I saw that his attention had drifted. I had no doubt he was thinking of that time so long ago, in a village in Ireland named for a pig, he'd once told me, Ballinamore or Ballinamuck, something like that. I had no doubt he was seeing the faces of that time, his youth. Perhaps he'd divined my true question: what did you want of life, what did you think the world would bring you?

I was about to say something merely to break the silence when he said, "She was unusual for her time and place. She had little else in her life, and I believe it pleased her, perhaps even made her proud, that I was 'different'."

Now he had my complete attention: here was the subject we'd danced around so long, that he was, indeed, "different," and this was as close as Farrell had ever come to addressing it directly.

"Why?"

"Well. She would have said it was the will of God. Many mothers would have been worried or uneasy with an odd child, but she was proud. I was a clever lad, and bookish, and no trouble to her. I wonder what she would have made of me, of my life." He shook his head and laughed. "Oh, Thomas, there is nothing like the mothers, poor things. The closest human beings ever come to experiencing unconditional love."

Outside, the wind put its shoulder into the window of the diner, making the glass bend visibly. Farrell began telling me a story of his early days in America, just after "the War", as he called his terrible war. He talked and at one point put his hand on my sleeve, he poked my hand with a finger to make a point, eventually rested his hand for several seconds on mine. I leaned back in the booth and a general drowsiness washed over me. My lungs seemed to open up, and I sucked in a breath so deep it left me giddy, and I coughed, not so painfully now. The turmoil in my stomach began to settle and I stretched out my legs, aware that for the first time in days my knee had stopped throbbing.

I knew what he had done, that the story had been merely a pretext. In my own long-ago past, in what seemed another man's life I had seen the power of his hands more than once, and he had used it now on me. Years before, he had intruded himself into my life, violated my life, as I saw it, and now he had imposed himself into my life again. Another man might have been enraged, but I doubt it. I feared my impending death, Farrell was right about that. He had caught me in free fall, and I had no doubt he had been looking for me. How he managed to track me down on Skid Row, how he even knew I was back in Chicago, was merely a manifestation of his peculiar gifts.

The room closed in on us. I was conscious of the night sounds of a small diner, the clanging of pots against a hard sink in the kitchen, the clatter of plates, the tough small talk between waitress and short order cook. I lost all track of time and the waitress was in no hurry for us to leave. I drank more coffee and then had a piece of peach pie. Farrell sipped his tea, bantered in his quiet way with the waitress, whom he called "Young Lady," and eventually ordered rye toast for himself, with marmalade. "A lovely girl," he pronounced her, though she'd never see fifty again. He made a child's long face when he tasted the marmalade – he'd always told me you couldn't get a proper marmalade outside of Ireland.

He ate and spoke, but the night and the late hour wore him down at last, and the silence between us was like a labored breathing. Finally I saw a place for my question.

"I thought I saw something tonight. In a tavern."

"What did you see?"

"People. A tavern filled with people, in a place that's probably been empty for ten years. And I've seen other things, too," I began, then stopped, unwilling to give voice to these things. He nodded and frowned as though this made troubling sense.

"You have these too, don't you?"

He shook his head and said, "Your visions are all your own, lad. 'Tis the way of it."

"The way of what, Farrell?" I heard the hostility in my own voice. In a calmer tone I asked, "The way of what? What would you call it – whatever is happening to me, or whatever you've caused in me?"

"I? No, lad. I've nothing to do with this. You still have – questions about me."

"You might say that, Farrell. Yeah, *questions*."

He grew silent then. I'd managed to kill conversation, but he had always been comfortable with long silences. I caught him studying me, assessing the damage, no doubt, but something else as well. He had something more to say, something to ask me, and he was reluctant to speak of it.

Finally I asked, "What have you been doing since the shop closed?"

"Closed? No, not closed. I've merely moved it. I have a shop now on Clark Street. Up by the Cathedral. You should come by."

He spoke the last words carefully, diplomatically. I wanted to say something but began coughing and he waited, concern in his face, until I was finished.

"You should wear a muffler around your neck, boy. Keep your throat covered or you'll have pneumonia to add to your troubles."

I think I smiled at that, at his well-meaning suggestions for my health, at his odd speech – "muffler" for a scarf, and his old country pronunciation, "throath" for "throat." But I said nothing and after a few seconds of his own silence he went on.

"And Meyer – well, Meyer we've already discussed," he added. He stared off in the direction of the street for a time. It struck me that I might offer some small consolation here, that I might remind him that there was little chance that harm could have come to Meyer, for I believed him to be, in the most fundamental sense, nearly indestructible. But Farrell knew that as well as I did, and indestructible or not, Meyer was apparently gone.

Before we left he tried to give me money. I refused and he stuffed a bill in my pocket. We parted without any talk of further meetings. As I left it struck me that Farrell had not asked me whatever he'd wanted to ask back there.

Once into the wind again I coughed, but it was a reaction to the cold air. My lungs were better, I no longer felt sick. I reflected on what he'd done to my physical condition. I had seen Farrell do things that suggested abilities uncommon to the species, seen him heal injuries great and small and once I am certain I saw him revive a dying man. Time and again I had seen him work his unsettling changes in what I understood as reality.

And try though I might, I could not suppress the recollection of another chill night, of Farrell coming out of an alley where he'd left a man dead, dead, I had no doubt, of the touch of those same hands. I wondered not for the first time about the nature of evil, and Arthur Farrell's relation to it. But I was too tired and in truth too grateful for what he'd wrought on me to think much about it tonight. I put my head down into the stinging wind and made my way to the barren room on Green Street where I was still attempting to cling to the world. I slipped past the landlord's door and into my room. With fingers stiff from cold I untied my sodden shoes, then looked around at my room. It was little bigger than a closet, it smelled of ruin, and I was suddenly aware of every shabby detail of it as though my vision had somehow been sharpened. The sordidness of it, the realization of how far I'd fallen, became oppressive, and I wept. And I am certain that this final vision of the evening, this sudden confronting of my own reality, was the night's last small gift from Arthur Farrell.

Twenty: A Task

After that night, I did not seek Farrell out again for several weeks. Despite his small kindnesses, our encounter had the effect of reawakening old fears, and I decided to avoid him. But perhaps our meeting had been fortuitous in other ways. I seemed to catch a second wind.

I hit the pavement the day after my encounter with Farrell and decided to take whatever work I came across. Not far from the diner where I'd let Farrell buy me food, I found a day labor place and made a few bucks on different work crews. I lucked into a job down at the Haymarket, where a guy with a heavy Greek accent gave me $25 a day to unload trucks of produce. I got three weeks' pay out of him, then turned around and blew half of it on a car. It seemed the most remarkable piece of luck, a way into a new life, and I recalled the long ago moment when Roy's purchase of a car had signaled to us that we had managed some small prosperity. My car was a '63 Buick with bald tires near to bursting, and just the right color: an unlikely amber that hid the rust gnawing at it. I thought of climbing into the Buick and taking off. And in my darker moments I told myself that a fellow with a car would always have a place to sleep, come Hell or high water.

Eventually the bleakness of my prospects wore me down: I was perhaps two days' minimum wage from being evicted from my room on Green Street, just about that far from living in the Buick. Late one afternoon I decided to find Farrell's new digs.

The slush of March was gone, and with it, finally, all trace of winter but the wind blew like February and smelled of fish. I knew the shop would be on a certain rundown stretch of Clark Street – trendy and gentrified now but the seediest of streets then, rows of desolate taverns and pawnbrokers and junk shops. On every block there was at least one building that would collapse before anyone got around to rehabbing it. There were bookstores here, for some reason, three or four of them, as if this were the place where old books went to die. On my peregrinations I'd been inside most of them, had even been thrown out of one by its paranoid owner who decided I was either stickup man or shoplifter. He was a small thin man who smelled of sweat and watched me with the eyes of a raptor.

I drove slowly up Clark Street and then I saw the shop. It was on the east side of the street, and I let out a gasp. I pulled over and stared at it. It was the same shop: not just the business, the shop itself. It was the same in every possible detail, the same hand-printed sign, the same window display in the same storefront, in the same low, flat building. On the weathered wood just inside the doorway I could make out the old tin thermometer with its faded salute to Birely's soda. It was the same shop.

I parked and crossed the street, oblivious to traffic, expecting as I got closer a clarified image to show me that I had just imagined things, but it was true, it was the same shop, down to the smallest detail, here some four miles from the original.

Farrell was behind the counter, paging through a guide to old coins, and he squinted at my backlit image to see who I was.

"Well, young Thomas, so you – "

Before he could say the rest of it, I said, "How did you do this?"

"What?"

"It's the same shop."

"'Tis. A grand location, why I'm right down here just a stone's throw from Marshall Field's and the other fine stores."

I ignored his wishful thinking about this street of dead places. Marshall Field's, the *Grande Dame* of Chicago stores, was in the Loop, on the far side of the river and it might as well have been in another state.

"No, that's not what I meant, it's the exact same place it was on Addison. Like you just moved it through the air."

"Through the air, is it?" He gave his silent laugh. "How would I do that?"

"My question."

"I don't understand." He frowned, shook his head. "But come sit down, have some coffee – do you have time for a cup of coffee? I have some back there."

Indeed, the air in the shop had the scorched smell of coffee to take the barnacles off ships, but it sounded, as he would say, *"Grand"*.

"Sounds good, Farrell."

He busied himself with the coffee and as he did so, an odd buzzing sound came from the rear. It took me a few moments to realize that this was Farrell humming tunelessly.

He knew enough not to pry, and he had little interest in small talk. And so he let me drink my coffee, and then I realized why I had come.

"Last time we talked, I think you had something to ask me. What was it?"

"Ah," he said, as though just remembering. "And so I did. I wondered if you would do something for me."

I looked around the shop and he laughed. "Not around here, lad, I don't need an apprentice in the business. But I am in need of a favor."

"What kind of favor?" I began, and already an odd look had come into his eyes, a look that might have given me pause if I'd had the time to think about it.

He ran his hand across his hair. "It concerns Meyer."

"What about him?"

"I want you to find him. I'll pay you for your time."

"You told me you didn't know where he was."

"True, true. No one knows where he is. But I have some ideas on the subject."

"No, I mean, how would I begin to look for him?"

"Well, I'm sure you'd figure it out, you've done this sort of work, it's just the sort of thing you're good at."

"Where would I even look?"

"Well, various places. Around the country."

"Around the country? You want me to go wandering around the country? What do you think I've been doing all this time?"

"I don't know that I'd call it wandering. And I should think the idea would appeal to you, you'd have a task to accomplish, d'you see?"

"If it's such a great idea, why don't you – "

"Because I am too old. I cannot do this."

I looked away. He had never spoken this way of himself and I wasn't sure what it meant.

"I am not Meyer. You are a young blood, you can do this. And why not?"

He looked at me under his great thatch of eyebrows and did not have to explain the question. Why not indeed, since I was little more than a derelict?

"I don't know." After a moment I said, "I'll think about it, Farrell."

"That's all I ask," he said, and took my cup to freshen my coffee. When he came back, I made a show of changing the subject, and even as I did so, I understood that I would do this for him and that he knew it as well.

I asked him about the old customers and street people, and he began to relate their stories. Once or twice I laughed, for the first time in many months. I felt myself relaxing in his company. At some point I began talking, about where my life had gone, about my hardest moments on the road, my fears, my experiences both terrifying and puzzling, the strange glimpses into other lives, my troubling "visions", and if I said a single thing that shocked or surprised him, he never showed it. I spoke of my mother and her barren life, I told him of the ambush that morning in the clearing, what had transpired, about watching the boy beside me die, trying to prevent his death, console him; I told him how close I felt I had come to death, how I felt I was near death now. He urged me on, encouraged me, said just enough to make it a conversation but never enough to halt my torrent of words. And finally,

280

I never saw it coming, I wept. Not at any particular story I was telling him or at any personal suffering of my own, or even at the memory of my mother, but I wept for it all, I wept as though overcome by the world's innate sadness. And when I was done I was of course mortified. Dumbstruck with embarrassment, I got up to leave.

"Sit down, boy, sit down."

"I don't know what's going on with me."

"There's no shame in crying, lad. I envy you."

"What? What's there to envy?"

"Tears are catharsis. I long ago lost my ability to weep."

I looked around me then, at the remarkable sameness of the old shop, improbably turning up in another part of town like the leavings of Dorothy's tornado. I was about to ask once more about the shop, then saw the truer question beneath it.

"What's happening to me?"

"Ah, you've just had a hard time of it."

"That's not what I mean. What's happening to me? Am I losing my mind? The things I've been –experiencing – "

"And why would I know?"

"You if anyone, Farrell."

"I know what you know, lad. You are in a period of change in your life. Your way of interacting with the world is changing."

"My *way of interacting*? God, Farrell, I'm seeing things, I told you that, hallucinations, for Christ's sake. Jesus, that's the one thing I couldn't bear, if I knew I was losing my mind."

"We all have moments when we fear we've lost our

hold on reality. In truth, every man has a time when he's not fully sane. You're as sane as the next fellow, Thomas."

The doubt was clear in his voice. I laughed then, and a look of relief came into his eyes, and I saw that I'd reassured him in some small measure about my mental state.

"You'll be all right, lad. I'm sure of it."

It struck me that this was a rare vulnerable moment, a time to ask my many questions about him. In the end I came at him obliquely, asking instead about the other great puzzle we knew in common.

"What's his story, Farrell?"

"Whose? Meyer's story? You mean, why is he the way he is?"

"Something like that."

"He has seen too much of the world, too much of humanity, far more than you can imagine."

"Meaning what?"

He gave me an annoyed look. "I think you know. He has seen the kinds of things that calcify the heart, many things, and terrible. And he has been able to do nothing to change or stop what he has seen."

"I would bet you've seen pretty much what he's seen."

"Not precisely. Meyer has led an eventful life. An involved life. He has made choices and decisions I have not. They have – " I watched his cautious search for a word. He settled for " – changed him."

"How?"

"So many questions, Thomas."

"You want something from me, you need to answer my questions. So. Changed him how?"

"His experiences and his actions diminished him. Sapped him."

I misunderstood. "Have you ever thought, then, that maybe because of all of that, he's just crazy, that no matter how understandable his reaction, that he's simply insane?"

"I suppose Meyer has his moments when, by most people's measure, he is not quite sane. Most people do not march into a crowded church to harangue the priest in the midst of a service. But as you grow older, you will come to see that 'sane' and 'insane' are elusive concepts."

"Is he dangerous?"

"I think you know the answer to that yourself." He raised the eyebrows again and I wondered if Meyer had told him of that long-ago fight in the bloody snow with the two punks, and who had witnessed it.

"Tell me this, then: who is he?" And the subtext: *And who are you?*

"He is an old man who has outlived most of the people he ever knew. He is just Meyer. He is who he is. And he is who you see. He is an old, very angry fellow refusing to 'go gently into that good night,' as Dylan Thomas wrote. Quite literally, in Meyer's case. Do you know that poem?"

"Only from hearing it quoted. I still don't read much poetry, Farrell. I know you tried, but it didn't take. I've just never seen the use." The last part was a lie, something I threw in to annoy him. We both knew how much poetry he'd selectively sent my way, and that most of it had taken hold of me the way he'd intended, Dickinson and Owen and Hardy and all of them.

He muttered something about my stubbornness.

"You told me once Meyer was angry with God."

"Not far from the mark, that."

"And you, Farrell, are you angry with God?"

"What would be the point?"

I snorted. "Is there a God, even?"

"You would know as much as I would about that." He smiled. "It seems we've had this conversation before, long ago."

"Yeah, more than once. You answered in riddles or referred me to weird old books. But I want to know: do you believe in God? Any kind of God?"

"On certain days, I do, yes. On others, I hope there is one. In my darkest moments, I fear there is not."

"What kind of God do you believe in?"

He gave me a surprised smile. "What an excellent question. The road and your – experiences have made you thoughtful. Well. What are the possibilities, Thomas? The old one is of course a God who is all-powerful, all-knowing, who is in all places simultaneously." Farrell frowned and looked off into the room. "Another is the one imagined by some of the Gnostic sects in ancient times, that there were actually two gods, the older vengeful God of the Old Testament and the newer God, the benevolent deity of the New Testament. The possibility then follows of gods locked in struggle with each other. 'Tis also possible that a god-being created the universe and died, or ceased to exist."

"God is dead, right? Who said that, Nietzsche?"

"He was speaking figuratively. He wasn't a believer in any sort of God. But there are many possibilities to consider. Perhaps God does indeed exist in a heaven of some sort, or a place beyond us, in another dimension.

There is even the possibility that a god of some sort lives amongst us, and is not a creator but a being of power or knowledge beyond ours. That he lives amongst us and we are not even aware of his presence. The possibilities are endless: a benevolent God or a powerless God or an interested bystander of a God. A God who merely watches our lives transpire or a God who takes sides, helps when he can. A God who controls all things or a God who has lost his power. Multiple gods, dead gods. Even a sorely tried God, a God who is up against it, as the saying goes."

"But you're convinced there probably is a God?"

"Convinced is too strong a word. Inclined to believe, because of what I take to be the evidence for him."

"Where have you ever seen evidence of God?"

He gave me his look, he knew I was baiting him. I could see him debating half a dozen responses. Then an amused look came into his eyes and he said, "Meyer."

"Meyer? Jesus, I don't think he even believes in God."

"When you know more of Meyer you will understand what I mean."

"Meyer is your proof that there's a God?"

"Proof? What a single-minded bucko you are! There's proof of nothing, my boy, read the great philosophers, read enough of those lads, Kant and Hegel and Schopenhauer and the rest, and they'll make a fine mush of your brain, they'll have you doubting your own existence."

"So Meyer reassures you there's a God?' He shrugged.

"What else?"

"Other – things I've seen. A couple of acquaintances I've made over the years." He stopped and looked at me, and I was certain he had just stopped himself from adding, "*And you.*" In the end, he smiled and said, "And the Rings of Saturn. Yes, the rings."

I remembered his telescope, Meyer ridiculing him for it.

"You still have the telescope?"

"Indeed I do. And on clear nights I use it. Sometimes I walk down to the lake where the city lights aren't so strong and I set it up. People think I'm the great eccentric, or they think I'm some sort of local astronomer. There's a fisherman down there who addresses me as 'Professor'."

"What's special about Saturn? I mean, I know about the rings – they're just rocks and debris. Gravity keeps them in place."

"Rocks and debris and gravity, indeed." He smiled. "See them yourself sometime, Thomas. Then tell me what you think. Speak to me then of gravity, lad."

Our talk began to wander but we kept at it, talked deep into the night, and at some point I fell asleep. Several times I awoke: once to find him leaning forward in his chair and looking at me, with concern. Another time I opened my eyes and he dozed in his chair, and I saw that he had covered me with a scratchy Army surplus blanket. In the morning he fed me toast slathered with butter and his cherished marmalade, and hot tea thickened with milk and sugar. When I was finished I told him I had to go home and change. It was understood that I had agreed to do what he'd asked.

When I returned there were customers – Little Ray, shooting the breeze about the old days, and a stranger ogling the lurid cover art on Farrell's paperback books.

286

Little Ray greeted me shyly, then withdrew from the field as Farrell and I tended to our business.

He gave me a piece of paper covered on one side with his writing.

"Here."

"Here what?"

"Well, you'll need to know where you're going. Here are the places to look."

I scanned the list – to this day I can see it, the old-fashioned cursive of another time, a script I would see on old postcards addressed to *"Molly McAvoy, 145 S. Wabash, the City,"* or *"Mrs. Annie Blakely, Genoa City."* And like all other things he wrote, it was in pencil. It was a list of names and places, and before I could even ask him about them, he had pulled the paper from my hand to add another.

"Mannheit," he said to himself. "That was the fellow. Don't recall the first name, though."

He did the thing with the pencil I'd seen both my parents do, touched the pencil to his tongue and added the last name. Then he handed me an envelope thick with money, like a Mafia don commissioning misdeeds.

"There, now. You've got what you need. You may wire me for more if it runs out."

I studied his list. Bergson, no first name given, Arlene Roenicke, Georg Glasner, and Mannheit. Bergson's address was given as a retirement home in Racine, Wisconsin. Arlene Roenicke lived on Bell Street in Galena, Illinois. Glasner lived in Sheridan, Wyoming. Mannheit was listed in Belton, Montana. Only Arlene Roenicke had an address.

"This is it?"

He blinked with the effort of remembering – the first time he'd ever seemed old to me.

"There was a fellow named Bednarik."

"No address for him or these other ones? What – do they live in refrigerator cartons in the alleys?"

"There aren't any alleys in some of these places."

"How do you expect me to find these people?"

"You will use your wits, your well-honed but not always utilized wits. You will rely on the skills acquired on your many travels." I heard the slight emphasis on *travels*, his polite euphemism for *while you were on the bum*. "And you will have an opportunity to use your knowledge of detective work."

Now he was amusing himself.

"All I learned about detective work is that I'm no good at it." I studied his list again. "None of them east of here."

"He would not go east. It is the direction he came from."

"So who are these people?"

"His friends."

"His *friends*?"

"You have trouble believing he could have friends. You still don't care for Meyer."

"Who would?"

"Consider the man's situation, Thomas. Put yourself in his circumstances. If you'd seen what he has seen of humanity, of this world, if you had outlived anyone you ever cared for, you might be a hard man as well. If you knew a little about Meyer's past – well, I don't promise that you'd like him, but you would think of him in a different way."

"What about you, Farrell?"

"What do you mean? Am I fond of old Meyer?" Farrell made a small sideways nod. "He is like a difficult younger brother, a mulish, contentious, intemperate, intractable, most difficult brother."

"Well, I don't know anything about Meyer, I don't know what he has seen. I only know what he is."

Farrell half turned and gave me a long look. "Someday he will take you into his – confidence."

"I'm not looking forward to it."

He shrugged, nodded, looked away. At that moment I was close to asking him the things I'd wondered about for years. But he gave me his back and there was a message there. He'd done me kindnesses, and it was clear that I owed him something. Perhaps when I'd performed this task, or at least tried, he'd owe me, and that would be my moment.

"Sometime, Farrell, after all of this is done – "

He watched me to see how I would phrase this.

" – I have questions." I thought of a dead man in an alley. "As I'm sure you know."

"All in good time," he said, his tone polite, evasive, dismissive.

"All right, Farrell." I held up the list. "And you believe he is with one of these people."

He hesitated before answering. "In the past he has gone away for weeks or months at a time. Without a destination, I believe. But if he has actually gone to seek out someone, it would be one of the people on your list."

"And if I don't find him?"

"Cut your losses, then, lad. Come home."

"And then we'll talk about other things."

"Sure, lad," he said, as he'd speak to a child who asked too many questions.

I looked again at the four locations and pictured a map in my head. "Exploring the frontier in search of Meyer. I feel like Lewis and Clark. I hope my car holds up."

"What sort of car is it?"

"A Buick."

"Ah, well, those are lovely cars. Do they still have the nostril-things along the side?"

"Sure."

"I had a Buick once."

"I can't picture you driving, Farrell."

"Ah, well. I drove it into a tree, you see."

I had a sudden image of a terrified Farrell holding the steering wheel in a death's grip as it ran into a tree trunk, and I laughed.

Later that night as I collected my meager belongings for my trip, I thought of what Farrell had said about Meyer, about his solitary life, about being the last, and wondered if he was taking a rare opportunity, not simply to enlighten me about his difficult companion but to explain, if only in the most reluctant, the most circuitous way, something about himself. And when I'd put some miles between myself and Chicago, it was plain enough that the search for Meyer was to accomplish several purposes, and not the least of these was giving me a chance recover something of myself.

290

Twenty-One: Bergson

1 found Bergson without much effort. The retirement home smelled strongly of disinfectant and roach killer and had the unfortunate-sounding name "Setting Sun Homes". I wondered if the name reflected an owner with an unholy sense of humor.

Bergson – first name "Edwin," the young attendant at the desk informed me – was sitting on a bench in the common area on the second floor. He was alone, perched at one end of the bench as though leaving room for me. A few feet away, a pair of women slept leaning against one another on a second bench.

"Mr. Bergson?"

He blinked, looked straight ahead, his gaze missing me. He blinked again and eventually found me, and smiled.

"Hello, son."

For a moment I couldn't speak, and Bergson simply held that smile, showing crooked teeth and a gold filling. His hair was white, the whitest hair I was ever to see in life, and it fell across his forehead and nearly hid one eye. Blue eyes, bright, a boy's eyes. His skin was red, as though he'd been in the wind and elements so long they'd stained him, and he was big – wasting now with age but in his youth he had been a tall man, heavily-built. His hands were enormous.

"Hello," I said.

"I don't know you, I don't think. Can't always remember who I know and who I don't," he said, and laughed silently.

"I'm a friend of Meyer's. Do you remember – "

"Meyer! Crazy Meyer. I wonder if he's dead now."

"Maybe not. I'm trying to find him. I'm looking for his old friends, anybody that might have seen him. So he didn't come to see you?"

"I don't think so. Why don't you sit down here," he said, patting the bench, and I realized I was down on one knee in front of him.

I took a spot on his bench and we looked at each other. He hadn't stopped smiling. In another bench-bound old timer I would have assumed senility, or perhaps simple giddiness at a visitor, but there was something else behind the smile. I would have been hard pressed to give it a name: simple kindness came close but it was something more.

He waited for me to speak again and I was about to explain my fool's errand when he surprised me.

"You've had a hard time of it, haven't you, son?"

Embarrassed and off-balance, all I could say was "Ups and downs, you know. Like anybody else."

"You're not like anybody else, though. Everybody's different. You've had a tough time, and you're alone, and you have no home." He seemed to remember where he was. I watched him look around at the dark hall of the retirement home and I wondered if he was content to be here or horrified when he recalled where he now resided. Then he surprised me again, he patted me on the shoulder.

"But you'll be all right. Probably not soon, doesn't ever really happen that way, does it?"

"No, it sure doesn't."

"So you know Meyer."

"I do."

"And he's not dead?"

"Well, I don't know. He might be."

"Should've been dead three or four times over. You know that, don't you?"

"I've heard something about that, yes. I was hoping he'd been here."

"Could have been. He's been here before. I have no concept of time, you see. And I don't know if I could do anything for him. What will you do now?"

"I have other places to look. Other people: a woman named Roenicke, someone named Glasner. Mannheit?" I watched him but these names meant nothing to him.

"Why are you doing this? A young man like yourself?"

"I told someone I would. Farrell."

"Ah, Farrell's looking for him." He nodded as though this explained much.

"Do you know Farrell?"

"Of course." He regarded me as though he were observing something about me, then added, "And now I know you."

Bergson closed his eyes, still smiling, and in a few seconds he was asleep. I looked down and saw his big red hand on the bench and put mine over it. I spoke to him but

293

he didn't open his eyes, and for no reason that I could have explained I decided it was only proper to stay there, to keep this sleeping old man company. For a while I watched him in sleep, and gradually I sank back against the hard back of the bench and closed my eyes. I drifted off, and dreamt. In my dream I saw a young soldier sitting on a boulder at the edge of a wood. He was filthy, his uniform torn. An American soldier, and of course when I managed to make out his features through the grime and a heavy growth of beard, it was Bergson. His rifle leaned against the boulder, and in his hand he held an unlit cigarette. Around him was nothing but death. The bodies of half a dozen doughboys lay where they had fallen, and ten or more German soldiers lay among them, corpses in khaki, corpses in gray. In my dream it was clear that Bergson alone had survived this, the horror of hand-to-hand killing. And then I saw movement among the dead. One of the Germans rolled painfully onto his side, then onto his chest. He raised his head and looked around him, a terrified-looking man made boyish by a shock of red hair. When he saw Bergson he climbed to his knees and felt around for his rifle. At almost the exact moment that the German found his weapon, Bergson saw him.

The German got to his feet and brought his rifle up. Bergson stood and picked up his rifle, casually, and held it across his chest. Then he stared at the German. The other man wet his lips and took a step back, white-knuckled grip on the rifle. Bergson met the German's nervous eyes, then looked around him at the clearing. He looked at each dead man in turn, then back at the German, and though his lips never moved I heard him speak, I heard him say, *I will kill no more*. He cradled his rifle and met the German's gaze, and then the German bolted into the forest, helmetless and terrified and, I now saw, bleeding from a wound near his neck. Bergson sat down again and this time he lit the cigarette.

In the dream the world was enveloped in darkness and fog, broken only by the sliver of the moon. Shapes emerged from the dark, soldiers moving, plodding, mindless, faint with exhaustion. And I saw that one of the men was an older Bergson. They trudged along and gradually one man a few yards ahead of the rest said something and I saw several of the men go through the tired motions of bringing their weapons up. They came to a stop and watched something ahead of them. Refugees. Half a dozen skeletal men, two with weapons: partisans. In their midst, two of them supported a third, a bony corpse of a man in a bloody jacket. One of the armed men moved up closer to the Americans, a strange small man, little more than a boy he seemed, with long arms and bulging eyes, and I understood that he would fight all these well-fed GIs if need be. This man looked Bergson in the eye, nodded and stepped back. I saw Bergson push forward to examine the wounded man. As he peered at this man in the gloom the wounded man raised his head as though waking to a new sound. And even before he showed his face, I knew that this man so near death was Meyer. The other men, soldiers and partisans both, crowded around him, and I knew from the looks in the eyes of the GIs that they were seeing in Meyer's half-closed eyes what I had more than once seen there: violence, the purest hostility, something more, something they might have called evil. In my dream, Bergson stepped forward and examined Meyer's wounds. His face was calm, and I had the distinct sense that he had expected this dark encounter on a foggy road.

I woke disoriented. Bergson was still out, and an amused-looking young woman in white ignored my embarrassment and told me Bergson would sleep that way until dinner, which wasn't for another hour and a half. She anticipated my indecision.

"He won't remember you were here. He'll think you just arrived." Then she laughed, a lovely laugh that made my heart ache because this small-town nurse was not of my world. "And you'll have to have the whole conversation all over again." I laughed with her and her face changed slightly. I don't know what she saw, but I sensed her pity for me, and was mildly humiliated. Her glance went from the sleeping Bergson to me.

"He's the best thing for you."

I blinked and for a moment thought to correct her, to point out that the visitor was usually the tonic for the patient, especially in a place like that, but I had the feeling that she'd somehow seen into me. I could also see that she was embarrassed by what she'd said. Mumbling about her many tasks she hurried away.

I stayed for a while longer, studying the white-haired man on the bench beside me, and was certain he was soon to die. When it was clear he would not wake up any earlier than predicted, I took leave, reluctant leave of Edwin Bergson.

Twenty-Two: Roenicke

From Racine, Wisconsin I drove the web of country blacktop to Galena, Illinois — river country. In another age, it was Grant's town, the place he retired to, now a tourist town just a few miles from the Mississippi. It is built onto bluffs, its main streets connected at intervals by improbably high staircases. There are no skyscrapers, high rises, or even arches of gold.

I found Arlene Roenicke easily, for hers was the lone address Farrell had provided: a small corner tavern at the far end of one of the main streets. The tavern was called "Elmer's". Like the town it inhabited, Elmer's was a time capsule.

Every face in the room turned when I pushed my way past the heavy door. A roomful of men, none of them young: one or two didn't like my looks but I hadn't started trouble yet so no one stared long, that is except the woman at the end of the bar. Indeed, I had the feeling that half the men in the bar had been looking at her before I walked in, and now merely resumed looking. She was pushing 60, give or take, no beauty, and I would have bet solid money she had never been one. But there was something riveting in the face, more than anything else in the eyes. I'd seen such eyes in children, eyes that danced in anticipation, whether of fun or devilment. If you weren't looking directly at Arlene Roenicke's eyes, she was a forbidding figure: well over six feet tall, big-boned and angular, with a wide mouth that might have been startling in itself without the splash of dark red lipstick. Her hair was dyed an improbable red to match the lipstick and was kept out of trouble in a hairnet. I hadn't seen one since my days in Millie's diner. When I stopped in the empty center of her bar, she called out, "You gonna stand there or join us?" Her voice surprised me, a younger woman's voice, a bit hard, sure of itself.

The man on the nearest stool said, "We don't bite," and someone laughed.

"That's what they all say," I told him, and this was apparently the proper response, for the man next to him smiled and winked at me.

"Got a wiseguy, fellas," the woman said. "Wiseguy in an Army jacket. Sit down and take a load off, smart aleck."

To make conversation I asked what sort of beer she carried, and saw as soon as it was out of my mouth that she would have fun with this, too.

"Got cold beer. Got beer that's not so cold. Got cases of beer out back in the sun, so that's actually hot."

I glanced up and down the bar and saw what they were all drinking, and ordered a Blue Ribbon. This seemed to convince them I was of their species and they all went back to their talk and their business. As the woman served me, I looked around and waited to speak.

"What else, my young road-weary friend?"

"Well, I'm looking for Arlene Roenicke."

"Nice work. You found her. We haven't met, so why were you looking for me?"

"I was told you could help me track down a guy named Meyer."

"That so? And what do you want with an old man like Meyer?"

The voice had changed, gotten older and lost its humor, and I could tell without looking that a couple of the men had renewed their interest in me.

"Me, personally, nothing. But I told his friend I'd try to find him."

"This friend – "

"Farrell, another old guy."

She nodded. "In Chicago."

"Where I'm from."

She shrugged. "When you're not wandering. You do a lot of wandering."

"You read minds or what?"

"I know the look." She grinned and took twenty years off her face. "I know all the looks, kid."

A man down the bar held up his empty bottle and she was gone, not to come back for nearly ten minutes. This was the time it took her to serve a beer, listen to a joke and top it with one of her own. When she came back I decided it was time to talk.

"So how much did I miss him by?"

"Who says he was ever here?"

"Your face when I mentioned his name."

Another smile. "Not bad." She lit a cigarette – a Lucky, unfiltered, like somebody out of a forties movie. She smoked while she considered whether to lie to me, then made a little shrug and said "You missed him by a couple of weeks. He didn't stay long. Never does."

"I can't imagine him in a place like this."

"Actually he likes the country. But what's inside of him keeps him around people most of the time. I know," she said when I rolled my eyes at this. "I know, least sociable guy on earth, he's got the sociability of a mass murderer. But it's what he needs because – well, it's what he needs."

She gave me a look and I knew she'd just decided to withhold information.

"So why would he come here in the first place?"

"To visit a good-looking girl," she said, and plucked at the elastic of her hairnet. "No. We knew each other in the old days."

"In what old days?"

"The war. I was a nurse."

A customer called out to her and she left. Deliberately she stayed at that end of the bar for the next fifteen minutes. When she finally returned she had made up her mind not to speak to me.

"Another beer?"

"Can you tell me – "

"No. I can't tell you anything. That's not what this place is for, kid. People come here to get things off their chests, to have somebody listen to them, be nice to them if they got nowhere else like that. Not to get information. You wanta ask people private things, be a cop."

"I wouldn't pass the physical."

She shrugged: not her problem. I finished my beer and left. I found a tiny grill up the street and had the same

300

hamburger I could have had in any diner in Chicago, and then I walked around Galena, gradually becoming aware that I was as out of place there as I could have been anywhere. It was a pretty place, even in the growing dusk, just narrow streets and old buildings packed next to one another, and long stone staircases to take you up the side of the hill to the next narrow winding street. It was too early in the year for the tourists, and I am certain I stood out, with my limp and the army jacket and hair that hadn't been cut in months. But the natives went about their business. I wondered what they had made of Meyer.

I climbed the stairs all the way up, until I was at the highest level and could see not only the old town below but the hilltops around it and the river, and although I have been the outsider in more places than it is healthy for me to recall, I have never felt more alone. I would not have been surprised if the place closed in upon itself as soon as I left and disappeared, like Brigadoon's plain sister. After a while I went back down to the main street and peered in antique store windows and killed time. At about ten-fifteen the last customer left Elmer's Tavern, and the tavern went dark. I could see her straightening up inside, putting the stools upside down on the bar. I saw her lean against the bar for a moment to catch her breath.

I knocked on the door.

"We're closed," she yelled over one shoulder.

I knocked again. She turned, impatient, taking no shit, but her face fell when she saw me. She hesitated. I nodded toward the stools and she came and opened the door.

"I got nothing for you, kid."

"You need a porter, lady."

301

"Can't afford one."

"You can afford one that works for free." I pushed past her and began putting up the stools.

She leaned on the bar, watched me as she smoked, and finally said, "He headed west. That what you want from me? Headed west. He likes it there, I think."

I continued putting the heavy stools on the bar without comment, and she misunderstood my silence.

"He wouldn't tell me where he's going – I don't even think he knows, poor thing."

I put the last one on the bar. "Where's your broom?"

"I'll get it." She came out of a back room with an old pushbroom. "I'll take care of this mess here," she said, indicating a pool at the far end of the bar. She sprinkled cleaning compound on it and it began to cake a dull orange color.

I began sweeping. "Learned to do this in a Chicago diner. And 'west' I think I could have figured out myself. What I think I'd like to know is why."

"Why do you need to know that? What's that to you?"

"I have no idea. I'm going to look for him one way or the other, I told Farrell I would. But I'd like to know – I want to know about Meyer."

She went behind the bar and came out with a beer for me. Then she made herself a drink, Evan Williams on the rocks.

"I don't know much more than you do. I don't know if anybody does – except for this Farrell."

"Do you know him?"

"No. He sent me a letter once. When Meyer went off on one of these – when Meyer disappeared for a while.

302

Sounded like a courtly old gentleman from another time."

"Sometimes he is. Other times I'm not so sure. So you met Meyer when you were a nurse." She tightened slightly and another thought came to me. "You nursed him."

"I nursed a lot of guys. Some of them made it and went home, some didn't make it out of the tent." She rattled the ice cubes, sipped her bourbon and went on posing.

"How many of them do you remember?"

"Most of the ones that died, they were so young. And like that, in a foreign country so far from their homes. Broke my heart. I wanted to quit. Actually did once, just started walking, walking out of Germany. Got almost two miles, too, before they stopped me. Bunch of GIs saw me crying and looking a little bit crazy, and turned me around."

"But you remember Meyer."

She looked at me now. "Oh, honey, if you were there, you'd remember him, too. I saw worse wounds, I saw boys shot open, boys with half their faces gone. I saw a nurse get the top of her body blown off. But I never saw anything like this, I never saw the *damage* in one human body that was still breathing. He'd been shot, him and a handful of other men for being partisans or Jews or maybe both. S.S., I think, on the run from our guys. They did that all over Europe when it looked like they were going to lose: they tried to kill people faster, all those Jews, POWs, everybody. Some of 'em, they shot knowing we were a couple hours' march away. Only reason we found anybody alive at the camps is the Nazis ran out of time." She shook her head, then recovered.

"Bunch of our guys brought him in with half a dozen

other men, partisans, you know. None of them in good shape, but one guy with a chest wound, a bad one, and we strip off his shirt which is just rags, and there's the bullet hole, seeping blood, but there's all these other holes, these scars, this old guy's been shot and slashed and stabbed it looks like half a dozen times. And old. An old man, even then. Looked sixties easy, maybe older."

She looked at me, daring me to question this. When I said nothing, she went on. "So we're trying to stop the bleeding from this hole that should have killed him and I – I see these scars and holes and it just seems like one man should not go through this much. I guess I must have been frozen there and the doctor notices. He's just turned from one patient to another, his hands are bloody from the last kid he worked on, and he looks at me and says 'Nurse?' and I just say 'look at him.' And he gives me this look, I see he's going to humor me, and he looks at Meyer and says 'My God.' And he starts working on Meyer. We worked for half an hour to find the bullet, then we couldn't stop the bleeding, then we get him bandaged and the doctor looks at him and shakes his head. He looks at me and I swear, that arrogant asshole, this was the only time I ever saw him without all the answers. Then he's off to another bleeding guy. And I stood there looking at this old man, we had cut off his shirt by this time so even with all the bandaging you could see the scars. And I could see places where he was still a little bloody, so I started wiping him off with a towel and next thing I knew, I was crying, dripping tears on this poor sonofabitch. And he woke up. He opened his eyes and said something like 'What's wrong?' He mumbled it but I heard it, and it was English, which took me by surprise. The ones that brought him in didn't know English. And I just looked at him. The guy's dying on a cot and he wants to know about me.

"So I told him I was okay but that I was just a little worried about him, he needed to rest and not talk. And he gave me this look, this street-wise look that said he could tell when somebody was bullshitting.

"'Stop crying,' he says. Then he goes back to sleep.

"We had to move after that, the Army was pushing the Germans back and the hospital units had to keep up, more or less, so we left those wounded behind. But I visited a couple of them, real young kids, teenagers we're talking about here. And Meyer. I told him the Army was moving and the staff were going too.

"'Wish I was going with 'em,' he says. At first I thought he meant he wanted to be with the same medical staff and then I saw the look in his eye. He wanted to fight. Then he grinned at me, all yellow teeth and gaps in his mouth, a face to scare the shit out of little kids."

"Still," I agreed.

"And just as I'm leaving, he says, 'You were crying. I saw you. The last person to cry tears over me is dead fifty years, more. You're a nice girl.' I think of him like that. Just a little old man with some kind of European accent, maybe Russian, maybe from Yiddish – he's lost most of it now from living here all these years. A little old man shot full of holes, smiling at me.

"'What's your name?' I said. He said, 'Meyer.' 'Your first name?' 'Don't have one.' And I looked at him and he just broke into this ugly grin and said, 'We were poor. Could only afford one.'" She laughed at the recollection.

"When the war was over and I got home and I didn't need to be afraid anymore, I spent a day walking around the lake in Chicago thinking about all the people I knew that died, all the boys that died. And I thought of that old man who lied about his name, yeah, even back then, just a green kid but I knew he was making up a name. And I assumed he was dead, too. So the first time I saw him back here I thought I was looking at a spirit or some damn thing, or maybe I was dead, like that lady in the old Twilight Zone story who dies but doesn't know she's dead. But it was no ghost, and I wasn't dead."

"How did he find you?"

"The first time? Who knows? It's just one more thing about him that there's no answer for."

"So now I know why he comes here. Did he stay long this time?"

"A couple days. I put him up in the back. I fed him. Tried to give him clothes, clean him up, but I know a lost cause when I see one." I smiled but she tilted her head and gave me a look that said I might be another such lost cause.

"So in all these years – "

She got there first. "Four times, I think. But he's – hard to say this about such a tough old sonofabitch, but he's weaker. Seems like a funny thing to be saying about Meyer but he was frailer. I got the feeling I wouldn't see him again. Like maybe that's what he's doing, going off to die somewhere."

"But you don't know where." A shake of the head. I threw some of the names at her: Bergson, Glasner, Mannheit.

"Sounds like a U.N. meeting."

"And you don't know about – *him*, I mean – "

"All I know is each time he's been here, I have trouble thinking about the world the same way. And him, there is something so *lost* about him that I almost wish he could stop, just stop."

"And die."

"Yeah." She surprised me then with a short smile. Then she shrugged. "But I don't think he actually wants to, not yet. Maybe soon. I know I'd want to, if I saw what he'd seen in his life."

I thought about this.

"How do you know what he's seen?"

"Honey, it's all over him. You've seen it, don't tell me you haven't."

"Maybe." I took a last swallow of my beer. "Well," I said, putting the bottle down and making ready to take my leave.

"My question," she said, "is what a young guy like you is doing looking for him."

"I told you. Farrell asked me to."

"Because why? Because you had a lot of time on your hands and this will keep you out of trouble?"

I laughed. "Maybe."

"And why is that? Why so much time? Why not a life?"

"That part's harder. I'm getting in shape for that."

This answer seemed to please her. "And after you find Meyer – then what?"

"Excellent question."

"Ain't it, though. Well, when you catch up with him, tell him I said 'Hi.'"

307

"What makes you think I will?"

"I told you, I know all the looks. Yours tells me you'll keep at it."

"I think it's what I'm supposed to do." My answer surprised me. I wasn't even certain I knew what it meant. But apparently she did. She nodded.

"Good for you, kid." She finished her whiskey and nodded toward the back room. "You can have the guest room. There's actually a cot there for over-served patrons."

"That where Meyer slept?"

"Yeah – but don't worry, I cleaned it up. Took a flamethrower to the sheets," she added and laughed her raucous barmaid laugh.

And so I slept the night in accommodations unique in that town of bed-and-breakfasts. In the morning I had a coke and helped her put the tavern together for the day's business. When I was ready to hit the road, I thanked her.

She shrugged. "It's what I do. You gotta know what you're good for, kid."

"See you around."

She looked at me with a little tilt of her head. "I doubt it. Hope you find the old shit, though. Go with God, kid."

"Don't know anything about God."

"Who does?" she was saying as the door closed behind me.

Twenty-Three: Survivor

1 t rained most of my way west, for four days and nights running, including the single day I spent looking for Georg Glasner in the town of Sheridan, Wyoming, a day as filled with blank looks as any I ever spent. I had nothing on him, no address or P.O. box, the name meant nothing to anyone, and I earned more than one dubious frown when I couldn't come up with a description or tell anyone a single thing about Glasner.

Why would you be looking for someone you know absolutely nothing about? those looks said. Once or twice I threw in a question about Meyer but that seemed to make matters worse: a guy in a beat-up Buick with Illinois plates looking for not one but two men, both apparently strangers. I stopped for a cup of coffee in a big old-fashioned drugstore that smelled of breakfast. My waitress was a small pretty woman going gray, and when I asked her about Georg Glasner and then about Meyer, she gave me a long look, then said, "You a skip-tracer?"

I explained that I was looking for the first one only to track down the other, that people back in Chicago were concerned about him. She watched me for a moment and I pushed.

"The guy I'm really looking for is old, small, kind of bent over. He's also tough as a bad steak and he'd be wearing a long baggy overcoat and a hat, a fedora. He wouldn't do much for your lunch counter business."

She gave me the look again and said, "Him, I saw."

"When?"

"Week ago, week and a half." She shrugged. "He didn't come in here, though. I don't think he actually went inside anywhere."

"Where did you see him, then?"

She lifted the metal coffeepot in the direction of the street. "Out there one afternoon, for a long time, just walking back and forth. Talked to himself now and then, too, but I've seen lots of people that talk to theirselves."

"But this one, you noticed."

"Well, it was plain enough he wasn't from here, and he's old. All the old-timers I know, they sit and nurse a cup of coffee in a place like this, or if they've got a few bucks, they have a beer at the The Mint, or on a nice day they sit, two or three of them on a bench up the street. But I never saw an old man walk back and forth for so long, and fast, too, like he's got energy to burn."

"He does."

"Is he kin to you?"

"No. But I've known him a while."

"Well, I'm sorry you missed him."

"At least I know I'm still more or less going the same direction he is. That's something. No Georg Glasner, though, huh?"

"No. Never heard of anybody named Georg Glasner."

When I was finished I tried a couple more places, even

stopped a police officer, who had seen Meyer briefly but believed he was long gone. And so I left Sheridan and headed north to Montana, where I would try the last name on my list, Mannheit. Just Mannheit.

The rain came down harder and pounded the Buick, and I cranked the radio to drown out the noise. An Irish band called "Thin Lizzie" was cheerfully predicting a jailbreak. Maybe it was the music, or maybe I'd been driving too many days by myself, but I took a turn too fast and the Buick spun out. If there had been another car there I would have killed myself and anyone else involved, but there wasn't, so when the Buick did its 360 and came to rest, front wheels more or less in a shallow ditch, no one died. My head hit the door and my eye was cut, but that was about it. I got out and walked around to assess damage, but as far as I could tell, the Buick had escaped with a good scare, more or less. Then the oddness of my circumstances struck me: standing alone in a downpour the middle of Wyoming with a facial cut and a headache, trying to figure out if I was going to be able to make it out of the ditch.

I mopped my eye with a bandana and then became aware of the voices – I'd left the car running and the Irish rockers were still predicting, *"Tonight there's gonna be a jailbreak,"* and then I heard another voice. Someone was speaking to me.

For a moment I peered into the trees along the side of the road and then became aware that the voice was behind me. I turned to face a small man, sitting on a low tuft of ground at the far edge of the road. The overhang of an enormous ponderosa pine caught most of the rain so that he was nearly dry, and I became self-conscious of my soaked appearance. He sat in a curiously childlike pose, arms around his knees, and rocking back and forth. He had very little hair, which called attention to his bat-like ears. He gazed at me from beneath hooded eyes, and he was smiling. Had he not been so small and frail looking, I might have been a little spooked. As it was, he went on rocking and smiling for a moment and then spoke.

"You almost got killed."

"Yeah, I see that."

"Will it still work?" He thrust an arm out in the stiff pointing gesture of a pre-school child.

"I don't think I hurt it any."

"Hurt your head, though."

He crossed one of his bony knees over the other and his bare ankles showed thin and pale under faded brown pants. Long legs, though. Standing, he wouldn't seem quite so elfin.

"It'll be all right. I've been hurt worse."

I dabbed at my eye with a bandana, then wiped the rain from my face. Now that it had soaked me, it was letting up.

He looked at my army coat. "Were you in the war?"

"Yeah. I was in the war. Hurt more than my head, too."

He began rocking and nodding, and his gaze clouded, and I was certain he'd left me to go to a distant place. The hooded lids rose and he stared into his own thoughts with enormous dark eyes. He looked insane. As though he'd heard my thoughts he looked up.

"I was in the war, too. I got shot once. And I shot people."

312

"I'll bet you did."

I was of course humoring him, and now focusing on what sort of maneuver it would take to back the Buick out of its predicament. He was rocking again and, as I stared at the Buick's front wheels to measure how close she was to going farther into the ditch, I was struck by the strange notion that I already knew this little oddball on a country road.

I looked at him and he was nodding. Somehow it was coming back to me but on a different level I knew I had never met him before, I was sure of it. But now I had to stare at him. The rain picked up again, now gouging into the soft ground around him but he seemed impervious. Some of the rain made it through the branches onto him. He blinked and wiped his eyes with his fingers but kept his gaze trained on me.

"So we were both soldiers," I said.

This seemed to please him and he nodded.

"When I get the car out, you want a ride somewhere?"

"No. I like it here." For the first time I thought I detected just the wisp of an accent. He looked at the plates on the Buick and then searched my face for a moment. "You're not from here."

"No. Chicago."

"I knew that."

"How? The plates just tell you Illinois."

"Are you his friend?"

"Whose?"

His eyes clouded and he rocked for a moment, anxiously this time, and for a moment he was forgetting me, I could see it. I let him go on with his rocking and

313

waited.

"You know who."

"I'm looking for a man named Meyer."

The rocking came faster and he clutched his knees to him and he changed, became a hard little package with hostile eyes, a feral child.

"Why?"

"I told his friend in Chicago I would."

"What will you do with him if you find him?"

For that, I had no answer. In truth I had envisioned half a dozen different scenarios, quickly discarding one for another, and not a single version rang true. When I left Chicago I half expected to find him in the first couple of places I looked. Sometime in the past few days I'd begun to feel that the man I was following was not long for his hostile world, if he was not already dead. But I really had no idea what would happen if indeed I found myself face to face with Meyer.

"I don't know. I'll maybe see if he wants to come back to Chicago."

"Better not hurt him." The heavy lids hooded his eyes again and he was no longer an eccentric by the side of a road.

"I wouldn't hurt him. Besides, you know him, I think. How could I hurt him?"

He grinned and nodded a quick little boy's nod, then pointed a long finger at me.

"Meyer saved Ivy. When all the blood was coming out of the hole in Ivy's arm," he said, and I heard the accent again but could not place it. "The blood looked like a fountain."

"And Meyer stopped Ivy's bleeding? How did he do that?"

"He put his hands on the hole the bullet made when the Germans shot Ivy. He put his hands on it and he pressed down, hard. And he was talking and calling them 'bastards' and bad names, and when he was done, the bleeding was gone."

"And Ivy was not bleeding anymore?"

He pursed his lips and waited for me to grasp the significance of all this.

"So Meyer saved Ivy's life. With his hands. And this person Ivy – "

And here he put his hand over his mouth and became a child again, threw his head back and squeezed his eyes shut and laughed at another hopelessly stupid grownup.

"You're Ivy."

"For sure I am," he said.

A new thought struck me. "Are you also known by the name Glasner?"

He shrugged. "It's a stupid name. I don't like it. I got a new one now."

"Ivy's better. Good name."

He nodded again, then brightened. "Want to see me climb?"

Before I could answer, he had unraveled the long legs, chosen a nearby cedar and gone scrambling up the trunk like something out of my species. In my life I never saw a human being scutter up a tree like that, and I thought perhaps I understood his unlikely nickname.

He came down as fast as he'd gone up and stood there posing, hands on hips and waiting for approval.

"You're the best climber I ever saw."

He smiled and sat on a rotting log: a faintly menacing elf on a dark toadstool.

I took a shot. "You've seen Meyer lately."

"We had a visit," he said, and chanced a small smile.

"Is he all right?"

"He's just like he always is." A stupid question, his face told me. He shrugged.

"Where did he go?"

"I don't know."

"Do you know who Mannheit is?"

"No. That's a stupid name, too."

I'd introduced annoying subjects and he had gone sullen again. I got into the Buick, put it into reverse and gave it gas, carefully. One wheel caught, the other didn't, and I could see Ivy sitting on his log, giggling at my trouble like a small troll. I tried it again and the car moved back onto the road.

I got out and once more asked if he wanted a ride.

"I like it here," he said. "I come here all the time. I could hide here for years and nobody could find me if I didn't want them to find me. If Meyer doesn't want you to find him, he can hide, too."

"I know that. And if he doesn't want to come with me, he doesn't have to" I said. I wiped my face again with the bandana and realized that the rain had stopped completely. "Well, my friend," I said but didn't finish the sentence, whatever it was going to be. He was gone.

I spent a moment looking around me but he was gone. There was no movement that I could see in the trees beyond the road. I thought of looking for him, wondered briefly if this were merely a game, a game for the most childlike of men, but something told me Ivy was gone. That he had finished with me or had learned what he wanted to know.

I headed north, to Montana, to find Mannheit or if my luck was finally running, Meyer himself. The highway rose gradually. It seemed I was poised to travel the very spine of the earth, that the crust of the world had risen to meet me. I felt as far away from my own life as I had at any time since Vietnam. The thought of combat reminded me of my dreams, the strange, disconnected dreams that visited me the afternoon I visited Bergson. The scene came to me once more, a group of bloodied, filthy partisans meeting up with the American soldiers, and I saw their faces again. And now it seemed that there was more to it, as though I were viewing the scene in clearer focus. I saw Meyer, supported by a man on either side, and I saw odd, inconsequential details, I could see their breath, it was cold, and I saw that a man coming behind them had no shoes, his feet were wrapped in rags, and it seemed that every one of them was in some way wounded or injured. And I saw again the young one on Meyer's left. He was not much more than a child, but a child with a carbine, wary, hostile, poised for violence, his huge eyes missing nothing, and I realized why the strange little man called Ivy had seemed so familiar, for I'd already met him in my dream.

I became aware of my own quickened breathing, shook my head to clear it of this thing that I did not understand, did not want to understand. I hit buttons on the Buick's radio and found an old song by the Who. They were threatening that they could see for miles and miles, because there was magic in their eyes.

Meyer, I told myself to focus on Meyer. It struck me that I had but two more places to look, and then, whether I found him or not, I would have to return to Chicago and the bleakest of lives. There, I told myself, there was my reality, that life on the streets, not these dreams and the other things I chose not to think about. I saw myself as little more than a homeless man with a car. I drove on toward the purplish mountains in the distance and wondered, not for the first time, if I had lost all control of my own life. If asked, I would have said I was nearly finished with it all.

Twenty-four: Mannheit

1n the town of Belton, Montana, wedged at the mouth of Glacier Park, I asked for Mannheit at a gas station and drew a blank. In the town's only tavern a bearded kid bartender frowned at the name. I told him Mannheit was supposed to live around there somewhere, that he was a friend of a friend, and he was shaking his head when the only other customer in the place told me, "You want Mannheit, go down to the end of the street. Little gift shop."

I thanked him and left.

As he'd promised, I found a shop at the far end of the short street. A small bell tinkled overhead when I pushed in through the screen door, and I found myself in an odd little hybrid of a store, half gift shop for tourists, half grocery store – milk and bread and ketchup, essentials for a camper or a local who might run out of the staples of life.

A woman was sitting at a small counter with her back to me, painting a design on a black t-shirt.

"Be with you in second," she said over her shoulder but did not look at me. I waited by the door. The woman had silver hair and wore jeans and a work shirt almost identical to the one I'd been in for two days now. Then she blew on the paint, put the shirt aside and turned to greet me.

"Afternoon."

"Hello. The people in the diner told me I could look here for a man named 'Mannheit'," I began, and the amusement in her eyes stopped me right there.

"What was it you wanted with this gentleman? Did you want to order a shirt?" When I shook my head, she said, "It's one of the things we do here, so I thought that's what you wanted."

"No, I'm looking for him – for Mannheit because I trying to track down someone else."

"Track someone?" She gave me a careful look. "Sounds ominous. But perhaps I should set you straight: there is no Mr. Mannheit. I'm Mannheit. Last one left, actually, so if you're looking for Mannheit, you're looking for me. My name is Karen."

In a matter of seconds I'd made her go from amused to wary. I hoped she'd say something to lighten the moment but saw that it was my turn.

"My name is Thomas Faye and I have trouble putting this into a sensible form, but I was asked by a friend to try to track down an old guy from Chicago, and I was told that he – that this might be one of the places he'd go. I was given a list of names and places, and all over the USA I've been getting that look you're giving me now. But I'm not looking for trouble."

"Looks like you've managed to find some anyway," she said, looking at my eye.

"Ran my car off the road," I said, realizing as I said it how stupid that sounded.

"What's his name, this man you're looking for?"

"Meyer."

"And who is it that really wants to find him? You?"

This made me laugh. "Not really. Frankly, he tends to piss me off. A man named Farrell wants to find him."

"Why?"

"They go back a long time. They're friends, more or less."

She seemed to pause before each of her questions – whether to make me uncomfortable or give herself time to consider my responses, I wasn't sure.

"And this man Farrell wants to find Meyer to do – what?"

"I think just to make sure he's all right. More or less." This earned a half smile.

"I'm glad you added the 'more or less' part. You know he'll never be all right. But he's alive and kicking. So. What happens if you find him?"

"That's all I have to do. Find him. I think Farrell is a little bit concerned that maybe this is the time Meyer will lose it, that he'll just go away somewhere and maybe drop off the earth."

"Maybe he will. But he hasn't lost it, not yet anyway. He just came out to visit my father."

"That's the Mannheit I was supposed to find?"

"Yes. He died a little over a year ago. Sit down."

It came out as a command rather than an invitation, and I looked around the close, cluttered shop for the first place to sit.

"I meant here." She pulled out a stool and invited me to sit at the narrow counter where she was painting. She busied herself moving the paint cans and the t-shirt to the far end of the counter, and when she'd thus cleared us a space, asked me if I wanted a cup of coffee.

"Sure, thanks."

"Been on the road a while, huh?"

"Couple weeks, give or take a day."

"That's not what I meant," she said, and I had the impression she'd just made a small joke at my expense. She disappeared into the back of the shop with her cup and emerged a moment later with two.

"You take anything in it?"

"No, black is fine."

She slid gracefully onto the stool while sipping her coffee and positioned herself with one leg under her. Up close I saw that the silver hair had given me an erroneous impression: she wasn't more than forty: laugh lines and crows' feet but I could still make out the faint freckles of her youth, and she watched me with large, luminous green eyes, a young girl's eyes. At twenty, this woman would have stopped traffic. At 60 she would probably still turn heads, and I grew suddenly conscious of my lived-in clothes and my need of a shave and a haircut. I have been uncomfortable with women in my life but never so quickly.

"So you've come all the way out from Chicago to find Meyer?"

"Yes. Unfortunately, not in a straight line."

"And you still haven't caught up with him."

"No, but he's running out of geography."

She smiled at this but looked off into space. To make conversation, I complimented her on the little shop.

"It was my father's. His pride and joy. Doesn't seem like much of an achievement but he was happy here. Happy in Montana after a miserable life in New York and Detroit and – other places."

"Other places meaning?"

"The road. The War – the first one. He was gassed. Most of the men in his unit were killed. He said he'd never seen a worse death, started trying to describe it to me and began to cry. I read a poem about it once, death by poison gas."

"Wilfred Owen. *'Dulce et Decorum Est.'*"

She looked surprised, cocked her head to one side. "A man of letters?"

"Not really. Mostly I've read a lot of things nobody's ever heard of. But I've read Owen."

"I've read all of his poems. And Siegfried Sassoon – for a while I read everything I could about that war, trying, you know – " She waved at the air.

"To get inside your father's head."

"Of course. But I never did."

"How did he know Meyer?"

"After the war he spent a while in France, convalescing in a military hospital. When he got out, he felt like a character out of old stories: no family, he had most of his army pay, he decided to see the world. So he set off hiking through Europe. It was not at all what he'd expected, though. A lot of Europe was in ruins. He had adventures, he told me about some of them, the funny ones and odd ones.

"Eventually, he made it all the way into Russia, but that was a disastrous mistake, the Civil War there was in full swing. Twice people shot at him without even knowing who he was. That's where he met Meyer. He got lost, wandered into an area that he didn't know, ran low on food. Then he happened upon the scene of a fight in a clearing. There were bodies of men, dead horses, the place was full of flies, and Meyer was going through the knapsack of a dead soldier. For just a second he thought Meyer was going to kill him. He said Meyer was wearing a dark coat a couple sizes too big, and he gave my father the look of an animal when it growls, he sort of bared his teeth –"

"I've actually seen that look on his face."

She shook her head and smiled. "Poor Dad said he thought he'd run into some Russian version of a werewolf. Then Meyer straightened up and he saw this was just a crazy man, a hungry, very crazy man. And he thought that after surviving the whole war he was about to be killed by some Russian he couldn't speak with, so he asked this man if he spoke German.

"'Russland. Das ist nicht Deutschland!' the man said."

"Meaning?"

"'*This isn't Germany. It's Russia!*' And then, under his breath, he thought he heard Meyer call him an asshole. In English." She laughed, a young woman's laugh.

"Then Meyer sat down *on the body* and began eating from a tin of meat he'd taken from the man's saddlebags. My Dad tried to sign his thanks and Meyer said, 'I speak English,' and kept on eating. After a while, he looked up at my father and asked him what he was looking at.

324

"My Dad said, 'How can you eat here, how can you sit on a dead man's body?' And Meyer said, 'He don't care, he's dead. They're all dead. And you got to eat, or you'll be dead. Americans are stupid.' And with that he threw my father a tin of food, and my Dad was so faint from hunger that he dropped his moralistic objections and started eating, digging some kind of tinned meat out with his fingers and shoveling it into his mouth. He looked across the way and there was Meyer, growling and snorting his way through the food. After a while Meyer got up and searched the bodies, and found more food, and he tossed some to my father. Dad said after a while he stopped eating and watched Meyer. It was clear Meyer had, at least for the duration of lunch, lost all interest in him. My Dad offered him a drink from his canteen, and that was the beginning of what my father always called 'the strangest of all friendships'."

"So they bummed together?"

"Yes, but not for long. They parted company somewhere north of where they'd met. But over the years they kept running into one another in odd places: my father worked for an importer, the job sent him all over Europe. So he ran into Meyer in Istanbul, in Sophia, Bulgaria, in Tirana, Albania, and each time he said Meyer had a different name."

A brief shadow fell across her face.

"A different name but the same face, or almost. My father said when he met Meyer, he would have put his age at around 50. And the last time was just before World War II, in 1938, my father was in Bohemia just before Hitler took it over, and he ran into Meyer again. He said Meyer looked the same as he had back in 1919. Sitting there, grinning at him, on a park bench."

"I'm surprised it wasn't in an alley."

She laughed. "Actually, he ran into him in an alley here in the States. Years later, after the war. My dad was doing social work then, working with the skid row people. He did that in Detroit and Chicago, and saw Meyer in both places. I think something drew them together."

"Any idea what?"

For the first time she was hesitant. I could see her debating something with herself.

"My father had certain abilities that helped him with people. Well, that's not even the right word, because these were not actually things that he *did*. I mean, it was his presence. People felt something in his presence. And he had the ability to sense when people were in distress. Dad always felt that Meyer did not take well to people's attempts to help him, but he thought Meyer was comfortable in his company. I know that doesn't sound like much of a gift, but – "

"Actually, it's hard for me to imagine Meyer comfortable with anyone. Comfortable, for that matter, anywhere in the world."

For a moment I considered the images she'd presented, saw Meyer roaming first Eastern Europe, then the alleys of American cities, and recalled one of the earliest things Farrell had ever said about Meyer: *He can never find any peace.* I thought of old Edwin Bergson and what I'd felt in his presence, and I had a vague notion of what had sent Meyer traipsing across the continent, one old man seeking peace from another, and perhaps sensing that this might be his last chance to do so before they were all gone.

"And you had to be the one to tell Meyer that your father was dead."

"Maybe. I mean, yes, I told him. But I had the vague sense that he already knew before he even got here, though there would be no way for him to have received that information."

"No normal way."

I watched her react to that. She shrugged but looked away. I sipped my coffee and relaxed, and had the sudden notion that perhaps Meyer had come out certain in the knowledge that his old friend was dead, but equally certain that his daughter shared her father's gift.

As though reading my mind she looked at me directly and smiled. She took a sip of her coffee and I noticed her long, delicate hands, lovely hands, and as she set down her cup she made the simplest of movements, a gesture I will remember to my last moments: with the tips of her thumb and forefinger she undid the top button of her shirt. She looked at me again and it was all I could do not to gasp.

I couldn't meet her eyes. For a second she surveyed her shop, then said, "I have a lot of work to do. I'm actually in the middle of inventory, among other things. But if you come back later, 6:30 or 7, I'll make you dinner."

"As it happens, I'm free."

"I thought you might be."

I took a room at the closest motel, if only to gain access to a shower and a mirror, and then showed up at her place in a wrinkled but clean shirt. She gave me an amused look and I was afraid to ask her what was so funny.

Dinner was pasta, sauce from a jar, her own

mushrooms and green peppers thrown in, and a bottle of chianti that might have been good or might have been vinegar for all I knew about wine. We made small talk until the food was served. She announced that it was ready, that she was no cook but probably wouldn't kill me, and then we ate in silence. For a moment or so I was uncomfortably aware of my inability to make conversation and then I realized it wasn't needed. After the second glass of wine she had me talking, and though I couldn't have said how, she managed to get me to speak of my mother and Vietnam and the wasted years in between, and from there it took no effort at all to tell her of a strange shop full of old men of uncertain character and questionable nature.

We moved to her couch, sat just a foot or so apart, and though I was acutely aware of her faint perfume, of her physical presence, I did not stop talking. At some point I understood that she was not paying attention in quite the same way anymore – still listening to me, though, to what she was learning about me. Here and there she asked me questions, enough to reassure me, keep me going – and I could not ever remember a night when I had felt so compelled to talk, to speak of these old painful things.

Finally she put down her wine glass, took mine from my hand, leaned forward and pressed her lips onto mine.

She said, "It's late," and before I had a chance to misinterpret, she took my hand and led me to her room.

Her room, her bedclothes smelled of lavender, and as I sank onto the bed beside her my strength seemed to leave me. I know that I let out a small groan and she went up on one elbow and asked if I was all right.

"Just tired," I said, and that was the unadorned truth:

in that room and in her presence, her salving presence, I understood how bone-and-soul weary I had come to be. She put an arm across my chest and kissed me lightly on the cheek, then on the lips. It was not, of course, my first time with a woman, nor was it to be the last, but there would be only one other time in my life when I would feel that I was in the sole place on the face of the earth where I was intended to be.

In the morning she made me coffee and scrambled eggs and for the second time in twelve hours I took a shower. Living in my car would never be the same. Except for the few questions she asked me about Meyer and how I proposed to find him, we ate in the calm silence of people who are at ease in one another's presence. As I looked around her small apartment I allowed myself the small fantasy of seeing a life there, at the edge of Glacier Park, with this unnervingly calm woman. A story came to me then, a Robert Block short story in a collection of fantasy and science fiction Farrell had given me. In the story, a man – a fellow without family, like me – makes a deal with the devil, that he can have anything he wants, can keep it if ever he comes to a moment when he can say, "Stop, this is the moment I will live in forever." The devil, of course, understands that no human can ever say, "This is all I want, I need no more," and will take the unsatisfied human soul with him.

Had I been the man in the story, with the same deal, I would surely have told the devil that I had found the time and place to inhabit forever.

"Maybe," I began, sounding tentative even to myself, "after I find Meyer, I could come back –"

But she was shaking her head before I'd even arrived at the main clause.

"I won't be here. I'm closing up for the season. Winter comes early this side of the mountains and the park shuts down. The grizzlies more or less take it over."

"Where do you go?"

"I have a friend I visit in New Mexico. We roomed together in school, and now we room together five months of the year. Ever since she threw out her husband. For five months we get along perfectly, like sisters."

"When will you be back?"

She looked at me for a long moment. "I'm going to shut it down. It's wonderful here but this is not the life I should be living."

"What is, then?"

"I don't know. But I'll never find it living here, more or less marking time. I think I'll move somewhere where I don't know the patterns of every single day."

"You've been planning this awhile, then."

"No. It came to me last night, while I watched you sleep." She smiled. "So I have you to thank for that. I think you brought that to me, that thought."

I had the sense not to press unlikely possibilities, no matter how golden they seemed at that moment. Instead I asked a more modest question.

"Think we'll see each other again?"

She thought for a moment. "Every time I've met someone I liked, it seemed obvious I'd see him or her again. Almost never happens. So who knows?"

"You think everything happens for a purpose?"

"Heavens, no. But some things, some things do. Seattle

now?"

"I think so. For no logical reason – there are after all, farther places he could be heading for. Alaska, for example. Or just to piss me off he could leave the continent."

She laughed, then leaned over and kissed my cheek, close to my ear, and said, "Good luck, Thomas, my love."

On an impulse I kissed her forehead. I don't know why, but it seemed precisely the thing to do.

Twenty-Five:
Edge of the World

1 more or less followed the railroad tracks to the end of the continent. But now I had run out of names to look for, now I was just looking for Meyer. Spokane and Yakima cost me time: if he'd been to those places, no one had noticed. I followed narrow roads all the way out to the final point of land in the state of Washington, out by the reservation of a local tribe I'd never heard of, literally at the place where the known world ended. I bought a carton of cheap smokes from a stand at the edge of the Res. Then I backtracked.

Just outside Olympia I had an odd experience. A local cop told me he had rousted a bum on a deserted stretch of beach and though it didn't sound at all like Meyer, I decided to take a look. The sun was already setting when I got there, and my presence spooked a pair of teenage lovers, who picked up their shoes and blanket and moved off toward a clump of trees. That left me alone there with a dozen noisy gulls and the solitary landmark of that stretch of Puget Sound: an abandoned freighter, dark and rusting.

It hung onto the edge of the sand like a lost cause. For a long time I stared at it and then I did what I thought Meyer might have done, I ignored the signs around it telling me of its many hazards and looked for a way in. Inside I found the signs of others before me, kids who'd left beer cans and shoes, and a tin of chili that told me more than one man on the bum had spent a night there.

While I explored the old ship it made its noises, frightening noises, the sound of metal straining to give way, the creaking of plates and rivets forced too long to hold together. The ship rocked with each slap from the waves and eventually it spooked me, and I clambered down the way I'd come.

For a time I stood there looking at the ship in the fading light. I was fading as well, I felt light-headed, washed-out, off balance. I became conscious of the isolation of this place and my own solitude, not just at that moment but the solitary nature of my whole life. I was indeed the perfect soldier for this fool's errand of Farrell's, for I had no life that would be inconvenienced, no schedule to contravene.

I sat on a rock and had a smoke and listened to the old ship make its night noises. As I did, I had the powerful sense that I was not alone. I tossed the cigarette and looked up and down the length of the beach. There was of course no one there, but I decided to leave that lonely place. A waste of time, this small detour to the ocean: Meyer was not a man for lost beaches and dead ships, he was an alley rat and I'd find him in a city. I'd find him in Seattle. For some reason this seemed a certainty.

As I left the beach I thought about my feeling a few

moments earlier that someone else was there. Not Meyer, no. I had the inexplicable notion, ridiculous but impossible to shake, that, if anyone, it was Farrell.

In Seattle I avoided the tourist haunts and instead made the rounds of the small diners and dark taverns full of sailors. In one of them I got lucky: a young guy remembered Meyer, a young guy with a gift for description: *"Old guy, short? Bad teeth, needs a shave, smells like bad onions, old-time fedora with sweat stains?"*

Meyer, it seemed, had been in twice, each time nursing a single glass of cheap red wine for an hour. I returned to the bar twice the next day, early and again near closing time, no luck. I had a couple of drinks and left.

They must have been in a doorway, and they caught me before I could get to my car. I took a couple of punches to the face, one to the back of my head. Kids, maybe three of them, and they had numbers and the advantage of surprise but they'd never fought anyone like me. Somebody put me in a headlock and I bit into his chest, caught skin through his t-shirt and sank teeth into it, and he howled and let go. I came out of a crouch, swinging at anything I saw, and I caught one of them in the nose and it sprayed blood. Then I was hit from the side, a good punch just above the ear and I was down on one knee, then keeling over onto the sidewalk and one of them was kicking me in the back. I covered my head with both arms. Then I heard a smack and a snarling noise, I heard someone say "Shit!" and the sound of a blow landing. Then a boy's voice cried out and they were running. I heard a voice say "Little bastards," and then he, too, was gone, but I'd recognized the voice and I would have

334

known that smell anywhere.

In the motel room mirror I saw a creature out of bad movies. The cut from my spin-out in Wyoming had healed to a black scab, and part of it had reopened in the fight. My nose was red and swollen, but nothing like the purple mound of flesh where my left eye had been. I got ice from the machine at the end of the hall and put it on the bruise until you could see that there was an eye there after all. Then I drank.

In the morning I spent a half-hearted hour looking around for Meyer until the rain drove me into a donut shop at the foot of a long sloping street near the waterfront. The walls of the place were covered with huge photographs of John Wayne in his various film personas, and the proprietress even looked a little like him, a cheerful older woman with small smart eyes and a wide smile that held even when she looked at my face. Like Arlene Roenicke back in Galena, this lady had seen all the faces and was fazed by none of them.

"Rough night in Jericho?" she said

"It's a tough town."

She eyed the long gash and said "You could've used a couple stitches in that one."

I said, "That's my souvenir from Wyoming. The eye is from here."

And now she laughed. "You been fighting your way across the U.S.A.! How about a donut?"

I ordered coffee and a couple of her homemade chocolate donuts, and a glass of ice water. She watched me guzzle the ice water and understood that, too. I wanted to ask her about the John Wayne pictures but that would have meant conversation and I wasn't sure I was competent. And so I kept my head down and ate her excellent donuts and drank her not-so-good coffee and made eye-contact with no one. I neither noticed nor cared when a man sat down on my right. It was the smell that told me the karma of my morning had evolved: wet wool, dirty cotton, an unwashed body, wood smoke, tobacco smoke. Still I ignored him.

He watched me eat for a while and then offered a judgment.

"You look like shit."

It would not be accurate to say I was elated – I was too banged up for elation. But I had a sudden sense of completion – the first thing I'd actually accomplished in years. Something else came to me at that moment, seemingly unrelated: the certainty that I was going back to Chicago, no matter what. And I might yet have something like a life.

"You want a cup of coffee?"

"Yeah. Couple of them donuts, too. Chocolate."

I looked for the donut lady but of course she was already watching us, for a streetwise woman like her would have spotted Meyer before he'd made it through her door. She came over and I gave her Meyer's order. She turned to walk away, gave Meyer a quick glance over her shoulder and looked at me.

"I run with a wild crowd," I told her and she nodded.

"You still look like shit," Meyer said, oblivious to his surroundings.

"So do you. But your company is the price I pay for being rescued."

He shrugged. "Now we're even."

"For what?"

"That time when you were a kid and I was fighting them two punks. You were watching my back. You were just a kid but you were watching out for me. Most places I been in my life, there's been nobody to watch out for me." He looked around at the shop and added, more to himself than to me, "Been fighting all my days, everyplace I ever went."

The woman brought his coffee and donuts and before her hand had completely cleared the area Meyer was pouring cream and sugar into the cup. He poured till the coffee was the nearly color of butterscotch, added at least six teaspoons of sugar and then dunked a donut into it. He made wet sounds chewing and coffee dripped down his chin. In seconds he'd consumed the first donut and started on the second. As he chewed, he looked around now, frowned at the John Wayne pictures but didn't ask, glanced out at the street.

I waited. He had come close, just now, to speaking of himself, and I gave him time for more.

When he finished the second donut, he wiped his hands on his coat.

"You want another one?"

"Yeah."

I held up one finger for the donut lady and sipped my coffee. She brought him his donut and he remembered enough of his manners to nod thanks.

Meyer paused with the new donut halfway to his mouth. "You're waiting for me to ask you what you're doing here. But I know. He sent you. Farrell. Still, I didn't think anybody could find me. So if that's what you're waiting for, yeah, you surprised me, kid."

"I should have just come here. To the edge of the continent. Edge of the world, for that matter. I don't know why it didn't occur to me sooner."

He snorted. "Edge of the world? This? There's places where you can be so far from other people you think maybe you left the whole world behind. I been to 'em."

"I've been to the edge of the world, Meyer, but it wasn't a place, it was a state of mind."

He gave me an interested look. "I guess you have." He eyed the army jacket, then looked into my eyes. "You got shot over there? You got shot and you thought you were gonna die, right?"

"Right. How did you know I got shot?"

"Who knows? Farrell. So you thought you were gonna die. Probably wasn't the first time, either."

"What does that mean?"

He shrugged. "So. You turned into a juicer."

"A what?"

For a moment he looked confused. "You know, a lush. Ain't that what they call it anymore? I get mixed up with the slang. A boozer. You turned into a boozer. Hey, it's not a big deal. Your old man was a boozer, right? It wouldn't be the first time a boozer's kid turned out to be a drinker."

"I never thought of myself as 'a boozer's kid'."

"Don't take it personal. There's worse things than being a drunk."

I laughed. "That's what I've been missing all this time, Meyer. Your social graces. Your tact, your sensitivity, your kind heart."

"I say what I think. Why waste time on bullshit?"

"Who told you these things about me? Farrell?"

"Yeah, maybe. I mean there was a time back when you were young, right around when your Ma died. She was a real nice lady, by the way. But I don't need anybody to tell me when somebody's a juicer. I know the look. You got it."

"I do, huh?"

"Yeah. You're hung over now. That's what the ice water's for. I watched you from outside, you already had two glasses of ice water. But you got the look. You're what – in your twenties? And you've already got little broken veins in your face. Somebody sees you for the first time, they'd think you been around the block, all right."

I'd seen enough people give me a second look to know there was something in what he said. He picked crumbs off his plate and without asking, I ordered him another donut. The proprietress came over and refilled out cups, giving us both a curious look this time.

Meyer looked at his donut and then gave me a little nod of approval. He went through the cream-and-sugar routine with his coffee again and I watched him. Then it came to me, unsought as ever, a sudden lightheadedness and Meyer seemed to fade from me. A new image came, a younger version of him, perhaps in his thirties. He was walking down a narrow road that cut down through a rocky slope, walking heavily and carrying a sack over one shoulder. The light was faint, dawn, perhaps. As I watched this vision of Meyer, I came to understand that he was tired and thirsty, that he had come a great distance and the end was just as far. It seemed that he alone inhabited this craggy landscape. He came to a small orchard, an apple orchard or the leavings of one, for it was clear that it had been ravaged. Several of the trees were barren and scorched black, and animals or men had stripped the smaller ones of their apples. A poor orchard on its best day, and now the skeleton of one. Meyer climbed over the low stone wall separating the orchard from the road, and for a time he searched the trees and the ground below. I saw him pick several fragments from the ground. He stuffed a withered apple into his mouth and put three or four into his sack. He wandered in and out of the stunted trees and found more rotting fragments of apple, eating several on the spot. For a moment he leaned against the wall, clearly refusing to let himself sit, lest by resting he might lose whatever will he had left. Then he moved on, head down, plodding, the sole human form in that empty place.

He caught the distant look in my eyes.

"What?"

"Nothing."

He shrugged. He had finished the donut and now was using his spoon to dig up, from the bottom of his coffee mug, the slush of four donuts. He brought it up in dense gouts of brown mush and slurped it off the spoon. It dripped onto his coat and he dug at it with a finger, then licked the finger. I watched in amusement and, a few feet away, the donut lady stared somewhere between fascination and horror. Meyer caught me staring and said, "This is the best part." He drank and scraped and slurped and did everything but belch. He stared childlike into the bottom of the mug and seemed genuinely disappointed to be done. The image came to me again, of Meyer alone on the road by the ravaged orchard, and I wanted to say something.

"I know about your – about the people you visited. I know why. At least I think I do."

"No, you don't." Then he gave me a measuring look. "Unless Farrell told you."

"No. I – I just know. I put it together. And some of it just came to me." *In dreams and visions,* I said to myself.

For a long time he said nothing. He looked at me, then played around with the cup again, scraped it with his spoon.

"You seen all of 'em?"

"Bergson," I began, and he seemed to coil as he watched me. I wondered if he would attack me. I shook out smokes for both of us and lit them.

"Visited a bit with Arlene Roenicke. Talked to Mannheit's daughter. Met Ivy."

That broke the spell. He grinned. "You found fucking Ivy? You're good, kid."

"I think he found me. I put my car into a ditch on a back road, and there he was sitting there, watching me. As if he'd been waiting for me to come along."

"Spooky, ain't he?"

I was amused that Meyer did not see the irony in this observation, but I kept it to myself.

"That's one word for him. Is he dangerous?"

"I wouldn't want to be the guy that jumps him in an alley. He's not what he looks like."

"Actually, I think he is. We talked about killing. About dead Nazis and people who could stop somebody from bleeding to death with just their hands."

341

He gave me a sour look. "Wasn't like that. I just put pressure on the wound – they teach Boy Scouts how to do it. I got lucky. Sometimes it don't do anything. There's holes you can't stop." He watched me to see if I was buying any of this. I met his eyes for a moment before answering.

"He thinks he was dying."

I got the one-shouldered shrug. Meyer puffed at his cigarette for a while, then jammed the butt into the side of his mouth. He squinted at me through the smoke and said, "So you talked to Bergson?"

"No. He couldn't really talk to me. Not much, anyhow."

"He don't anymore. Couple words, that's all. Don't even know you're there some of the time. He won't be around much longer, either, Bergson."

"Farrell gave me another name but I never ran that one down: Bednarik."

"He's gone. They put him in a home – in Milwaukee. He got out four times. The last time, he decked the security guy." Meyer gave a short laugh. "Fucking Bednarik. Someday somebody'll run into him in the woods and they'll think they caught a fucking werewolf."

"Was he there with you, that time when you nearly died? When you were shot up? I know Bergson was there, and Arlene Roenicke. And Ivy."

He laughed. "Lotta moments when I nearly died, kid."

"But this was the worst you were ever hurt?"

"Fuck, no. There was two or three times I shoulda died. One time a camp guard put two rounds in me from close up, that should have finished me. And it didn't. But the time you're talking about – which by the way I know Farrell had to tell you about because you couldn't have figured it out and I don't think any one of those people could tie it all together – "

"Farrell just gave me names. He never said a word about them. Think what you want."

"How do you know about this?"

He waited and I just stared at him. I felt a quick surge of satisfaction that just this once I'd caught him off his guard. Then he nodded, to himself, it seemed.

He stared a moment longer. "I was shot and left for dead more than once, I'll tell you that. But that one time, was maybe different."

I looked out the window at the rainy street beyond, and then it came to me: I saw them again, the GIs encountering the partisans, the murderous Ivy and his compatriots carrying Meyer, I saw Bergson step forward and this time I saw him put his hand on Meyer. I saw Meyer look at him, barely alive but acknowledging the man's touch. In Meyer's eyes I saw something I had never seen there: if I had to put a name to it, I would have said it was recognition. Then the scene changed and I saw the nurse looking at him in horror, Arlene Roenicke. Staring and then snapping out of it as a doctor began working on Meyer.

A thought struck. "Those other times, it just happened. And this one time, other people pulled you through." When he said nothing, I nodded. "That was it. These people saved your life, and you're not certain you would have made it without their – intervention."

"What intervention? You don't know nothing. You

343

don't know shit."

"So who was Bednarik?"

"He had nothing to do with all that." Meyer half turned away as though offended. He shook his head, then faced me.

"Where did you know him from?"

This time I saw the resistance in his eyes. For a half-second I thought he might throw a punch.

"Poland. Where do you think you'd meet a Polack? Warsaw. We fought together. When the Nazis destroyed Warsaw. Don't ask me no more about that."

"Take it easy."

He shrugged and took a final sip of his coffee, pointed to the cup and said "Thanks." Then he left. There was something casual about it all, so that it didn't seem final. I wandered Seattle the rest of the day, killed time at the waterfront. When it grew dark I headed again for the small tavern where I'd been looking for him when I'd gotten jumped.

He was sitting near the door, drinking red wine from a small tumbler. He wasn't even surprised when I sat down beside him. A washed-out looking man behind the bar raised eyebrows at me and I indicated a wine for myself and another for Meyer. It was, predictably, bad wine, and its dreadfulness drew out his first small gesture toward conversation.

"Horsepiss, right?"

"Yeah. But who's fussy?"

I drank bad wine and was careful not to press him: I'd never thought to get this far with him. Three glasses of cheap red into the night and I finally found his weakness:

he couldn't hold liquor. After the third he began to lose focus, to have trouble finishing his sentences. More than once he repeated something he'd just said. I forced another wine into him and he began to slur his words.

I took him to my motel room – surprised that he did not protest – and helped him onto the bed. He sat at the edge of it, refusing to go any farther. I took the chair from the cheap desk and faced him.

"Now what?" He teetered there, ran his tongue across his lower lip, squinted at me.

"Now go to sleep. I'll sleep on the floor."

"I don't wanna go to sleep. I'm not tired."

"Oughtta be. You've covered enough ground to tire out anybody."

This struck him funny. "You don't know the half of it, kid." Then he sank onto one elbow and gradually closed his eyes. I waited for him to fall backward onto the bed but he just stayed there in that improbable position, and just when I thought this might be how he slept, he opened his eyes.

"I ain't going to sleep. I don't like it here."

"Suit yourself." I leaned back and closed my eyes, hoping to wait him out. I thought he would eventually collapse, if only from the wine.

When I opened my eyes to steal a glance at him, he was watching me.

"Now what?" he said for the second time, and I understood he wasn't speaking of the moment.

"That's up to you, I guess. He sent me to look for you, and that's what I did."

"So you're supposed to give Farrell a report or

345

something? Or you gonna truss me up and throw me in the trunk of that car?"

"Hadn't thought that far."

"Think you can?"

"No. But it would be a better fight than you think."

He liked that. He grinned. "No, don't think I underestimate you, kid. But this is what I'm asking: what did he send you out here for?"

"I told you. I think he wants to know you're all right."

"That's all bullshit. He knows what he needs to know. He can't tell the future, nobody can do that, although there's been times he could tell something was coming. But I think he knows where I am and what I'm doing here. At least he's got some idea. So I'm asking, why did he send you?"

"Because he knew I – "

"To give you something to do, kid. That's all it was."

I had no response to that. "You think whatever you want, Meyer. Right now, I need to sleep."

I made a complicated show of getting ready for bed. I hung my pants over the corner of the bathroom door, got a spare blanket and a pillow from the tiny closet and made a place to sleep on the floor.

I closed my eyes and tried to will myself to sleep, but he'd gotten to me, a part of me already believed what he'd said. I lay there stewing and gradually the cheap wine dulled the edges of anger and I drifted off. I woke once to use the toilet and get a drink of water, and the room was dark. Meyer was sleeping in that same strange position, up on one elbow like a fighter trying to decide whether to beat the count. He breathed through his mouth and made

346

strange wet noises. The room was rank with his smell.

The next time I woke it was because of movement in the room. Faint light was beginning to seep in from the street, and I could hear a bird announcing the dawn. Meyer was going through my pants pockets. He found what was left of my roll, then picked up my jacket and I heard his fingers working through the change in the pocket. He took out his hand and squinted into his palm.

"Yeah, take that too, there's about a buck in there."

He looked at me without expression, impossible to startle. "You're awake," he said, in a voice that knew no shame.

"What are you doing, Meyer?"

"What's it look like?"

"Give me the cash, Meyer."

"I need money."

"You're a piece of work."

"I left you a couple bucks. And you got a car," he pointed out.

"You're a prince of a guy."

He looked out at the street and said, "I'm tired." Then he turned to go.

"Meyer, I'll tackle you right here."

He paused and gave me an interested look over his shoulder. Then he turned back and reached for the door.

"Meyer!"

I got to my feet, and my own anger surprised me, I was light-headed with it, and I was speaking before I realized what I was saying.

"Tell me one thing."

"What?" He saw something in my face. His eyes

narrowed.

"That guy that used to watch Farrell's shop. That guy I told you about. He told me something."

"Yeah, he said I should be dead. He's right."

"I never told you exactly what he said. But I know about you, Meyer."

"You don't know shit. You couldn't find your dick in a dark outhouse with both hands."

I ignored him. "This was interesting: he said wherever you showed up, people died. He said you were some kind of angel of death. That you did nothing but bring death to people."

He blinked. "He was nuts. And so are you."

"Did you kill people in those days, Meyer?"

"Yeah." He turned and faced me, slowly. "I did. So what?"

"Stupid question – after all, I know how you took care of that poor sonofabitch. But did you cause the deaths of those people he talked about? The women, children even? Just like the Nazis. Were you one of them, Meyer?"

And that was all it took. He threw the money at me and then he was on me like a cat, snarling and clawing at my face, clubbing at me with his fists. I went down on one knee, grabbed his legs and tipped him onto his back. He hit the floor hard and I half-expected the sounds of old bones cracking. He sputtered and swore and pulled tufts of my hair out, and even on his back he was pummeling me. I let go of his legs and threw a long right hand that landed high on his skull with a sharp smacking sound. He growled, bounced a bony fist off my face and then we separated.

I got up on one knee and he pulled himself into a sitting position, breathing heavily. I saw with some satisfaction that I'd opened a cut high on his forehead. For a moment he said nothing, then he muttered something in another language, something like "*pomylony*", and then he snorted.

"Fucking kid," he clarified. He leaned back with both hands on the floor and then seemed to notice the money spread everywhere.

"Now your money's all over the goddam room," he said, as though he had had no part in that.

I felt around and found scratches on the side of my face. There was no serious bleeding though places on my head would soon grow lumps. I no longer felt any anger.

"So what do you want from me?"

"You were ripping me off. I thought I had to do something about it."

"I don't think you give a good shit about the money. What do you want from me?"

"I want to know who you are."

He nodded. "That's what I thought. I'm an old man with a million miles on his bones. That's who I am."

"And you're not coming back to Chicago with me."

"No. But you may see me there sooner or later. Siddown." He looked around the room and felt for his smokes, then remembered he'd been bumming mine. I tossed him my pack and he lit up. I got up and found him the ashtray. He got slowly to his feet and fell rather than sat on the edge of the bed. Then he began to tell me his long dark story. A million tales have been told in the darkness of a cheap motel room but I'm certain, absolutely certain, that none of them was ever a tale like Meyer's.

"You don't need to know all of it, I don't even know if you need to know any of it. But I'll tell you enough so you'll get straight about me." Then he gave a short bark of a laugh and started coughing. "That's if anybody could ever get really straight about me."

He cleared his throat. "And don't ask me no questions, 'cause I'm telling you what I want to tell you and nothing more."

Twenty-Six: Meyer's Tale

Meyer settled back and smoked and fixed me with a thoughtful look, and just when I thought he'd changed his mind, he began.

"My father was a wanderer, a tinker, he made his living out of a wagon, and that's where I was born. There was never a time when I belonged to one place. My mother died young, of some sickness, and I had a brother who didn't live through his first year of life in a wagon. The night my mother died I sat in the dark in the wagon and stared at her, listened to her breathing, and when my father told me she was gone I already knew it, even though I was only a little boy. She was very young and, like any boy, I thought my mother was beautiful. She could make things, my clothes, our blankets. I still think about her after all these years."

"Where was this? Europe? Asia?"

"Everywhere. And it's all one place, look at a map, Europe runs into Asia. It's all the same place."

"What was your mother's name?"

"You don't need to know. Believe it or not, I liked the wagon. My father's tools and his wares made a clanking sound, I used to think of it as our drums, our chimes. So now there were just the two of us, and he taught me his skills and gave me the one thing he had of any value, his gift for languages. He could learn any language and he gave me that, so later, no matter where I went, I could pick up enough to get by. That I think you know about."

"Yes. I've heard you in the shop."

"And if it was a language similar to the ones I already knew, I could speak with people in no time. To me all the Slavic languages are just one language. If I told you how many languages I've spoken in my life, you'd call me a liar.

"My father died fixing a wheel on that wagon. The thing fell on him, crushed the life out of him. I was there: he looked surprised, but he was dead in seconds. I was a young man by then, I had outgrown the wagon, so I sold it, and his team of horses and started off on the road, on foot." Meyer puffed at the cigarette, blew out a lungful of smoke. "I been walking ever since.

"When my money ran out, I had no trouble finding work in the fields or in cities because I had already discovered something about myself, that I had no end of energy, I could do three times the work of another man without being tired. People noticed, it gave me value. But I wasn't interested in staying in any one place for long. Or I couldn't, maybe that's closer to the truth. I needed to see all of the world, every place I could," and here he paused and aimed a yellow-nailed finger at me, "and that's how I know about you. Anyway, I began to roam, and I will tell you I have seen places that other men only read about in books. I have seen every kind of land there is, and every kind of people, and I've even been places that people never knew about."

"But none that you ever wanted to stay in."

"Not then, no. But I picked up things, skills and abilities, I was clever with my hands. I had my old man's gift for fixing things as well as his languages, and I made my living. Along the way I learned other things about myself: other, you know, 'talents', you might call them. I could sense things about people, feel their emotion, I could tell when someone was lying, or wished me harm. Helpful things for a man who is forever alone. Eventually I also learned of the other 'gift', if it is a gift, I understood I didn't seem to change, to age, not like other men did. Other things I knew by then, too."

He paused and touched his hand to the cut on his head. It had stopped bleeding, already beginning to close.

"People notice these things. And it was this that guaranteed that I would never settle down in one place, because when you don't grow old with your neighbors, they'll burn you at the stake. Once I made a mistake, I showed another – whaddya call it? A special talent. A village on the Turkish border, this was.

"There was this young kid out working clearing brush or something, cut his own arm, God knows how. Bad cut. He was just lying there bleeding just beyond this hedge, all alone – so I thought. And I was there looking at him, and he was hurt bad. I don't know what I thought I was doing, I'd never done this to anyone, but on an impulse I knelt down beside him and put my hands on the gash. Long fucking cut, I couldn't keep it closed all the way, blood still coming out fast, but I stayed with it. I willed it to close. I didn't have any great miracle in mind, I just didn't want this poor kid to bleed to death. I held it until it wasn't bleeding no more. I closed it. Then I heard voices behind me. I look up and there's half a dozen men watching me, looking at the kid.

"'*Sihirbaz*,' I heard one of 'em say. '*Sihirbaz*' – it means, like, a wizard. Then a couple of the other men said it. And it wasn't a compliment. I saw they were afraid of me. They gave me some cheese and a drink of some kinda plum brandy, but I saw how they looked at me. I left as soon as I could, went as far as I could from that place."

He stubbed out his cigarette and shrugged. "So I kept going. And I never stayed anyplace. That was my life for many years. Once or twice things interrupted it. I got conscripted in the first war, into the Russian goddam army, of all things! That's where I was at the time, Russia. So they put me in a green uniform and gave me a rifle. I didn't soldier for long: a year into the war, a fucked-up army, one disaster after another, incredible fucking casualties and freezing cold, and finally here and there the line started to cave in. My whole regiment pulled out. It's easy to desert when your regiment is doing it, and that's what I did. I found a dead man lying in a wagon track a few days after we pulled out and put on his clothes.

"I went back to work as a tinker, I learned to fix watches and clocks, and this allowed me to go into the big cities where there was always call for somebody who could fix things. I was in a city when the Revolution came, and I ran like hell, but you can't outrun that kinda trouble. The whole country was in chaos, and it got worse when the Civil War broke out. I was chased by the Reds and the Whites, both, they both shot at me, a bunch of Red partisans wanted to hang me. But the officer's watch saved my ass."

"His watch?"

Meyer laughed silently. "Yeah, I saw him shaking it and frowning at it, and I told him I could fix it. I did. This seemed to amuse him, he was a typical Russian officer, a vain asshole. He let me go. An ugly time, that was. Everywhere I went, I saw dead men, whole patrols of dead men and horses. The men's boots were gone and their guns and the saddles, and whatever food they had. The horses were butchered for the meat. And sometimes I saw dead women, too, and kids. And once I found a soldier, a Red Army man, lying behind a rock, and he was dying. Just a kid, fifteen or sixteen. In the Ukraine, this was. They'd cut him up, him and three other men, but he was still alive. Kinda whimpering there while he bled to death."

Meyer gave me a hostile look. "Don't laugh at me."

"I haven't heard anything funny. What are you talking about?"

"Well, if you do. Anyway, I found some things in the woods, I knew about these things from my father, and I made a poultice. You know what a poultice is?"

"More or less."

"I tried to slow down the bleeding, and stop the infection. And it wasn't doing nothing. This cut, I couldn't close. But I got this idea, that I could save his life if I – if I could give him some of my life. Some of the force of me." Meyer watched me for a reaction. I nodded and he went on.

"So I sat next to him and I put my arms about him and I squeezed his body so hard I thought I'd crack his ribcage open, and I sat like that for hours, and I willed him to live. I willed him to live. And by morning he was better." Meyer flicked a two-inch ash on the carpet of the motel room and took a long drag on what was left of his cigarette. "But I felt like shit. I was weak, it seemed I couldn't get air into my lungs. Like I'd transferred that kid's death to me. I even thought for a minute or so that that was what I'd done. Fucking superstitious notions we get. But I got better. It took time, for a while I wasn't sure I was going to be the same. But it passed. This thing that I did, this thing that happened, I didn't know what to make of it."

"You found that you had what Farrell has."

He blew smoke and gave me a wave of irritation. "Fuck, no. I couldn't cure sickness and I couldn't stop death. I found that out later." He glared as though I were responsible. "Listen to me, kid, no one has what Farrell has. He is – well, that's between him and you, what he is. He can tell you. But nobody has that ability, or at least, what he once had. Some of it is gone now. It's a thing that doesn't stay."

"Why?"

"Nothing lasts forever. It takes something from you. Like I said, ask him about it. But I put the life back into that poor kid in the Ukraine, and when he could get to his feet he was gone as fast as he could move out. He didn't know who or what I was, but I'm pretty sure he knew what I'd done."

"Is this is around when you met Mannheit?"

He shrugged. "Later. That was in Russia."

"You were sitting on a corpse and having lunch."

"First food in days."

"I wouldn't eat on a dead man."

"You're stupid. But we established that already. Anyway, yeah. Mannheit with his – his strange open heart, he embraced the fucking world, kid. I liked him. He thought everything was interesting, that all people were worth finding out about. And no matter where I went, he kept turning up. It was pretty funny."

"Or it was fate."

"No. Fate is two guys having a smoke and a bomb drops on 'em and they're dead, but a third guy overslept so he didn't make it. That's fate. You met Mannheit's daughter. She's something."

"She is."

"She'll be gone if you go back there," he said, and I was strangely irritated that he could know this, or that he knew I had thought of going there.

"That's what she said."

"So I was in Poland – "

"This is when? Right after you brought this kid back from the dead?" I said, to piss him off.

"He wasn't dead. Don't be foolish. And no, this was later. Time makes no difference to me but it was later. Maybe ten years. I was traveling between two villages in Poland when I was robbed. They beat me, stabbed me in half a dozen places and left me there to bleed to death. A man and his son found me and brought me to their house and tried to take care of me themselves because there was no doctor. They were Jews, these people, and when they saw how badly I was hurt, they called for the rabbi. A rabbi!"

Meyer grinned at the absurdity. "He sat up with me all night, that rabbi – little man with the thickest eyebrows I ever seen, and he never left my side. Once or twice I came to and he was there, praying but also watching me like you watch a thief in your store. I don't know exactly what he saw, but he saw something. He stayed there by me, the little rabbi whose name I don't even remember, and I woke up to find out he'd gone to sleep. But I was healing. I mean completely healing – my wounds were closing up. I had a gash along one arm and it had begun to scab over, it looked like it was a month old. I just sat there staring at it. But it made sense to me: if my body could do certain things, it might do others as well. I still looked more or less the way I had looked before conscription, so why shouldn't I have this, too, the ability to – "

He waved a hand in the air as he searched for the word.

"Rejuvenate," I said.

"Good, kid. The ability to rejuvenate. Anyhow, when the rabbi woke up he was spooked, and then he thought better of it, and pronounced it God's work."

"Maybe it was."

He gave me a look. "Yeah? And the times when I came across a hundred bodies in a clearing, all of 'em murdered, was that God's work, too?"

"I don't know."

"Don't irritate me. So this rabbi calls in the other heavyweight in town, the priest. Orthodox priest. You know what they look like, right? You seen pictures. Tall guy, black whaddyacallit down to his shoes – "

"Cassock."

He nodded. "Yeah. And a bunch of dark hair looked like it would bust a comb, and a beard growing all the way up to his eyes, he looked like the fucking Wolfman. And they confer over me in Polish, but I know enough Polish so I know they're going through the possibilities to see if I was a miracle. Never could decide in the end, but they both thought it was pretty interesting. This family that found me was called Brotman. Brotman," Meyer said again, slowly. "The father was the town blacksmith, for everybody, for the Jews and for the Poles on the other end of town. But he was sickly. He was training his kid but the boy was about fourteen or fifteen, and small, so their business was, you might say, in the shitter. As I recovered, they took care of me and I decided to pay 'em back, so I worked at the old man's forge. I had actually done that work once, I done everything at least once, so I knew what I was doing. And business was good: the next town over, their blacksmith up and moved, so there was work, and money coming in for the Brotmans."

Meyer looked past me and though his face did not change, his eyes seemed to take on a softer focus.

"I'm not a guy for towns, but after all those years alone, after the road, it was a good place. The Brotmans were good people: six of 'em, there were, the man and his wife, two boys, one girl, the *babcia* – Grandma – none of 'em gonna live out what was coming. Next war. Anyway, I stayed there, working and pretending I was part of a town and a family. I told them my name was Osip. They called me 'Wujek Jozek'. Which is something like 'Uncle Joe'. The other people in the town, they weren't so sure they liked me, but they liked the Brotmans so I was tolerated.

Some of them called me 'Cygan'. Gypsy." Meyer allowed himself a small chuckle. "Gypsy – that's not bad, when you think about it, not far from the truth.

"But that wasn't my life. The old man got a little better and his kid got bigger, and I know I coulda stayed with them, they liked me." Meyer's look dared me to contradict this unlikely idea. I just nodded.

"But that wasn't my place. So I said good-bye to that town, those people. Last thing I saw, the damnedest thing, kid. On the far edge of town, sitting on a bench, was the rabbi and the spooky- looking priest. They were playing chess. When I went by, they both waved and told me good luck. Powodzenia."

Meyer stubbed the butt of his cigarette out and looked at me. "When the Nazis came through that town, first thing they did, they took that priest and the little rabbi and a couple other leading people of the town, brought 'em to the town square and shot 'em all. To discipline the Untermenschen. They did it all over Europe, but they did as much to the Poles and the Polish Jews as they did to anybody. Anyhow, I left that little town and I was already feeling funny about it. You know me, kid, I got no time for sentiment, but I missed the Brotmans already. Funny thing is, I was gonna see 'em again. About ten years later."

Meyer paused to run his stained fingers through my pack of smokes and I knew I wouldn't be smoking any from that pack again. "Why don't you keep that pack, Meyer. I got more."

He shrugged, pulled one out and lit it.

"I don't know what else there is to tell," he said, and I could have choked him.

For a while I let him smoke, then I thought of a way to draw him out.

"You once showed me the number on your arm. Where's that in your story?" And unbidden, another question: *And the man in the alley, with his number.*

Meyer looked at me like a man who's just been cheated at cards.

"People that were in the camps, they don't talk about the camps."

"You're not quite like anybody else."

"That don't make it any easier." He puffed at the cigarette. "The next nine, ten years, I lived on the edge of life in Europe, back and forth from one place to another. Poland, Romania, Czechoslovakia, Moldova, Armenia. Other places, too."

"And you ran into Mannheit again, in all those places."

He gave me an odd look: he was just realizing how serious I was about trying to put all these stories together.

"Yeah. I met Mannheit in some of 'em. He called me *'the bad penny'*. So anyway, I roamed Europe and made my living, and I watched and I listened. And I knew what was going on, what was gonna happen, before the people who started it even knew what they were gonna do. So I was there in 1939 when the shit hit the fan. I was in western Poland, to be exact, I was there when the Nazis came through and took over all those towns. German army units every place I went. German settlers coming in, too. They took the Polish farmers and the people from the towns, the Jews from the shtetls, and shipped 'em all off to the cities. *Lebensraum*, that was what they were up to: *Room to Live* for the German people. Shipped hundreds of thousands of people off to the cities and to the new camps. Emptied whole towns. Never saw anything like it in all my days, and people here don't fucking know about any of it." He glared at me as though this were my fault. "And the Jews they put into ghettos in the cities. When I heard that, I knew what was in store for those poor fuckers. Just a matter of time.

"So the Brotmans were gone, and that whole town with 'em, except for the ones the Germans shot on the spot. Warsaw, they sent 'em to Warsaw." He took a long drag on his cigarette butt, blew smoke into the already-clouded air of the small room.

"About a week later I found the body of a German courier in a ditch. He'd been dead a while, the body was already bloated and collecting flies. I took his canteen and his rations. There were dispatches in his bags. I tore 'em up. A few days later, a patrol stopped me, found the courier's stuff, and they arrested me. I told 'em I found the stuff. They debated about shooting me, then took me in, and I was put in a labor camp. It was full of Poles and Jews, mostly men and some women, and we worked on the railroads the Germans were building. They worked us to death, literally. Men and women died working, or later, in their sleep, from exhaustion and starvation. It was a camp for slave laborers, and when we weren't working, they made sure we had no illusions about what kind of life was left to us. The guards had enjoyed tormenting the Jews. They didn't like me much better: I had this Ukrainian name – Osip – and I gave them lip, and they beat the shit out of me, busted my nose, knocked out a tooth.

"One morning I got sent out on a burial detail with some other men, to dig graves for the ones that had died the day before. One of the men on the burial detail ran and most of the guards went after him. Two of them stayed with me, a corporal and a private. The corporal went into the trees to take a piss, and I hit the private with a log. I took his rifle, and when the corporal came running out of the trees, I shot him. I took both rifles, and some cigarettes off the corporal, and I ran into the woods. They looked for me for days, but I went so far into the woods that I thought I'd never be able to get out. That was my first time escaping from them. Not the last. Not my last time in a camp, neither."

He watched me and saw something in my face. "Ask me what you want to know. If I don't like it, I'll just say, 'fuck you, kid'."

"The one who told me about you, the one who watched the shop. He said he saw you shot. He said you should have been dead."

"Another time, another fucking camp. What else he tell you?"

"I told you. That you were some kind of bringer of death. That you were evil. You and Farrell, both."

"Bringer of death, huh? Sounds like Genghis fucking Khan. Well, he's right about one thing: I shoulda been dead. Bullet went through me here." He pointed to his chest. "Went in my back, blew out part of my lung, came out my chest. When I was on the ground, the officer in charge went up and down the line with a pistol and put a round into each of the men. There was seven of us – a luger held seven rounds – and he went down the line to finish all of us. I still got a piece of that bullet in the back of my skull." He turned slightly, touched the back of his head, just behind the ear.

"See that?"

He moved his matted hair away from the ear and I could see an irregular lump there.

"I see it."

He looked at me and for a moment I feared he would ask me to touch it. Instead he nodded.

"Then they threw dirt on us. They buried us. I don't know how long I was there in that ditch with those other dead men, maybe a day, maybe a week. But whatever it was, I woke up under the dirt, and I could smell death. I started screaming, I thought I was buried alive. I was screaming and the dirt filled my mouth, I couldn't breathe, and I just started clawing at it and kicking. That's the only time I ever screamed for fear. Fear for myself, at least.

"Turns out the other men who had to bury us did a half-assed job – whaddya expect from men that think they're gonna be dead themselves in a couple days? I dug my way out. When I had my face above the dirt, I saw it was night. It was night and I was still alive. The back of my head was like it was on fire, I could hardly see straight, and when I breathed in, I couldn't take in enough air. My chest felt like it was full of water, I gagged on it and spat it out, and it was blood, already clotting. So I pulled myself out of that grave and sat with my back against a tree, and I decided I would die there, sitting up. At first light I heard the birds and realized I hadn't died during the night."

Meyer shook his head and gave a short chuckle. "Birds. You know, I always hated birds, noisy little fuckers, they

364

irritate the hell out of me. And there I was hearing the birds and I knew I was gonna live. Only time I was ever glad to hear a bird. I couldn't quite stand yet, so I crawled on all fours into the trees beyond the ditch. That night, I got on my feet and left that place. All I could think of was water. I needed water. My head still hurt and my chest, and it was still hard to breathe, but I had the notion if I found water I was gonna live. And I found it, a shallow stream full of moss and dead bugs and shit, and it was the coldest, most wonderful drink I was ever to have in life."

He stopped and looked around the room, licking his lips, and I started laughing.

"Hang on. There's a glass in the bathroom." I brought him a glass of water and he sucked it down with the noise of a slurping dog. He stared owlishly into the glass as he drank. When he was done he held it out for another, and I took a long drink from the faucet myself.

He belched, then watched me for several seconds. He pointed a finger at me. "Here's the thing, kid. After I drank that mossy water, I started to burn up, like I was gonna die of fever. I ripped off my shirt and threw myself in that shit water, and rolled in it like a kid at the beach. And for a while it didn't seem to help. Then, gradually, I started to feel a little better, but I had this strange itching all the places where I was hurt. And I looked down at the bloody fucking hole in my chest, and it was closed, it wasn't even a hole anymore, just a round mark with nasty rings of scarring around it. And when I felt the wound at the back of my head, my hand came away with pus but no blood. I was healing. In those places where they shot me, I was healing. I scrambled out of the water and hid behind a tree. I have no idea who I was hiding from, I think maybe from myself, I didn't want to admit this. This thing I had found out."

"That you couldn't be killed."

He made a choking sound. "You spent your whole life reading bullshit and now your head is full of it. That's not what I thought. But I began to put it all together, how I seemed to age so slow, how I recovered from the knife wounds when the Brotmans found me, my, my strength, and now this. All those other things, there coulda been some explanation, blind chance, maybe, but this time I shoulda been dead."

"And it never occurred to you it could have been a miracle."

"No." He pointed at me again. "And don't say it was magic fucking water from that stream, which *goats* pissed in, I am certain."

"I wasn't thinking that. I was thinking you had to have experienced something like this before."

"Some. All the way back to childhood, kid. I once cut myself fucking around with the old man's tools and slashed my finger. Thought I'd cut the sonofabitch off. I wrapped it in a rag and hid it from my family, went to sleep with it throbbing and bleeding. In the morning the cut was closed up. My cuts always healed fast. I learned to keep 'em bandaged so people wouldn't know. But bullet wounds aren't cuts."

He puffed at his cigarette.

"How much time passed between your escape from that first camp, and this time when they tried to kill you?"

"I told you, time has no meaning for me. But probably

a couple years. Coulda been three. All the years of my life run together, kid."

"All right, how many camps?"

That made him smile. "Ah, smart kid. Five camps in all. Two labor camps, three that were, you know, the real deal. Death camps. Piles of dead people. You never think you'll see something like that, and believe me I'd seen everything people can do to each other, least I thought I did. But I never thought I'd see piles of dead human beings, naked, shot, tossed into a ditch like meat scraps. Yeah, camps I can count, although I'll tell you, after a while there's a sameness to them, too. Same shit. Same dying people, same smell of filth, death, decay. Same guards, even when they weren't German. Ukrainian guards in one place. Dull-witted, bigoted fuckers. All the same. And I got out of all of 'em. One time they chased me, seemed like forever they chased me. Brought out the dogs, chased me deep into the woods. And there I had the advantage." Meyer slapped his chest. "I had it, 'cause I'd already had to live in the woods more than once, I could kill something and eat it raw, I could go without food for days, without water. And they couldn't. Finally they started to turn back, all except for one man. He kept coming after me, with a dog, just one dog. I went farther into the woods, where it was so dense there wasn't even a deerpath. I killed that guy. Killed the dog, too."

He gave me a long suspicious look, as though I might protest the dog's death.

"Wound up in the city of Lodz. They'd already started putting the Jews into specific places in the cities, all the cities. Thousands and thousands of Jews crammed into a single neighborhood. Walls around 'em, barbed wire. In Lodz I met a Pole from the town where the Brotmans had lived. He told me they'd been taken to Warsaw. He said he thought the Jews were going to have to live in ghettoes in the cities until the Nazis deported them. I told him I thought they were just going to kill them all.

"'So many?' I remember that: '*So many?*' Naïve sonofabitch." Meyer fell silent.

"So you went to Warsaw," I prodded. "To find the Brotmans."

"Yeah. I went to Warsaw. I found the Brotmans."

Twenty-Seven:
"The End of the World"

For a long time Meyer said nothing. I leaned back and closed my eyes to show that he could stop if that was what he wanted. When I stole a glance at him he was smoking and looking round the room. Then he fixed me with a shrewd look that told me he knew I'd been watching him.

"I seen the end of the world."

"What does that mean?"

"I'll tell you about Warsaw, and then I'll stop. You don't need to know everything. Just like I don't know everything about your life."

"Fair enough."

"So I thought about the Brotmans, and I went to Warsaw. For a while I moved around the city as a tinker, I sold trinkets, I repaired shoes and boots. Once I fixed the boots of a German officer while he stood a few feet away in his stocking feet, smoking and pretending I didn't exist. I could've killed him.

"For a month I lived in the back streets of Warsaw, I

learned that city like someplace I lived all my life. I can still draw you a map of Warsaw the way it was then, every street, the buildings and alleys. I put on my collection of accents, all of 'em, told the Germans I was a Bulgarian named Ioan. Told 'em I was a Romanian named Anton. Sometimes I walked with a limp, sometimes I faked I had some kind of palsy in my arm. I learned those streets, I *haunted* those streets. At night the Jews came out of the ghetto, children mostly, sent out by their parents to scavenge. One night I saw a boy, a little boy, couldn't have been more than eight, looked like a skull with legs, foraging through the garbage. A pair of German sentries caught him and smacked him around, called him a fucking little Jew, then took him away.

"A short time later, I let a German patrol find me going through the trash outside a restaurant popular with German officers. I admitted to being a Jew, and on the spur of the moment, gave my name as Meyer. I don't know even where that came from. Meyer. From that point to this, that's who I been.

"They threw me into the ghetto, and what I saw made me sure there ain't any hell, 'cause there couldn't be two places like that. Hundreds of thousands of people crammed into space for about a tenth of that. And they were dying already. That first day I saw a body in the street, just a dead body, flies all over it. Clothes were gone – people were already getting desperate about pretty basic things, like staying warm. Starved to death, this person, the body was just a skeleton with skin. And it was only the first one I was to see there. The Nazis were starving those people to death. It was a little city within a city, a town of dead and dying people who spent their days digging and clawing and begging for food. And there was sickness, all the kinds of sickness you get in a crowded place where there's no sanitation, no medicine, no food. In the morning there was almost always a body in the street, some days there'd be a dead person on every corner. Men would come by with a two-wheeled cart, and pick up the dead. I can still smell that smell. I can still smell Warsaw.

"The Nazis had put up a ten-foot wall around the Ghetto, and put barbed wire and shards of glass, big chunks of sharp glass, on top of that, but people still got out almost every night or sent their children out, to scrounge for food in the neighborhoods around the ghetto. They went over that wall or down into the sewers, or they found little places where a kid might squeeze out. The Germans caught most of 'em, took what they'd found and brought 'em back into the Ghetto. The children they just knocked around. Adults got it worse, and one guy they just shot on the spot, I don't know what he took or what pissed them off. They shot him and threw the body just inside one of their guard posts.

"After a couple days I found the Brotmans. The father was dead, the grandmother never even made it to Warsaw. Died on the road. That left the woman, her name was Miriam, and two of the kids, the girl, Hannah, she was a young lady now, and the younger boy, named Myron. Older boy was already gone, he went off to fight as soon as the Germans brought their troops up to the Polish border. They were living in a one-room apartment in a building so crammed with Jews I thought it might collapse into the street. And they were all dying, the Brotmans, that was

371

plain to see. The mother would go soon, I could already figure she was giving most of her food to the two kids. But they offered me some of their food and their putrid drinking water.

"'*Wujek Jozek,*' the girl said when she saw me. They all hugged me, I could feel the bones through their clothes, and the kids acted like I was the best news to come their way in months. I looked Miriam in the eye, though, and there was a different message: *now they've got you, too, Jozef,* that's what her eyes said. Later that day I overheard the girl say to her kid brother, 'Uncle Jozef will help us now.' I didn't have food for her, or a weapon, except my tools. But I knew Warsaw from my, whaddya call 'em, my explorations. So I started going out at night."

"How did you get out?"

"I went over the wall. In those days I could climb like a fucking mountain goat, and I could ignore cuts from the glass." He gave me a quick, challenging look. "The barbed wire was no big deal – I had clippers in my pack. And I was careful to twist the cut ends of the wire back together when I came back, so the Nazis wouldn't see where I'd gotten out. I went out and I found them food. I broke into shops and stole food, I took food scraps from the trash behind cafes and restaurants. For weeks I did that, slipping out every night, coming back before dawn with food. The two kids acted like I was some kind of character out of fairy tales. Like I was a hero. And once or twice I even tossed a scrap of food to one of the other families living on the same floor. One of the Brotman kids must have told them I wasn't a Jew, because they started calling me *Zigeiner.*"

Meyer laughed. "This is Yiddish for Gypsy. I think it's Yiddish. Gypsy again! *Cygan, Zigeiner.* Anyhow, they came to me for things, for advice. Had me fix things, which I did in return for food if they could afford to give any up, or for free, which was most of the time. Came to me for protection." He snorted. "Like I could give them protection against an army. And one night, a woman who had lost everyone but her small son came to me to heal him."

"To heal him?"

"Don't ask me why. She was going mad, she got it into her head I had some kind of magical ability because I could get out without the Germans seeing me. Came and begged me to help her son. I went into her place and there was this little boy dying of, I don't know, dysentery. He had sunken dark eyes, he looked haunted. And he knew he was going to die."

Meyer glared, daring me to question this. I nodded and he went on.

"So I sat by his bedside, this little kid shivering and moaning, his bowels leaking onto his cot even while I sat there with him. And he hurt, I could see he hurt, and I never for a second in my life thought I was any kind of healer, not even that time in Russia when I brought that kid back. I don't even know what that was."

He shrugged, and his shrug said it was all beyond understanding.

"But I thought I could do something. So I sat with him and put my arms around him and tried to keep him warm. That seemed to settle him. I stayed that way with him for hours, and near dawn I felt him moving, shuddering. I felt dizzy then, and I sank back on the floor beside his cot. And I slept that way, sitting up. When I awoke, his mother was cleaning him, putting on fresh clothes, to bury him.

"I told her I was sorry. I swear to you I thought my fucking heart would break." Meyer glared in his embarrassment, then looked away. "She shook her head and said, 'You gave him peace. He said my name. He spoke to me, he smiled his first smile in many weeks, and he died in peace.'"

Meyer stopped, and I sensed that he had something else to tell that made him uncomfortable. He asked me if I wanted one of my own smokes.

To give him time, I took one out and lit up. He nodded in approval, as though I were eating my vegetables. He clasped both hands around his own cigarette and pointed them at me. "Listen to me now, kid," he said, as though I had been doing anything else. "I wanna get this out. It's plain I never had a life like other people, not a normal life. But there, in the middle of all that fucking squalor, those crowded starving people, most of 'em terrified about what was gonna happen to 'em, there, I felt like I had a place that I belonged to. In the stink of that place full of dead people, in the middle of the Jews of Warsaw, who were all about to die, all of 'em, I had some kinda life. And I thought it was pretty certain I'd die with 'em. But I belonged there. I did.

"A little while after the boy died, I went out on one of my food raids and I jumped a drunken German officer. This was as far away from the ghetto as possible, so the Jews wouldn't be blamed for it. I took his pistol and a pouch of extra bullets. And back in my little corner of the

Brotmans' room, I sharpened one of my leather-working tools into a knife. At night I went from one street to another, I walked for hours, you know how I can walk, kid. I patrolled the Warsaw ghetto like a – a – "

"Guardian angel."

He gave me a long, slow look, and I thought we might go at it again. Then he pointed a finger at me. "Don't start with me about angels again. Don't be funny or I'll – "

"Take it easy."

"And don't fuckin' tell me to take it easy," he said but he was calming down. "There was no angels in the Warsaw ghetto, boy. Just the Jews that would be dead soon and the German soldiers outside the walls that were gonna kill them all. And me, the one – "

His voice trailed off but mentally I finished the sentence for him: *the one who belonged neither to the one nor the other.*

"The weather warmed up, and with it came a new feature of life: the Germans started rounding up the Jews, sending 'em off on trains. To be resettled, was what they were told. People seemed to take hope from this, they were so desperate they wanted to see possibilities instead of probabilities. Then we heard they were taking them to labor camps, to work. But I had lived in the camps, I knew that there were no camps where the people were expected to go on living beyond a few weeks or a few months. It took a while but eventually word spread that these people were being taken to Treblinka, this was the big camp, and they'd be killed there.

"At night they sat around in their crowded smelly rooms and talked about what was happening, about the ones that had already been taken off to be executed, and who might be next, and who the Germans might leave alone and who they might use for a work crew and stupid shit like this, because some of the people didn't want to accept that the Nazis were gonna come for 'em all. But I knew what was coming. Three or four times more I went out and took weapons from German soldiers."

Meyer gave me a look rich in malice. "Always officers. Always. Those sonsofbitches. Pretty soon word got around that I was armed and somebody came to me and told me to be ready. There was a resistance movement there, they were arming themselves and they were waiting for the right moment. Anyhow, one day a young guy named Mordecai – Mordecai Anielewicz, his name was, him I remember – this guy starts calling out on the street for people to resist, says they're gonna fight this shit. Some of the people, I could see in their faces, they didn't think anybody was gonna stand up to the Nazi army. But sure enough, next morning when they came for that day's 500 doomed Jews, these young badass Jews opened fire on them. They'd been collecting weapons, same as me, and they killed a bunch of S.S. troopers that day. And that was the start of it. The long streetfight in the Warsaw ghetto.

"We fought every foot of the ghetto, from behind fences and boxes, we fought from the buildings we lived in, we fought from holes we dug in the ground and basement windows. We killed Nazi soldiers every single day until the fight was over. One of those times they caught a bunch of us in a hallway in a tenement, about a dozen of them, ten or twelve of us. They rushed in and there we were. We all fired at the same time, there was smoke and you could smell burnt cloth from the shots fired at such close range, and a couple of us rushed them and grappled with them, you could smell sweat, ours and theirs. I grabbed hold of a guy's shirt and put my knife in him, and we were all so crowded together he couldn't go down at first. That hall was so packed with bodies fighting and dying nobody could get out even if he wanted to. We fought till they were all dead."

He pulled at his lip and gazed into his past. I could hear his raspy breathing. "In the end, they brought in a full S.S. division to fight a couple thousand untrained Jews, set fire to whole blocks, trained their tank guns and artillery on the apartment buildings, bombed and burned us out, all of us, until the Warsaw ghetto was just a pile of old bricks and burnt lumber. And they took the rest of the Jews, all of 'em, to Treblinka. Men, women, children, babies. Not the Brotmans, though. They were all dead. Killed when a Panzer tank blew their little room to pieces, with them in it."

"And you?"

"We were in a little dead-end alley between two buildings, five of us. When the pile of dead S.S. men at the mouth of the alley got their attention, they brought in a machine gun and finished us off. I woke up in a pile of the dead. It was the middle of the night, and for the second time in my life I was in a mound of dead human beings and my body felt like it was on fire, I was shot in a couple places. I felt myself drifting off again and thought I was finished. Sometime near morning I woke up again and knew I was gonna live. When I was sure there was no guard watching the dead, I crawled out, made my way into the woods and escaped. Once again. This time it took me a little longer to recover from my wounds. And one other thing I noticed, I was starting to age a little more. The skin of my hands seemed a little more wrinkled, I thought I saw age spots that hadn't been there before. Later on, when I finally got hold of a mirror, I could see my face looked older. Not much, but a little. I remember that. I was actually glad about that.

"I got in with a bunch of Polish partisans. I stayed with them for a time, we blew up trucks, killed sentries. Twice we ambushed patrols and once we had it out in the woods with an SS unit that'd been sent after us. They killed a lot of our people, and we killed most of them. A few months after that, word came to us that there was gonna be another fight in Warsaw. This time the Polish Home Army was gonna make their fight, all throughout the city, in every street. I went back to Warsaw. "

"Why this time?"

He raised his eyebrows. "Why do you think?"

"For the fight. You went back just to fight."

He gave me a curt nod. "The Poles were ready for their fight and I was gonna be in it. I'll never know for sure why they didn't all fight when the Jews inside the ghetto fought, maybe they weren't ready yet, and some of those Poles had no fondness for the Jews. But about a year had passed since the ghetto was massacred, and it was their time. And that was a fight, kid. That one got their attention, the Germans."

Meyer held up two fingers. "Two months we fought 'em. We fought 'em all of August and all the way until October. A whole German Army, special SS units, rockets and mortars, all that shit, tanks, thousands of soldiers. We fought street to street, took over public buildings, lost ground, regained it. At some point the Germans started massacring people whether they were fighters or not, women and children, old people. Killed hundreds of people in a hospital. Rounded up all the people on one street and shot 'em in the center of it.

"I fell in with a bunch that included a couple of absolutely crazed Jews, they'd lost all their people in the ghetto rising, and some hardcase fucking Poles."

I thought for a moment. "Bednarik."

"Yeah, him. Marek was his name, Marek Bednarik. He was a badass. And the last time we fought, it was in a crowded street and the Germans had both ends blocked off, and we were shooting one another point blank. And there were some civilians caught in the middle, trying to get out of a building, women and old people and a couple of small kids, and they were all down in a matter of seconds. We fell back from the Germans and guys were falling on all sides of me, and then we broke out of that street and ran into people that were running out of a narrow alleyway, and I heard one of the women call out, 'It's the end of the world'."

He looked at me. "*The end of the world,*" he repeated, and chuckled quietly. And I got to tell you, kid, it felt like that. It was a time of madness, I saw hundreds of people die that day, Germans and Poles, we fought all that day, hand-to-hand we fought. Some of us got caught in a little courtyard, and an SS unit came at us, and we were all mixed together, no lines of separation, just a bunch of people shooting. I fought a big SS sergeant so close I could smell his breath. He hit me with the butt of his rifle and I clawed at his eyes and I beat his face with my bare hands, I fought him till I thought I'd faint, but he gave out first."

As he spoke, Meyer's eyes bulged and he literally spat his words out, his spittle flying. He paused and wiped his mouth on a sleeve.

"In the middle of it all I saw this kid, just a boy, I don't know how he got in with us, this was just fighters by this point, I told him, 'Stay by me,' and as long as I kept him right behind me, he was okay. I had a handful of his shirt and I kept him there, and he was okay. Small kid, skinny – I'm sure his people were all dead. Then somebody hit me from behind and we got separated. I got up and I could see the kid, and an SS trooper coming for him. And just for a second I thought I'd get the SS guy but my shot went wide, I was no marksman. No marksman, just a fighter."

The look in Meyer's eyes was as close to an apology as I'd ever seen there.

"There was firing all around me, people being shot, but I watched and I saw that Nazi bastard shoot the kid, I saw the kid die with this look of surprise on his face. Then the Nazi looked around to see if anybody grownup might've seen him, seen what he did, and he saw me. Last thing he saw in life. I didn't use no gun."

For a moment Meyer was silent, his breathing heavier as though from the exertion not of the telling but of the remembering, and Farrell's words about him came back to me:

"He has lived an involved life."

"That night what was left of our group, maybe a dozen guys and two women, we crawled into what was left of a shelled building and I remember I could hear us all breathing like we run a long race. Somebody passed a jar of water, I don't even know where it came from. I wanted to drink it all, I felt like I was gonna die of thirst, just like that time I drank out of that stream. I just took a sip. The next day we went out to fight again but it was pretty much over for us.

"By this time most of Warsaw was burning – the order came down to destroy the city. The air was fucking clotted with smoke, you could smell people burning like roast meat. The Home Army surrendered, and the people that were still armed marched out and became prisoners of war. They marched 'em off, to all the different camps. Not all of 'em, though. Some of the fighters made it out of Warsaw and into the countryside. A few snipers kept at it."

"And you?"

"I slipped down into the sewers with Marek and another guy. We stayed there for a couple days, in the sewers. You'd be surprised how far you can go in the sewer system of a city. While it was all burning we slipped out, out of the city. Eventually we joined up with a partisan group – " He smiled and pointed at me. "This is where I met little Georg – Ivy, that crazy fucker."

"He said you saved his life."

"He's goofy, he don't know what he's talking about." Meyer shrugged, gave me a quick glance to see if I'd bought it.

"Anyhow, he was about fifteen then, an orphan kid from the very first days of the war, he'd been livin' on his own for almost five years. And the rest of the group was nearly as nuts as him. I stayed with them until the last days of the war, and we fought more or less constantly. Every day we fought the Germans, kid, every day."

And he stopped then, and I was aware that he was breathing audibly as though the telling had exhausted him. For a long moment he looked off into the corners of the room. He seemed more pale, and a haunted look came into Meyer's dark eyes so that for just that one moment he seemed a very tired old man, of no menace to anyone. Then he brought himself out of it.

"When it was over, I went from one place to another, I saw people trying to start over like nothing had happened and other people that were just lost, and every place I went, it seemed I could remember somebody from there that died in the war. All of those people, all dead. And it seemed to me then that everything I did in the war was without a point. Everything was foolish: I didn't accomplish nothing, it was all bullshit. They all died, just as they would've died without me being there." Then he gave a slow shake of his head and looked at me.

"So I ask you, kid, where is the point in all of it? Show me."

"I don't know."

He shrugged. "People don't even remember now. And the ones that saw it, they're all dead or dying. So what was the point?"

His voice had grown softer: he posed the last question to himself.

"It couldn't be pointless, there has to be some purpose to it."

I wasn't even sure I believed that, I spoke just to be

saying something.

"There does, huh? Ask Farrell if there has to be a point. Ask him about the Somme, kid. Ask Farrell about the fucking Somme."

"Why the Somme? I mean, I know that's where he was wounded – " I began, then stopped. I had wandered into a minefield.

Meyer grinned, as close to a smile of perfect malice as I had ever seen. "Wounded? Arthur Farrell was killed at the Somme."

"What does that mean?"

He gave me a long look and then shrugged, clearly losing interest in baiting me.

"Ask Farrell. I got no time for this. You should sleep now."

"It's almost morning," I heard myself say. "Besides, I'm afraid you'll be gone when I wake up."

"So what?"

"What will I tell Farrell?"

"Tell him to stop being a fuckin' old lady. I'm fine."

"Anyhow, I gave you the bed. So you should sleep."

"I got to go."

"Where?"

Meyer shrugged. "Somewhere I never been. Maybe the desert. You didn't think I was gonna ride back to Chicago in that car, did you? You and me in a car for all those miles?"

"I didn't actually have an idea how this would all play out. I just did what I was asked to do."

He made a short nod and said, "Maybe I'll close my eyes." And with that he stubbed out his last smoke of the long night, then fell back onto the bed. In seconds he was snoring, a loud, grating, startling noise that filled the room. For a time I watched him and saw again some of the violent images he'd conjured. And almost as troubling, I recalled his sneering look as he'd told me about Farrell and the Somme. But I was exhausted as well, and I was asleep in the chair not long after he dropped off.

When I awoke daylight filled the room and he was standing in the middle of the floor watching me. I had the impression he'd been in precisely that pose for some time.

"I was waitin' for you to wake up."

"Yeah. I'm up. And you're leaving."

He nodded. "Can I take your smokes?" He held them out.

"You've got them already." Meyer had a slight red mark on his cheekbone where I'd landed a punch during our fight but his cut was nearly gone. I touched the side of my head and found a tender spot where he'd landed one of his own.

"You all right?" Meyer asked.

"I'll live."

He shrugged as if this were no gift. For the first time since our scuffle I realized that the money we'd fought over was still scattered on the floor all over the room.

"Take money."

He shrugged, bent over and grabbed a ten and a couple of twenties, jamming them into a pocket.

"I gotta go."

"Take it easy, Meyer."

He turned and with his back to me gave me a short wave. Then he was gone.

I spent my last morning in Seattle wandering around near the waterfront. Tucked between a tavern and a diner I found a tiny bookstore, presided over by a birdlike little woman who seemed to spend most of her time arranging and sorting her books, adjusting and readjusting the spines till they looked as though no human had ever taken them off the shelves. I saw her give me the look when I entered, and I couldn't blame her: a thin guy with a battered face and a beat-up Army coat lurches into her shop when she's alone. So I looked her in the eye and said, "Hello."

In a fine display of old-time manners she ignored my bruises and just said, "Good morning, sir."

I stood in front of a tall bookcase of fiction, saw a book by H.G. Wells and reached out for it, then pulled my hand back – I would have to mess up the perfect order of the little woman's shelf.

"Go ahead, they don't bite. At least not right away." She regarded me over her glasses with a look I recalled from the nuns in grammar school.

"I didn't want to spoil the symmetry."

She smiled. "The symmetry is my job. Were you looking for anything in particular?" She squinted at the book I had been reaching for. "H.G. Wells. Are you interested in that sort of thing?"

"I like his stories. And I've read parts of his *History of the World*."

She looked at me with renewed interest, and then a new thought came to me. I suddenly needed the sort of book all readers come to need at some point. Just as in those early days in Farrell's shop I had wanted to read about boys of the street, Studs Lonigan and Danny O'Neill and hard-luck families, now I wanted to see myself in the pages of a book: I wanted to read about men who do not belong anywhere, or who feel that they do not fit anywhere.

"Actually, I was looking for something else. Can you suggest a book about a character who needs to see the world? Kind of a wanderer."

Her face did not change but her eyes did. She looked at me with a cautious curiosity, blinked several times and then bustled over to another section of her shop, beckoning me with a simple crook of her finger.

She stopped in front of another bookcase. "Have you read Conrad or Maugham?"

When I told her I had not, she pulled several books from different shelves. To her credit, a couple of them were small, well-thumbed paperbacks – she wasn't trying to sell me *The Book of Kells*.

"Wanderers, you say? Not explorers? Because if you want explorers and adventurers, then you should read Conan Doyle and Jules Verne and Stevenson. Even Kipling – *The Man Who Would Be King*, for example."

She looked pleased when I told her I'd read it and enjoyed it, and mildly surprised. I doubt very much that I looked like a reader of Kipling.

"Right now, I'm more interested in wanderers."

She glanced at my Army jacket and looked quickly away. "Then it's Conrad and Maugham, and the others." She moved back and forth, her eyes scanning the shelves, and when she was done, she had seven or eight books. I was about to protest that I really didn't have money to buy a lot of books when she said, without looking at me, "I know you don't want so many books but I want to give you a choice, a selection."

She showed me novels by Joseph Conrad – *Lord Jim* and *An Outcast of the Islands* and *Almayer's Folly*, and a collection of stories by Somerset Maugham called *Ah, King*, and a novel called *The Razor's Edge*. From a bottom shelf she produced *South Sea Tales* and *Martin Eden* by Jack London.

"What do you recommend of these? Which ones are best?"

"In my view *Lord Jim* is the best. But people find Conrad difficult: dense, complicated writing and lush description. But his characters tend to stay with one for years and years. Yes, *Lord Jim* is the best of these but you should read it later. When you are more settled."

I couldn't tell whether this was shrewd observation or merely a comment on the literary tastes of the young.

"Also, his books are essentially sad, for so many of them are about failed men, you see. His wanderers are men who feel they have no place, or they've fled the place they belonged to. There is little in life so sad as a failed man." Here she paused to add, "Or, more accurately, one who concludes that he is a failed man." She said this with the certainty of experience. "I'd read Maugham first. You'll enjoy him – a very underestimated writer, in my opinion."

In the end I took the two Maugham books and the Jack London stories and – for later – two books by Conrad. At her desk she wrote down the name and price of each book in a thick notebook with yellow pages, and I saw that she had filled many such pages. Then she took each of my purchases, stuck a small bookmark in it and wrapped it in thick beige paper. She settled each book carefully in the bottom of a paper bag, then rang them all up on a great cast iron relic that may have been the ancestor of all cash registers.

I thanked her, and she said, "Vaya con Dios, as the Mexican people say. Lovely expression: 'Go with God'."

"I would if I could figure out where he is."

"God is elusive, young man."

"Never thought of him that way."

This seemed to please her. She told me to come back some time, if I ever made it back to Seattle. I had no idea how she knew I was from another place.

As I left, a small scholarly-looking man in a dark suit and homburg entered the bookstore. He could have been her fraternal twin. He touched his hand to the brim of the hat as we passed, made polite eye contact and I nodded. He broke into a shy smile when he saw the proprietress and called out, "Hello, Mildred, I've finished the Durrell books."

At the door I stole a glance at her, and she was beaming at him, and there was no doubt in my mind that this was some autumnal courtship.

Twenty-Eight:

In Praise of Failed Men

1 drove more or less straight back to Chicago, sleeping in the car by the side of the road. In sleep I was visited again by the dark images of Meyer's tale, and twice that first night on the road I awoke in a night sweat, heart pounding over dreams I couldn't recall. I made only one real stop, at the Badlands of South Dakota, and on that day just before sunset, deserted. It is a desolate, scarred place, as though God himself has clawed the ground. It is possible to stand in such a place and imagine a world in the earliest stages of its life, empty of man. I enjoyed that thought, and the odd notion that soon followed it, that here was a place scoured of the past, so that a man who emerged from it might indeed start over in the truest sense of the term. I thought of the little bookseller and her comment about the sadness of failed men and it struck me that she was attempting with great delicacy to head me from that path. I wandered there for nearly an hour, in that place where time seemed to begin, and only turned back

when I startled a small snake, which in turn scared ten years' growth off me.

I drove into the city in the dense dark middle of the night when the big trucks feel they own the highway. The last time I had come back to Chicago I had been little more than a derelict, hitching rides and bumming cigarettes and lying to strangers about my name. That other time the city had seemed a place of menace to me, a dark looming shape on my horizon that promised me no good, as it had done me injury in the past.

But this time, as I drove in with the Buick's windows open, I felt slightly giddy to be back. It was an alien feeling, the closest I had been to elation in years. For the longest time I had had the unshakeable belief in my own impending death. Somewhere between Edwin Bergson and my long night with Meyer I'd stopped thinking I would die soon, but I couldn't have said where it had happened – in the soft company of Karen Mannheit perhaps, or on that desolate stretch of beach at Puget Sound.

Knowledge. I felt that at long last I had received knowledge, I was closer to understanding all the mystifying things I'd seen and experienced. As I drove I could hear Farrell all those years ago, counseling me to be patient.

And now, Farrell, I said to myself, *is the time for patience.*

I got myself a room in a transient hotel on Halsted. The walls were cardboard and I swear the bathtub was made of plastic. The handle came off when I opened a drawer in the dresser. Somewhere down the hall a guy moaned in his sleep while another guy watched the White Sox, I could hear both of them simultaneously. My room had one useful feature, though, a full-length dressing mirror, and after a shower I stood naked in front of it and assessed what I was.

The man in the mirror had the same unruly brown hair I could see in my childhood pictures, the same serious look around the eyes, but he'd been busted up some, this fellow. The cuts and bruises of my recent sojourn in the West were indistinct, all of them healing in one way or another. And as they healed, they left a sort of patina of hard use on my face. I noticed other things now. For perhaps the first time in long years I saw the person others might see: a tired-looking body and a face already showing scar tissue like a boxer of limited gifts. Pale and scarred and underfed, this man, and damaged in ways large and small. He stood with weight slightly to one side in deference to the bad leg, that knee actually slightly larger than the other – all these years later it remains more or less permanently swollen. An image came to me then of Meyer, of what his bullet-pocked body so much older than mine, so much harder used, must look like in a mirror.

One more change I noted, and not one I could see in the mirror: for reasons I could never have put words to, I felt a sense of almost physical relief, as though I had come through the worst of a long illness. And that, that was in the eyes.

Farrell was standing at one end of his counter buying old books from a thin woman in a man's raincoat. I saw him give her $20, and as she left the store I saw her peek into her pocket, as though to make certain the bill hadn't jumped back out.

Something made me pause at the door. I watched him put the books on a table for later sorting.

Arthur Farrell was killed at the Somme.

He looked up. "Hello, lad," he said. "This is a lovely surprise."

He seemed genuinely glad to see me but I doubted it was any sort of surprise. He set down the book and studied my face, my bruises and whatever other baggage I'd earned.

"You've changed. Grown older in some way. That's good."

"I've put on some miles," I allowed.

He gave me an expectant look. He leaned forward, searching my eyes, then smiled, and I understood we would now engage in that sort of talk when what two people say has nothing to do with the heart of a matter.

"How are you, Thomas?"

I decided not to play. "You wasted your money."

"Why? Because you couldn't find him?"

"Oh, I found him. You knew I'd find him, I think."

An impatient shrug.

"But I couldn't talk him into coming back, and you knew I couldn't make him come back against his will. And now we have no idea where he is. Again. So what did I accomplish?"

He nodded, as though he'd been paying no attention. "You spoke to Meyer, then. How was he?"

"All the usual things: rude, belligerent, what you'd expect."

"And nothing else, lad?"

"No, well, not at first. He seemed more or less the way he has always been. I spent a day with him, I let him spend a night in my motel room, so in a sense you paid for his – "

"His lodging?" This seemed to amuse him, and I was quickly growing frustrated.

"So you don't think this was a great waste of your money and my time?"

He gave me an owlish look. "No. I – "

"Ah. I get it: you didn't expect me to find him in the first place."

"Oh, but I did, lad. Yes, indeed, I did. I knew you would employ your several gifts, and you would find him."

"Gifts again. I have no gifts, Farrell."

"You have some experience of the road, you have your – your detective skills." He smiled as though he'd made a fine joke. "You are dogged in your pursuit of things, you are in a queer way tireless with your constant questioning, your endless walking – I can imagine you chasing him down on foot across the continent, a matched pair. You have curiosity in larger measure than most. And although I have no proof of this, I suspect that people will speak frankly to you more often than not. They will tell you things out of proportion to your familiarity with them. That, my boy, is a gift."

I ignored all this and instead contemplated the unspoken answer to my question: he had never meant me to bring Meyer back – at the very least, bringing Meyer back would have been an unsought bonus.

"The trip was the thing, wasn't it? The trip itself was the point."

He looked at me for a moment and I saw that he would rather I come to a certain conclusion without his being forced to admit it.

"A part of it, yes," he said hesitantly.

I suddenly saw Meyer sitting on my bed in the motel room, staring off into the vast spaces of memory and thought I understood. To spite Farrell I changed the subject.

"Got any coffee?"

"Of course. There is always coffee." He bustled around in the room behind the shop and returned with coffee and a bowl of sugar cubes and a small carton of half-and-half.

The coffee was burnt into another substance but I drank it anyway. Farrell glanced at me several times but did not force the conversation. We both knew he'd wear me down.

"So here is what I think, Farrell. I mean, for a while I tried to convince myself that you really needed me to go out there, that there was nobody else you could send out into the country looking for Meyer – what with me being a gentleman of leisure – perfect person to do you this favor. But I see now that you were doing me the favor. This was your way of getting me off the street for a while, maybe give me a chance to think about things, about where I am, what next, et cetera. Is that about it? Or part of it?"

He surprised me by nodding. "Yes." He sipped his coffee, made a face, said, "I beg your pardon, Thomas, this is quite terrible."

"Forget it. Well?"

"Yes, of course I wanted to – to extricate you from your unhealthy circumstances. Morbid circumstances. You would do the same for me, I believe."

"I like to think I'd stand you to a meal and slip you a few bucks, but then be able to see the difference between your business and mine. You're not a man who minds his business."

He gave me Dickens: "'Mankind was my business.'" I looked into my coffee cup and he dropped Marley's ghost and came back to the point.

"I said, lad, that the trip was a part of it. Not the whole of it. The trip was just one thing. To help a fellow get back on his feet, as we used to say in the old days."

"Which old days, Farrell?" This was malicious and I regretted it immediately. He ignored the unkindness.

"Back, you know, in the Depression. A time of failed men, Thomas. Women as well, for the country seldom remembers the women. It seemed half the people I knew were living on the very edge of things. And some went over it. Poor people, dying largely from an acute sense of shame. And we used to say, all of us, 'If I could just get back on my feet,' or "I just need a couple bucks to get back on my feet.'"

I smiled: he'd slipped into a perfect American accent, the nasal speech I heard in old movies, he could have been James Cagney.

"Another hidden talent, Farrell?"

"Oh, just something for my own amusement. But you asked me a serious question and you'll have your answer. Yes, the trip was a part of it, to get you off the street and break your patterns. A man's patterns are the thing, lad, and half the time if a fellow in trouble could only break them he would survive. But they are invisible, you see.

You can't see them at all."

"But they're there when you look back."

"Indeed, they are. So that was part of it, to break your patterns, though, fair play to you, Thomas, you had already broken them somewhat when you came to me: you were working and you'd put aside a few shillings to buy the lovely Buick – did it come back with you or bleed its last on a Western highway?"

"I ran it into a ditch in Wyoming, but that was the worst of it. I still have it."

He pulled at his lip. "I wouldn't mind a short ride in your car some afternoon. As a young fellow I was fond of cars."

"And hitting trees with them, as I recall."

He heard the small truce in this and smiled.

"But breaking your patterns was just the smallest part of it. An urgent part, it seemed to me at the time, but in the long run not the most important." He sipped his coffee and added, "I believe you are aware, on some level, of the other – aspects."

"Other aspects?" I snorted and drank some more of his dire coffee to buy time. But now a spate of images came to me, faces and things said, things said to me, impressions. Impressions of Meyer, of his life. I'd spent weeks going from one place to another, to meet with people who could tell me about a moment in Meyer's life.

"Meyer. You wanted me to know about Meyer. You hoped I would learn from his – his friends about what he's been through in his life. You wanted me to understand Meyer."

Farrell gave me a sideways nod: I was getting some of

it, but only some.

"When you met up with him, how was your meeting? Did it go smoothly, Thomas, or were there difficulties?"

"We tried to punch each other out, is that what you mean? We fought in my motel room."

He sighed. "A donnybrook. Did he hurt you?" He squinted, noticing my facial bruises.

"Not much. Most of this is from other sources."

I saw him mouth the words *"Other sources"* and give a slight shake of his head. "Good lord, Thomas, what have I put you through?"

"I'll live."

"You cannot fight your way through your life. It would be a form of suicide."

"My impression is that Meyer has done exactly that."

"Yes, and look at him. The poor man is a walking mass of scar tissue. And his physical injuries are not half of it."

"I know. He told me, at least some of it. Some of his experiences."

Farrell did not exactly brighten – he was too deep into the moment for that, but a change came into his face, a touch of optimism, a sanguine moment.

"And *that*, Farrell," I said, pointing a finger in his face, "was the real point of this. You hoped that would happen, that I'd hear his story."

"Aye. So I did. His story, indeed. Or at least a portion of it – he would not tell you all of it, and I don't think another man could bear to hear all of it."

He gazed at objects around his shop and to a stranger would have seemed distracted, but by now I knew at least a few of his thousand strategies of disputation, and I knew this silence was meant to force one more admission from me, that I had not yet reasoned out the final objective of my journey. At first I was unsure what he wanted from me. I heard the ticking of his clocks, the tinkling of his spoon in his cup.

Then it came to me, a long train of images, of what I had seen and felt, inexplicable things, unsettling things. I remembered odd experiences, the sense of Farrell watching me at the abandoned ship in Washington, Ivy appearing seemingly from nowhere and yet knowing where I was from and who I sought. And I recalled how people had reacted to me, heard again what they said: Arlene Roenicke's greeting of *"My road-weary friend,"* and her comment, *"You wander a lot."* I remembered the odd glimmer of knowledge or recognition in Karen Mannheit's lovely eyes. But most of all I remembered what I had felt in the presence of old Bergson, his words to me: *You've had a hard time of it, haven't you, son?"* And perhaps even stranger, the words of his young nurse: *"He's the best thing for you."*

I saw now that my trip had merely confirmed what I had long believed, that I experienced things that simply did not happen to other people, and that they were not a function of my imagination, or depression, or alcohol or even the stark loneliness of my existence. And other people, a handful of people, were sensitive to these things about me in ways they should not have been.

I considered the sum of these strange moments and saw what they revealed and refused to give Farrell the satisfaction of admitting that I'd learned anything about myself. I said nothing. And for once in my long involvement with Arthur Farrell, I forced him to speak when he would have preferred silence.

"I'm sure there were other things you learned, Thomas, were there not?"

"Such as?"

"Well – I hoped you would be able to answer some of your life's questions."

"My life's questions? What questions would those be?"

"Ah, you'd know more about it than I, lad. But all the young men have questions: will I find a girl? Will I be successful? Will I have money? Will I have a long life? And the more generous, they ask, Will these ones I love, will they live long lives? Will they be well?

"But you, Thomas, have an entirely different set of questions, colored by your experiences, your – nature." He shot me a quick look as he added the last part, but continued as if worried I might interrupt.

"Your questions are about the past, and about the present. You ask 'Why?' about so many things. Why has my life been what it has been? Why have I not had a life like other young men? Why have I seen the things I've seen? What has happened to me? Or what is happening?"

I set down my cup but he held up a hand to forestall objections.

"These are the constant questions of your life, and I had thought to assist you in answering some of them through this – this endeavor. But I don't know if anything came of it. You'd be the one to say that."

"If you mean, have I gotten my answers to these things – no. At least, I'm not certain of that. I had hoped you'd see your way clear to answering some of them for me."

"Don't assume I have these answers. This knowledge."

"You do, I think. You've caused some of it."

"I told you before, Thomas, I have no such powers or abilities. That's not the way of it. I've caused nothing. Except for your numerous injuries, lad, for which I am sorry."

"They're not important."

But he seemed genuinely troubled that he might have caused me suffering, and I saw his distraction, I saw an opening.

"Tell me about the Somme, Farrell."

He shot me a suspicious look, then understood.

"What did he tell you?"

"Just the basic facts. That is, that you were killed at the Somme."

"Killed?" He made a show of confusion, then amusement. He muttered, "*Amadan*," and I wasn't sure whether the *amadan* – fool – was Meyer or me.

"Manifestly, I was not killed, lad, for here I sit, not five feet from you."

"He would do many things for his own malicious amusement, Farrell, but after all he told me that night in that motel room, after we tried to beat each other's brains out on the floor, I just don't see Meyer lying to me. So what did he mean?"

Farrell brushed his hair back from his face. "He meant nothing. 'Tis a great lot of nonsense." But in his face I saw genuine distress. He got up, shaking his head, and went into the back room and I heard him boiling water for tea and knew he would speak of this now. He would speak to me of himself.

Twenty-Nine: Shanachie

Farrell went through the ritual of his own personal tea ceremony and I knew not to disturb him. He doctored his tea, sipped it, added milk, sipped again and nodded. He set down his cup, cleared his throat and leaned forward, his hands on his thighs.

"I have never felt a part of anything, you know. You've heard people say of someone odd or very old fashioned, 'He was born too late,' or 'there's one born out of her own time.' Well, that is not exactly the way of it with me, but I understand the saying. I understand a person not part of his time or his people.

"You yourself, you've learned what it is to be out of step with the world, my friend. You as well as anyone. I have ever been out of step with the world. 'Tis why I first left home, why I left Ireland, why I kept moving and wandering over the years till I could take no more of it."

I thought I heard an oddly plaintive note come into his voice with the phrase *"why I first left home."*

"Did you have to leave home? I mean, was it really necessary?"

"Yes. If not then, well, soon after. Folk in our small village had long marked my abilities, admired them, in fact: I could read before any child in the village, I could memorize improbably long lists, poems – I still can, you know." I nodded, this I had seen.

"As the youngest, I had a whole house full of sisters – " He paused then, remembering his sisters. " — of sisters to stand up for me, but I was 'a quare one,' as the oldest girl would say. They doted on me, but my oddness did not go unnoticed.

"And as I got older people noted my idiosyncrasies more than my small talents: I read constantly, borrowed books from the local schoolmaster, from the parish priest – I devoured the Bible, Thomas. I read the Bible so many times I have it by heart. I spent all my time alone, I had no interest in others my age, including the girls. Not that I did not find them appealing, but it seemed they were not for me." He frowned, then raised his eyebrows.

"Though it might surprise you to know I had for a time a –a romantic involvement. In New York when I first came here between the wars."

"It didn't work out?"

"She died." He looked off into the room for a moment. "She was a fragile girl, physically as well as emotionally. I knew from the first time I met her that she would not have a long life. I saw this," he said pointedly. "I saw it."

As you see such things, his look said.

"But it was just as well, you know, for she would have grown older and seen that I did not."

"Yes." I was startled. There it was.

"But we were speaking of my small village in Leitrim.

402

There was an incident: a child was hurt playing in the woods not far from the field where I was working, and they brought him to me for no other reason than that I was there. A simple cut on his knee but a bloody one so he was frightened by it and the other lads thought it worse than it was. A comical scene, really, all of them terrified by the blood, and the little fellow sobbing so. You'd have thought he'd lost a finger. I told them to let me have a look at it. I wiped some of the blood away with a handkerchief and then the impulse took me, I wanted to help him, I wanted to show off my worth. I'd once closed a cut on my brother's arm, but he was too young to realize what had happened. And so I pressed my fingers onto this child's cut knee and the wound closed up so that there was nothing but a small ridge of scar to show where it had been, and even that was faint. They ran off exclaiming at what they'd seen.

"Later that night a group of mothers and fathers from the town came to call on my mother, to ask about me, whether there was anything about me they should know. She told them they were all a great bunch of ninnies and fools and not to bother her with such nonsense. But when they left I saw the fearful look she gave me. A few days later the priest came to our house. He spoke not with me but with my mother. The following day he contrived to speak to me in the street. We sat down on a small bench and we spoke of everything from the weather to the local footballers and when I thought he'd simply wanted someone to chat with, he asked me about the cut, and the healing. He asked if I'd ever done that before, and I told him of my brother. And that I did not know how I'd done these things nor even if I could do them again.

"He asked me his questions and listened and showed no emotion. He was a phlegmatic fellow, taciturn, not the best traits for an Irish village priest so that he was respected but not actually liked. An outsider, he was, like me. But a good man, and no fool – he'd lived in Sligo and Dublin, no bumpkin, this fellow. He did not believe in witchcraft or any of the other nonsense that festers in small places. It was clear that in his eyes this was a significant thing I'd done. And so I asked him if I should stop this, never do this sort of thing again. I knew he'd give me the straight answer.

"And he laughed at me."

"'D'ye know the Corporal Works of Mercy, bucko?' says he. 'Yes, Father,' says I. 'Well, this is one of them, and no mistake. But this is not the place for it. And too small a stage for a clever lad. In the old stories, the lads go out and seek their fortune. You should seek yours.' And the priest got to his feet and brushed off his cassock and left me there. And when he'd got a few feet away, he turns and adds, 'And send home money to your mother. There's a good lad.'

"I was sixteen. My mother was mortified, and relieved. She feared for me, and her own brothers had gone off to the city for work, so this was a bit of a family custom. She made me a fine bundle of food, and a second parcel containing the herbs and leaves she used in her own remedies, her many remedies. Then she hugged me as though she'd crush the life out of me, and saw me off."

Farrell paused, sipped his tea and looked away, unable to speak for a moment, and I understood that he never saw

404

her again.

"I did not make my way to the cities, not at first. I traveled the length and breadth of my small country and learned what I could learn. Here and there I dared heal a small wound, always taking care to combine my touch with a salve, or a drink of some nostrum of my own device. And who knows? Perhaps Mother's remedies played a role. For a time I made a modest living that way. And I'm happy to say that on one or two occasions, I sent money home to her, and small gifts as well.

"And then I fell in with the Travelers. Do you know them, Thomas?"

"No."

"Some call them the Tinkers. The older Irish call them *an Lucht siúil* – which means 'the Walking People.' They are nomadic people, Irish gypsies, though they are not at all related to your gypsy folk that come out of Europe. Just a wandering sort of Irish people. They lived and traveled in wagons with rounded sides and they spoke to each other in a sort of dialect called the Cant, or Shelta, an odd stew of English and Irish and words of their own. Like the true gypsies they are not trusted or accepted. But they took me in – found me, quite literally, by the roadside where I'd come down with an injured knee."

"*Cygan*," I said.

He frowned. "What was that?"

"It's what the Jews of Poland called Meyer. I think it means 'gypsy'. You became a gypsy."

"Ah. Well, not quite. They were kind to me and saw at a glance that I was, like all of them, something of an outsider. 'Twas clear I was not one of what they called 'the settled people.' And I was of some small use to them: I could heal the occasional cut – a talent which impressed them only slightly, for there had been some Traveler woman earlier who'd been able to do the same thing and with serious wounds – and I was another able body to help when the wagon sank into the mud, and I could read. Most of them could read nothing, and so I had value to them. And they to me: they taught me their own store of folk medicine and the head of the clan that took me in, fellow called 'Marius,' taught me sleight-of-hand and the showmanship that goes with it. And for a time I enjoyed their peripatetic life.

"In the end I made my way to the cities. I lived in Limerick, then in Cork City, and finally in Dublin, and I exhausted a succession of careers: I set type for a printer of children's books, I performed street magic for pennies, I dispensed medicine. And for a brief time I taught school in a village in Wicklow where the schoolmaster had run off with a fellow's wife. I thought for a time that would be the place for me, the life. But I was beginning to note other things about myself."

"What things?"

"I was not aging, at least not in the normal way. At thirty I looked twenty. So I took myself to Dublin again, this time to stay there, where I thought to hide among a larger population. But Ireland is a tiny country, and more than once I saw a fellow frowning at me in the street, and once I am certain it was a man from our village, wondering if the lad he knew had sired an identical son or had made a pact with the devil. I wrote home to say I was going to London. I received a short note back from my eldest sister wishing me well and telling me that my mother had died some years back.

"And so I lived in London for quite a long time. And it came to pass, as they say in the Bible, that I began to feel haunted."

"By the strangeness of your life."

"No. That, I accepted rather early on. No, Thomas, I became haunted by two things, by the unending solitude of my life, and by a crushing sense that there must be a purpose to this, that I had some task to perform and had not done it yet, had not even learned what it was."

Farrell paused here and gave me a long look. I did not bite.

"The War came, our war. There was grave debate over whether Irishmen needed to be answering the call of an English king but thousands volunteered nonetheless. And I recall telling myself, 'This madness is nothing to do with me.' And I'd no sooner told myself that, than I had the odd sense, unshakeable, that this was how my questions were to be answered, all of them.

"I had no interest in soldiering, I'd carry no weapon, that was certain. And so I volunteered for medical service in the British Army. For a time I worked as an orderly in one of the hospitals in the rear, in a Belgian chateau. Already the horrific nature of the war was clear to me, equally clear that I must somehow participate. I volunteered to become a stretcher bearer, and was attached to a brigade of Irish regiments that included the Second Dublin Fusiliers. The Dubs. They liked me, those lads. I looked and sounded like one of them, and they'd no way of knowing I was twice their age. The very first day with them I saw men shot, and a short time later, at Ypres, the lads were gassed by the Germans. I caught a lungful of it fetching our wounded, it hung in the air and I wore no mask. I remember hoping I'd be able to carry the wounded lad back behind our lines before I died. But I did not die. Unlike the other poor devils who died that horrible way," and here he looked at me, to see if I recalled the poem. I nodded.

"But I recovered, remarkably. Men told me I'd been lucky. 'Lucky Paddy,' some of the English called me. Some luck! Fortunate to survive so that I could live to see the Somme. The blackest day of the war." He sipped his tea and then surprised me by asking for a cigarette.

I gave him my pack and he lit one up and puffed a couple of times, then looked at the cigarette.

"Woodbines, we smoked back then. Short, dense-packed cigarettes, they were. In the hours before the Somme, it seemed every man smoked a Woodbine. One of the lads near me said, 'I just want to be the toff that makes these,' and the other lads all laughed. In two hours almost all of them were dead. There was a mist that morning. A fine soft morning, it was, and then the sun came out. And so the lads waited on a beautiful July morning in France, waited for the greatest artillery barrage we'd ever seen to finish wiping out the Germans. Then the shelling stopped and there was a strange moment of quiet anticipation. I had the sudden ridiculous notion that we'd ended the war, followed by a sense just as strong that I was soon to die. And then the oddest combination of noises: the officers climbed out of our trenches and blew their shrill whistles for the men to follow in the assault, and just up the line from the Dubs I heard the bagpipes of the Scots regiments. Whistles and bagpipes under the blue French sky.

"And so the British Army marched out in perfect restraint, men five yards apart, at a relaxed pace, lads on parade. The officers carried walking sticks, Thomas. Those in the Irish regiments carried blackthorn sticks. And each man in the line wore a shiny piece of tin on his back, 'twas supposed to help the spotters see the extent of their progress, the sun shining on the little tin squares. And when they had gone a few hundred yards the Germans opened up, thousands of machine guns, none of them silenced by our guns. We soon found that our terrifying shelling had done nothing but crater the lovely French soil: it had neither killed Jerry nor blown apart the miles of barbed wire strung thick across that field. And I tell you, Thomas, I could not witness a day like the Somme again for it would leach the life from my heart.

"The Germans later said you didn't even have to aim your weapon, just point and fire. Our lads fell in waves, lay on the ground like piles of dead leaves. Men were shot as they tried to climb over the wire and their bodies hung there like the leavings of the crows. In the sector where the Scots fought, the Gordon Highlanders charged into battle in kilts. In kilts." He shook his head. "Their kilts caught on the wire, and many of them died frantically trying to tear themselves free.

"We stretcher bearers ran out to them. I have no idea how many times I went back out into that carnage. No lack of dead and dying – half the men who left our lines were shot the first hour: twenty thousand died that morning, three times that many wounded. Killing and suffering on a

409

scale I'd never imagined. Some units lost ninety percent of their men. As our lads pushed on, they fell farther away and we had to follow. Twice the other stretcher bearer with me was killed. All the rest of that awful morning I brought in the wounded and the dying, many of them my lads the Dublins. Once, a man died on my shoulder: shot again even as I carried him. If the shot had passed through him, it would have killed the both of us. At some point I lost some of my hearing, from the incessant firing, but it might have been that I willed it, to block out the shrieks of the wounded and the dying. Poor souls."

The horror of that time was plain on Farrell's face, and I noted as well that, as he fell deeper into his tale, his eyes grew more distant, and the Irish crept back into his speech.

"We came upon a man whose face had been blown off. The rest of his body was untouched but he had no face. The other man with me began to sob. He collapsed on the ground and I left him because there was a wounded lad nearby. Just a boy, this one, and bleeding to death. He lay on his back, looking up at the sky. White as bone, from shock and loss of blood.

"I pulled back his blood-soaked shirt and saw his wounds, shrapnel wounds they were, and one in the center of his stomach. The blood seeped from it, but the killing wound was at the base of his neck, where the blood spurted and gushed. I pressed against the gash with all my strength, I put my weight on the poor boy's neck, but the blood came through my fingers. And suddenly it seemed that the whole point of the battle came down to this moment, that I could not save this boy whose life literally gushed out of him. I believe I began to weep, and I could not look at the boy, could not meet his eyes in my failure. I pushed and squeezed and held the gash closed and sobbed in rage as I lost my grip again and again on his skin that was slick with the bleeding. I pressed against the wound as though to push in my own life force. But I could not stop the bleeding. I stayed that way till my body began to cramp and my hands grew stiff, I stayed there till I grew faint and my hands could no longer grip the boy's skin. And I wanted to scream at my failure, I called on God to give an account of himself if he was there at all, told him to show himself. I was losing my head, d'you see, Thomas?"

I nodded, for indeed I saw what he described and considerably more, for as Farrell told his tale his face grew pale, his skin slack as though he were exhausting himself in the telling. His breathing was audible. He looked at me with red-rimmed eyes, and I'd never seen him look so vulnerable.

"D'you see?"

"Yes."

His cigarette, hardly smoked, was just a column of ash and he looked around to find an ashtray. I laughed inwardly at this: in a shop filled with a hundred ashtrays, brass and steel, novelty ashtrays and ashtrays of all the fifty states, he could not find one to use. I took one from a countertop and pushed it toward him.

"Oh, not that one, boyo, that's from the World's Fair of 1933."

I laughed and he gave me a sudden self-conscious smile. He found an ashtray more to his liking and put out the cigarette. I held up the pack and he waved me off.

"So he died, the boy," I said.

Farrell blinked, then shook his head. "No. No, he did not. The bleeding had stopped, you see. The bleeding stopped and I pulled back my crippled fingers and the gash was closed. But closed as though it had a month in the healing. I said something to the lad but he was unconscious, breathing evenly as though he'd just gone off to sleep. I looked again at the fine scar line of his wound and wondered if I'd imagined all of this, but I had his blood to show for it, on my hands, my wrists, the sleeves of me shirt were matted with it. I stood up and found that I was wobbly, dizzy and half-deaf and it seemed my vision was clouding, and I looked for the other stretcher bearer to get the boy off the field. He was lying on his back a few yards away, dead with a dark crusted wound in the side of his head. No saving that poor fellow. So I carried the sleeping boy back to our lads and went out again, for it was clear that was what I should be about."

Farrell watched me for a reaction and then went on.

"Twice more that ghastly morning, Thomas, I *ministered* to the dying, and pulled them back from death. And each time I felt more exhausted, more drained. Once I fell onto the field and could not get up for some time, wondered even if I were meself dying, that I'd burst my heart somehow with all of this. When I did get to my feet again, I staggered back toward our line, for I knew I was finished. I saw the way the other lads looked at me as they passed, the other stretcher bearers, the men looking for their mates.

"I was perhaps half the way back to our lines when I thought I heard someone calling my name. I turned and felt a great force strike me in the chest. It put me back on my heels and as I looked down in wonder at the hole that had appeared in me chest, a second shot took me in the shoulder. I found myself knocked back on me buttocks, and I recall thinking this was no way for a fellow to die, falling onto his arse. But it was clear to me, Thomas, that this was it, I'd got my killing wound. I had no doubt I was dying."

"What – what did it – ?"

"What was it like? Not the wound, of course, for you'd know about that. Death, you mean, the feeling of dying. It was like nothing. It was death. I felt the life leaving me and for once, just that once, young Thomas, I felt peace. But I saw nothing, no lights at the end of a long corridor, no happy faces of the long-dead waiting to welcome me into the afterlife, none of that. Although I did think of my mother. A fellow will think of his mother, even so many years later. I heard more than one dying man that day calling for his mother. And another sound I heard as I lay there, my lad, that I would not hear again. Strange to tell you, perhaps it sounds mad to say so, but on that field where 20,000 men of ours had died in just a couple of hours, I heard the sounds of their souls, the anguished souls. Nothing will ever convince me otherwise, I heard their souls. But I lay there dying and could comfort none of them.

"Later that day, when the guns fell silent men came out among the dead and dying and looked for men who could be saved. They found me, bent over me and I heard one say, 'He's gone, not a pulse in 'im.' 'Oh, Jaysus,' says the other. 'Tis our Farrell.' He kept his hand on me and then the other one said, 'This lad's alive over here,' and the fellow moved off, away from me, and I understood there was no more to be done for me. Then I felt nothing.

"When I woke it was dark, but time had passed. Days. I could smell the dead, their bodies beginning to decompose. I was face down on the field, my face pressed into the dirt, I was half covered with it, perhaps from a shellburst. The smell of gunpowder still hung on the field and I could smell the essence of the earth churned by a half million explosions. I remember wanting desperately to call out, to raise my face out of the dirt. And I could not. There was firing in the distance, and heavy shelling began, so that even if I found me voice, I would not have been heard.

"When I came to again, I was lying on the ground with a blanket over my face. I pulled it off and heard a man shout "Jesus the Christ!" and I wanted to call out to him with some fine joke about Jesus but I could not speak. In the end, I was in hospital for five weeks. My greatest shock came the first time I was able to shave meself: the face in the mirror was mine, but 'twas a gray-haired man that looked back at me. Before the Somme my hair had been black, darker than yours, Thomas, and now I looked more or less my true age. Men who'd known me stopped by and marveled at it. The doctor who attended me wasn't interested in my hair – common enough, he said, for a man in terror to age overnight, he'd seen lads of twenty come out with white hair. But he could not decide which was the greater miracle, that I'd survived wounds that should have meant my death, or that I'd recovered in so short a time. Just before I was released he came to see me. He regarded me with a not unkind look as he shook my hand, a look that said he knew I was beyond his experience.

" 'Good luck to you, Arthur Farrell, and don't let Jerry shoot you again, for you could not be this lucky twice. Or perhaps you could – but 'twould be better not to count on it.'

"Once more after that I was to witness combat, once more to stop a lad's fatal bleeding. A year later, at Paeschendale. He was some distance away from me, a gutshot boy, sitting with his back against a shattered tree trunk and holding himself. I saw him there, suffering not only the pain of his wound but the loneliness of his dying, just a boy sitting against a tree with the life leaving him and no one of his mates there to see. I made for him. I heard the bullets rip the air around me and the bark of the trees and I did not care. He saw me coming, started to say something and stopped. I don't know what he saw, Thomas, but it frightened him. If he'd been able to move, he'd have run from me.

"'There, now, lad,' I says to him, 'we'll have a look at you.' And I put my hand on his shoulder until I felt him relax. And I stopped his bleeding. I believe I fainted then, Thomas, and when I awoke, the wounded soldier was still asleep. I put 'im over me shoulder and took 'im back to the dressing station. That was my last action. I spent the remainder of the war attached to various field hospitals and dressing stations. I did what I could."

"Meaning?"

"I worked no more 'magic' – but I found that I could give peace with my hands, that men responded to my touch, particularly those who suffered inwardly, who had lost hope. I could calm them, it seemed, merely by laying my hands on them. But I closed no more mortal wounds, I saved no more dying men. Later, on those few occasions over the years when I called upon it to save someone, I saw that this, this power or ability had its own mercurial character, came and went from me with no pattern that I could discern. And as had happened at the Somme, when I was able to – to fight off a person's dying, it weakened me, diminished me."

I noted the word he had once used to describe Meyer: *diminished.*

"And worst of it was, I saw no sense in it, I could not see my purpose."

"Your purpose?"

"Yes. Why give a man the *occasional* power over death? Why? That was the question that haunted me. That and the lives I could not save. So that was the Somme, Thomas. That is my tale."

Farrell's eyes took on a distance, I'd lost him to his own history. He thought for a moment, then made a dismissive wave like a man refusing the offer of food. He leaned back in his chair, breathing heavily. He was finished – literally. He looked drained, heavy-lidded. He sipped at his cold tea and put the cup down, and even as he watched me I saw him begin to nod off. With a start he caught himself and apologized.

"Time to go, Farrell. I'll stop by again."

"Good lad. After all, we didn't answer your other questions." I ignored the sly look that had come into his eyes, tired or not.

"I only asked you the one, Farrell," I said, and waved at him as I went out the door. A customer was entering

416

just as I left, a man with a bag of books and nervous eyes. I remembered a man in another time, lying in an alley, and tried to make sense of it all.

Thirty: Clark Steet Boogie

Of course there were other questions, and only one was about Farrell, but I stayed away from him for a time and walked the streets if only to give myself time to digest what I had heard. Now these things were out in the open, and even though I had long suspected some of them, it was no small thing to accept them. Harder still to accept what it all meant for me, for I doubted another person on earth had heard both these tales. It seemed I was no longer the boy in the corner of the shop reading comics. What I had become, that was the question. At night in my rented room I listened to music on a cheap transistor radio I'd bought and thought about what I'd heard. There were many more aspects of Farrell's life that I wished to know about, but I had the sense that sometime when I least expected it, Farrell would instead tell me about myself. I thought of the strange experiences I'd had in the past year and I realized I was afraid to know about these things.

Other concerns I had as well: the need to come in from my existence in the dark margins of life. So I spent some time looking for work. For a month I earned grunt wages, put some away, drank less, bought clothes and new tires for the Buick, and when I thought I'd pulled myself out of the mud, I decided to show myself to someone. On a hot muggy afternoon I took in a movie at the old Clark Theater, where the moviegoer was always guaranteed adventure, and not necessarily on the screen. The double bill that day was *Gunga Din* and *Zulu* – dead Englishmen on two continents, Her Majesty's unemployment program in high gear. A trio of pickpockets roamed the theater looking for guys who were asleep, went through pockets, took wallets and cash. They saw me watching, and when I left they followed. I spoke to the manager who shrugged and said, "Place like this, whattya gonna do?"

I had coffee in one of the old DeMars grills, then drove up the late afternoon circus of Clark Street.

Farrell stood in front of his counter, an expectant look in his eyes.

I said "Hello," and pulled the door closed behind me.

"Hello, Young Thomas, an unexpected pleasure," he said, and I heard the preoccupied note in his voice. His gaze remained fixed on the street but he recalled his manners and forced himself to look at me.

"There's coffee. I hope you'll stay awhile."

"Sure."

People came in, a woman looking for mysteries and old Pickett, the retired man of the sea, whom I had not seen in years. We sat in a corner on folding chairs, sipping Farrell's toxic coffee. Pickett inquired about my "travels" as he styled them, and we chatted about the mountains and the badlands, and trains, he was a great lover of trains. And all the while I was in his shop, Arthur Farrell watched

419

the street. It began to rain, and customers scurried in, strangers soaked through their clothes and laughing over it. I saw how they looked at the shop, as though they'd found themselves in Oz. An hour or so after I arrived, the door opened and brought a wet ghost into the shop, and all of us, Farrell, Pickett, myself and half a dozen others, all of us turned to face the newest refugee from the rain, all of us drawn to this late arrival.

I looked from the newcomer to Farrell, who said merely, "Well, Meyer."

And Meyer, hatless and so looking smaller and vulnerable, shook the water from his coat and said, "Got any food?"

"I'm sure we have something."

Meyer nodded and seemed to recall his rudimentary manners and said, "Whaddya say, Farrell?"

He nodded to Pickett, then saw me. He gave me a shy smile and said, "Fuckin' kid."

Farrell shook his head at this language but this was merely a formality: I could see in his eyes how pleased he was. He looked at me and nodded as though I'd done this thing. I shrugged. Farrell called Pickett over to introduce him to another old sailor, and I sat in the corner sipping coffee.

Gradually, piece by piece, a new scene of surpassing strangeness assembled, like a play putting itself together: four or five more customers came in, including Leo the Professor, compensating for the baldness of age with a massive fringe of electrified looking hair, a cab driver from the old days, and a wizened bag lady I didn't know. A short fat priest came in followed by an apparition from my past, Father Mackin, gaunt and pale and sunken-eyed, looking like a refugee from a vampire movie. And Madame Volga, Madame Volga the Clark Street fortune teller, bent and frail but bustling into the shop and calling out greetings in a voice that could have stripped the bark off a tree. She still wore her improbable turban and wig, the blue-and-silver cone that added four inches to her height.

She called out "Hiya, Farrell," and "Meyer, long time no see," and gave off a smell of violets and mothballs.

I made the rounds, greeted the ones I knew. Father Mackin introduced me to his stout companion as "the boy who used to take care of me when I gave my retreats. The soup boy."

"So you're the soup boy," the other priest said, nodding, and I laughed.

Father Mackin asked how I was doing. As I spoke I realized from his ashen pallor that he was dying. Dying, yes, but interested primarily in how I was faring in life, and smiling, the smile never left his face. He asked odd but clever questions of me and nodded as I told him what he wanted to know.

Someone called for music and Farrell turned on his old Crosley radio behind the counter. He motioned me over.

"A favor, lad. It appears a gala has erupted. We need sandwiches."

He took out his old money clip and gave me cash, added to it from the great iron box of a register and sent me off to a nearby diner for food. I was to decide what to bring back. Half hour later I returned soaked to the skin but laden with a dozen hamburgers, some fries, a couple

421

of bowls of chili, and for Farrell, a Denver omelet sandwich, and I entered a room gone dense with cigarette smoke and the smell of burnt coffee, and the noise and the odors of wet cloth and mothballs.

I set the greasy bags on Farrell's counter and looked around me. The room was alive with a half dozen arguments too loud for a bystander to focus on any one in particular. On the far side of the room someone had put Glenn Miller on Farrell's old record player, and I heard Tex Beneke's breezy baritone singing "Chattanooga Choo-Choo".

I stood at the end of the counter and gazed around at the debaters, some of them arguing with cigarettes in clenched teeth, Meyer and the Professor and the unknown bag lady and Madame Volga and the two priests and a tall man with wild eyes, all their images softened by the thick blue smoke, as though they grew less corporeal by the minute. Two strangers came in and joined arguments in progress. I let myself stare off into space and listened, amused, to the shards of conversation and the odd fragment of poetry or song that made their way through the babble.

"How could there be no God? What about miracles?"

"Ah, your man Frost gives all these lads a run for their money."

"—and if it wasn't for the unions, we'd all be working like slaves, like slaves."

" – could actually tell your fortune by looking at the lines at the corners of your eyes, she was that good."

"Sweden? A world power? In what world?"

"Miracles? It's a miracle nobody decked you yet!"

"— but the man's language is so perfect you don't know you're hearing actors read iambic pentameter."

" 'A thou-sand Swedes ran through the weeds, chased by one Nor-wee-gian —'"

"— small islands that no one has ever mapped, I saw them myself in my Navy days."

The noise swelled to a physical presence and I would have sworn the building was swaying. At some point the clocks all began striking five, and I heard Meyer say "Oh, shit, here we go." For a moment the multifarious jangling and bonging of Farrell's clocks drowned out Meyer's muttering and the debaters and Glenn Miller's trombone, and then in the small space after the chiming, the band moved on to "Kalamazoo" and Madame Volga began to dance.

She shuffled around the room with half-closed eyes as though jitterbugging with an imaginary partner, and as she moved, her great turban began to slide off and she pushed it back atop her head. From across the room, Meyer broke off a complaint against God and startled me by dancing across the room toward her. He matched his movements to the music, did not miss a beat or a step, and when he reached her, grabbed the turban from her and placed it on his own barren head. The woman gave him a smile impervious to such foolishness and went on dancing. Without her wig she was tiny, nearly bald now. But wig or no, she boogied. She danced, Meyer danced in his turban like some deranged dervish and the debaters left off their arguments about God and Robert Frost and unkown islands and watched, grinning. Toward the end of the song Meyer grabbed his partner and spun her around

423

till she shrieked like a young girl. I had to laugh. At the other end of the counter Farrell was watching me as he took the food from the bag. I met his eyes. He shrugged and shook his head, and smiled what seemed a tired smile.

Between songs he called out, "Young Thomas has brought us some lunch," as though it were my idea, and the party paused for refueling. They fell on Farrell's banquet like ill-mannered children, laughing and murmuring at the food. I watched them eat, ignored Farrell's invitation to join them until I was certain there was an extra burger, and then I plunged into the party. Someone turned up the music once more and now a second couple took the floor, the bag lady and Professor Leo, and a moment later Madame Volga dragged Meyer out once more to show his moves. He danced with a cheeseburger in one hand and gnawed at it as he spun his partner through the room.

Farrell glanced from them to his counter top, now coated in grease and spilt mustard and chili and shrugged, content to have them trash his shop, thankful at the return of his Prodigal Son.

It seemed a good time to leave. I nodded to him, went to the door and took a last look around me at the Clark Street party. As I watched them all through the haze I thought I saw the shop grow dark, empty, I saw it as it would be if all those present were long gone, Farrell and Meyer and the rest of them, I saw its remains, and I was surprised at the ache the image caused me. I waved to no one in particular and left.

In the weeks after the impromptu party at Farrell's I

managed to put something like a pattern into my life. I jumped jobs again: I found work first in a rambling used bookstore on Lincoln Avenue and, two weeks later, in the huge Kroch's and Brentano's on Wabash. Neither paid much but each gave me twenty or so hours, and I was not hauling junk or working on dying cars. I found that I wanted to be around books, and my employers were pleasantly surprised that I knew something about them. The people at Kroch's insisted on a coat and tie, and the dress code gave me an excuse to drop the Army jacket and the ragged flannel shirts and see myself as something else. With steady work and little to spend it on, I put money away. I found a small cheap apartment and furnished it from resale shops. Carefully and slowly I constructed a life, ever conscious of what had gone before, and how close I'd likely come to dying in a furnished room on Green Street.

Without making a conscious decision about it, I kept away from Farrell's shop. When I realized what I was doing, I saw the necessity. Farrell and his mysteries were hopelessly intertwined with the bleakest times and darkest elements of my old life. I was no longer that Thomas Faye. Indeed, I was no longer troubled by my odd "visions" or the unsettling moments of insight into other lives.

More than once during this time I thought of women, of relationships, and certainly many women came into the places where I worked. But always I held myself back, as though this was something that could not fit into the odd patterns of my life. I threw myself into my jobs, intent on absorbing every single detail of the business of books, for I had determined that someday I would sell books, in a shop of my own. I settled into something like contentment, even if the ghosts of my past nature gnawed at the edges of it. Sometimes at night I would wake in my small apartment in terror, beset by inexplicable fears, night sweats, by the sense that all the tranquil order in my life was illusory, or at best, that my modest success in constructing a normal existence would pass.

One night in late November, when a low sky made noises about snow, I left the used bookstore and began the long walk to my apartment. It was past nine, and on a long stretch of Lincoln Avenue the lights had gone out. An empty street, black as a tunnel. At some point I realized I had been hearing the same sharp footsteps for more than a block. I looked over my shoulder just in time to see a tall figure slip into a doorway. I picked up my pace. The person on my tail followed suit. A man who has been mugged in the street more than once will develop strategies for such moments. The thought of dashing into traffic or simply running seemed oddly undignified – I knew how to fight, after all. Somewhere up Lincoln I could see a Hamm's sign but it was more than a block away. At the corner I turned up a side street where the lights were working, planted myself in the middle of the sidewalk, took my hands from my pockets and waited for him. I heard him pick up his pace. His footsteps made an odd clicking sound that I couldn't quite place and then it came to me. A sound out of my childhood: cleats. He was wearing cleats, small steel plates once worn on men's shoes to slow down the wear of the heels and the tips of the soles. A sound from the past, on an empty street. His footsteps grew nearer and chilled my heart.

Then he turned the corner and I got a look at him: a tall one with a cocky strut, underdressed for November in Chicago: a flat Irish cap and a long scarf, a tweed jacket. Young and by his step aggressive, and oddly foreign. Though I could not see his face clearly I would have said he was good-looking, sure of himself. Then he saw me and stopped, caught short. I waited for him to do or say something, I prepared to fight. Then he made a little sideways nod as though I'd made a fine play indeed. He gave me the faintest of smiles and just as I moved forward, not to fight but to see him better, he spun on his cleated heel and was gone.

I ran to the corner and he was already halfway down the darkened block. His scarf fluttered behind him like a banner and he ran with a long-legged stride that I'd never catch. I ran a few paces after him and then gave it up. As he drifted into the darkness I saw him give me a last glance over his shoulder. I was certain he smiled at me.

Not the first time a mugger had been caught out and decided to change his plans, and so I thought nothing of it until about a week later, again late at night, and this time I trudged home through the first fat flakes of snow. I delighted in it, in the oddly clean smell of the streets as the winds of November scoured them and lay down a white cover. And then I heard the man in the cleated shoes. I spun around and startled a young woman, apologized and stood aside. She passed quickly by, huddled into the thick fur of her collar. I looked around and then I saw him on the far side of the street, walking more or less parallel to me.

He could have been any other man hurrying to get out

of the cold: hands thrust into his pants pockets, chin tucked into that long scarf. Indeed, he did not glance my way, showed no interest in me whatsoever. But it was the same man and so I stepped off the curb into the traffic and crossed the street to cut him off.

Before I could reach the other side he broke into his long-legged run and though I ran hard I could not close the gap between us. But I kept at it, even after he ducked down a side street. It struck me that he might tire, slow his pace, and then I'd catch him. And so we ran together, block after block through the thickening snowfall, the only sounds now the click of his shoes and my own breathing. And finally the gap between us closed, he was slowing down, and when we'd gone three or four blocks that way, he made a sudden cut through a gangway. I slowed down and ducked into another one a few houses before the one he'd disappeared into. I made my way through the snow-silent yard and out into the alley, and he was there waiting for me, shoulders hunched against the cold.

Despite the darkness I could see him smiling as he had that earlier time. It was a most singular, troubling smile that seemed to mix shyness with expectation, like a man uneasy about his welcome.

For a time I waited for him to speak, and then I blurted out, "What do you want?"

He made an odd shrug, as though my question had confused him. His smile faded.

"Who are you?"

He stared at me, then took off the flat cap and hit it against his knee to get rid of the snow. Before he put the cap back on he brushed his hair back in a gesture I recognized. I moved closer to get a clear view of his face. As I did so he moved back into shadow and his face and image became blurred. I kept moving forward and suddenly I stopped short. The dark figure in the alley faced me, his hat and shoulders coated once more with snow, and despair emanated from him. It seemed that his shoulders slumped with the weight of his distress, his almost palpable sorrow, and I understood it.

To feel fully, perfectly, the pain of another will scar your heart, and I understood his, my chest actually ached with it. I had known nothing like this in all my unasked-for visions of the lives of others. I was in the presence of a soul in nearly perfect loneliness.

I heard myself say, "I'm sorry, I had no idea," and I allowed him to back away.

I trudged on out the way the man in the cap had gone before me, and saw without surprise that there were no footprints in the fresh snow. And of course it was Farrell that I had seen.

Thirty~One: Seraphim

h e was sorting through a tray of his old silver dollars, his favorite among all the coins. *"For the heft of them, Thomas. Money once had heft to it."* Sorting his silver dollars, but he was waiting for me.

"Open late, I see."

"And yourself, Thomas, out late."

"Should I lock it?"

He made a wave in the general direction of the door and I slipped the bolt across.

"Where's Meyer?"

"Out 'cutting a rug' somewhere," Farrell said, and smiled.

"I might live to see stranger things, but I doubt it." He went on arranging the coins. "You know, I've never asked where you met him."

"Here. He come into the shop muttering his complaints about the weather, and asked if I had any coffee." Farrell put on a belligerent face and said, *"Got any coffee?"* in Meyer's own voice.

"And this was the first time you saw each other?"

"No, not quite. Once many years ago, in Europe after the war, my war this is, we – saw each other. I wandered

430

for a time after the war. I had a sense, you see, of looking for a singular place, a place I would see as the one I was destined for, where everything would become clear to me, all of it. It was no good, of course. I just wandered, made it as far as North Africa. Had a few adventures, as you might expect. And one day – I'd made my way back as far as Romania – 'Rumania' in those days, and they had a king, King Ferdinand. All the small countries still had their odd little kings: the Serbs had King Peter, there was Tsar Boris of Bulgaria, and for a time, King Zog of Albania. Little kings, such illusions we create.

"I found myself at the edge of a small orchard, and the apples had already begun to fall so that the ground was carpeted with them. Indeed, a deer was eating the apples off the ground, and I startled him when I entered. I was hungry meself, so I took up a few of the apples to put into my sack and I bit into one. It was a lovely moment: a warm day, and the tart smell of the apples on the ground, and there were bees hovering. I saw a perfect apple in a low branch and I was reaching for it when I realized I was not alone. Just a few feet from me was another man. Meyer. He was eating and watching me. He never took his eyes from mine. I nodded to him and he gave me the most reluctant wave of his apple. We exchanged no words and, indeed, when I looked up again he was gone. But I knew I would see him again. I understood I'd seen another like me. And thirty years later, he comes into my place of business looking for food."

Farrell shook his head, smiling, a silver dollar still in his hand. He seemed to recall what he'd been doing. He replaced the coin, peered in at the contents of the case, then shut it. He made the motions of dusting the glass cover but said nothing, forcing me to come to the point of my visit. I remember wetting my lips repeatedly, fumbling over a way to begin.

"What do you want from me, Farrell?"

"I?" An innocent look. "I'm not aware that I want anything from you. Do you want a cup of tea?"

"No. No tea ceremonies."

"It'll just be a moment. Cold night," he said, and disappeared. For several minutes he bustled around in back. I wondered if he was even aware of the apparition in the alley, of what I'd seen.

"How about an answer to an old question between us: who are you, Farrell?"

"Ah, now we're getting to the heart of the matter – though that is not the question that most troubles you."

"But –?"

"Yes, but 'tis a start. Who am I? No, *what* am I? – what you really want is a name, names are the way we try to understand things, we give them names and think we've sorted them out. So the clever lad in the village who learned how to foretell rain and predict an eclipse, he earned himself the title 'wizard' or 'shaman' or 'magus'. And many's the name folk have put on me – I've been called 'healer' and 'sorcerer' and as you've doubtless guessed, 'devil'. And if once they'd given me a name that I thought took the measure of me, I'd have worn it like a favorite hat."

"But you are a healer, you've told me, and I've seen that as well."

"At times. As I've tried to make clear to you, Thomas, it

comes when it will and goes again. And that day at the Somme the use of it again and again might have drained the life from me if I hadn't been shot."

"I saw you use this thing once, on the street, I saw you – do this. An old man – that old ragpicker that used to come in."

I'd thought to surprise him but he just nodded.

"All those years ago. Aye, I knew you were there, Thomas. I could not see you but I knew you were there. I was angry: I didn't think you were ready for it. But you saw."

Then he said again, "It comes when it will and it goes again. Though I still retain that small measure of it in my touch, I have ever had a calming touch. We've spoken of this."

I remembered the night he'd found me on Skid Row, Farrell allowing his hand to rest briefly on mine. "And I know about it."

Farrell leaned forward now, an urgent look in his eyes. "I can do no harm with it. Nor would I, if I could."

"I understand now."

"'Tis what you saw that night in the alley. That poor soul. He was dying, d'you see, he was suffering the greatest misery and pain, he wanted to die, and I calmed him so that he would have peace in his final moment. But I did not take his life. It was leaving him already."

"I'm sorry."

"Ah, you saw a terrifying thing and put a name to it."

"Nonetheless, some would say these things make you a healer." He shrugged, unimpressed. "And of course, you are a skilled magician."

433

He took this as it was intended: he smiled. "Aye, a magician. As if there were such a thing."

"Isn't there?"

"Not since Merlin. Just the ones in the old tales, lad. I know only of old conjurers like m'self."

I became conscious of the ticking of his several clocks, cars passing by, tires hissing on the wet streets, and I realized I was frightened of this moment. I sought to buy time.

"What about Meyer?"

"Ah, he's no conjurer. A man of no artifice is our Meyer. He is what you know. A man of diminished gifts, you might say."

"Why diminished?"

Farrell looked at me for a moment, considering his answer. "The great violence of his life has altered the essence of him."

"What is he then?"

"Now? He has seen more of life, of our poisoned century, than anyone alive. I believe that is his purpose, if that is what you are asking. He is now the witness to all he has seen, a tireless, seemingly indestructible witness. Perhaps destined to be the last. *But what are we?* the lad asks. One of the several things he wants to know. We are a pair of strange old men. A couple of fellows destined to be forever apart from the rest of humanity. And from each other, Thomas: you'll have noticed we share very little beyond our longevity."

"But you share something."

"Yes. Our common straits. But you're still looking for a name. There is no name for us. In ancient times men might have called us any number of ridiculous things. This is how the world creates its legends: dragons, ogres, trolls, elves, leprechauns."

He watched me for a moment, then leaned forward again, a tutor about to make a point. At that moment I was vaguely fearful of him.

"I want you to imagine, Thomas, a time when simple people found themselves in the presence of power, of a man or woman with genuine power, not tricks nor play-acting nor predicting the simplest of the earth's patterns but genuine power beyond that of a normal human being. Someone touched by this thing. This power."

"No, you're asking me to accept something else first: that such people could exist. Human beings with powers beyond the human."

"After all you've seen, all you've experienced, lad? Can you have any doubt?"

"I know only about you, Farrell." He raised his eyebrows at this but said nothing. "I've never actually seen Meyer do anything – anything really supernatural."

"No more, no. But his very existence is beyond anything 'normal' or 'natural' or whatever else you would call it. His age alone, Thomas, the fellow's indestructibility – No, there are such people and perhaps there have always been, and men have named them odd names: witches and warlocks, wizards, seers, shamans, magi – "

As he spoke an odd small moment returned to me from an earlier time: a page marked for me, the passage in H. G. Wells, Sir Harry Johnston's rumination on the possible origin, in man's first contact with the Neanderthals, of our cherished myths of ogres. I had not understood the passage, nor Farrell's intention in marking it, but now I understood its application to so many things. An image came to me of a simple man in primitive times encountering someone like Farrell, with traits and talents beyond those of normal men, and I understood the names this man would give to such a being.

And so to Farrell's list I added " – seraphim and cherubim and thrones and dominions. And archangels."

To my surprise he smiled at the interruption. "Indeed. Angels. One more name among many for what they could not fathom."

"Angels," I repeated, and thought of Meyer's anger on that long-ago day in the church.

He watched me with a look of almost clinical interest. The room seemed very cold. I began to see a dark pattern emerging, and I sought to conceal my growing fear. I gave him a casual shrug.

"So there's no actual answer to my question, Farrell. No simple answer, at least."

"None that I would pass on. And the simple truth of it, Thomas, is that no name would apply to us, for a name would imply that we are the same, Meyer and I and – and the others."

"The others? What others? How many others? How many like you have you – found?"

He pursed his lips and squinted as though the recollection were complicated. He tilted his head to the side and ran his hand through his hair, and I saw that I'd caused him discomfort with this question.

Finally he said, "Four. I have met four."

"Tell me about them."

"Well, Meyer, of course. And an ancient fellow I came across in North Africa – there was your healer, Thomas, I've no doubt of it. He made his way across the continent healing the sick and comforting the dying. When I saw him he was himself near death from the exhaustion of it, but the happiest man I ever encountered. Near death and therefore, he believed, nearer to his god." Farrell paused, and when he resumed, he spoke more slowly, as though the next recollection pained him. "And between the wars, a Belgian nun who went on to save many lives, a very young, very holy woman."

He gave me a sheepish look. "Had she not been a nun, I should have been wild in love with her, Thomas."

"Is she still alive?"

"No. She disappeared in the final days, like so many. In those times I met people and understood they would be lost. The young woman, I knew she wouldn't live out the next war."

He sipped his tea, sipped it again, smacked his lips uncharacteristically, waited for me to ask the obvious question. And so I did, I owed him that much for his candor.

"And the fourth, Farrell?"

He paused with the cup halfway to his mouth, held the cup that way and one finger came free, he pointed to me. I thought of half a dozen incredulous responses, I wanted to curse at him. I said nothing.

"You, lad. You. I knew it the day we first met. As did Meyer."

I recalled the first thing I ever heard Meyer say: "*Another one.*"

My stomach churned so that I thought I would be sick. My breathing came faster. I wanted to run from the room. He watched me with concern, with sympathy, he waited for me to speak.

"But I'm not like you. I'm – I don't have these – powers." I started shaking my head and the words came out in a torrent, just as they had on that drunken night so long ago when I'd first confronted him.

"I have no powers, I've healed no one in my life, I never could. Jesus, Farrell, if I could have healed somebody I would have healed my mother. I would have healed that kid that died next to me in Nam, I would have *done* something in my life."

"Your life, I suspect, is far from over."

"But I don't have any of these – " I stopped myself, looked away, determined not to lose control, not to weep.

"You have abilities, you see what others cannot, you've told me of your visions, your experiences. Think, Thomas. Reflect for a moment on that day in the clearing in Vietnam. See it again, see the small details. What happened?"

I remember shaking my head to dispel the image but it came nonetheless: I saw the kid Kloppstein dying, weeping, shuddering, then becoming calm as I placed my hand on him. From my touch. I recalled the Vietcong soldier with the blood-filled eye, I could see again the look he gave me, a look that might have been recognition. And I remembered *his* touch. Whether the moment was just the surreal aftermath of a short, one-sided firefight or the unlikely confluence of like-gifted strangers – I couldn't have said.

"You see into people's lives, Thomas."

"What kind of a gift is that? What good is that?"

He ignored the petulant tone. "Think, lad. Lonely creatures, we are, and the saddest aspect of human life is our inability to read each other's souls. You, Thomas, you see into their souls. It has been given to you to see their moments of pain, to sense the depths of their unhappiness. This seems a gift to me."

He tilted his head to one side. "And more than once people have sensed this about you. As I have. As did Meyer, the very first time we saw you."

"How?"

"It is difficult to put into words. But the first moment I saw you, as you stepped inside my door and stopped there, for just a second I could not see your face clearly, as though something disturbed the air around you. The way distant things are distorted in sunlight. Your features were, quite literally, a blur, while I could see the rest of you perfectly."

"And Meyer, that day in the apple orchard?"

"A look of recognition. Something in the eyes."

I felt a sudden urge to resist, to debate him, to ridicule all of it. But I had no heart for debate. I knew it was true, all of it, at least in the most general sense, and I'd known before he opened his mouth, before I even went there that night, that there would be one explanation for all the things that troubled me, and that Farrell would provide it.

In the end, I chose to say nothing. I feared my skull would erupt with my questions and the great sense of dread that now came over me. I drank my tea, suddenly quite thirsty, as dry as though I'd been the one doing all the talking. I drained the cup, he pointed to it, I nodded for more. He took his time to give me a moment to compose myself, indeed to compose one question of my hundreds. When he returned with the tea I drank mine too fast, burned my lips, swore, felt foolish. Farrell waited.

"I can't believe – I don't want to believe this, any of this."

"I know."

"But what would be the point? I have not saved a life, I have changed no one's future, I cannot recall a single moment when I did something to someone that changed anything."

"So far as you know."

"Except for the smallest, most common acts of kindness, as far as I can tell I have never done a bit of good for anyone, I've displayed no abilities to change lives, I've – "

"And how would you know?"

"I'd know."

He shook his head. "Think, boyo. That day at the Somme, of the men that died that morning, I believe I saved three. Three of 20,000! And for years I asked myself what the point of the thing was, why those three, why not three others, why not three hundred? And the thought even struck me, Thomas, that at least one of those three boys was more than likely killed later. And the few times over the years when I was able to do something like that again, and not always when I wished – your mother, lad, I would have cured that good woman if it had been granted me – but in all those years I waited to see the pattern, the point. And finally, whether through the acquiescence of age or simply the gradual emergence of some sort of wisdom, I accepted all of it: what it has been given to me to do, and the limitations of the thing. I came to know that it is not possible to see what point my existence might have had.

"Perhaps one of the lads I pulled through the war accomplished some fine thing, perhaps he just lived to be a good man and raise children like him. Perhaps my reason for existence was the day I met the lovely young Belgian nun, to encourage her in her perilous work against evil. Perhaps I was meant only to look after poor mad Meyer, a hapless fellow if ever there was one."

He gave me an arch look and I smiled in spite of it all.

"More recently, though, I've come to suspect that I had another purpose, that the point of it all was to be there in the old shop that long ago day when three young thugs chased you in from the street."

"Some destiny."

"'An ill-favored thing, sir, but mine own,'" Farrell quoted. "And there is the chance, Thomas, that you will never know the why of the thing."

"I understand that."

He studied me for a moment. "Crestfallen, you are. Don't be afraid of this, of your – your nature. It is not without its benefits. I have little doubt, for example, that it is why you did not die that day in Vietnam."

"It's actually something else that I'm – "

But he read the unfinished thought, my greatest fear, and laughed.

"'Tis immortality you are fearful of. You would not be like old Meyer and meself, living long past your time."

441

"Yes."

"I have little fear for you on that score. Look in the mirror, lad. You actually look older than your years: the road and the drink and your interesting propensity for pugilism have all marked you. It is what a fellow might call a 'lived-in face'. Meaning no disrespect, Thomas. So you'll likely be spared that, at least, the long loneliness of outliving all your – your people."

There seemed little one could say to that. I drank the rest of my tea in silence. Farrell sipped his and watched the street, an odd look of contentment on his face. I realized I would not mention what I thought I'd seen in the alley that evening. I had little doubt I'd been granted a glimpse into his soul's more despairing moments.

We drank our tea and I watched him, and for the first time I understood all of it, the old errands, the books left open to odd passages and lines of poetry, the people and experiences he sent my way. Half of it so that I'd understand him, half to prepare me for what was to come.

I offered to get us sandwiches. He brightened at the thought, not of food, but of company. At that moment the clocks rang and buzzed and chimed, and he smiled.

"I am always disappointed when Meyer is not here for the clocks."

As I put on my coat I gave him my final question of the night.

"What if there is no point to any of it?"

"Of course I've thought of that many times. In that case, the opportunity to do good, that would be the point of it, simply to do good. Good, like evil, is a great contagion. It spreads like a sickness. You have the

442

opportunity to do good."

"And God, Farrell? What about God? Where is he in this?"

"He has chosen to remain anonymous."

He shrugged and put away the teacups. I went out for sandwiches.

Thirty-Two: A Gift

I spent the better part of the next week alone. Despite the coming of winter I took long walks along the lake, watched the dark water pile up against the rocks and freeze. Curiously, it seemed that when the sun shone brightly I could convince myself it was all nonsense, that most of my experience was the product of an imagination steeped over the years in vodka and panic. For the next month I nearly wore myself to exhaustion in a manic attempt to demonstrate to myself my own normality. I worked longer hours, read everything I could about the book business. I bought clothes, spent money on things meant to dispel the gloom of my apartment, I socialized casually with co-workers, went on a pair of dead-end dates. I visited used bookstores and began a modest collection of books about Chicago or by Chicago writers.

On a cold evening I stopped in the DeMars Grill on Ashland for a cup of coffee. A man in a nearby booth gave me a furtive look and then turned so that his back was to me. Too late, for I'd recognized him, a guy named Dan whom I'd known casually in high school. And in the moment of eye contact I'd seen something else as well.

I had a sudden sense that the room was slowly turning,

so that I had to sit back in the booth and close my eyes. I'd seen his life, not a single instance from his past but a series of images, as though I'd been shown a dark collage of a life: I saw this man's childhood, I saw a kitchen not unlike the one I'd known as a boy, and the man across from me was a boy watching a man and woman fighting in it, literally wrestling, the woman with some sort of knife; I saw the boy, older now, running down an alley, I saw him in a strange city on a street corner and he couldn't have looked more alone, I saw him in a hospital room, staring out at the darkness. I saw images of violence and drunkenness and loneliness, and if asked to name the aura, the sense I had of this man across from me I would have said it was desolation.

The waitress took my order and I turned to the other man.

"It's Dan, right? From Lake View?"

He nodded and I told him my name and he smiled. We forced small talk. He watched me with his careful eyes and I noted the red rims, a man not far from weeping, and finally I got him to talk, the two of us sitting at the edge of our respective booths. And Danny spoke of Vietnam and family long gone and alcoholism and a failed marriage, and I noted that he spoke calmly, slightly embarrassed but without self-pity. The waitress brought my food and I saw his gaze rest on my hamburger. On an impulse I told the waitress to bring him whatever he wanted. He didn't argue.

When his hamburger came he moved across from me in my booth, ate fast as though the waitress might change her mind, and we talked of the old times. The theme, if there was one, seemed to be how far from our expectations life takes us.

I watched his face as he spoke, he was pale, his cheeks slightly sunken, his lips chapped. I noted that he'd shaved carefully, he was still putting up a fight. But he was a sickly man. When he was finished eating he took out cigarettes, offered me one and was glad when I accepted.

I paid the bill and got up to go. "It was great seeing you again, Dan," I told him, and though it was not my custom I felt compelled to put a hand on his shoulder. I felt him move slightly, a man unused to human contact. And I felt something else as well, a sudden pulse of something like heat. Danny was looking down but I saw him blink, twice. He sank back into the booth as though the conversation had exhausted him. At the door I took a last look at Danny. He was sipping the remains of his coffee. His cheeks were flushed.

On a cold Saturday close to Christmas, in a shop no larger than a walk-in closet I found a 1902 edition of Tennyson's *Idylls of the King*. It was bound in red leather, and illustrated in the grand old way, and despite bent corners a steal at twenty bucks. The proprietor wore a derby and dark glasses, and he sang along with the Grateful Dead – "Jackstraw" – a hobo-jumping-the-trains song, and as a former drifter I took it for an omen. When I handed him the money he smiled and said, "I could get fifty for this from a dealer downtown but I need the money for drugs."

I wrapped the book and went to Farrell's. On this frigid afternoon an odd group had assembled: two college-age girls I'd never seen, Leo the Professor, Meyer, Pickett.

Farrell was in "serious" negotiations with a homeless man who'd brought in a lamp, a joke of a lamp, the cord frayed to the point of uselessness. He gave the guy a dollar and Meyer made the farting sound with his lips.

Farrell shrugged. At the far end of his counter he'd set out a pot of tea, a bottle of cheap Scotch and a bottle of Powers Irish Whisky. In the background, his old Crosley was tuned to a station that played '40's music and old radio shows. I handed him the package. He nodded toward the liquor.

"Help yourself, lad. I've turned the shop into a *shebeen*. There's better money in it."

"A bold career move, Farrell. Oh, and nice job decorating for the holidays."

He shrugged. He had hung a single wreath over the front door, and taped an aluminum star to the cash register.

I watched him open the package. For a moment he stared at the cover and then simply said, "Ah."

He paged through it, nodded, found a favorite passage and read it to himself.

"A lovely gift, Thomas. Thank you."

"What have you got there, Farrell?" the Professor asked and Farrell held up the book for his admiration.

"Your man Tennyson. Come have a look."

I left the two of them to contemplate the lovely cover and soon they were quoting Tennyson to one another.

People came and went and, though no party erupted on this occasion, the press of bodies in that small space, combined with the old music and Farrell's liquor touched the day with a barely suppressed giddiness. I helped myself to the Powers – Farrell had long ago told me there was no point drinking Irish whisky unless it had a bite to it – and sat to one side, eavesdropping on the talk in much the same way that I'd done all those years ago. Through it all Meyer remained near the front window, exchanging no more than a few words with anyone. At one point I saw him move his head to the music – Benny Goodman's band – and for just a moment I thought he might dance again. But there was no Madame Volga to partner with this time.

I poured myself a second shot, tossed it into a cup of Farrell's bituminous coffee.

Leo the Professor left, nodding to me as he hit the street. We'd never exchanged a single word but were now old acquaintances. Gradually the shop cleared out until only Farrell, Meyer and I remained, along with the two young girls. For a time Farrell held court as they asked him about his shop and his life.

A question from one of the girls sent him to a far shelf, looking for a book. At the front of the shop, I saw Meyer buttoning up his coat. At the door he paused and looked back at Farrell. Though he had his back to Meyer, Farrell turned at that moment and looked at him. From where I stood I could see them both. Meyer nodded, once, and put on the ruined hat. Farrell raised his hand in a wave and held it there as Meyer went out the door. I saw how Farrell watched the street after Meyer had disappeared from view and gradually understood what I'd witnessed. I went over to Farrell.

"He's gone again, isn't he?"

Farrell nodded and gave me a faint smile.

"For how long this time?"

He looked back out on the street. "I will not see him again."

I stopped myself from asking how he knew. In the context it seemed the most foolish of questions.

"Are you going to be all right?"

"Of course," he said. "The finality of things, even when expected, well, it is disquieting. Disquieting."

Then he turned and looked slowly around him at his shop, his gaze resting on all the different parts of his odd enterprise. "But I would ask a favor of you, lad."

"The Northwest Passage again, Farrell?"

In spite of the moment he laughed silently. "No, no, we're through with the wandering, the both of us."

"What is it that you need me to do?"

"I thought now, with your knowledge of bookstores and grand enterprises, that you could help me put some sense into mine."

"Like an inventory?"

"The very thing, an inventory."

He nodded, smiled in the direction of the young girls, muttered "inventory" to himself as though mightily pleased at my word choice.

I told him I would stop by the following week and took my leave. Farrell nodded in the direction of the two girls – and pretty girls, they were.

"Not for me, Farrell. I'm twenty-six but I've got the soul of a fifty-year-old."

He shrugged and thanked me again for the gift. When I left he went back to the girls but I saw him glance one time more at the darkening street, looking, I knew, for Meyer.

Thirty-Three:
Last Things and Reckonings

We began the inventory of Farrell's shop toward the end of January, two nights a week. I had no illusions that any legitimate purpose was served by this process, only that it pleased Farrell. At first I imagined that he hoped to see a semblance of order come to his shop, but it was not that at all. Among other things, he wanted a document to vouch for all his efforts to collect interesting and worthwhile things. As he explained to me the value and provenance of objects I'd long since stopped noticing, I understood his pride in the ten-thousand-and-one items he'd managed to find in a long life, and more than that, I realized that a good many of these things had been brought under his roof, not with the goal of selling them but to preserve them, like a man taking in strays. Indeed, he'd done what he could, consciously or unconsciously, to avoid selling some of them: a small painting of an Irish village was tucked behind a larger print where no one could see it. It reminded him, of course, of his own village, of his mother. A small tattered volume of his beloved Frost held a place of honor on a high shelf but was priced –

preposterously – at forty dollars, so that there was small chance anyone would take it but a high likelihood that it would be noticed.

As we worked through his "holdings", as he called them, I became engrossed in the work. Two nights a week proved a feeble commitment in the face of the simple enormity of the shop's contents. Soon I was there most nights, even before the day's last visitor had left the shop. At first Farrell sat beside me to identify the things on his shelves and trays. Soon he withdrew, busying himself in the far corners of the shop. I called out my questions or held up odd objects and he glanced at them, squinting, and told me what he recalled. Some of the items had a long history and for others the tale of his acquisition was more interesting than the item itself. And since by now I knew that Farrell never did anything without multiple motives, I saw that he was laying before me the outline of his life. Indeed a subtle pattern emerged from the boxes and shelves and cases: here and there he paused over an object, held it in his hands and turned it over and studied it. These things, all but buried amidst the clutter, had been his own possessions: a polished stone, a tie pin, a folding magnifying glass.

He watched my reaction but said little. At times I felt his gaze on me and looked up, and he quickly looked away or pretended to be deep in thought. Once I caught him smiling.

"Look at you, Thomas, how far you've come. Dressed like a lord with your tie and your fine coat. How far you've come from that other fellow, the one in the Army coat. A bruised and battered lad that was."

"That guy's still inside here, Farrell." I tapped myself on the chest. "There's not a day that goes by that I don't wonder if I'll look in the mirror some night and see him again."

"Certainly the thing's possible," he said with a surprising candor. "But I doubt it."

Last of all we catalogued his books, and for these Farrell pulled up a chair across from me and as we went through them he made certain I understood not only what they were but what to look for, and why one book might have more value than another. I knew some of this already from my work in the bookstores but his knowledge was far more comprehensive, and he knew more of the actual making of a book, of bindings and paper choice and the subtleties of fonts than anyone I'd encountered. And as we did our cataloguing of his books there was no doubt that imparting this knowledge to me was at least partial payment for my services and for my friendship, such as it was.

The inventory took me well into the spring. At some point he gave me a key so that I could get into the shop even when he was on one of his odd and uncommon errands. Eventually I finished. I handed Farrell the thick listing of the contents of his shop and he beamed at it, and then at me. To celebrate, he poured each of us a whiskey.

We downed our drinks and he tried to give me money for my work.

I refused and we compromised. I let him take me to dinner – downtown at the old Berghoff, where we had wiener schnitzel and 14-year-old bourbon – and the following day, a ball game. On a dank April afternoon

Farrell and I sat in the drizzle of Wrigley Field and watched Willie Stargell and his friends demolish the Cub pitching staff. I recall shivering for most of the afternoon. Farrell seemed not to notice. When the game was out of hand he amused me with his anecdotes. It began to rain and I suggested that we find a place that sold coffee. He would not hear of it.

"We've not even sung the song yet, lad. And they sell coffee here."

And so we stayed through the rain and had a cup of ballpark coffee, surely one of the world's unknown toxins, and we stood for the 7th inning stretch so that Farrell could sing in his reedy voice "Take me out to the ball game." And when he came to the line, *"I don't care if I never get back,"* I understood that he meant it quite literally.

After the game, soaked and both of us smelling like wet sheep, I drove him back to the shop and stopped in for a quick cup of tea. When I was leaving, I called out, "See you around, Farrell."

"Aye, lad," he said.

And I was halfway through his door when I heard him cough, I heard Farrell cough. I stopped and turned. He met my gaze, raised his eyebrows and shrugged. I had never heard him cough. He coughed again, not a deep cough but real enough. He smiled like a man who has discovered money in an old coat.

Later in the week I contrived to stop by the shop and he was bustling among the shelves, sorting books and dusting – dusting! – and humming an old song. Though it was still chilly outside the sun had come out and he'd propped the door open to let in the wet smell of the lake.

The shop was cold.

I raised my eyebrows in question and he shrugged.

"To let the spring inside. We've all made it through another winter, Thomas."

He offered me a cup of coffee and we made small talk, and I heard the cough again.

"You getting sick, Farrell?"

"It is just a cough, lad, no more."

He looked away when he said it, and I decided not to push it. When I got up to leave, Farrell said, "Thank you for stopping by, lad. But you don't need to be looking after me."

"I just stopped in to say hello."

He gave me a dubious look. When I was at the door he added, "Trust your instincts, Thomas."

I had no idea what he meant. Outside the shop I paused for a moment and Farrell looked up. He smiled and raised his hand. I waved back. Something made me hold that pose for a long moment. Then he turned away.

On Saturday he failed to open and I let myself in. Farrell had been making coffee – gotten as far as opening the can and then collapsed. He had managed to crawl to a sitting position, propped up against a chair but too weak to climb onto it. It was clear enough that he was dead, but I touched him all the same for I have long believed that someone should touch a dead person, just because it is right. I let my hand linger on him for a long moment but it was clear not even Farrell himself could have revived this dead man with a touch.

Then I did what I thought Farrell would have done. I finished making the coffee, called a funeral home, and waited for his guests. I tended to the shop the rest of that day, broke the news to them. When the last one left – Leo the Professor – I sat in Farrell's chair and read once more the Eliot poem "The Journey of the Magi," understanding for the first time the line, "*No longer at ease here in the old dispensation.*"

Meticulous to the end, Farrell had left instructions – to me, in a letter tucked under the drawer in the cash register: he asked that I "look after his things." He also asked that he be cremated, his ashes to be scattered at the lakefront spot near Montrose Harbor where he'd often set up his telescope; that I see to the sale of his "holdings"; and that I consider keeping his shop, if it suited me.

Of course it did not suit me. There was no place in the life I was trying to put together for this relic of a shop with all its dark associations. Of course it did not suit me.

I held a small Irish wake in the shop and was startled at how many people showed up. Then I shut the place up, cut off the utilities, put it to sleep.

In the last week of May, I went walking along the lakefront. An uncommon day, gray and cold, and a fierce wind came off the lake and sent the waves slapping high up onto the rocks. Thirty or forty feet back from the shore you could still feel the spray on your face. As I stared out at the gray-green surface of the water I became aware of another man nearby, a dark-haired man of middle age. He stood on the rocks, watching the waves, never once looking my way, and as I watched him I felt a spasm in my chest as though a terrible sadness had gripped my heart, and I knew this man was there to kill himself.

Then he lowered his head like a man charging an

enemy and lunged off the jagged boulders into the lake. He went under, came up gasping for breath, went under again, and when he came up I saw that he was weeping. He reached for the rocks, fought for purchase on the slippery surface, lost his grip and went under again, and I heard him choke in mid-sob as he took in water. I began running toward him. I slipped on the wet surface and went down hard on my hipbone. When I got up again I could not see him. I threw off my jacket and my shoes and went out onto the rocks and he was there, his body wedged between two of the boulders, his face in the water. A wave hit then, a wall of icy water that pushed me backward over the rock I was standing on and almost sent me into the lake. When it receded, I scrambled down to the edge of the rocks and got a grip on his coat and pulled at him in vain. Then I slid barefoot into the freezing water and pushed and tugged at him as though it would save my own soul, and gradually I felt him come free. I slid backward onto the rocks and pulled him after me.

I took a moment to get my breath and then turned him over. It was clear that he was dead, that he had managed to take his own life as he'd intended. But I remembered his sobbing face before he went under for the final time and knew he'd embraced life at the last moment.

I put him face down on the pavement and tried to pump the water from his lungs. Then I lay him on his back and tried to force my own air into him, my mouth on his cold lips, and it was useless. I remembered his heartbroken face and took the dead man into my arms and held him. I don't know how long we stayed that way. Gradually I came to realize that I was rocking back and forth, and crying. From somewhere behind me I heard voices and then a group of people, several of them women, came running toward us. They called out to us, called the dead man by his name and I pressed him to me as though I could squeeze him back into life. I crushed him against me, and he moved. He moved, little more than a shudder, and then he gasped and choked and coughed, and he was alive. My vision seemed to fail, things grew faint. I loosened my grip and they were pounding me on my back and hugging me, and one of the women said something in Spanish that I didn't understand, and called on Jesus and Mary and the saints.

They huddled around their stricken loved one and I got to my feet. I retrieved my shoes and jacket and slipped away. I had the most distinct sense that my own life was fading from me. A short distance from the lakefront I staggered into an underpass where I'd seen homeless people huddle in the winter and here I stayed, pressed against the cold wall, too weak to walk further, chilled to every part of my body. The irony of the thing occurred to me then, that in saving this unhappy man from his death I had likely brought about my own. I felt myself drifting away.

When I awoke it was night. I got to my feet, reeled, caught myself against the wall. I stood there until I thought I could walk. Several times I was forced to stop and hold onto a tree or a post, but I made my rocky way home and threw myself into bed, naked, my damp clothes dropped on the floor. When I finally awoke I had lost a full day.

I spent three weeks wrestling with the inevitable and

then, in June, put a sign in the front window that Farrell's shop would be open for business again, just two afternoons a week.

Epilogue

For the next three years I lived a life quite different from the old one. I worked my two jobs, held court at Farrell's shop two and sometimes three times a week. Where other men my age would have spent a few bucks upgrading to a decent apartment, or courting young women, I put away every spare nickel. I even held onto the Buick, a car as near death as one could be, kept it together with little more than duct tape and good intentions.

By the third year I was able to buy a moribund bookshop on Belmont from a pallid-faced man whose shop smelled as though things had died there. I got his inventory, his location, and his troubles for three thousand. I handed him my check and I could see him suppressing the impulse to dance out of the shop. I sold off most of his books and set about remaking the shop, specializing in hard-cover books on geography, history, archaeology, and the sciences.

My hours at Farrell's shop were irregular, by design. On some nights or on Saturday afternoons, there might be a few actual customers. At other times the place filled, as was its tradition, with the eccentric and the homeless. For a time my life was without extraordinary moments, I had neither vision nor adventure. Nor miracles. Indeed, after that day at the lake, I half convinced myself I'd exhausted whatever there was of what Farrell had styled my "gifts". Once or twice I looked unwittingly into a face and saw sorrow or despair or a jumble of painful images, but nothing more. And at these times I looked quickly away. All this would soon change.

My mother, that poor simple woman, always saw patterns where none existed. She'd once told me that significant things happen in threes. Two celebrities would die and she would then wait for the third – even if the third death came a month later, and then she would call the sequence to my attention.

In the spring of 1979 I was visited by my own triad of events, each startling in a different way.

The lake smells promised spring, and I had just propped open the door to Farrell's shop. Three customers came appeared in a matter of seconds. The first two were older men. I was shelving books on the far side of the shop and so did not see the third newcomer for a moment. When I turned she was standing more or less in the middle of the room, staring about in obvious wonder. A woman my age, dark hair streaked with early silver, a good-looking woman with what Farrell would have called "a lived-in face." A ridge of bone showed where her nose had been badly broken, and as I looked at her, I felt it then, the old sudden constriction in my chest, and a blur of jarring images came to me unbidden: I saw her getting up from a kitchen floor holding a bloody hand to her nose, I saw her lying awake in the darkness, staring at the ceiling, I saw her as a thin girl sitting at the edge of a bed where her mother had died, I saw her fighting with me, I saw myself pushing her down on a bed and leaving her life.

She turned then and saw me. Her face was, just for a moment, a wondrous mix of confused emotion: pleasure at finding Farrell's shop, shock at seeing me, pain and embarrassment from old wounds.

For several seconds neither of us could find language, let alone composure, and then I found myself laughing. "Rachel."

She shook her head as if to clear it.

"Yeah," I said. "One of those moments."

"You – you work here or you – ?"

"I'm the, ah, proprietor."

"He's gone. Mr. Farrell."

"Yes. Six years now."

"And the other one – Meyer?"

"He just left one day and disappeared. It's what Farrell always thought would happen."

"And Farrell left you the shop?"

"Yes."

She nodded but said nothing to tell me what she thought of that. At the same moment, both of us looked around, suddenly aware of the other two customers. In the small silence that followed, I realized I wanted to keep her there for a few minutes, I hoped for a chance to learn more about her. And so I backed off.

"Why don't you have a look around. I've got a couple of things to do."

I puttered around behind the counter and hoped she wouldn't take the opportunity to leave. For several minutes she stood stiffly in front of the bookshelves, her discomfort manifest. I realized that she could probably feel my eyes on her, and so I went into the back room and stayed there to let her make her decision. In the end the shop wore her down – impossible to leave a place you thought gone forever. When I looked out, she was moving about the room, looking into Farrell's old cases and trays, revisiting the past.

She stayed in the shop for nearly a half hour. One of the men had left and the other now made a purchase. She waited patiently for me to finish taking care of him, then moved awkwardly up to the counter with two books. She handed me money and my hands were shaking when I took it. We both saw me shaking. I put the bills in the register, shut the drawer and then remembered that she had change coming. When I glanced at her face she was smiling. I put the coins in her hand and my fingers touched the skin of her palm. I remembered the feeling of her skin now, I swear I remember the first time I touched her hand. For just a moment she stood stiffly, she remembered it as well. Then she put her change into her small purse but dropped half of it on the counter. I caught a quarter before it could roll off, and handed it to her. She fumbled to close the purse. She blushed.

I was about to blurt something out, I didn't know what, when she got there first.

"How are you, Thomas? I mean, are you all right?"

"I am. And how is your life?"

She gave me a sardonic look. "You know the old Beatles song, 'It's Getting Better'? That's more or less how my life is. It gets better."

"Good," I said, and wondered if it sounded as trite to her as it did to me.

She got a look into her eye then and I knew she was remembering what our history was. I believe there are moments when we can all of us read minds and I read hers then, I saw the look and the set of her jaw, and I know she was going to say one of those stiff things we say to show distance to a former lover, to a most disappointing former lover. But there are people for whom honesty is a second skin. She opened her mouth, thought better of whatever was ready to come out, looked around the shop. Then she looked at me.

"Can you make a living? I mean, does the shop – ?"

"Does it do enough business to support me? No, not even close. I have another job – a shop of my own, actually. A bookstore."

She smiled, then, a slow genuine smile of relief, and I understood that, all these years, all her trouble, and she was worried about me.

"You should stop in and see that one. My other shop."

"Oh? Why? What's so special about that one?"

I was fighting to come up with something witty and she held up her hand, smiling.

"I was just having fun with you. You're proud of it, your shop. I'd like to see it."

"Here," I said, drawing a card from the register.

"You have a business card!"

"Such as it is," I said, handing her my minimalist business card. It read, "Thomas Faye, Bookseller," and gave an address and phone number. I took it back and wrote down the hours that I was usually there.

She looked at the card, smiling and shaking her head. "Oh, Thomas, I'm so happy to see you, and to see – well, that you're alive. Don't be offended, but honest to God, you were so tough, so destructive, I thought you'd be dead in a year. For a time I read the paper with a feeling of dread, expecting to see that you'd gotten yourself killed."

"You have no idea how I tried."

I saw the quick glance she gave me. She saw the scarred knuckles and god-knew-what-else but opted for a discreet silence. It struck me that she'd managed not to tell me a single thing about her life. I thought of the painful images I'd seen of her life.

As though she could feel me probing, she said, "I have a child. That's one good thing I can speak about, one thing I'm proud of. Her name is Annie. She's eight." She saw me doing surreptitious math and shook her head.

"She's not yours."

"Of course not. And is there a husband?"

She pointedly touched the broken ridge of her nose and said, "No."

There wasn't much to say to that. The moment came back to me then when I'd left her: about to be abandoned by her lover, she'd been most concerned about what would happen to me.

"You won't have a home anymore."

"Well, I'd like you to see my shop. My other shop."

"I'll come by next week."

I smiled, composed myself. I noticed that my heart was racing. "Maybe we'll have a chance to talk. As a matter of fact, there's a small coffee house down the street from my shop, maybe I could buy you a cup of coffee."

Her face was clouding before I ever reached the end of my sentence. She shook her head, once.

"I don't think that's such a good idea."

I was on the verge of blurting out that I understood, and of course I did, but I caught myself.

"I didn't say it was a good idea. I don't know anything about good ideas. I just thought it might be nice to sit down in a warm place and talk if only for a few minutes. No strings attached, nothing – "

"Thomas, there are strings attached to us all the time, to every single thing we do."

She looked off in the direction of the bookshelves. I'd managed to cause her distress in just a few minutes.

Before I could mutter "I'm sorry" she turned and said "A cup of coffee. Okay."

And about a week later, Rachel came to my shop. She walked from section to section, took random books from their shelves, admired the pristine jackets and old binding. She smiled and shook her head and finally just said, "I'm proud of you."

Over coffee we made small talk and, completely against my better judgment, I admitted to her that my youthful, drunken, violent misadventures, my "lost years," as I sometimes styled them, were not even the most troubling elements in my past.

"My life is not normal. I'm – I'm not entirely normal, I don't think." I heard the ineptness of my explanation, as though the very strangeness of my life made me simple-minded when I tried to speak of it.

"Have you killed anyone?"

"No. As a matter of fact, I saved a man from drowning

once. Even that was disturbing."

"Why?"

"That's for another conversation."

She smiled. "Tell me what's 'normal,' Thomas. Look at my life. Do you remember the first time we saw each other? I was sitting in a window next to my dotty old aunt who thought she was a fortune teller. A fortune-teller's apprentice!" She laughed.

She laughed that musical laugh of a young girl and as she was laughing I asked her to dinner. She looked away, nervously rubbing her arm. Then she looked back at me.

"Isn't it inevitable?"

A wet Saturday morning a few days later, and I was standing in the window of the shop, staring out at the street, thinking of second chances. As I watched the people walking by, I saw a child standing just outside the shop. She stood back from the window and looked warily inside. I thought I saw her gaze come to rest on me, and as I watched her I felt a small shudder, though I could not have said why.

She peered in again and I could see her gathering the nerve to enter this strange place, and then she came in. She closed the door behind her and stopped there, uncertain whether to go any farther. She was perhaps twelve, a girl of mixed race, slender and large-eyed and quite pretty, and shy about herself and the place she found herself in. I studied her and as she turned her gaze on me I saw her face change, just for a tiny sliver in time, her features blurred and a faint aura of color played across her face. The air around her seemed then to shimmer, like the distorted horizon on a hot day, and I understood what Farrell and Meyer had seen on that long-ago afternoon when I came into the old shop. My breath caught in my chest.

I heard myself mutter, *"Another one."*

To the girl I said, "Hello."

She gave me an uneasy smile and walked her tentative walk to the far side of the shop, to the books, to the magazines, to Farrell's vast stack of *National Geographic*, a leaning yellow column threatening to collapse onto the floor. She took one, looked around for a proper place for a young lady to sit. A few feet way was an unpacked box.

"You can sit on that."

The diffident smile once more, and then she settled herself in with her magazine, this haunted child. I looked at her and saw the images of her life, the faces of the people in her life, and understood I would see her again many times. I had no idea what her peculiar gifts might be, what strange course her life would take, only that I was intended to be somehow a part of it.

So this is how it begins, I thought.

I wanted to call out, *"I don't know anything about this, I don't even know about children,"* but I held my tongue. When she left, she waved and gave me a small smile.

I was late closing the shop that day. I stood behind my counter brooding on the girl, on my role, on the strangeness of my life. It began to rain and what few people were left wandering my disreputable block of Clark Street hurried by.

The door opened and an old man came in. I bit back the impulse to tell him I was closing. Ten more minutes wouldn't hurt, and this one looked like he could use ten minutes under a roof, any roof. He shuffled in, bent over, soaked to the skin, and shook himself like a wet dog. He was wind-burnt and filthy and the sleeves of his heavy coat were in tatters. He wiped the top of his bald head with a soiled handkerchief and looked at me. I could smell him from twenty feet. He grinned then, this orphan of the street, showed me a mouth full of blackened teeth. He nodded and laughed silently at all of it, at himself and the look on my face and the great joke of life.

I nodded back, and laughed. I said, "Hello, Meyer."

The End

ACKNOWLEDGEMENTS

Special thanks to Peter Raleigh for his help with the manuscript – and to old Casey, whose small, cluttered junk shop under the tracks on Addison so many years ago was the inspiration for this story.

BIO

Michael Raleigh is the author of seven previous novels, including IN THE CASTLE OF THE FLYNNS. He has received the Eugene Izzi award for crime fiction and four Illinois Arts Council awards for fiction. He teaches writing at DePaul University and lives in Chicago with his wife Katherine and his three children.

Other novels published by

Harvard Square Editions

All at Once, Alisa Clements

Gates of Eden, Charles Degelman

Trading Dreams, J. L. Morin

Patchwork, Dan Loughry

A Weapon to End War, Jonathan Ross

Spiders and Flies, Scott Adlerberg

CPSIA information can be obtained
at www.ICGtesting.com
Printed in the USA
LVOW11s1023170917
549031LV00001B/48/P